REMAIN SILENT

Books by Robyn Gigl

BY WAY OF SORROW

SURVIVOR'S GUILT

REMAIN SILENT

Published by Kensington Publishing Corp.

REMAIN SILENT

ROBYN GIGL

KENSINGTON
PUBLISHING CORP.

www.kensingtonbooks.com

KENSINGTON BOOKS are published by

Kensington Publishing Corp.
119 West 40th Street
New York, NY 10018

All Kensington titles, imprints, and distributed lines are available at special quantity discounts for bulk purchases for sales promotion, premiums, fund-raising, educational, or institutional use. Special book excerpts or customized printings can also be created to fit specific needs. For details, write or phone the office of the Kensington Special Sales Manager: Attn. Special Sales Department. Kensington Publishing Corp, 119 West 40th Street, New York, NY 10018. Phone: 1-800-221-2647.

Library of Congress Card Catalogue Number: 2023930909

The K with book logo Reg. US Pat. & TM Off.

ISBN: 978-1-4967-4176-9

First Kensington Hardcover Edition: June 2023

ISBN: 978-1-4967-4178-3 (ebook)

10 9 8 7 6 5 4 3 2 1

Printed in the United States of America

For Abigail, Alice, Caroline, Gwendolyn, and Madison

CHAPTER 1

Wednesday, May 27, 2009, 10:30 a.m.

ERIN EYED THE CAMERA IN THE CORNER OF THE CEILING. AFTER ALmost twelve years as a criminal defense lawyer, she had been in enough interrogation rooms to know that it probably wasn't the only one focused on her.

She brushed her copper-colored hair back off her face, willing her expression to conceal the emotions roiling inside. She glanced to her left at her law partner, Duane Swisher, hoping to find solace in his commanding appearance, but as she studied his face, she found it inscrutable. Duane, who had spent seven years as an FBI Special Agent, had mastered many tricks during his time with the Bureau, one of them being the art of hiding whatever he was thinking.

The door to the room suddenly swung open, and a man swaggered in, followed closely by a woman.

"Ms. McCabe, Mr. Swisher, I'm Detective Adam Lonza with the Cape May County Prosecutor's Office. We spoke yesterday. And this is Detective Emily Carter with the Avalon Police Department," he said, extending his hand and shaking Duane and Erin's hands in turn, with Carter then following suit.

Lonza looked to be in his early thirties, with close-cropped black hair and brown eyes. His broad shoulders and barrel chest certainly looked like the by-products of many hours in a gym.

Carter appeared older—mid-forties perhaps—her brown hair pulled back in a tight ponytail. Despite the fact that Carter was there to interrogate her, Erin was immediately curious about Carter's backstory. It wasn't easy for women in law enforcement, so if Erin's guesstimate of Carter's age was close, it meant she had gone through the police academy when there were very few women recruits.

"Thank you for coming in," Lonza said, dropping a folder on the table in front of him before sitting opposite them.

Thank you for coming in, Erin thought. *Not like you gave me much choice.*

Lonza folded his arms across his chest. "You're both experienced lawyers, so let me be clear. Ms. McCabe, you have the right to leave anytime you'd like. This is not a custodial interrogation. We're just trying to gather information on the murder of Bradford Montgomery."

Duane leaned forward in his chair, narrowing the space between himself and Lonza. At six-two, with broad shoulders and a hard body, Duane's size was imposing, a fact he wasn't afraid to use to his advantage.

"Since we are, as you said, experienced lawyers," Duane said, "I will likewise presume you and Detective Carter are experienced detectives. So, let's lay our cards on the table, shall we. We're in the county prosecutor's office in one of your interrogation rooms, meaning this is all being video-recorded and probably monitored by others sitting in another room. Your preamble about Ms. McCabe being free to leave is just your way to avoid providing her with her Miranda rights. That way you can always claim it wasn't a custodial interrogation. Which means that if you so choose, you can cherry-pick her words and use them against her." Duane stroked his goatee and leaned back. "Do you think Ms. McCabe is somehow involved in Mr. Montgomery's death?"

"Let's just say she's a person of interest," Lonza responded.

"Let's just say," Duane said, feeding Lonza's words back to him, "legally there is no such thing as a person of interest, Detective. Either Ms. McCabe's a suspect or she's not, and we both know there are different ramifications."

Erin watched her partner, still trying to adjust to her unexpected role in this unfolding drama. She was supposed to be the one fencing with the detectives, parrying the lunges at her client, but not today. *In this morning's performance, the part of Erin McCabe will be played by Duane Swisher,* she thought. And yet as much as she hated being the understudy, there was no one she trusted more than Duane. He was not only her partner, he was her best friend. When he left the Bureau six years ago, he could have gone anywhere, but to Erin's surprise, he agreed to become her partner, and together they started the firm of McCabe & Swisher. Of course, at the time, Erin was still living as Ian McCabe. A year after they formed the firm, Erin had come out as a transgender woman, and even though some of Duane's friends had given him a hard time for staying partners with the "trannie," Duane hadn't wavered, and the firm, and their friendship, had flourished.

"Mr. Swisher, we can put Ms. McCabe in Mr. Montgomery's home around the time he was murdered. Perhaps Ms. McCabe has an explanation for that, perhaps she doesn't," Lonza said, his tone pleasant, but his eyes betraying his suspicions. "But since you and Ms. McCabe were kind enough to drive all the way down here, I presume it wasn't to turn around and drive right back. So is Ms. McCabe willing to talk to us or not?"

Duane gave Lonza a sly grin. "Why don't you talk to us first, Detective? I was with Erin when she spoke to you on the phone yesterday. Based on that, you already know that she met Mr. Montgomery for the first time Monday evening. She also told you that she met at his request for a consultation. I would add that Mr. Montgomery was very much alive and healthy when Ms. McCabe left him. You've said Mr. Montgomery was murdered. How did he die?"

"Ms. McCabe . . . and Mr. Swisher," Detective Carter interjected softly, allowing herself to fall smoothly into the role of "good cop," "I'm sure you can appreciate that at this stage of the investigation we cannot divulge the cause of Mr. Montgomery's death. We're just looking for information that might be helpful." Turning to face Erin, Carter continued, "Mr. Montgomery's surveillance videos show you arriving at his house around seven thirty in the evening on Memorial Day and the two of you walking down toward the beach about thirty minutes later. There's no video of either of you reentering the house at any point. From a security camera on Fiftieth Street, we see your car leaving around 8:20 p.m. Mr. Montgomery's body was discovered in the dunes between his house and the beach yesterday morning. The medical examiner estimates his time of death to be between seven and ten p.m. on Monday. In other words, right around the time you were together. It certainly would be helpful if you could explain why you were there."

"Detective," Erin responded, "as I told Detective Lonza on the phone, I can't reveal why I went to see Mr. Montgomery. As you know, I'm an attorney, and despite the fact that Mr. Montgomery is deceased, I'm not relieved of my obligation to maintain his confidence as a client. All I can tell you is that he called my office on Friday while I was at home, packing to head to the Shore, and left a message that he needed to speak with me as soon as possible. When I called him back, he asked me to meet him at his place in Avalon for a consultation. At our Monday meeting, we talked about why he wanted to see me. Afterward, he showed me his house, and then we walked down to the beach to continue our discussion. While we were talking, he received a phone call on his cell that he ignored. It then appeared he received a text message, followed by a second call, which he did answer. When he hung up, he told me he had to go and showed me where to leave the beach at Forty-eighth Street. When I looked back, he was standing by the water, watching me leave. That's the last I saw or spoke to him."

"Do you know what number you called him at?" Carter asked.

Erin removed her BlackBerry from her purse and scrolled through her recent calls. "973-555-0100."

As Carter jotted the number down, Lonza opened the file in front of him and slid several photographs across the table to Erin.

"Do you recognize these?"

Erin looked at the photographs. The first group of photos appeared to be dated, having an almost vintage quality to their appearance, perhaps copied from some website or a publication of some sort. The others were more recent. Erin had seen law-enforcement surveillance photos in any number of cases, and these had the same feel—surveillance photos taken using a tele-photo lens. They were all of a woman. And as Erin studied them, she realized all the photos probably depicted the same woman, each group separated by several decades.

"I've never seen these before," she answered.

"Do you recognize the person in the photos?" Lonza asked.

Erin glanced down at the photos. "I don't believe I've ever seen this person before," she replied, looking up at Lonza.

"What if I told you they were all pictures of Bradford Mont-gomery dressed as a woman?"

She looked down at the pictures again and then back to Lonza. "Okay," she said.

"Okay, what?" he said accusingly.

"Okay, nothing," she responded. "I met Mr. Montgomery once, for less than an hour. That's the only time I've ever seen him. He was dressed in khakis and a golf shirt. If you're telling me these are pictures of him dressed as a woman, I'll accept your represen-tation. It doesn't change the fact that I've never seen these be-fore."

"Don't you find it strange that Mr. Montgomery is found dead after meeting with you, a well-known transgender, and pictures of him dressed as a woman suddenly surface?"

Erin cringed at Lonza's misuse of the word "transgender" as a noun, but she knew this was not the right time to be pedantic. "Detective, I find it strange that Mr. Montgomery has been mur-dered, period, full stop. But I can assure you, these pictures have nothing to do with me."

"We have reason to believe that you, probably at the behest of others, were trying to blackmail him with these photos because of his involvement in Arnold Welch's campaign for governor. What do you say to that?"

Erin stared at Lonza, suddenly aware of what it felt like for her clients. She'd lost count of the number of times she had watched an interrogation video in disbelief as a client, sitting in a room just like this one, tried to talk their way out of the jam they were in. And each time, she'd scream at the screen, "Shut up and take the Fifth, you idiot!" But they rarely did. And on those rare occasions when they did, it was usually too late. Now she understood the temptation—the feeling that all she had to do was explain what happened; then they'd understand their mistake, and she'd be done with all of this. But that was a fool's errand.

"What do I say? I say I think you're crazy, Detective," she finally said. "That, and I think it's time for me to go."

Duane pushed his chair back from the table. "Unless you have a warrant for Ms. McCabe's arrest, we'll be leaving now."

Erin held her breath, waiting to see if they had a warrant. She didn't think so; otherwise, they would have Mirandized her. But Lonza struck her as someone who didn't always color inside the lines, making the sudden appearance of a warrant possible.

"If you leave now, you'll be missing your one and only opportunity for Ms. McCabe to come clean and work out a deal," Lonza snapped at Duane. He then turned to Erin. "Your story doesn't hold water, McCabe. The only cell phone found at Mr. Montgomery's was in his living room, and there were no incoming calls or text messages between six and nine thirty p.m. So, where's the phone you say he got these calls on?"

Don't engage, she thought. As crazy as it seemed, Lonza appeared to truly believe she had killed Montgomery, and it was clear from his demeanor that nothing good was going to come out of any further conversation.

Lonza pointed his finger at Erin. "Prison life can be really tough on people like you. If you cooperate, tell us who you're working with, we can make it easier. Make it so you do your time at Edna Mahan, the women's prison. But if you walk out the door, all bets are off. Who knows, maybe you'll wind up at Northern State or East State. The guys there will have a lot of fun with you."

She glared at him, trying to ignore his comments and focus on what was important. They didn't have a warrant, so they weren't arresting her. She moved her chair back from the table and stood.

Lonza's smirk quickly morphed into a scowl, the veins in his neck pulsing noticeably. "Remember, McCabe, this train is leaving the station. This is your one and only opportunity to get on board. The next time I won't call and invite you down for a talk; I'll show up with cuffs. You understand that?"

She tried not to roll her eyes at the number of clichés being thrown at her.

"Have a nice day," Duane said, then gently took Erin's arm and steered her around the table heading toward the door.

Lonza shot out of his chair and hurried over to block their way. "I meant what I said, McCabe. I'll have fun watching you sit in the men's jail. I have to admit that, for a guy, you're pretty attractive. I'm sure all the guys in state prison will be happy to see you."

"It's Ms. McCabe to you, Detective," Erin said. "And as far as your threats . . ."

She walked around him, opened the door, and looked back over her shoulder.

". . . You can go fuck yourself."

CHAPTER 2

Two days earlier, Memorial Day, May 25, 2009

As Erin headed south on the Garden State Parkway, she couldn't help but notice the traffic crawling north. Sooner or later, that was going to be her fate. There was no way to avoid it. It had been a glorious Memorial Day weekend, and the beaches up and down the Jersey Shore had been packed. She and her boyfriend, Mark Simpson, had enjoyed the weekend at the condo she owned in Bradley Beach. They had been dating off and on for about two years, and Erin had finally begun to feel confident that their relationship was going to last. Somehow, Mark had gotten over the fear that many heterosexual men had when they found themselves attracted to a transgender woman. What did it say about their own sexuality? There had been a few bumps in the road, but Mark had come to see her as the person she was—a woman—and not the person she had once forced herself to be. Of course, his mother and brothers were a different story. His relationship with them since he'd started dating her was strained; her relationship with them was nonexistent.

Normally, after a weekend at the Shore, she would have headed north to Mark's house in Clark, where they lived together, but today she was driving to Avalon to visit a new client, Bradford Montgomery. They had spoken for the first time on Friday. He told her that he needed to meet as soon as possible and gave her the address of his place in Avalon. Since he didn't want anyone to know they were meeting, he asked her to park on Fiftieth Street and follow the path that led from Dune Drive to the beach. Then, about fifty yards down the path, she'd see a smaller path on her left, marked with PRIVATE PROPERTY NO TRESPASSING signs. She should take the smaller path, which snaked about thirty yards through the dunes and ultimately led to his backyard. Aware that he was asking her to make a four-hour round trip on Memorial Day weekend, he had offered her a three-thousand-dollar fee, which, after Erin had agreed, he wired to her firm's account.

After their call, she had done a quick Internet search on Montgomery. Apparently, he was the owner of a financial services company located in Hoboken, but what had startled her was that he was a financial adviser to Arnold Welch's campaign for governor. Welch, who was running against Senator William Townsend to be the Republican nominee for governor, was, in Erin's opinion, a little bit to the right of Attila the Hun. Unfortunately, the racist and xenophobic undertones of his rhetoric seemed to be striking a chord with a segment of the electorate.

It was almost seven thirty p.m. when she parked on Fiftieth Street, walked across Dune Drive, and followed Montgomery's directions. When she stepped into the small clearing behind his house, she was overwhelmed by the size of his home—it was enormous. Montgomery was sitting on a deck that wrapped around the entire second story; when he saw her, he immediately jumped up and came down to meet her.

Based on the little she had found on the Internet, she guessed Montgomery was around sixty. Up close, however, his unwrinkled face made him look like he was in his early fifties. *Clean living or a good surgeon*, she thought. He was dressed casually in khakis, a Lacoste golf shirt, and Top-Siders. After introducing himself and offering her a drink—she accepted a Diet Coke—he led her back to the deck.

"May I call you Erin?" he asked, as they sat across from one another.

She smiled politely. "Of course."

"I guess you're wondering what this is all about?"

"I am," she replied.

"I'm not sure what you know about me."

"Honestly, not too much," she said. "I presume you know that there's very little available about you through an Internet search."

"That's good," he said with a small grin. "Unlike some of my flashier contemporaries, I like to fly under the radar. But as you can see," he continued, allowing his hand to sweep around in front of him, "I've done okay. I give people investment advice and, if they want me to, invest on their behalf. The folks I invest for are part of a very select group of high-end investors, including Arnold Welch, who, as I'm sure you know, is running against William Townsend in the Republican primary for governor. I will confess, I'm not a huge fan of Arnold's politics, but he has been a client for years, and I want to keep him happy. Candidly, I didn't think he had a chance, but apparently there are a lot of people out there whose politics are as crazy as Arnold's. I now find myself in a very awkward place. I'm not sure I want him to win, but I'm even less of a fan of Senator Townsend."

"Have you ever thought about voting for a Democrat?" she interjected with a broad smile.

"Good God, no!" he said with a chuckle. "My father would haunt me."

"Can I ask why you're not a fan of Senator Townsend?"

He took a deep breath, and Erin sensed he was weighing his words. "I've known Will Townsend for many years. We don't exactly run in the same social circles—I'm more New York, he's more Philly—but we both have money, so we know a few of the same people. Let's just say I find some of his business practices . . . unsavory. He's got enough lawyers and accountants that I assume he never breaks the law, but he certainly knows how to bend it, and it seems like it's the little guys that do business with him who often wind up getting screwed." He shook his head. "I know I'm not the poster child for altruism," he said, gesturing to their surroundings, "but I've tried my best to avoid taking advantage of people." He grew silent. "But to each their own."

"I'm sorry, I interrupted," she said. "You were telling me about Mr. Welch."

He shook his head as if waking himself from a trance and ran his hand along the back of his neck. "On Thursday, Arnold called me. His research team had been doing oppositional research on Townsend, and a case you were involved in came up." He hesitated. "The case involving the death of Townsend's son."

Erin nodded. "Okay?"

"There was a settlement of a civil case with Ocean County. It appears that money was paid to your firm's attorney trust account and that simultaneously there were nondisclosure agreements entered into by you, your partner, and a Tonya Tillis, the guardian ad litem for Sharise Barnes. Although the criminal case against Ms. Barnes received a lot of notoriety, this settlement received no press. Any idea why no one knows about it?

Erin snorted. "Probably because there's a nondisclosure agreement."

"Arnold believes that the nondisclosure agreement is hiding dirt on Townsend's son and perhaps on Townsend too." He stopped, his look betraying his hope she would add to his statement.

"Mr. Montgomery . . ."

"Please, call me Brad," he interrupted.

"Brad," she repeated, "there's nothing I can say. There is a nondisclosure agreement, so legally there's no information I can provide other than what's already part of the public record."

"Erin, I understand that if you breach the agreement—or I guess if your firm and Ms. Tillis breach the agreement—you may all be required to return whatever amounts you were paid. But suppose I were to say that, in return for the information, I'd be prepared to pay your firm, and Ms. Tillis, double whatever it is you have to return."

Erin was momentarily stunned, and she could tell by his expression that she had not done a good job of masking her reaction. After considering her options, she finally said, "I'd say that would be very generous of you, but it's an offer I couldn't accept."

"And why is that?" he asked, matter-of-factly.

"A number of reasons, I suppose. First, I have no desire to help Mr. Welch get elected. In my humble opinion, he's a racist, a xenophobe, and a misogynist—no offense," she replied.

"No offense taken—he certainly can sound that way at times. Although, on some issues of importance to you, you'd be surprised to know that he's more nuanced than you may think."

"Nuanced is not something I associate with Arnold Welch," she said. "Not to mention the fact that I'm supporting Marie Honick for governor."

"Fair enough," he replied, his tone gracious.

"As for my other reasons not to accept your offer, there is the little detail of researching whether the payments you propose would be in violation of campaign-finance laws. But, most important, I signed an agreement, and my firm is ethically obligated to honor its commitments. Besides," she added before he could respond, "based on my experience, William Townsend is a dangerous man, and I honestly don't want anything to do with him."

Montgomery stood and walked over to the railing of his deck, leaning against it as he looked at her. "I appreciate your principled position. Not too many people, especially lawyers"—he flashed a grin—"would turn down an opportunity to double their money, no questions asked. I also agree that Townsend is a dangerous man. As for Ms. Honick . . ." He let out a small laugh. "I hate to break it to you, but the Democratic bosses will never let a woman beat Henry Nestor in the primary. I suspect it will be Nestor against Townsend, and as much as I don't like him, it's in my interest if Townsend wins. My taxes are high enough now."

She got up and walked over, so she was standing next to him at the railing, gazing out at the ocean. "I don't know, as I drove around Avalon, it didn't look like there were too many people being taxed into the poorhouse," she said, a tinge of sarcasm in her voice.

He turned so he too was facing the ocean. "Touché," he replied. "Is there any information you can give me on Townsend?"

"I'm afraid not," she replied.

"I will confess I'm disappointed, but I respect the position you're in." He cupped his hands over his mouth, as if weighing what to do next. "Perhaps I could interest you in taking a walk down to the beach before you leave? There are a few other questions I'd like to ask you." His tone seemed cautious, almost apprehensive.

"Sure," she replied.

He led the way inside and showed her around the house before they made their way along the path to the ocean. They stood looking at the waves crashing on the shore when he turned to her. "I hope you don't mind, but the questions I'd like to ask are personal."

"Like?" she replied.

"I know you're a transsexual—I mean, don't get me wrong, you're a beautiful woman, there's nothing about you that gives you away—but I did read about you on the Internet, and, well . . . I was wondering if you'd had the change?"

"The change?" she repeated, unsure of what he meant and struggling with his reference to her passing and his use of "transsexual," a term she didn't use.

"You know, the surgery?"

"Um, yeah, I did," she replied, trying to figure out where this was going.

"Are you happy as a woman?" he asked.

"Very," she replied.

Again, she noticed him staring at her, but this time there was a different quality to it. His look appeared wistful.

"Is our conversation confidential?" he asked.

"Of course," she responded.

He turned back to the horizon. "I've been a crossdresser for years. Back in the seventies, I was part of a sorority for crossdressers. Most of us were married, or were at the time, and it gave us a chance to dress up and have some fun. We'd have events in different places, and sometimes our wives even joined us. In the beginning, my wife tolerated my 'little quirk,' but she eventually tired of it, and we divorced in 1982. At the time, it cost me a pretty penny to buy her silence. But I have to give her credit; she never betrayed me. After we were divorced, I thought about going through the change, but my career on Wall Street was really starting to take off, and I knew my father would disown me." He stopped and slowly turned back to her. "So I just stayed in the closet."

He fell silent, and Erin was at a loss as to what to say.

"Was it hard for you—I mean your transition?" he asked, ending the awkward silence.

Now it was her turn to look wistfully out to sea. "I lost most of my friends, but the hardest thing was losing my marriage. I loved my wife, Lauren, very much, and I hoped we could stay together. But she's not a lesbian, and she wanted to be with a man. I get it. I just didn't fit the bill anymore. My dad and brother struggled with it. But my brother and I are okay now, and things with my dad are getting better. My mom has been very supportive, and that's been really helpful. My law partner has been great, so at least I didn't have to start over again professionally. There were some bumps, but things have definitely gotten better."

"I'm glad to hear that. I'd like to hope that things are getting better for transgender people. Back in the seventies, when I thought about going through the change, being transsexual was almost unheard of. I saw what happened to Renée Richards, and I decided I wanted no part of being in the limelight." He inhaled. "I don't know; it just wasn't an option for me. I did what I needed to do to survive."

The sound of a phone ringing startled both of them. He reached into his pants pocket, took out a cell phone, looked at the display, and hit IGNORE. Before he could even return the phone to his pocket, it vibrated. Again, he looked at the display, his face contorting with confusion. Then the phone rang again.

"Who is this?" he demanded, spinning around to peer over the dunes at his house. She could hear a muffled voice on the other end but had no idea what they were saying. After several seconds, Montgomery disconnected.

"I apologize," he said. "But I was just reminded I have to meet with someone. I think it's best if you leave by going off the beach at the Forty-eighth Street exit," he said, pointing in the direction of the exit. "Please don't take it personally, but it's best if my company doesn't see us together." He looked at her, his eyes conveying his disappointment. "I was hoping to take you out to dinner and continue our discussion. Perhaps we could meet for dinner one night up near my home in Short Hills. I think we'd have a lot to talk about."

"I'd love that," Erin replied.

He shook her hand. "Until then."

"Until then," she replied with a warm smile.

CHAPTER 3

Tuesday, May 26, 2009, 1:30 p.m.

"PUT ALL THIS SHIT IN ENGLISH FOR ME," WILLIAM TOWNSEND demanded as he paced behind his desk.

Milo Corliss, Townsend's campaign manager, looked down at his laptop, making it clear that he expected his assistant, Sarah Meadows, to deliver the bad news. Corliss was no fool. He knew it was hard to deal with Townsend when all they had was good news—and this was decidedly not good news.

After an annoyed look at him, Sarah sighed. "Will, what our polling is showing is that four weeks ago you had a ten-point lead over Welch among likely Republican voters, with a margin of error of plus or minus three points," Meadows hesitated. "Unfortunately, as of our last polling, which was tabulated on Friday, you are only holding a four-point lead. Given the margin of error, that means it's now an extremely close race."

"What the fuck!" Will exploded. "How can that little shit be catching up to me? Damn it, Milo. I'm paying you good money. What the hell is going on?"

Corliss, who had handled all six of Townsend's successful campaigns for state senator, took a deep breath. Will Townsend was one of the wealthiest and most powerful politicians in the state. He could literally make and break careers, which meant he was not someone you wanted to piss off.

"Will, you are a middle-of-the-road conservative Republican. Welch is far to the right, but some of the things he's saying are appealing to a vocal minority of the party who are now calling themselves Tea Party Republicans. They love the guy. He probably doesn't have a snowball's chance in hell of winning a general election in New Jersey, but folks are paying attention to him. And Terry is considered even more liberal than you are," he added, referring to Theresa Posten, who was Townsend's running mate.

"They're right, Will," Michael Gardner said from where he was sitting in the back of the room. Reed-thin, and with tufts of salt-and-pepper hair on either side of his bald dome, Gardner had a well-lined face, square jaw, and thin lips that appeared unfamiliar with the concept of smiling.

Corliss turned in his chair to face Gardner. He had known Gardner since he had become Townsend's personal lawyer about nine years ago. Exactly what that role entailed, Corliss didn't know, and he was happy to keep it that way. Gardner's eyes were cold and dark, devoid of emotion, and as much as Corliss found Will Townsend intimidating, there was a different air about Gardner. He scared Corliss. But for now, to have Gardner on his side was a plus.

Townsend stopped pacing and stood next to his chair. "For Christ's sake, Welch is nothing but a fucking bigot who's never been elected to anything. He couldn't even win a seat on his town council. I've been a state senator for twenty-two years and control just about every Republican county chair—certainly, everyone south of the Raritan. And now you're telling me I could lose to this . . . to this idiot." Will plopped down into his desk chair. "This is fucking crazy."

"Will, Miles and I have talked about a strategy for you," Sarah began.

"That's right," Miles interrupted, sensing that, with Gardner on their side, this could turn into good news—no sense letting Sarah get credit for that. "My thought is that all you have to do is track to the right a little bit on some social issues to take the steam out of Welch," Corliss continued, drawing a glare from Sarah.

"You're not going to lose any votes from the people who know you, and you can win back some of the social conservatives that Welch has been syphoning off from your base."

"What? What do you want me to do, suddenly come out against abortion? You do realize that sixty percent of New Jersey voters favor abortion rights, don't you?" he asked dismissively. "That's the only fucking reason I picked Terry—to have a fucking woman on the ticket. Well, that and the fact that she's from Somerset County and I need votes out of Somerset."

"No, Will. We weren't thinking abortion rights. We were thinking about the homosexuals. You know maybe you start by criticizing the homosexual lifestyle, or the attempts to allow gay marriage."

"How the hell is that supposed to help me? Besides, I do pretty well with gay voters. I'd probably wind up losing more votes than I'd gain."

"Will, this is just for the primary. Once you win the nomination, you can soften your rhetoric again," Corliss offered. "Look, you're an incredibly successful businessman, and one of the most powerful politicians in the state. You're not going to lose the well-educated voter on this issue. But you need to find an issue to appeal to those who are . . . well, how should I put it? A little bit more socially conservative."

Gardner rose from his chair, causing Corliss to momentarily fear he had overplayed his hand.

"Sarah, Milo," he began. "I think what you're saying has merit, but rather than going after the gays, I say we go after the trannies. Will's right; he has some really good backers who are gay men. We don't need to alienate them, but even a lot of the gays have no use for these trans characters."

Corliss, relieved Gardner was still on his side, stole a glance at Will, whose scowl at Gardner conveyed his displeasure with Gardner's suggestion. Shit, Corliss thought, the last thing he wanted to do was wind up in the middle of a disagreement between Gardner and Will.

"Milo, let me speak privately with Will. I have some thoughts. After Will and I chat, I'll give you a call to discuss messaging."

"Of course," Milo agreed, happy to get out of the room in one piece.

It was all Townsend could do to hold back his temper until Milo and Sarah left. The memory that his only child had been stabbed to death was still fresh in his mind.

"Do you mind telling me what the fuck you think you're doing? I know I don't need to remind you that some trannie whore killed my son and was defended by a trannie bitch of a lawyer. Drawing attention to what happened to Bill three years ago can't help me. As it was, that case almost destroyed my political career. I'm not going there. You know better than anyone that there are secrets buried there that I can't allow to be unearthed."

Gardner took the seat Milo had previously occupied. "How was your Memorial Day weekend?" he asked calmly.

"What? What the hell does that have to do with anything?" Townsend asked. "Have you been listening to me?" Townsend glared at Gardner, his annoyance unabated. They had been through a lot together, all the way back to Vietnam, when Gardner had been Townsend's executive officer and Townsend had saved Gardner's career. After Gardner left the military, he had gone to law school and then went to work for the government, first at the CIA and then the NSA. Throughout, the two had stayed in touch, and when Gardner retired, Townsend hired him. Not only could Gardner be trusted, but his years at the CIA and NSA had taught him how to read between the lines, something Townsend needed from time to time.

"Will, I don't need to be reminded of what you went through with Bill, both his death and the fact that if McCabe had ever been able to expose him, it could have destroyed your political career. But for now, you need to be focused on your future, not your past." He crossed his arms across his chest. "So did you have a busy weekend?"

"If you really must know, I spent most of it at fucking parades, shaking hands and kissing babies. Then I get here this morning and find out I'm in a horse race with a political nobody."

"Then I presume you haven't heard about Bradford Montgomery yet?" Gardner asked with a smirk.

Townsend's forehead wrinkled. Normally, he wouldn't give a damn about Montgomery, but the fact that he was a major financial supporter of Welch put him near the top of Townsend's shit list. "No. What about Montgomery?"

"He was murdered yesterday."

Townsend's head snapped back. "Murdered. Shit; how come you know this, and I don't?"

"Let's just say I have insider information from a very reliable source," Gardner responded with a small chuckle.

Townsend looked at his former XO suspiciously. "And what other information did your *source* provide you with?"

"It happened late yesterday. He was found stabbed to death in the dunes outside his house in Avalon after meeting with a lawyer," he paused. "A lawyer by the name of Erin McCabe."

Townsend pushed his chair back from his desk, stood up, placed his hands on his desk, and leaned forward. "McCabe! Why the fuck was he meeting with McCabe?" he screamed. "What the hell is going on, Michael? You know more than you're telling me."

Gardner gave Townsend a wry smile. "Of course, I know more than I'm telling you, Will. That's my job—to insulate you. Let's just say that based on some emails acquired from Welch's campaign, I learned that Montgomery was trying to see if he could get dirt about Bill, his murder, and about you."

"What? They can't do that. There's a settlement with a nondisclosure agreement."

Gardner's look revealed he was enjoying himself. "The plan was to offer McCabe and Swisher more than double what the case settled for. That way, if the settlement had to be repaid, they'd still come out ahead."

Townsend took a deep breath. "Do we know if McCabe gave him any information?" he asked, a whiff of panic creeping into his voice.

"Don't know. But that's why I handled it the way I did. Even if she did, it doesn't matter because Montgomery met his demise before he even got back to his house. And," Gardner added, "this is the pièce de résistance—there were pictures of Montgomery in drag at the scene next to his body."

"Pictures of Montgomery in drag?" Townsend asked, running his fingers through his hair. "Come on, isn't that going a bit too far? Won't the cops be able to figure out they were doctored?"

"No, because they're not doctored."

"Jesus, Michael. Are you telling me Montgomery was a drag queen?"

"I don't know what he was, but the photos of him dressed to the nines are real. I had someone start doing surveillance on him when he was in Avalon after he started backing Welch's campaign."

Townsend dropped back down into his seat and sat in silence, processing what Gardner had told him. "I never liked Montgomery, and I always thought he was a bit of a poof, but I would never have pegged him for a faggot like McCabe. Any chance we can set McCabe up to take the hit for the murder?"

Gardner's sneer was evil. "Working on it. I'm assuming Montgomery's house has security cameras, so the videos should show her as the last person to be with him when he was alive, making her a likely suspect. We'll have to see how the investigation plays out, but perhaps there are ways we can help focus it on her."

"You know how much I want that bitch to suffer, don't you?"

"Yes, Will. I am well aware of your feelings toward Ms. McCabe," Gardner said, placing added emphasis on the *Ms.* "I have no love for that faux bitch either. Remember, I was the one who suggested that she should be eliminated three years ago."

"You don't need to remind me." Townsend ran his lower lip between his fingers as he mulled over his options. "Let me reach out to the first assistant prosecutor in Cape May. I suspect he's interested in the top job, so maybe, as a favor to me, he can make McCabe's life miserable." He nodded his head slowly and then said, mostly to himself, "This could be good."

"Shall we go back to discussing getting you elected?" Gardner asked.

Townsend shook his head. "That would be nice. None of this matters if I don't win. So why the fuck are you agreeing with Corliss?"

"Because he has a point—you need to get to the right of Welch on some social issue, at least through the primary, and I think this trans thing has potential." He quickly held up his hand before Townsend could speak. "And do it without drawing attention to Bill's case."

Townsend snorted. "And just exactly how do we do that?"

"We go after the kids."

"The kids? What the fuck are you talking about?"

"Do you know that a boy can now play sports as a girl with a note from a doctor that says they think they're a girl?" Gardner asked. "And if the name on the kid's birth certificate is John, his parents can get a judge to change it to Mary—crazy, right? But that's where we are in this state, Will."

Townsend shrugged. "Okay, so it's crazy. But how does that help me politically? You were the one who said nobody gives a shit about these people."

"You know the American Liberty Defense Alliance?" Gardner asked.

"Sure. They're a bunch of nutjobs who believe everybody should be free of government oppression, unless it's something they want oppressed, like abortion or queers," Townsend replied.

"I got a call last week from Dave Mallory, their legal director. He's looking for financial and logistical support on a case they'd like to get involved in on behalf of a father to prevent the mother from changing their kid's name."

"Why do we want to get involved in a family dispute?" Townsend asked.

"Because the kid is eleven years old, and Mom wants to change his name from Nicholas to Hannah. The American Liberty Defense Alliance wants to fight it and help the dad get custody to prevent Mom from turning him into a girl. Mallory wants money to help fund the litigation. He also wants you to speak out publicly about how what Mom is doing to the kid is child abuse and shouldn't be allowed. He thinks the case could be huge for their national fundraising efforts. As to how this helps you," Gardner continued before Townsend could ask the obvious, "you do a couple of appearances, and in return, the American Liberty Defense Alliance endorses you over Welch, boosting your credibility as a conservative voice the Tea Party crowd can vote for in the primary."

"I don't need to do this shit," Townsend replied. "Just about every Republican county chair in this state owes their position to me. All I have to do is squeeze them by the balls, make sure we have street money available for them come the primary, and I'll be fine."

"Will, you dropped six points in four weeks. You picked one of the most liberal Republicans in the state as your running mate. The primary is three weeks away. You have to do something to stop the bleeding and turn things around. The Republican Party is changing—you can't just be for lower taxes and against the public employees' union and expect to win. These Tea Party folks would rather lose the election than compromise their principles, and they don't give a shit what the county chairs say. You need to throw them some red meat to get them behind you," Gardner suggested. "And if some of the photos of Montgomery happen to leak to the press, along with the fact that he was working for Welch . . . I'm telling you, this could be a win-win for you."

Townsend sat in silence, rubbing the back of his neck. He had plans—big plans. Other than Obama and the first Bush, every president since Carter had been a governor. But if he didn't win the governor's election, his plans would go down the toilet. "Get Mallory in here so I can talk to him," he finally said. "I want to know how crazy he is before I get in bed with him."

Gardner gave a small snort. "I actually think you'll like him. He doesn't believe half the bullshit he says, and he knows the other half are lies."

CHAPTER 4

"REALLY? 'GO FUCK YOURSELF'?" DUANE SAID ONCE THEY WERE out of the prosecutor's office and safely in his car. "You couldn't stay quiet for another ten seconds?"

Erin cocked her head to glare back at him, her anger still on full display. "You heard what he said—his transphobic bullshit. Not to mention, he was threatening me."

"Yeah, and it worked," he replied. "He got under your skin. And if I hadn't been there to steer you out the door, God knows what else you would have said."

"What's that supposed to mean?"

He snorted. "It means that yes, he was goading and threatening you, but when you're the client, and not the lawyer, you keep your mouth shut."

"You don't understand what it's like to—"

She stopped when she saw his sardonic smile appear.

"Really, I don't understand?" he said. "I'm Black. Trust me, I get it, E," he said, using her nickname. "It doesn't matter if it's racism or transphobia; it's infuriating, and it hurts. But there are times when you fight back and times when you just have to take it. Obviously, no one's ever had to have the 'talk' with you, but every Black kid learns at some point that sometimes, 'yes, sir, no, sir' is the safest response. And when someone is looking to charge you with murder—well, that seems to me to be a pretty good time to hold your tongue and take it."

She hung her head, embarrassment replacing her anger. "You're right," she replied sheepishly. "It's just all so bizarre. First, Montgomery being murdered and then Lonza thinking I'm involved." She sighed. "If nothing else, I now have a much better understanding of what it feels like for our clients."

"Any thoughts about what is going on?" Duane asked as he backed out and headed toward the Parkway.

She rubbed the side of her neck. "I have a theory."

"We have a two-hour drive. I'm listening," Duane replied.

"Actually, are you in a rush?" she asked.

"No."

"Good. Then when you get to the Parkway, go south and take the Stone Harbor exit."

"Why?"

"I want you to see the scene of the crime, but I'm not walking around on the beach in a skirt and heels. We can stop at Wave Runner, a store where I can pick up some shorts and a top."

He gave her a sidelong glance. "How do you know the stores in Stone Harbor?"

"When I was in law school at Temple, a lot of folks from the Philly area would come to this part of the Jersey Shore—Ocean City, Sea Isle, Avalon, Stone Harbor—so I made it down here a few times." She hesitated. "And Lauren and I came here a few times when we were dating and after we were married."

"So you get shorts and a top, and I have to walk the beach in a suit and oxfords?"

"They sell men's clothes too," she replied with a wink.

He shook his head. "Fine."

She and Swish, as his friends called him, both because of his last name and because he had such a sweet shot from three-point range on the basketball court, made an interesting pair. They had met while in college, Swish at Brown and Erin at Stonehill College, because the women they were dating at the time—in Swish's case, his wife, Corrine, and for Erin, her ex-wife, Lauren—were college roommates at Brown. Swish, who was thirty-eight, with dark brown skin and a well-trimmed goatee, would probably still be at the Bureau if he hadn't been forced to resign when he was set up to be the fall guy for a leak of classified materials involving the illegal surveillance of Muslim Americans after 9/11. Having been an All-Ivy basketball player at Brown, he kept himself in great shape by playing in various adult basketball leagues. Erin, on the other hand, even though only six months younger than Swish, was often mistaken for being far younger. At five foot five, with a dusting of freckles that ran across the bridge of her nose, a slim athletic figure, and girl-next-door looks, her youthful appearance belied a seasoned attorney with a unique backstory.

An hour later, they had exchanged their business attire for shorts, T-shirts, and flip-flops. Duane parked his car on Fiftieth Street, just as Erin had done on Memorial Day.

"That's Montgomery's house," she said, pointing to the top of a huge home that was visible over the pines.

"Nice digs," Duane said.

"It's even better when you see all of it," she replied, leading the way toward the hard sand trail. Even though the scrub pines on either side of the path were stunted by the sandy soil, they were still tall enough to obscure the huge house off to their left.

About fifty yards down the path, they came to an opening blocked by several rows of yellow police tape emblazoned with CRIME SCENE DO NOT CROSS strung between the pines, blocking access to a smaller path.

"It leads to the backyard of Montgomery's house," she said, nodding to the trail closed by the police tape.

They made their way down to the beach and turned so they could look back at Montgomery's house tucked in the dunes.

"That's some place," Duane said.

"It is. It has to be six or seven thousand square feet," she replied. "But check out the dunes between here and the house— plenty of places to hide."

Once they reached the water's edge, she pointed out approximately where she and Montgomery had stood talking. Duane glanced back over his shoulder at the house.

"That's a good distance between here and the dunes," he said. "If there was someone watching you from back there, I suspect they had binoculars." He squinted, then looked at Erin. "Kind of like the person watching us from Montgomery's house now."

"What?" she said.

"There's someone up on the second floor."

"How can you tell from here?" she asked.

"I saw the sun reflecting off the lens," he replied, then grinned. "FBI training. It's got to be law enforcement. They're the only ones who would be cleared to be at the crime scene."

"Or someone with enough juice to get the gendarmes to let them on the premises," she said with a sidelong glance in his direction. "Want to have some fun?"

"What do you mean?"

"Let's turn around and wave. If it's the cops, they'll know we've seen them."

"And if it's not the cops?" he asked.

"Then they'll know we're not going to be intimidated," she said with a mischievous smile.

They looked at each other and exchanged nods, and when Erin counted to three, they turned in unison and waved.

After their wave, they made their way toward the Forty-eighth Street exit from the beach, following the path Montgomery had sent her down two days earlier. Halfway down the path, Duane headed off to search the dunes, while she continued down the path to the street.

"You find anything?" she asked when they were back in the car and headed to the office.

"Clearly lots of people have been walking around in the area between his house and the ocean, so it's not a pristine site, and if there was anything there, it's long gone."

"If it was a cop who was watching us from Montgomery's house, they'll probably send you a ticket in the mail for walking in the dunes," Erin said. "You know it's against the law in Avalon?"

"Yeah, I saw the signs," he replied dismissively.

"Quite cavalier about breaking the law, aren't we now?"

"Says a woman who is suspected of murder," he responded.

"Ouch," she said. "Maybe I need a new lawyer. One who be-lieves in my innocence."

"Or maybe one who can prevent you from telling the lead detective to 'go fuck himself.' "

She was about to quip about making one small mistake, when it occurred to her that if she was truly the target of the investigation, she couldn't afford to make any mistakes—not even small ones.

"Let's be serious. Do you think you should consult with someone not as close to you as I am?" Duane asked.

She studied Swish's profile as he drove. She knew there were lawyers who were more skilled than they were, but she didn't know a better team than the two of them. She was confident this would blow over quickly, but if it didn't, she wanted Swish at her side. "If you'd rather have someone else involved, yeah, let's talk other options, but there's nobody I want or trust more than you. If you're okay handling it, I'd really like you to represent me," she said.

"Whatever you need," he replied.

"Thanks," she said. "Where do you want to start?"

"What do you make of the pictures and the missing cell phone?" he asked as he merged onto the Parkway.

She thought for a moment. "His phone was just a basic cell phone, nothing fancy. I would have expected a guy like Montgomery to have either the latest BlackBerry or one of the new iPhones. And since they found a phone in the living room, I'm guessing the one that I saw on the beach was a second phone—maybe even a burner. I asked Cheryl to check our incoming phone logs from Friday, and the call that came in from Montgomery was on a blocked number."

"So there'll be no number on our phone bill," Duane commented.

"Correct."

"And you're thinking that whoever killed him took the phone you saw?"

"Yep," she said. "As for the pictures, I'm not sure. Some of the photos seem consistent with what Montgomery told me about being active in some of the crossdressing events held back in the seventies. There were organizations founded by men who considered themselves heterosexual crossdressers. Remember, this was way before the Internet, so when they attended these events, they'd print up newsletters. Some of the photos look like they may have come from there. Other photos were more recent and looked like they were taken from the dunes with a high-powered lens while he was at the window or on the deck. Clearly, someone was surveilling him."

"But why leave them at the scene?" Duane asked.

She took a deep breath. "Sounds weird since he was already dead, but my guess is it was revenge. One of the cruelest things you can do to someone in the closet is 'out' them. So, in this case, it's not only are we going to kill you, it's 'we're going to out you and ruin your reputation too.'"

"Sounds like you don't think the pictures are related to why he was killed?"

"I really don't think they are," she replied.

"Then what do you make of the phone calls he got when he was on the beach?" he asked.

"Whoever called him killed him—or at least was setting him up to be killed. When he took the call, he looked around, like he thought whoever had called him was nearby. He also didn't look or sound happy, and based on him saying he had hoped to go to dinner, it wasn't a call he expected."

"But the question remains, who killed him and why?" Duane asked.

"I don't know the *who*, but I think the *why* was to stop him from disseminating the dirt on Townsend."

"But you never gave it to him."

"Whoever killed him didn't know that. He was killed before he even got back to his house. So, from the killer's perspective, if he got the information, it died with him. And if he didn't get it, that was the price he paid for trying to get it."

"And a message to us to keep our mouths shut," Duane added.

"Yep—loud and clear."

When she walked in the house just before six thirty, she was greeted by the smell of roasted garlic.

"Smells good," she said, putting her leather satchel in the closet and making her way to the kitchen, where Mark was busy making shrimp scampi. Unlike her, Mark was not only an excellent cook, but it was something that he loved to do.

Even though they had been living together for about six months, whenever she came home and saw him, her heart still did a little dance. He was six feet tall, with jet-black hair that was disheveled in a way that suggested he combed it with his fingertips. He somehow always managed to have just enough stubble to be sexy without looking grungy, and his green eyes sparkled.

She walked over, stood on her toes, and gave him a kiss on the cheek.

"Dinner in five," he said, shaking the pan as he gave her a warm smile. "Nice outfit," he added, catching a look at her shorts and flip-flops. "Thought you had a big meeting this morning."

She grabbed two plates out of the cupboard and placed them on the counter, then took out silverware and napkins, quickly setting the table.

"I'll fill you in shortly," she said, ducking into their bedroom.

When she returned, she had changed into a pair of jeans and a Pittsburgh Marathon T-shirt. She poured two glasses of water and carried them to the table.

"How'd things go in Cape May?" he asked as he stirred the rice one last time and plated it.

"Ah, not so great," she replied, uncertain about how to respond.

"*Por que?*" he asked innocently.

She watched as he spooned scampi sauce over the shrimp and rice. "Looks great," she said, taking the two plates to the table and waiting for him as he washed his hands.

"Bon appétit," he said, taking his seat and picking up his fork. "So what happened?"

"Well . . . they think I murdered my client," she responded with a shrug.

His look betrayed his skepticism. "You're kidding—right?"

"Not really," she answered half-heartedly.

"What!" he said, dropping his fork on his plate.

"Apparently, from his home security system, we're seen leaving his house together, and he never returns. According to the medical examiner, his time of death is around the time we were together."

Mark got up, walked over to her side of the table, and gave her a hug. "Are you okay?" he asked.

"Thanks," she said, leaning her head into his chest. "Yeah—I'm okay, I guess. I know he was very much alive when I left, but I will confess it's disconcerting to know I'm in the crosshairs of the prosecutor's office."

"What are you going to do?" he asked.

She gave him a weak grin. "Eat before it gets cold. It looks really good."

"You seem pretty unfazed about this. Aren't you concerned?" he asked, going back to his seat.

She thought for a moment. "Yeah, I am, but probably not for the reason you might think. I can't help but think that Senator Townsend is somehow involved, and if he is, I know he'll do anything to get back at me for defending Sharise. I'm not worried about the truth—just that the truth has never meant much to Townsend and those who do his bidding." She took a forkful of shrimp and rice. "Thank you for cooking, by the way."

"My pleasure."

"This is delicious," she said, as she considered how to broach the next difficult subject—their current living arrangement. Back in January, before she had moved in with Mark, she had renewed the lease on her apartment, and it ran for another seven months.

"I still have my apartment in Cranford," she said. "Maybe I should move back there until this blows over. If I'm right about Townsend being involved, I may be in his crosshairs, and I don't want you to get caught in the middle. He's dangerous."

This time, he gently placed his fork on the side of his plate.

"And you living by yourself is somehow supposed to make me feel better?" he said wearily. "We both know that if someone wants to come after you, one of the ways is through me, even if we're not living together. Neither of us has forgotten that you saved my life," he said, referring to an incident when Erin was able to surprise two thugs posing as police officers just as they were about to abduct Mark in an attempt to silence her. "And don't you dare go to where I think you're going. You broke up with me once trying to protect me from my own family's transphobia. Breaking up with me again isn't going to protect me from crazy people out to get you. We've been through this before. You don't get to make decisions for me—only I do."

She rubbed the back of her neck with her hand, hoping her expression didn't reveal that she was guilty as charged—that's exactly what she had been thinking. A little over a year earlier, she had called time on their relationship because Mark's family had given him such a hard time about dating her. Now, with the exception of his sister, Molly, and her wife, Robin, things were still tense. She already felt guilty enough about his estrangement from his family; the thought that he might also be hurt or killed because of her was horrifying.

"Let's hope this is over with quickly and we never have to worry about it," she said in a tone that was neither encouraging nor convincing.

He squeezed her hand reassuringly. "I'm sure it will."

CHAPTER 5

Thursday, May 28, 2009, 10:00 a.m.

GORDON PATERSON COULD COUNT ON ONE HAND THE NUMBER OF times he had spoken to Will Townsend and, up until yesterday afternoon, on one finger the number of times Townsend had called him. That call had been to express his condolences when Gordon's father, State Assemblyman Ray Paterson, had died suddenly.

It was no secret that Gordon, who had been first assistant prosecutor in the Cape May County Prosecutor's Office for the last five years, coveted becoming prosecutor, but he had just assumed that, with his father gone, he didn't have the political juice to get the nod. All of which made Townsend's second-ever call, requesting to meet with him, even harder to fathom.

Townsend had made his fortune in the commercial real estate business and then parlayed that wealth into a political career as a state senator and power broker. The combination of his wealth and political clout had given him a hand in just about every political appointment in South Jersey. He was a good person to know because he had the connections to make things happen, but if you crossed him, there was no chance of being appointed to anything.

The meeting had been set up at an office building in Atlantic City owned by one of Townsend's companies. As was his habit,

Gordon arrived early, and the young receptionist took him to a conference room that could easily seat twenty people. Gordon was already sipping his coffee when Townsend walked in carrying a small manila file folder.

"Gordon, you're early—I like that. So nice to see you again," the senator said, with an informality that seemed both disarming and disingenuous.

Gordon stood quickly to shake Townsend's hand.

"It's been far too long—your dad's wake, wasn't it?" Townsend asked, taking a seat opposite Gordon.

"Yes, sir. I believe it was."

"Your dad was a good man," Townsend said with a small nod. "Please, sit—and call me Will. 'Sir' makes me think that I'm back in the military," Townsend said with a small chuckle.

"Yes, si—ah . . . Will," Gordon said, stumbling to correct himself and trying not to show his indignation at the reference to his father.

Townsend waved a hand. "I'm sure you're very busy, what with Bradford Montgomery's murder and all. Although Brad and I sometimes disagreed politically, I considered him a friend. If there's any help your office needs, please know that I am here to help however I can."

"Thank you, si—Will. Much appreciated."

"If you don't mind me asking, are you personally overseeing the investigation?"

"No . . . Will. Assistant Prosecutor Tom Pendergast is supervising."

Townsend's head tilted slightly. "I see," he said. "Gordon, far be it for me to tell you or Prosecutor Musgraves how to run your office, but I have been looking at your background for reasons we will discuss in a minute," he said, tapping the manila folder on the table in front of him, "and I know before you became first assistant, you spent time as the assistant prosecutor in charge of Major Crimes, and before that you were the trial team supervisor, not to mention all the cases you tried when you were assigned to the trial team. You've been in the office for, what, fifteen years?"

"Actually, eighteen. Nineteen on September first, sir."

"Nineteen years, congratulations. You're a lifer," Townsend said, using a term sometimes applied to a lawyer who made their career out of being in the prosecutor's office. "Good for you. Anyway, as I said, I don't want to tell anyone how to handle Bradford's case, but because he was a friend, I have a personal interest in seeing that his murderer is brought to justice, and it seems to me that, given your experience, you're the best one for the job. I mean no disrespect to Mister . . . whoever you said is handling it, but perhaps you should consider taking over the case. It would mean a lot to me personally. And, I hope it goes without saying, it could mean a lot for your career."

Gordon hadn't expected this. There was no doubt that Montgomery's murder was a big deal; unlike in some counties, his office had relatively few homicide cases each year. But it sounded like Townsend was suggesting this was his ticket to the top job.

"That's actually the reason I asked to speak with you—your career," Townsend segued before Gordon could even respond to Townsend's suggestion that he take over the investigation. "As you know, I'm running for governor, and I will be looking to appoint the best and brightest once I win. I have to confess that the reason I'm familiar with your career is because your name has been mentioned for the prosecutor's position. No offense to Lena, but I am not terribly impressed with the job she's done over the last five years as prosecutor. She's a politician, not a lifer like you. You have all the credentials to make an excellent prosecutor, which is why I asked to meet with you. I see you have a wife and two children. It can be a demanding job, with long hours. I certainly wouldn't blame you if you didn't want to take on that kind of commitment at this point in your life." Townsend gave Gordon a quizzical look. "Would you be interested?"

Gordon took a deep breath. *Don't screw this up.*

"Yes, sir. I'm very interested. It's been a lifelong dream of mine to become the prosecutor."

"That's wonderful. I also see that, like your dad, you're a registered Republican." Townsend chuckled. "Makes my job a lot easier."

Gordon gave a small snort. "Yeah. Kind of hard growing up in my household not to be a Republican."

"Terrific." Townsend pushed back his chair and slowly stood. "I really do appreciate you taking the time out of your busy schedule to meet with me. I look forward to a more formal interview after the election."

"Thank you, Will. It's been a pleasure," he offered. "And, of course, once I get back to the office, I will take a long, hard look at the Montgomery investigation. Rest assured, we will solve this case."

"Thank you, Gordon. I really appreciate your personal commitment."

They were almost to the door when Townsend stopped.

"Can I ask you something—off the record?" he asked.

"Of course," Gordon responded.

"I understand through the grapevine that an attorney by the name of Erin McCabe was with Bradford the day he died. Is that true?"

"Yes, sir," Gordon replied cautiously, trying to avoid revealing confidential information, while at the same time curious as to why Townsend had circled back to Montgomery's murder. "Our investigation does confirm that information. As a result, she is certainly a person of interest in our investigation."

Townsend inhaled deeply. "I'm not sure if you know this, but she's the lawyer who represented the person who killed my son."

"I am aware of that—yes."

Townsend put his shoulders back, his chest expanding, his military bearing suddenly coming to the fore. "Promise me that if she was involved in murdering Bradford, you will lock her up and throw away the key."

"Anyone who was involved in Mr. Montgomery's murder will be brought to justice," Gordon said firmly. "I can promise you that."

"Thank you. Just knowing that you will be taking over gives me a great deal of confidence it will be solved." Townsend reached into his pocket and took out a business card. "Thank you, again. I certainly wouldn't want you to do anything improper, but if you could let me know periodically how the investigation is going, I'd appreciate it. Here's my private number."

"Thank you," Gordon said, placing the card in his billfold. "I don't see why that should be an issue," he lied, knowing that ethically he couldn't provide confidential details of the investigation to Townsend.

"Perfect," Townsend said, patting Gordon on the shoulder. "Oh, one last thing. Given that Prosecutor Musgraves has no idea that I won't be renominating her if—or when—I get elected, I'd ask you to please keep this little meeting confidential. I wouldn't want word getting back to Lena. At least not until it's a done deal."

"Of course," Gordon replied. "You have my assurance this will remain just between us."

Gordon made his way to his car that was parked on the second floor of the public parking garage across the street from Townsend's building. Once inside his car, Gordon removed the micro-cassette recorder from the inner breast pocket of his suit jacket and took out the tape. He then opened the glovebox, located the envelope, placed the tape inside, sealed it, wrote his name, the date, and the time on the sealed flap of the envelope, and placed the envelope in his briefcase that was lying on the passenger seat. It had been a last-minute decision, but knowing what happened to his father, he wanted to make sure he had a record of all his dealings with Townsend.

Sorry, Dad, he thought. *I know you wouldn't want me to do this, but it's what I need to do.*

Two hours later, Gordon had the Montgomery crime-scene photos spread out on a table in the rear of his office when Assistant Prosecutor Tom Pendergast walked in. Thirty years old, with the looks that matched his passion for surfing, Pendergast had been with the office for five years, and he didn't lack for self-confidence, which, in his case, often crossed the line into arrogance.

"What's up?" Pendergast asked, plopping down in a seat.

"Bring me up to date on the Montgomery investigation," Gordon requested, trying to mask his interest and make it sound routine.

"Nothing really new. ME says cause of death was a sharp-force injury, a single stab wound under the right arm that severed Montgomery's axillary artery. Likely the weapon was a stiletto or switchblade, with a blade approximately five to six inches long. It appears the knife entered the center of the armpit and then was either pulled or pushed toward the front of the torso. Based on a very short trail of blood, it looks like he tried to get to the house but quickly collapsed. Given the nature of the wound, ME says Montgomery would have bled out in about two to three minutes. No murder weapon found at the scene, but there was an envelope that contained pictures of Montgomery dressed as a woman. Montgomery's hand was resting on the envelope, as if he had been trying to get to it. We sent the envelope and the pictures to the state police lab to see if there are any prints or DNA on them. We did a cell-phone extraction on the cell found in Montgomery's house. Still going through it, but no calls in the period from seven to nine thirty. Out of an abundance of caution, we got warrants to seize his home and work computers. Because he has a lot of his clients' confidential personal information on his computer network—social, financial records, stuff like that—we're working with the company lawyers to make sure we only access what we need."

"Why does Lonza like McCabe for the murder?" Gordon interrupted.

"She was admittedly at the house with Montgomery near the time of death. Her prints are in the house, and on a glass, and E-ZPass records confirm timing consistent with time of death. The last toll she went through on Monday was Toms River northbound at 11:02, which is consistent with there being very heavy traffic northbound. It appears that at some point she got off the Parkway, and based on the fact that she owns a condo in Bradley Beach, we're guessing she headed there Monday night, because Tuesday morning her E-ZPass records show her going north again on the Parkway and going through the toll plaza at Asbury.

Again, consistent with her heading to her office in Cranford or an apartment she has in Cranford.

"She claims he called her office on Friday, but there's no record of a call to her office on his cell. But there is a call from her cell to his cell on Friday."

"He could've called her from work," Gordon suggested.

"According to his staff, he headed to Avalon on Wednesday."

"How about from the landline in Avalon?"

"Again, according to the folks at work, he canceled his landline about a year ago. Also, our search of the house revealed no landline."

"Okay," Gordon said.

"And, like I said, she claims he got a call while they were on the beach, but his phone was found back in the house and shows no incoming calls during the time mentioned."

"A second cell phone?" Gordon asked.

"No records of one. Plus, the staff said the number for the cell phone we found in the house was the only number they had for him."

"A burner?" Gordon asked.

"Yeah, it's possible. But why would a guy like Montgomery use a burner? I mean, he's in financial services. Not exactly cloak-and-dagger stuff."

"Motive?" Gordon asked.

Pendergast hesitated before he answered. "We've discovered that Montgomery was the chief financial guy for Arnold Welch's campaign for governor. Lonza believes that McCabe must have learned through members of the 'trans community' that Montgomery was transgender, but backing Welch, the Tea Party Republican. After that, she had someone take photos of him. Then, when she set up this meeting to confront him with the photos, they got into an argument. When she threatened to expose him as trans unless he stopped financially supporting Welch, things got nasty, and she wound up stabbing him."

"What do you think?" Gordon asked.

Pendergast shrugged. "Too early to tell. At this point, she's the leading contender because she's the only contender, plus her story does seem to have some holes."

"You watched McCabe's interview when she came in, right?"

"Yeah. She's definitely been around the block. She didn't give anything up. Her partner also knows what he's doing. Lonza rattled her a little at the end—enough that she told him to go fuck himself. Bottom line is she's either telling the truth or she's a good liar—and since she's a lawyer, there's a presumption of the latter," Pendergast said with a smirk that suggested he was pleased with his own quip.

Gordon rolled his eyes. "Anything else?"

"After the interview, she and Swisher went to Avalon and took a walk around the beach by Montgomery's house."

"You had them followed?" Gordon asked.

"No, actually just kind of dumb luck. Detective Carter from Avalon PD was there and watched them from the deck. At one point they waved, so they knew they were being watched."

"Are we running down any other leads?" Gordon asked.

"Based on the fact that Montgomery was giving some financial advice to the Welch campaign, we've reached out to them to see what, if anything, they know. We've been trying to locate any security videos from homes in the area, but almost all these places are second homes, so getting in touch with the owners for access has been difficult."

"What about from the church—what is it, Maris Stella? They have anything?" Gordon asked.

"Yeah, that's where we got the video of McCabe arriving around seven thirty and leaving about an hour later. Nothing else unusual."

"How long is the state police lab taking these days?" Gordon asked.

"DNA is two to three weeks, more or less." Pendergast gave him a funny look. "I know we don't get a ton of homicides, but you have the crime-scene photos on your table, and based on the third degree, I suspect there's more to your questions than keeping tabs on a big case. What's up, Gordie?"

Gordon let out a deep breath. "Montgomery had some friends in high places, and we're getting some pressure. I haven't talked to Lena yet, but I may be taking over."

"Who the fuck is putting on the pressure? The guy was a fucking drag queen. Do these folks in high places know that?" he asked indignantly.

"No," Gordon replied. "I suspect they don't. At least not yet."

"Well maybe they should," Pendergast mumbled under his breath. "Listen, you're the boss. Just let me know. Anything else?"

"No. Thanks, Tom. That's all for now. I'll keep you posted."

"Gotcha," Pendergast said, quickly heading out of the office.

Gordon walked out of his office, drawing the attention of Nora Burns, who was the administrative assistant to both him and Prosecutor Musgraves.

"Is Lena in?" he asked.

"She just walked in ten minutes ago."

"She free?"

"Nothing on her calendar for the next hour," Nora replied.

"Thanks."

Gordon walked over and knocked on the prosecutor's glass door. When she looked up, she beckoned him in with a wave of her hand.

"Just had a meeting with the police chiefs this morning, and, of course, everyone wants to know what's going on in the Montgomery case," she said as he took a seat on the couch. "Rumors are spreading that it was a serial killer, or done by some anti-capitalist cult. Gordie, these new social media platforms are just breeding grounds for all kinds of crazy rumors. It's a strange new world out there," she said, twirling a strand of her long blond hair around her finger. "I saw you meeting with Pendergast when I walked by your office. Anything new on the case?"

He went over his conversation with Pendergast, then leaned forward, crossing his arms so his elbows were resting on his knees. "I'm thinking about taking over the case."

"Any particular reason?" she asked.

"I had a meeting with Senator Townsend this morning."

Musgraves leaned back in her chair and raised an eyebrow. "Really. I'm certainly curious to hear how that's connected," she said.

"Townsend knows McCabe is a person we're looking at in connection with Montgomery's murder."

"How's he know that?" Musgraves interrupted.

"I suspect that with his connections, along with the fact that it's no secret that he has a history with McCabe and despises her, someone here, or Avalon PD, got word to him."

"Okay. So why the meet and greet?" she asked.

Gordon sat up and rubbed the back of his neck. "He asked me to take over the investigation."

Musgraves gave him a wry smile. "Did he offer you my job if you nailed McCabe?"

Gordon shrugged. "I wouldn't say offered. I'd say dangled."

She shook her head. "So do you think it's McCabe?"

"I'm not sure yet. But both Lonza and Pendergast are so anxious to nail her, I'm afraid they'll move on her too fast and screw it up. I think there's a connection between McCabe and Montgomery, but . . ."

"Maybe it's the pictures of the victim in drag," she interjected with a chuckle.

He gave her a knowing look. "No, it's not that."

"You're not buying into these rumors, are you?" she asked.

"No. Nothing like that. But my gut tells me McCabe knows a lot more than she's telling us. She claims their conversation was an attorney-client conversation, but Montgomery had more money than God and enough lawyers to start his own law firm. Why was he calling McCabe, a run-of-the-mill criminal defense lawyer, on Friday of Memorial Day weekend, and demanding a meeting on Memorial Day? Her story just doesn't add up, but then, there's other things that don't add up either."

Musgraves nodded. "Gordie, you've been my first assistant my entire tenure. You know how much I want you to get the job when I leave."

"I know. And I appreciate you letting me know you weren't going to seek to be reappointed. At least I don't feel like I'm stabbing you in the back trying to get your job."

"Just be careful. You're getting in bed with the devil when you work with Townsend."

"Yeah, I know," he said, rising from the chair, his thoughts turning to what had happened to his father. "I know who I'm dealing with. Trust me, I know."

CHAPTER 6

Friday, May 29, 2009, 7:15 a.m.

ERIN WAS SITTING IN THE DINER'S CORNER BOOTH WHEN HER MOM arrived.

They tried to meet at least once a week to catch up, and Erin truly loved their time together. It had only been about six months since her mother had finished treatment for breast cancer, and the realization that her mother was mortal had shaken Erin to her core. As a result, no matter how crazy things were in her life, Erin had vowed to always try to make room in her schedule for time with her mom.

Her mother had initially struggled when Erin told her that she was transgender, wondering if, in some way, she was the cause. But over time, as they talked through things, her mother had come to accept that Erin hadn't chosen to be transgender; it was just who she was. And after Erin transitioned, they had connected in a new way. Maybe it was a mother-daughter bond, or maybe it was just a shared love that they hadn't expressed as openly before.

Although now sixty-seven, with her brown hair cut in a short bob and her almost wrinkle-free face, Peg McCabe could easily pass for someone in her early to mid-fifties. She still worked full-time as a guidance counselor at Cranford High School and stayed in shape mainly by doing yoga. Whenever Erin looked at her mom, she hoped the old trope of a woman turning into her mother turned out to be true. Resilient, attractive, young at heart, and a wicked sense of humor—not bad qualities to emulate.

"You're here early," her mother said as she leaned over and gave Erin a kiss on the cheek before moving to the other side of the booth. She put her purse down next to her, and when she looked up, the smile quickly faded.

"What's wrong?" she asked.

"Nothing, why?" Erin responded quickly.

"Oh, sweet Jesus. You are the world's worst liar. You look like your dog, Sparky, was just run over by a car."

Erin looked befuddled. "Mom, I never had a dog named Sparky. I never had a dog. I'm allergic, remember?"

"Of course, I know you never had a dog; it was just an expression." Her mother's face scrunched as if she had sucked on a lemon. "And by the way, you're not allergic to dogs."

"What?" Erin said, sitting back in her seat. "You told me my entire life I was allergic."

"Sorry. I made it up." Her mother quickly held up her hand. "Now before you go judging me too harshly, in my defense, your brother, Sean, wanted a dog, and I didn't want one, not because I don't like dogs, but because I knew I was going to be the one who'd get stuck taking care of it. So you became my excuse for why we couldn't get a dog."

Erin looked at her mother, shaking her head. "But I remember going to the allergist! Afterward, you said we couldn't get a dog because I was allergic. I distinctly remember that happening."

"It did," her mother agreed. "You did go to an allergist, and you were tested, which showed you were allergic to bees, pollen, and ragweed—I just added the dog part."

"You mean all those years that Sean blamed me for not having a dog, it really wasn't my fault?"

"I'm sorry, dear. Think of it as taking one for the team. I mean, did you really want a dog?"

"No. But—"

"So what's going on with you? You look awful," Peg said, adroitly changing the subject.

"My imaginary dog, Sparky, was run over by an imaginary car, and I'm distraught," Erin replied, giving her mother a *so there* look.

"Coffee, ladies?" the waitress asked, placing the menus on the table.

"Yes, please," they replied in unison.

"Talk to me," Peg said, her tone now serious. "Something's really wrong. I can tell."

"I'm involved in a new murder case," Erin finally offered.

"You've handled murder cases before. What's bothering you about this one?" Peg asked.

Erin closed her eyes and took a deep breath. "I'm the suspect in the murder, not the lawyer."

"Oh my God," Peg said, reaching across the table, taking Erin's hand and squeezing it. "I'm sorry. Tell me what's going on."

Over breakfast, Erin explained what had happened and, without going into detail, some of her thoughts on who might be involved. Erin had rarely seen her mother speechless, but when she was done, her mother sat in stone-cold silence.

"Are you okay?" Erin finally asked.

Peg shook her head. "How can I be okay?" she asked. "I feel horrible for Mr. Montgomery, and I'm worried about you. You've managed to make some serious enemies, and I know that sometimes powerful men can literally get away with murder. No. I'm not okay."

"Sorry," Erin said. "Hopefully Swish will do his magic and find something to show them that I didn't do it."

After breakfast, Erin made her way to the office, which was located on the second floor of a former Victorian home that had been converted into an office building over twenty years ago.

It was only eight thirty a.m., so Cheryl, their receptionist, secretary, and paralegal all rolled into one, wasn't at her desk yet, but Duane, having the daily job of dropping his four-year-old son, Austin, off at day care, would be there hard at work.

"How's it going?" she asked, standing in his doorway.

"Good," he said, gesturing for her to come in.

Duane's office occupied one of the former bedrooms and, unlike the clutter and chaos of Erin's office, was always neat and orderly, with everything in its place on his glass desk.

Erin dropped her purse on one of the chairs and lowered herself into the other.

They briefly talked about the status of some of their cases, but Erin quickly turned to the case that was foremost on her mind—hers.

"You find out anything?" she asked.

Duane's usually inscrutable expression was replaced by one of disappointment. "Sorry, nothing so far. I have calls into six different people with the Welch campaign, but no one has called me back. I did get a call back from counsel for Montgomery's company, but it was just to tell me that they were cooperating with law enforcement and had no desire to discuss the case with me. When I mentioned you had met with Mr. Montgomery on Monday, shortly before he was murdered, he said there had been no meetings on Montgomery's calendar for the entire weekend, but that if it was a social visit, it probably wouldn't be. Sorry, E, I got nothing."

"I feel like I should be doing something—I don't like sitting back and waiting," she said, chewing on her lower lip. "It sucks being a client." Suddenly, she straightened. "Do me a favor," she said. "Do a search for Bradford Montgomery's obituary."

Duane gave her a sidelong glance but typed in the search terms. After a few clicks, he started reading. "This is from the *New York Times* on Wednesday. 'Financial services consultant Bradford Montgomery died on Monday, May 25, 2009, the victim of a senseless attack at his beloved house on the ocean in Avalon, New Jersey. Mr. Montgomery was 60 years old. The founder and owner of BJM Financial Services—'"

"Any next of kin?" she interrupted. "And what are the arrangements?"

Duane scanned his computer screen. "'Bradford was predeceased by his parents, Aloysius C. Montgomery and Madeline (Davis) Montgomery. He is survived by his cousins James Montgomery, Allison Laurie, and Stephanie Calderon. Visiting hours will be on Friday, May 29, from 2:00 p.m. to 4:00 p.m. and 7:00 p.m. to 9:00 p.m. at the Cornish Funeral Home in Millburn, New Jersey. Funeral services and interment will take place Saturday, May 30, starting at 10:00 a.m. at Saint Stephen's Cemeteries in Short Hills. In lieu of flowers, please make donations to the Leukemia/Lymphoma Society.'"

"What are you doing this afternoon?" she asked, jumping out of her chair.

He gave her a look that slowly morphed into a grin. "I think I have a wake to go to."

"Worth a shot," she said. "Besides, I feel like I owe it to him to pay my respects."

"You really think we'll find anything out?" he asked.

"Hey, your friends at the Bureau used to always hang out across the street from funeral homes and check out who was paying their respects. If it's good enough for the FBI, it's good enough for McCabe & Swisher." Since it was a Friday, and she didn't have to be in court, she was dressed casually. "Let me take care of a few things, then, around lunchtime, I'll go home and change—need to look both a little more lawyerlike and a little more somber," she said. "We can then meet at your house, and we'll head over together?"

"Sounds good. I presume I should tell Cori that I might not be home for dinner."

"Nah, don't do that. It's a Friday night. You have a four-year-old and a four-month-old," Erin said. "You're entitled to spend time with your family, especially on a Friday night. We can head back to your place after the afternoon session, and, if there's any reason to return, I'll head back tonight by myself. Maybe I'll have Mark take me." She smiled. "Who knows, he might be up for a cheap date."

They had arrived at the funeral home a little after two p.m. They met the three surviving cousins, who made up a small receiving line near the casket, and then split up, trying to listen in as they made their way around the room, which seemed to be filled mostly with employees from Montgomery's company and clients of the firm. Standing near one group of employees, she overheard them discussing Montgomery's murder and speculating whether it could have been a disgruntled client, perhaps angry over some heavy losses in the stock market. But someone else in the group chimed in that the market was getting better, so it made no sense for a client to kill him now.

When the conversation drifted to more mundane issues, Erin made her way to the side of the room, where she found herself gazing at photos of Montgomery that were spread out on several tables. They included pictures from when he was a young boy, all the way through to several that appeared to have been taken shortly before he was killed. The photos depicted a privileged life, and by all outward appearances, a successful life—but life wasn't always what it seemed. As Erin studied the photos, she couldn't help but think of the set Lonza had showed her of him dressed as a woman. Other than Swish, of all the people in the room, she probably knew Montgomery for the shortest period of time—less than an hour. But the two of them shared something that perhaps no one else in the room shared—a gender identity in conflict with the sex they were assigned at birth. Yet even with that shared experience, their lives had taken different paths. She recalled his wistful stares and wanting to know about the "change," along with his acknowledgment of what would have happened to him if he had transitioned. Somehow, she had managed to encapsulate his fondest dreams and his worst nightmare. She was living the life he longed for but never thought he could attain.

She picked up a picture of him that appeared to have been when he was in his thirties, close to her age now. He was laughing, presumably at something off camera, offering no hint of his inner struggle. It was ironic, she thought, how an image could accurately capture a split second in time but actually tell us nothing. What was he laughing about? Was he happy with his choices? A wave of sadness gripped her. Montgomery seemed like a decent person, and Erin couldn't help wondering whether, if he had lived longer, he would eventually have allowed himself to live as the person *she* knew *she* was. Erin gently placed the picture back on the table, wondering if there was anyone else in the room who knew his secret.

Eventually, Duane and Erin took seats toward the rear of the room, comparing notes. Neither of them had heard anything that provided any clue as to what had happened or who was responsible.

Around 3:45 p.m., Erin noticed some whispering, and there was almost a sense of excitement that spread throughout the room. A moment later, Arnold Welch, accompanied by four of his campaign staff, walked in. On the shorter side, with a round face and small paunch, Welch had blond hair that was now flecked with gray. As he made his way toward the casket, a number of people greeted him warmly. Makes sense, Erin thought, realizing that many of Montgomery's friends and coworkers were probably Arnold Welch supporters.

Duane leaned over and whispered to Erin, "If we have any chance of talking to him, it'll be on his way out, when he's away from the crowd."

"Good luck," Erin replied sotto voce.

Fifteen minutes later, when Welch briskly headed for the exit, Duane was there waiting.

"Mr. Welch, my name is Duane Swisher," he said, with that special tone that conveyed *law enforcement*. "May I speak with you for a minute, sir?"

Welch stopped just long enough for Duane to continue.

"Sir, my partner, Erin McCabe, was contacted by Mr. Montgomery. He was trying to get information about Senator Townsend to help your campaign. They met to discuss the information the day he was murdered, and I have a few questions."

Welch cocked his head to the side, seeming to weigh his options. "I'm sorry. I have no idea what you're talking about," he said, moving again toward the door.

"I think you know exactly what I'm talking about," Duane said, trying to keep pace. "And I think you know that Montgomery's murder may be related to him trying to get this information."

Welch motioned to one of his staff, who looked like he was a cop working a side job as security. The man quickly stepped in front of Duane and put his hand on Duane's chest.

"This conversation is over," the man said.

Duane glared at him. "If I were you, I'd take your hand off my chest, unless you want me to charge you with assault—or break your fucking arm in self-defense."

Momentarily stunned, the man removed his hand from Duane's chest, but then his eyes narrowed, seemingly trying to gauge who would come out on top if things escalated. Duane, who had taken a business card out of his wallet while waiting, handed it to the man. "Here's my card. Please make sure you give it to Mr. Welch and ask him to call me."

The man studied Duane's card, then Duane, before heading out the door.

"That went well," Erin said from behind Duane.

"What?" he responded angrily as he whipped around.

She held her hands up. "Whoa, big guy. Just me."

Duane took a deep breath. "Sorry."

"No worries," she said, gently resting her hand on his arm. "I think we're done for the afternoon. Why don't we head back to your place, compare notes, and I'll head back later?"

When she returned in the evening, she was alone. She had decided against bringing Mark, since, no matter how remote, the chances to learn something were better if she was on her own.

Not that this strategy seemed to be working either. No matter how many conversations she listened in on, or how many times she lingered by the photo table, she was still having very little luck.

As she took a seat in the back row of folding chairs, she contemplated whether she should leave. She never knew how to feel about wakes, which were never for the deceased; it wasn't like Brad Montgomery was going to be thankful she paid her respects. No, wakes were for the living—a bridge, as it were, to help the living deal with the loss of their loved one. But this one seemed strange. The surviving cousins didn't seem particularly distraught over Brad's demise, and based on what she had overheard from the employees of BJM Financial Services, they seemed more concerned with the fate of the company and their jobs now that the head honcho was gone, as opposed to any personal loss.

She glanced at her watch and told herself to give it five more minutes.

"Excuse me, dear."

Erin looked up to see a tall, thickly built brunette who appeared to be in her sixties staring at her kindly.

"I saw you here earlier this afternoon," the woman said in a husky contralto. "Did you work with Bradford?"

"No, ma'am. I'm a lawyer, and I recently met with Mr. Montgomery about some issues he had," Erin replied, knowing her response was mostly true.

"Do you mind if I sit?" the woman asked.

"No. By all means," Erin replied, gesturing to a seat next to her.

"It's very sweet of you to give up your entire Friday to be here."

"It's the least I could do," Erin replied, feeling a tinge of guilt that her real reason for being here had little to do with paying her respects, and a lot to do with trying to find something that would get her off the hook for his murder.

"Did you know Mr. Montgomery well?" Erin asked.

The woman let out a small chuckle. "Bradford and I go way back, I guess to the mid-seventies," she said.

The date resonated with Erin immediately. That's when Montgomery had told her he had been involved in going to crossdressing events.

"I'm so sorry for your loss," Erin offered. "I only knew him for a short time, but he seemed like a wonderful man who . . ." She stopped, searching for the right words. "A wonderful man who had many different sides."

The woman's forehead creased, and her head tilted as if trying to weigh what Erin had just said. "Yes. That's true. He certainly was a multifaceted individual," she answered, caution circling her words.

There was something about the woman and the two-step they had begun to play that intrigued Erin.

"My name is Erin McCabe," she said.

The woman folded her hands in her lap, and her eyes seemed to smile. "Hello, Erin. Rachel—Rachel Stern. It's a pleasure to meet you."

"Nice to meet you as well," Erin replied. "I wish it were under different circumstances, especially given your long friendship with Mr. Montgomery. The fact that he was murdered is just horrible," Erin said, trying to study Rachel for a reaction, to gauge if she knew anything about the murder. But Rachel was looking past Erin toward the entrance. When Erin turned to see what Rachel was looking at, there, in all his glory, was William Townsend.

As Welch had earlier in the day, Townsend was surrounded by people as he made his way to the casket at the front of the room.

Shit, Erin thought. If her theory that Townsend was connected to Montgomery's murder was correct, she didn't want to be seen by Townsend, and especially not talking to a friend of Montgomery's—someone whom Townsend might view as trying to get the same information from her that Montgomery had sought.

Erin quickly took a business card out of her purse. "Excuse me, Rachel. I have to run. Here's my card. Perhaps I'll see you tomorrow at the funeral, but if I don't, please give me a call, I'd love to talk more about Mr. Montgomery."

Rachel gave her a quizzical look. "Is everything okay?"

"Actually, no," Erin replied. "I just saw someone whom I don't want to see, and it's better for you if he doesn't see us together. Best if I go."

"Of course, my dear. It's been a pleasure chatting with you,"

Erin exited the row so that her back was always to Townsend. *Damn it,* she thought, cursing the fact that he had shown up just as she finally found someone who might have helpful information.

The next morning, Erin took a seat in the last row of the nondenominational chapel at Saint Stephen's Cemeteries just as the funeral service was about to begin. Thankfully, Townsend was not present.

Montgomery's casket sat in the front of the room—open so that the upper half of his body was visible. She surveyed the crowd and counted about twenty-five people, which seemed woefully small, given his wealth and status. Welch was in the second row, sitting between two people.

One of Montgomery's cousins gave a brief eulogy, talking about Montgomery's willingness to always be there to financially help out distant relatives in need. He was followed by two employees of BJM Financial Services, who expressed their appreciation for what a generous boss Montgomery had been and how much they would miss him. Following that, a minister walked to the lectern and said a few prayers. When he finished, the funeral director walked to the center of the room, thanked everyone for coming and advised them that Mr. Montgomery was going to be cremated and that the interment of his remains would be private, for family members only. He then let everyone know that people were invited to walk by the casket and pay their final respects.

When people began to stand and file past the casket, Erin moved outside, hoping to catch Rachel as she exited. Welch and the two people who had been sitting next to him were the first ones to leave, making their way to a Lincoln Town Car and driving away. As other people trickled out of the chapel, a few mingled on the sidewalk, chatting in small groups, but most made their way to their cars and left.

When Erin saw Montgomery's three cousins leave, she walked back to look inside. Everyone was gone; the place was empty.

Rachel hadn't come to the funeral? Why? It made no sense. Montgomery was her friend for more than thirty years. Did something happen after Erin left the funeral home? Had Erin's fear of being seen by Townsend somehow spooked Rachel, or, worse, had something happened to her? *Damn it*, Erin thought. *This isn't good.*

CHAPTER 7

Tuesday, June 2, 2009, 7:30 a.m.

MICHAEL GARDNER PACED HIS ALMOST BARREN ONE-ROOM OF-fice, berating himself while he waited for a report that would let him know how costly his mistake might be.

Fuck! How could I have been so fucking stupid, making such a god-damn rookie mistake? he wondered. Sure, the emails his team had hacked into on Welch's campaign's email server referred to the campaign purchasing disposable phones for key campaign peo-ple, but he hadn't checked the phone number he had discovered for Montgomery in one of the emails. Instead, he had assumed that Montgomery was one of the people who had received a burner, meaning all he'd have to do was destroy the phone, oblit-erating the unblocked calls he had made from his burner to Montgomery when he was on the beach, and all record of calls would be erased. But Montgomery's phone wasn't a burner. In-stead, when he recharged Montgomery's phone to see if there was any valuable information on it, he had discovered that it was simply an inexpensive cell phone, which meant somewhere records of calls existed—records that would give *his* burner num-ber and location. It would take some work, but because he had got-ten several calls on his regular cell phone while he was in Avalon, if anyone ever obtained his cell-phone information, they could use the cell-tower information from his phone, together with the cell-tower information from the burner he used, to place him near the beach in Avalon at the time of Montgomery's murder.

Realizing his mistake, he reached out to a former colleague from his days at the NSA and met with him so he could download the data from the phone to analyze. Now Gardner waited impatiently for the faxed report.

After what seemed like an eternity, the fax machine—the only thing in the office that was state-of-the-art—chimed and suddenly sprang to life. Gardner walked over to the machine, taking each page as it finished printing.

Analysis of Telephone Number 732-555-0194

The phone number in question is registered to a Verizon Wireless account in the name of Rachel Stern. There's one other number listed on the account, 732-555-0110. The address on the account is 538 Seventh Avenue, Asbury Park, New Jersey. Billing is paper. No online account set up. According to records for Monmouth County and the City of Asbury Park, the property is owned by Stern. A search of the County Clerk's Office shows no recorded mortgage. The deed shows that title was taken by Stern in 2002 from a Jacqueline Ford, who had purchased it several months earlier. According to the New Jersey Tenant Registration Act, Ford is a registered tenant at the address, as is an individual named Julius Hayser.

All utilities are listed in the name of Rachel Stern. Based on credit reports, which go back seven (7) years, Stern is approximately sixty-one years old. She has a checking and savings account at PNC Bank and receives a pension from the Internal Revenue Service. Three credit cards, all opened in 2002 and paid in full on a monthly basis. Excellent credit score.

Regarding Jacqueline Ford, other than the property in Asbury Park, there are no public records identifying her. She appears to live off the grid. There are no employment records, banking records, credit reports, or any other public records dealing with Ford. Except for the house, she is a ghost who has no traceable history.

Most of the calls made to and from this number are from the other cell-phone number listed on the account. There are also six

calls to a number registered to the campaign of Arnold Welch; four
calls to a cell phone registered to Arnold Welch; one call to the num-
ber for the Law Offices of McCabe & Swisher, LLP; and two calls
and one text message from an "unknown" number.

Bingo! Of course, Jacqueline Ford was a ghost. Jacqueline Ford
didn't exist. The name was nothing more than an alias for Bradford
Montgomery. Made sense given his penchant for crossdressing. Obviously, whoever Rachel Stern was, she was close to Montgomery.
And since both phones were in her name, with the bills sent to
her address, there might be a very easy solution.

He picked up his burner and dialed a number that he knew
was secure.

"Crossman?" he asked, using the man's code name.

"Who's this?"

"It's Farmer," he replied, providing his alias. "You still have access to the SSI and IRS database?"

"Yeah. Fifteen hundred each."

"For Christ's sake. I'm only looking for information on one
name!"

"I don't care if you're searching your own name. Fifteen each."

"I need everything you can get me on a Rachel Stern, current
address 538 Seventh Avenue, Asbury Park, New Jersey. Apparently, she receives a pension from the IRS, so I'd start there. And
I need it yesterday," he added.

"You're a funny guy, Farmer. For information that was needed
yesterday, I needed payment yesterday."

Gardner flexed his jaw and took a breath. "Western Union in a
half hour."

"Excellent. Assuming you're correct, you'll have your information ninety minutes after I collect my fee. Same fax number as before?"

"Yes."

Crossman gave a small snort. "A pleasure doing business with
you, Farmer."

* * *

Three hours later, Gardner stood off to the side of the stage in Meeting Room A of the Lafayette Hotel and Conference Center in downtown Trenton, waiting for Townsend's news conference with Dave Mallory to begin.

There was a buzz in the room as the fifteen reporters and various cameramen milled about, shooting curious glances at the twenty or so supporters of the American Liberty Defense Alliance strategically positioned around the room.

As he waited, Gardner scanned the fax Crossman had sent, intrigued by what he read about Rachel Stern. Given her past work with the IRS, he'd have to be careful, but it was still smart to take care of this quickly. Townsend could be mercurial, and he wanted to be in the position that, when he told Townsend about the problem, he could present him with the solution at the same time—one he was now confident he had. That was his job, to come up with solutions. The only difference this time was that he had created the problem, and he was already mad enough at himself that he didn't need Townsend haranguing him over his fuckup. More important, Gardner needed to keep Townsend's political ascent on the rise, to ensure he reached his own goal.

There was no denying that fate had hitched Gardner's wagon to Townsend's star, starting with the fact that Townsend had saved his career by covering up what Gardner's company had done in Vietnam—something Gardner had never forgotten. Without Townsend's efforts, Gardner's career path would have been far different. Instead, with his honorary discharge, Gardner was able to attend law school and then join the CIA. Once in the clandestine world, Gardner's career had advanced quickly, first in the CIA and then after he went to the NSA, mainly because those agencies tended to reward people like him—those with a "the ends justify the means" mentality. But about ten years ago, some of his "means" had caught up with him, and his career at the NSA had hit a dead end. He and Townsend had stayed in touch over the years, and from time to time, Gardner had provided Townsend with information, some concerning criminal investigations of people politically connected to Townsend. Then, at a reunion of the 23rd Infantry Division, they had talked late into the night about Townsend's game plan to become governor of New Jersey and then run for president. A short time after that, Gardner had come to work for Townsend and had spent the last nine years as Townsend's personal attorney—actually more of a consigliere, a problem solver. And if things worked out as Townsend planned, Gardner had a potential path back to his own fiefdom as the president's National Security Advisor, a role that would allow him to lord over those who had sidelined him.

Gardner looked up at Townsend, who was now standing at his shoulder, ready to take the stage.

"This idea of yours better work," Townsend's voice a muffled growl in Gardner's ear.

"Trust me. It will," Gardner replied, deciding this was not the time to discuss Rachel Stern. Hopefully, the news conference would work as planned, and then he could broach the subject with Townsend when he was in a much better frame of mind.

Townsend watched from offstage as Milo Corliss slowly climbed the three steps onto the stage, lumbered over to the podium, and tapped the microphone a few times to confirm it was live.

As Corliss ran through his introductory remarks, Townsend tried to take the measure of his fixer—something was off. Gardner was tough to read under any circumstances, but he seemed distracted. This should be Gardner's moment; he and Corliss had convinced him to join forces with Mallory and the American Liberty Defense Alliance. But whatever the hell was on Gardner's mind, Townsend told himself he'd deal with that later. Now it was time for him to play the role his handlers told him would reverse his sinking poll numbers. They had better be right.

"Senator William Townsend," Corliss announced, stepping back from the podium.

Townsend strode across the stage like a lion returning to his pride, knowing he cut a sharp image in his bespoke, navy-blue suit and a pale blue Winchester shirt with contrasting French cuffs and collar. A yellow silk Turnbull & Asser tie and pocket square completed the ensemble. He carried no notes, having committed to memory what he wanted to say.

"Good afternoon," he said, letting his rich baritone resonate through the PA system in the spacious conference room. "As people who have followed my political career are well aware, I have always been a friend and supporter of the LGBT community. I have had, and hope to continue to have, the support of the State's Log Cabin Republicans, the country's oldest Republican LGBT organization. I supported civil unions for same-sex couples and fully support New Jersey's laws that protect gay and lesbian folks from being discriminated against in employment and housing." He stopped, eyeing the reporters, looking for any reactions. "But I've recently discovered that when we amended the state's Law Against Discrimination in 2006, we did a tremendous disservice to the girls and women of our great state by allowing a provision that permits boys and men to claim they're females, thus allowing them to use public bathrooms and locker rooms reserved for women and girls. I take full responsibility for not realizing the full scope of the change that was in the amendment, but having now realized my mistake, it is time I try to correct it."

He paused, willing his face to appear sincere.

"I mean no disrespect to any transgenders in our state, but our wives, sisters, and daughters deserve to be protected against biological men who seek to prey upon them in their bathrooms and locker rooms and take their places in our sports programs."

"How you doing?" Mary O'Connor asked.

Michelle Costello gave O'Connor a shrug. Up until six months ago, Michelle had never considered going to a therapist. But when her eleven-year-old child came out to her as transgender, she welcomed the opportunity to talk to O'Connor, whose patience and experience helped her face issues she had never even thought about.

"I'm okay, I guess," Michelle finally responded. "I suppose I'm nervous about the whole name change thing, but Nic—I mean, Hannah—I've never seen Hannah happier in her life."

"She having any trouble in school?"

"No. So far, the kids have all been great. And even his . . . Sorry, I still struggle sometimes with the pronouns."

"No worries. You're doing great," O'Connor said with a warm smile.

"Thanks. I try to be really conscious of it when I'm with her, but old habits die hard, and for the last eleven years, she's been my little boy. And sometimes when I use pronouns, it's just reflexive."

"How does Hannah react when you mess up?"

Michelle inhaled before responding. "She's usually pretty understanding. It also helps that she's looking more and more like a girl every day. Her hair's gotten longer, and she really only wears girl's clothes. So when I look at her, it's easier to get the pronouns right."

"You were telling me about school."

Michelle nodded. "Yeah, the principal pushed back a little in the beginning. But after Hannah and I met with him and the school psychologist, he's been okay. Unbeknownst to me, Hannah had come out to the school psychologist in the beginning of the year—four months before she told me. So she was really helpful in convincing the principal that Hannah wasn't faking this. It also didn't hurt that our lawyer wrote a letter to the school board's attorney, pointing out what the law says. And, I have to say, with one exception, her teachers have been great."

"The exception?" O'Connor asked.

"Her gym teacher, Mr. Scott. He refused to let her change in the girls' locker room and was making her go to the nurse's office to change."

O'Connor sat back, concern sweeping across her face. "Oh. That's not right."

"Actually, it ultimately worked out okay. Hannah had told the school psychologist that she didn't want to change in front of all the other girls, because she didn't have the right parts and she was embarrassed. They have a private bathroom near the office that the coaches use, and Hannah changes there. She's okay using the girls' room to go to the bathroom because no one can see her when she's in the stall, but the prospect of changing out in the open in front of all the girls was freaking her out."

O'Connor chuckled. "Sixth grade is such a tough year. I'm sure there's probably about twenty other girls in her class who wish they could change in private."

Michelle gave a knowing smile. "Oh, trust me, I remember. I didn't start to develop until the summer before my freshman year. Middle school was a nightmare. I wish I could've had my own bathroom."

Both Gardner and Mallory had emphasized that bathrooms and sports were the key points to hammer on. Mallory had shown him internal polling that ALDA had done that showed even people who didn't think transgender people should be discriminated against struggled with what bathroom or locker room a transgender person should use, especially transgender girls and women.

"New Jersey's law has been interpreted so broadly," Townsend continued, "that our youth and high school sports' governing bodies are using it to allow boys and young men to take the rightful place of girls and young women in youth and interscholastic athletic competitions and, in the process, marginalizing our wonderful, hardworking female athletes. This madness must stop, so I want to bring up David Mallory, the legal director of the American Liberty Defense Alliance."

Mallory bounded up the steps with the swagger of a bully heading toward his next victim. Like Townsend, his suit was custom-made and designed to accentuate his broad shoulders and barrel chest. His sandy hair was slicked back, and his eyes seemed to glow like a coyote on the prowl. When he reached the podium, Mallory allowed a tight smile to grace his lips.

"I personally want to thank David for bringing the full implications of the 2006 amendment to my attention," Townsend said as he shook Mallory's hand at the podium. "He and the American Liberty Defense Alliance are working tirelessly to defend the rights of girls and women. David's here to tell you about the profound impact this amendment is having on one family."

Townsend moved several steps away from the podium, allowing Mallory to step up to the mic.

"Has her father objected to the name change application?" O'Connor asked.

"No, but from what the lawyer tells me, he has until the end of the week. I don't think he'll do anything. He really hasn't been part of Hannah's life since we divorced. Honestly, Paul's not a bad guy, he just never wanted to have children. He had a horrible relationship with his own father, who was physically abusive to him, his brothers, and his mom, and, as a result, when I found out I was pregnant, he wanted me to have an abortion. But I believed it was my right to choose—after all, it is my body—and I wanted the baby. That was pretty much the death knell for our marriage. We separated for a few months, then we reconciled, and I hoped that once he saw the baby, he'd change his mind, but he didn't. I guess he was so afraid of being a horrible father, he thought Nicholas would be better off with no father. The irony is that, because of his experiences with his father, I think he would have been a great dad."

"When's the last time he saw Hannah?" O'Connor asked.

Michelle gave a small sigh. "Well, technically he's never seen Hannah. He came to one of Nick's soccer games about three years ago. We went out for breakfast afterward, and I think both of us thought that maybe after that Paul would be part of her life—but then, nothing. That was hard for Hannah. She blames herself for the fact that her dad doesn't want to see her. And as much as I try to tell her that it's not her, she's sure it's her fault."

"I'm sorry to hear that. Is it okay if I share that with Dr. Bradshaw?" O'Connor asked, referring to Hannah's therapist.

"Of course," Michelle replied. "I guess the only positive thing is that since he has no relationship with her, Hannah coming out as trans isn't going to impact it."

"Well, you never know how people will react. But hopefully,

based on what you've told me, he won't do anything to interfere with Hannah's transition."

"Yeah, I suspect he'll do exactly what he's done for the last eleven years—pay his child support and be invisible. He doesn't even want to acknowledge he has a child. I can't imagine him doing anything to try and interfere."

"Good afternoon, everyone, and thank you, Senator Townsend, for allowing me the opportunity to speak here today on the issues threatening our daughters, wives, and sisters. As a result of the 2006 amendment, young girls and women across New Jersey have to look behind their backs as they change in locker rooms just to make sure there isn't a confused man trying to catch a peek. We at the ALDA applaud your efforts to right this injustice." Bringing his hands together in prayer, Mallory turned, bowed his head to Townsend, then returned his attention to the audience.

Watching Mallory's showmanship, Townsend suppressed a smile—this guy is good, he thought.

"The other reason we are here today is to shine a spotlight on a related situation in which a mother, without the consent of the child's father, is attempting to change their child's sex and name. The ALDA has agreed to represent the dad and will not only oppose the application to change his child's name; we will be filing an action in the Family Court to remove custody of the child from his mother and give custody to our client to prevent irreversible medical procedures from being inflicted upon the child." Mallory gestured with a wave of his hand. "Paul, come on up."

A man with short brown hair, who looked to be in his mid-thirties, dressed casually in khakis and a button-down dress shirt, slowly made his way across the stage. He avoided looking out at the crowd, keeping his head bowed, his only focus seeming to be on making it across the stage in one piece.

"Folks, this is Paul Costello, the young man I was telling you about.

"Paul works hard every day as an electrician at the New Jersey Convention Center in Edison," Mallory continued. "Like many

Americans, Paul's marriage ended in divorce, and despite wanting to have a relationship with his young son, his former wife has done everything she could to prevent that from happening. As a result, Paul has only seen his son sporadically over the last five years. Recently, Paul learned that his ex-wife is attempting to turn his son into a girl and is seeking to have his name legally changed to a girl's name. Like any father, Paul is horrified and concerned for his son's physical safety and emotional well-being. That is why the ALDA has agreed to represent Paul.

"Unfortunately, Paul's son is emblematic of a much larger issue—the willingness of therapists, doctors, and even parents to allow and encourage young, impressionable children to believe that they are other than God made them. Folks, there are only two genders, male and female, and you cannot change who you are. Accordingly, we are thrilled to announce that Senator Townsend has agreed to sponsor legislation to amend the state's definition of 'child abuse' to include any attempts by a parent, guardian, or health-care provider to provide puberty blockers, cross-sex hormones, or genital-mutilating surgery to minors."

Mallory took a step back from the podium to allow Townsend to approach. This time, as they shook hands for the cameras, Townsend patted Mallory on the shoulder. Townsend then stepped up to the mic.

"In addition to the legislation, I'm also announcing that my PAC will be making a fifty-thousand-dollar donation to the ALDA to support its commitment to defending the rights of women and girls and preventing medical experimentation on young, confused individuals."

After Townsend finished, he and Mallory shook hands again, and then he stood at the podium, taking questions from the reporters. When they walked off the stage fifteen minutes later, Gardner was waiting in the wings, his face a display of self-satisfaction.

"I'm glad I introduced you to each other," he said.

"The pleasure has been all mine," Mallory replied quickly.

Townsend gave Mallory a sly grin. "If you ever decide to go into politics, Mr. Mallory, let me know. You have a natural gift for . . . how should I put it?"

"Bullshit?" Mallory said.

"I would have been more diplomatic, but bullshit works," Townsend replied with a laugh.

"Thank you, Senator. I do appreciate this opportunity, and I can assure you that we will work with Mr. Gardner and Mr. Corliss to make sure the ALDA's endorsement of you is timed for the maximum effect."

"Thank you," Townsend replied. "I believe Milo has the check from my PAC, so make sure you see him before you leave."

CHAPTER 8

Tuesday, June 2, 2009, 2:30 p.m.

T HE INTERCOM ON HER PHONE BUZZED. "ERIN, IT'S RICH RUDOLPH on line one. He said you'd know who he is. Do you want me to put him through?" Cheryl asked.

"Sure," Erin replied, wondering why Rudolph, a reporter for the *Newark Journal,* would be calling. She had known Rudolph since she was a public defender, but it had been during the recent trial of Ann Parsons's case in Union County when she had come to truly respect his journalistic skills.

"Hello, Mr. Rudolph," Erin answered with faux formality. "To what do I owe the honor?"

"Hi, Erin. I'm calling to see if I can pick your brain a bit, because, honestly, you're the only trans person I know, and I have some questions."

Curious about Rudolph's strange lead-in, she told him she'd be happy to try to answer his questions.

"To start with, since the last time we spoke, I have a new assignment," Rudolph said. "I'm now covering the governor's race, and I just left a news conference given by Senator Townsend and David Mallory, from the American Liberty Defense Alliance. I was wondering if you'd be willing to talk a little on background, and then, if I could get maybe some comments from you."

"Townsend and the American Liberty Defense Alliance?" Erin repeated. "Those are strange bedfellows," she said.

"That's what I thought," Rudolph replied. "Let me tell you what happened at the presser. Townsend announced that he will be sponsoring legislation to amend the state's definition of 'child abuse' to include any attempts by a parent, guardian, or health-care provider to provide puberty blockers, cross-sex hormones, or genital-mutilating surgery to minors."

"What!" Erin shouted. "That's crazy—genital-mutilating surgery! Give me a break."

"I'm not even sure I understand what that all means. Can you help me out?" Rudolph inquired.

"Rich, the first thing you should do is go online and search for the WPATH Standards of Care. WPATH stands for the World Professional Association for Transgender Health. Under the approved standards, minors don't undergo genital surgery, which in an adult would be called gender-affirming surgery," Erin offered. "And as for puberty blockers and hormones, they can save kids' lives."

"Why is that?" Rudolph asked.

"Rich, you're a guy; think about what puberty is like for a boy. The voice deepens, you start to grow a beard and body hair, you develop an Adam's apple—your body changes in profound ways. Now imagine that all those things are happening to you, and you know you're a girl—it can be devastating. Puberty blockers only delay puberty; they're reversable because if you go off them, you then go through the puberty of the sex you were assigned at birth. On the other hand, the effects of puberty are very hard to reverse."

"But do kids really know who they are at puberty?"

"Yeah—not all trans kids know, but many do. In fact, some kids know much younger. I knew from around the age of four. If you allow kids to delay puberty, it gives everyone time to make sure this is the right thing to do for the child, and if it is, then you're not trying to undo or override the changes that puberty has already brought. But, Rich, please keep in mind, many trans kids either can't afford those treatments or don't have parents or guardians who will allow it. Which means this will be particularly harsh because it will target those parents who not only want to help their kids, but also have the means to do so."

"Okay, thanks. Unfortunately, there's more," Rudolph said. "Townsend wants to roll back the provisions of the New Jersey Law Against Discrimination that allows people to use bathrooms and locker rooms in accordance with their gender identity, and he wants to prevent transgender kids from playing youth and high school sports in accordance with their gender identity because they're taking away spots from 'real' girls."

Erin closed her eyes and tried to take a breath. She felt like she was about to explode. *Why the hell was he doing this?*

"Erin, are you still there?" Rudolph asked.

"Yeah. I'm here," she replied. "Rich, let me ask you a question. Can you name one high school transgender athlete?"

There was a long pause. "I don't know of any," he finally said.

"Precisely. It's not an issue."

"I know that, several years ago, you represented Sharise Barnes, a transgender woman who killed Townsend's only son. Do you think there might be a connection between those events and Townsend's sudden interest in trans issues?"

"No," she replied quickly, certain Sharise's case had nothing to do with this. "No, this has to have something to do with the American Liberty Defense Alliance. What do they bring to the table?"

"Of course, that's it," Rudolph responded. "It's the primary. All the polling is showing that the primary race between Townsend and Welch is getting tighter, so the ALDA helps move Townsend to the right on a social issue few people care about."

Erin winced. "Rich, if you're trans or if your child is trans, you care deeply about these issues," she said softly, caught between the sting that no one cared and the realization that, in some ways, trans people would be better off if no one cared.

"Um, sorry," Rudolph replied. "I didn't mean that the way it sounded. I just meant that Townsend doesn't lose any votes going after the trans community."

"I get it," Erin said. "And you're right. That all makes sense."

"You willing to go on the record to talk about this?" Rudolph asked.

The safe response was "No." She knew if she walked down the hallway and spoke with "her attorney," Swish would tell her not to go on the record—nothing good could come of it. And he was right. If Townsend was involved in Montgomery's death and trying to set her up, she wasn't going to help herself by attacking him in the press. But fuck Townsend. He was going after the kids—kids who wanted nothing more than a chance to live their lives. For whatever reason, life had afforded her a platform, and despite her reluctance, if she didn't speak up, who would? It was a role she didn't relish, but it was one she felt she couldn't turn away from either.

"Sure. Fire away," Erin replied.

Hannah giggled, and Morgan burst out laughing when Jenna finished telling them her story. The three lived in the same neighborhood and had always been friendly, but after Hannah had socially transitioned, they had become inseparable. The previous Saturday had been Morgan's birthday, and she had a sleepover—it was the first one Hannah had ever been to. As soon as Hannah had come home on Sunday morning, she asked her mom if, when her name change was official, she could have a sleepover with Morgan and Jenna to celebrate officially being Hannah. Her mom had smiled and happily agreed.

As they turned the corner onto their street, Hannah noticed her mom's car in the driveway. It wasn't unheard of for her mom to be home before she was, but it was unusual enough that Hannah hoped there was nothing wrong. She quickly said goodbye to her friends and ran into the house.

"Hi, Mom. I'm home," she called out.

"I'm in the kitchen, Hannah."

Hannah dropped her backpack in the hallway and headed to the kitchen. As soon as Hannah saw her mother's face, she knew something was up. Her mom's eyes were red and puffy. Clearly, she'd been crying.

"Mom, what's the matter?" she said, rushing over to the table.

Her mom's elbow rested on the table, her hand covering her mouth. "Sit," she said.

Hannah pulled out a chair and took a seat. Her eyes were fixed on her mom, fear slowly churning her stomach.

"Hannah, honey, we need to talk."

"Okay," Hannah said, trepidation creeping into her voice.

"Honey, your dad has filed opposition to your name change."

"Opposition? What's that mean?" Hannah asked.

"It means he doesn't want you to be allowed to change your name to Hannah," her mother said softly.

"How can he do that? I never even see him."

Her mom took a deep breath. "Well, as your father, he does have the legal right to argue that your name shouldn't be changed."

"Why would he care?" Hannah asked, confused by what her mother was telling her.

Her mother reached out and took hold of Hannah's hand. "Apparently, your dad has teamed up with some folks who don't approve of transgender people, and I'm not sure why he suddenly cares, but I got a call from our lawyer about an hour ago, and your dad has filed papers to oppose your name change and . . . and to try and get temporary custody of you."

"Get custody? Of me? You mean, he wants me to live at his house? How can he do that? I've seen him like three times in my entire life."

Her mother sighed. "Honey, it's complicated. According to our lawyer, the lawyers representing your father are accusing me of abusing you by trying to force you to be a girl," her mother said, choking back tears.

The import of what her mother just said suddenly hit Hannah. "Mom, are you saying they want to force me to go back to living as a boy?"

Her mother nodded.

Hannah pushed her chair back and stood up. "No way! I won't do it," she said, running out of the room and up the stairs to her bedroom.

Hannah curled herself into a ball on her bed and began sobbing. She couldn't go back. Why was he doing this to her? He had never been part of her life, and now suddenly he wanted to try to take control.

Hannah felt the bed tilt as her mother sat down next to her and slowly began stroking her hair.

"It's going to be okay, honey. No judge is going to take you away from me." Her mom slowly stretched out on the bed next to her and wrapped her arm around Hannah. "I promise, I won't let anything happen to you."

Hannah lay there, swaddled in her mother's arm, trying with all her might to believe everything was going to be all right. "I'm scared, Mom. Who are these people helping my father, and why are they coming after me?"

"I honestly don't know, hon. It doesn't make any sense to me either. I'm supposed to talk with our lawyer tomorrow, and hopefully I'll find out more then."

Hannah rolled over so she was facing her mom, wiping a tear from her cheek. "I'm a girl, mom. They can't make me be a boy—they can't."

"I know, honey," her mother said. "I know."

Hannah pursed her lips. "I won't go back. I'd rather be dead than go back."

"Please don't say that, Hannah. I need you alive. You are my pride and joy. I wouldn't survive if anything happened to you."

Her mother pulled her close and kissed her forehead. "We'll get through this. I promise we'll get through it."

CHAPTER 9

Wednesday, June 3, 2009, 9:15 a.m.

Duane had the *Newark Journal* open on the top of his glass desk. The article on Townsend's news conference and proposed legislation was prominently displayed on page one above the fold. Fortunately, Erin's comments weren't on page one; unfortunately, they were on page seven. He knew if this had been any other client, he'd probably be having a conversation with them suggesting that if they weren't going to follow his advice, they should probably start looking for a new lawyer, but this was not any other client. This was the person who, outside of his wife and family, he was closest to.

Try as he might, he couldn't explain the bond that existed between them. When they had first met, almost twenty years earlier, they had connected as two guys whose girlfriends were best friends. At that point, Ian seemed like a regular guy. But after Erin had come out, been divorced from Lauren, and transitioned, Duane seemed to have nothing in common with her, other than both of them being criminal defense lawyers—and, in his case, that wasn't even his career choice. He had taken a fair amount of ribbing from his friends, some good-natured, some not, when he remained partners with her after she transitioned. And, if he was honest, there was part of him that had been upset that Ian hadn't told him before they became partners about being trans. But both Corrine and Lauren persuaded him to give the new situation a try. And as strange as it was to watch his friend morph into this new persona, Erin seemed so at peace with who she was that, within weeks of her coming back to work as Erin, they had settled into a new normal. He shook his head and smiled, trying to remember who she used to be. He had known her as Ian for almost fourteen years and as Erin for about six, yet he found it almost impossible to remember or see her as anyone other than Erin.

And now that bond between them presented him with another dilemma—representing a friend. The pressure of representing a client you truly believed was innocent, and whose life depended on your skills as a lawyer, was a lot to deal with in a normal case, but this was decidedly not a normal case. The pressure he felt in knowing Erin's very freedom was in his hands was almost unbearable. And as her fate weighed on him, there had been several times when he had come close to suggesting that she should retain other counsel. But, for better or worse, Erin had put her faith in him, and he didn't want to let her down.

"Hey, big guy," Erin said from the doorway. "Cheryl said you wanted to see me when I got here. I'm here. What's up?"

Duane motioned for her to come in. "Let me ask you a question," Duane said, as she took a seat in one of the chairs in front of his desk. "What would you do if one of our clients who, let's say, was under investigation for murder, was quoted in the newspaper talking trash about a very rich and powerful politician?"

"This is a hypothetical question, right?" she replied, cocking her head to the side, her eyes fixed on the paper in front of him.

He folded the newspaper so page one was on display. "You tell me—is it hypothetical?"

She looked down at her lap, her demeanor suddenly that of the child holding a cookie next to the broken cookie jar. "Can I plead guilty with an explanation?"

Duane closed his eyes and inhaled. "You're a difficult client, you know that?"

"I haven't seen the article. How bad is it?"

He picked up the paper and offered it to her. "What you said is fine. It's not the content. It's the fact that we both suspect Townsend is behind all of this, and yet you're poking at him. My question is why?"

Erin took the paper, scanning the front page and then opening it to page seven. As she read, she nodded along as if affirming her words. When she finished, she no longer looked like a guilty child. Now she looked like she was standing next to the broken cookie jar saying, "I broke it. What are you going to do about it?"

"Swish, you are one of the nicest people I know—other than on a basketball court," she added with a weak grin. "But the other day at the funeral home, when Welch's bodyguard put his hand on your chest, I saw your reaction. I won't pretend I know for sure, but I suspect your anger had a little to do with Welch not wanting to talk to you, but more to do with the fact that a white man was trying to make you back down. And what I saw—what I saw was there was no way you were backing down to the man. I understand my situation is much different, but by attacking trans kids, Townsend is being a bully putting his hand on the chest of my community, trying to stop us from moving forward. Sorry, but I can't back down either, not even if it makes me a shitty client. So if you want someone else to represent me, I understand, but I'm not going to shut up. Truth is, even if I sit here quiet as a church mouse, Townsend's still going to come after me. I can't hide from him, Swish. I have to push back."

Duane stroked his goatee, feeling a mix of resignation and pride as he looked at the defiant face of his partner. "You know, there's a fierceness to you now that I don't remember you showing before you transitioned."

She shrugged. "Maybe. I don't know. Before I transitioned, I was perceived as just a kind of bland, privileged white guy. To the rest of the world, there was nothing that made me stand out—I wasn't the other. Now, like it or not, I'm one of the others because I carry around an adjective. I'm the transgender woman, the transgender attorney—whatever it is, the adjective always comes first. I don't know, maybe going through the gender confirma-

tion process acted as a kiln, hardening me to help me survive."
She hesitated. "But why am I telling you? In this country, you're
not seen just as a man—you're always seen as a Black man. You
have your own adjective."

"Yeah, I do. And I get the similarity, but let's face it, there's a
major difference."

"How so?" she asked.

"Yes, I'm a Black man, but I'm always a Black man. No matter
what room I'm in, no one's ever going to mistake me for a white
dude. So whatever racial bias exists in that room, conscious or unconscious, it's going to land on me. On the other hand, no one
ever questions my authenticity as a Black man. They may hate me
for who I am, but they never deny who I am. For you, it's different. Unless you out yourself, you just blend in—people just see a
white woman."

She frowned. "You're right, I do sometimes have a cloak of in-
visibility you'll never have."

"But there's the irony," he said. "When people do know about
you, not only do some people hate you simply because you're the
other, but a lot of people won't even accept that you're a woman.
Like I said, no one ever denies I'm Black."

She sighed. "I sometimes focus on the shit I have to deal with
and forget the advantages I've had. I spent the first thirty-plus
years of my life being perceived as a heterosexual white guy—and
reaped the benefit of that privilege. I didn't face the same misogyny that cis women deal with growing up or the racial prejudice
you've faced. And even after I transitioned, I didn't lose the ben-
efits of a lot of what I obtained. Honestly, I'm one of the lucky
trans people. I still have my family, my career . . . and my law partner," she added with a wink.

They sat, not saying anything.

"By the way, you're not a shitty client," Duane replied, his
words slicing through the silence. "And I don't want you to get
another lawyer."

"Thanks," she replied, her eyes conveying her gratitude.

* * *

Later, back in her office, Erin picked up her BlackBerry from her desk and checked the display. "Hi, Mom," she answered. "Is everything okay?" she asked, concerned because her mother rarely called her during work hours.

"Yes, dear, everything's okay—well, mostly. Do you have a minute to talk?"

"Sure. What's going on?" Erin asked.

"I'm sorry to bother you, but . . . well, usually you let me know when you're going to be in the newspaper, giving me a chance to warn your father about what's coming. So I was surprised this morning when there was an article about Senator Townsend in which you're quoted extensively about how bad his proposals would be for transgender kids."

"I'm sorry, Mom. I should have called you last night, but I honestly had no idea it was going to be such a big article. Was Dad upset?"

"A little bit," her mom said, but her tone suggested that maybe she was understating his reaction. "You know your father is trying to be accepting, and he's gotten much better. But he doesn't understand why you always have to be so public."

Erin took a deep breath, trying not to get upset. It had only been in the last two years that she and her dad had begun to bridge the chasm that had opened up between them when Erin had come out as transgender and then transitioned. For nearly three years, her father and her brother, Sean, had refused to talk to her. It was only thanks to the persistence of her mother, Sean's wife, Liz, and Sean's two young sons, Patrick and Brennan, that their relationships had started to heal. But despite the progress, Erin knew her father still struggled, a struggle made even more difficult when she had started dating Mark.

"Erin, are you there?"

"I'm here," she replied, a weariness creeping into her tone. "Honest, Mom, I don't know what Dad wants me to do. People know I'm transgender. Besides, there must be a couple thousand McCabes in New Jersey. How is anyone going to know I'm related to Dad?"

"Honey, the article says you're an attorney in Cranford, with the firm of McCabe & Swisher, and your father used to brag all the time about his son, the lawyer. I'm sorry. It's just hard for him. He comes from a generation of men that struggle with LGBT issues."

"In other words, I embarrass him."

"Well . . ."

"What should I do, Mom—sit quietly in the corner and not say or do anything, so I don't embarrass anyone?" As the words left her mouth, Erin immediately felt a tinge of guilt for taking her frustrations out on her mom, who had always been her staunchest supporter. "I'm sorry. I'm not trying to take it out on you."

"I know you're not, dear," her mother replied in the calm, measured tones she reserved for most difficult conversations. "You have to do whatever you feel is right. But if you know something is coming, just try and let me know, so I can prepare your father. He really does love you, and his take on things is evolving. You have to admit he's much better than he was two years ago."

"You're right, Mom."

"Slow and steady does it," her mother replied.

"Um, well, there is something else that you should probably warn Dad about."

"What's that, dear?"

"My twentieth high school reunion is Saturday."

"Are you going?" her mother asked.

"Yeah, I was planning on it."

"Oh," her mother said.

"Why do you sound so surprised?" Erin asked.

"I don't know. I guess the fact that it's an all-boys school . . . well, I just thought you might be a little embarrassed to go."

"Oh, I'm sure it will be awkward," Erin said with a small snort. "I know Dad was very active in the Fathers' Club when Sean and I went there, and he's still friends with some of the dads of guys who may be at the reunion." She stopped. "I guess I may wind up embarrassing him again. Sorry, Mom."

"Thank you for letting me know," her mom replied.

They talked for a few more minutes about the Montgomery investigation and about them coming down to her condo in Bradley Beach for a weekend. When Erin hung up, her mind jumped back and forth between the newspaper article and her dad's embarrassment.

Cheryl's voice on the intercom broke her train of thought. "Erin, there's a Rachel Stern on line two for you. Do you want the call?"

"Yes!" Erin said, grabbing for the phone.

Adam Lonza knocked on the open door of Assistant Prosecutor Pendergast's office.

"Heard you wanted to see me?" Lonza asked.

Pendergast looked up from a stack of papers. "Yeah," he responded. "Come in and close the door."

"What's up?" Lonza asked, taking a seat.

Pendergast swiveled to grab a folded newspaper from his credenza. "I don't know if you get the *Newark Journal*, but take a look at the front-page article on Townsend. Your girlfriend McCabe's in there."

Lonza took the newspaper and glanced at the headline. "Well, I'm glad someone's doing something about this transgender shit."

"Read the story," Pendergast directed.

"What the fuck?" Lonza said as he got to page seven.

> *Noted transgender attorney Erin McCabe called Senator Townsend's proposed legislation "mean-spirited" and "a solution in search of a problem." McCabe observed that transgender people use the bathroom for the same reason everyone else does, to go to the bathroom. She said Townsend and others like him who attempt to link transgender people to assaults in bathrooms have absolutely no facts to back up those claims. "There is simply no evidence that transgender people engage in sexual assaults in bathrooms," McCabe said. McCabe pointed out that*

transgender people have been legally using bathrooms in New Jersey in accordance with their gender identity since 2007, and there are no reported instances of any problems. McCabe agrees that any sexual predator who goes into a bathroom to assault someone should be arrested, but to equate transgender people with sexual predators is a false equivalence. As far as prohibiting transgender children from receiving the appropriate health care, McCabe noted that "minors are not undergoing gender-affirming surgeries, and what other care they receive should be left to parents, guardians, and health-care professionals and not to politicians trying to score points in the midst of an election." McCabe stated, "By going after a vulnerable population, especially children, Townsend's actions will likely lead to more bullying and harassment because he is telling people it's okay to attack members of the transgender community."

Lonza let out a whistle. "Wow! She certainly didn't mince any words, did she? Townsend isn't going to be happy."

"You know him?" Pendergast asked.

"Townsend? How the fuck would I know Townsend?" Lonza said, confused by the question.

"I don't know. You tell me," Pendergast said accusingly.

"What's that supposed to mean?"

"It means I want to know what you're doing."

Lonza leaned forward. "What are you implying?" he asked, anger creeping into his voice.

Pendergast chuckled. "I'm not implying anything. I'm telling you flat out that I know you're leaking shit on the investigation."

Lonza stared at him, then rose out of his chair. "Fuck you. I don't have to take this shit."

"Sit," Pendergast commanded in a tone that left no room for negotiation.

Lonza warily lowered himself back into the chair.

"Relax," Pendergast said. "I'm not trying to hurt you. If you tell me what's going on, maybe we can work together. And before you go batshit crazy again, I'll lay all my cards on the table." Cuffing his hands behind his head, Pendergast leaned back in his chair. "A week ago, our wonderful first assistant prosecutor told me he's taking over as lead on the Montgomery case, because he's getting some pressure. Makes no sense to me—rich faggot gets murdered, who the hell would be putting on any pressure? But then I remember you telling me Montgomery was working for the Welch campaign, so maybe it's someone connected to Welch. Then, two days ago, Detective Carter wanted to talk to me confidentially, because she had been here the day before, running down surveillance videos. After you left, she saw that a fax you'd tried to send hadn't gone through. Thinking she was helping you out, she had the machine print from memory what you had sent." Pendergast opened his desk drawer and took out some papers and held them out. "Look familiar?"

Lonza eyed Pendergast suspiciously. He grabbed the papers, scanned the cover sheet, and laid them back on Pendergast's desk. *I'm fucked,* he thought.

"Who you helping?" Pendergast asked.

Lonza's expression looked like that of a boxer whose manager had just thrown in the towel. He slumped forward, defeat slowly sapping his energy. "He uses the name Farmer. What he told me is that he's tight with some politicians, and if things go right, he can help my career."

"Welch?" Pendergast suggested.

"No, it can't be."

"Why not?

Lonza exhaled. "You're not going to jam me up?"

Pendergast laughed. "Shit, no. If whoever you're dealing with is on the level and can help your career, then maybe they can help me too. I don't want Paterson to get credit for solving this case. My goal is to get his job—become first assistant, then after a few years, hopefully get a judgeship."

"What about Carter? How do we deal with her?"

"Already taken care of. I told her your fax was to a confidential informant you had in Welch's campaign. She bought it. So, what's going on?"

Lonza realized he had nothing to lose. If Pendergast was on the level, they both stood to gain. If he wasn't, he was already fucked because of the stupid fax machine.

"The day after we found Montgomery, I had just finished my workout at the gym. I'm heading to my car when a guy calls my name. It sounds like he knows me, but I've never seen the guy before. He walks over and tells me he works for someone with a lot of juice who's very interested in the Montgomery case, and he's looking for information. He tells me if I help him out and the right people get elected, I'll be a lieutenant in five years."

"Lieutenant in five years! And you fucking believed him?"

"As crazy as it sounds, he knew every detective's info, including when sergeants and lieutenants were eligible to retire on full pension. I'm telling you, this guy strikes me as a pro."

"So why don't you think he's connected to Welch?"

"Because we know Montgomery was connected to the Welch campaign, and this guy wanted to know if we had any dirt on Montgomery."

Pendergast cocked his head to the side. "Wait. Did you give him copies of the pictures?"

"No. I didn't have to. I showed them to him, but he said he already knew Montgomery was a fag and could find some of the photos on the Internet. He was looking to see if we had anything he didn't know."

"Did we?"

"No, not on Montgomery."

"What else was he looking for?"

Lonza put his hand in front of his mouth. "Basically, our investigative reports, especially anything to do with McCabe," he muttered.

Pendergast's face scrunched like he had just stepped in dog shit. "What the fuck is it with McCabe that everyone wants her to take the fall for this? Do you honestly think McCabe, someone at the head of the class in being a fucking pervert, is blackmailing Montgomery?"

For the first time since he came into the office, Lonza relaxed a little. "I don't know. What else do you make of the photos? Sure looks like someone was blackmailing him. Why not her? I think she was trying to get Montgomery to back off supporting Welch. Besides, based on what we have, she was the last person with him. I'd say she's still top of the list."

Pendergast chuckled. "Of course she's on the top of the list—she's the only one on the list."

"Makes it easy then, doesn't it?" Lonza suggested, giving Pendergast a conspiratorial grin.

CHAPTER 10

Tuesday, June 9, 2009, 7:15 p.m.

Erin had only seen Rachel Stern once, and even then, it was just for several minutes. Standing at the entrance to the Hotel Tides's small dining room, she hoped she would recognize her.

Sitting alone at a table in the far corner was a woman that fit Erin's mental image of Stern—sixtyish, with a round face and a prominent chin, the only difference being that Erin remembered her with brown hair, not the current auburn crown. Confident that it was her, Erin made her way toward the table.

"Good evening, Ms. Stern," Erin said. "Nice to see you again."

Stern gave Erin a warm smile. "Please, call me Rachel," she said, gesturing to the chair opposite her.

"Of course," Erin said, taking a seat. "Please call me Erin."

"Thank you for coming. I hope it isn't too far out of the way for you."

Erin grinned. "Actually, the Tides is one of my favorite restaurants in Asbury. I have a place in Bradley Beach."

"Oh. I had no idea."

"No reason you should've known."

An awkward fog of silence seemed to roll over them. Finally, Erin spoke. "I thought I'd see you at Bradford's funeral service."

Stern tilted her head. From Erin's perspective it looked like she was weighing her options.

"Ms. McCabe—sorry, Erin," Stern began, "let me be very direct. Bradford was one of, if not my closest friend. Someone murdered him, and I'm trying to figure out why. He was a very good person, and despite his success in business and his wealth, as far as I know he had no enemies—or certainly none that I'm aware of who had reason to kill him." Stern rubbed her hands together, her eyes narrowed. "I've done some research on you, and I know you're an attorney. I also know that you're a transgender woman. When we were at the funeral home, you told me you had recently met with Brad about some issues he had." She stopped, appearing to weigh her words. "Here's the thing, Erin. I am by nature a cautious woman, and at this point I have no idea if I can trust you or not. I suspect that if I ask you flat-out why Brad wanted to speak with you, you'd tell me it was privileged. So how do I figure out whose side you're on?"

Erin cupped her fingers around her chin. She had no idea what Stern's background was, but her manner gave off an aura of law enforcement.

"You're correct about the attorney-client privilege. That said, we're both here for the same reason—we're trying to figure out why Bradford was killed. You because he was your best friend, me because . . ." Erin paused, knowing what she said next could either break through the developing impasse or cause Stern to get up and leave. "Me, because there are members of the Cape May County Prosecutor's Office who think I killed him."

Stern's eyes went round, and her sharp intake of breath was audible. "And why do they think you killed him?"

"Because, according to them, I was the last person to see him alive. But I know I couldn't have been because he was very much alive when I left him."

"Wait. He was killed on Memorial Day. Were you with him on Memorial Day?"

Erin nodded.

Stern grew silent, seemingly lost in thought. "That's interesting. I had dinner with Ja—Brad here that Saturday, and he told me he was heading to Avalon because he was meeting with someone on Monday. The Welch campaign wanted information, and he had volunteered because he was interested to meet the person who had the information. That person was you, wasn't it?"

"I guess it may have been," Erin responded cautiously. "I have no idea who else Bradford met with on Memorial Day."

"Good evening," a waiter interrupted. "How are you, Ms. Stern? I apologize for the delay." After some chitchat with Rachel, he told them the dinner specials and took their drink and dinner orders.

"They know you by name," Erin observed. "You must come here often," she said.

"I do. I only live a few doors down, and even when I don't come to eat, I often stop by for a drink." Despite the momentary distraction, Stern picked up the thread of her previous inquisition. "It was you. You represented the woman who killed Townsend's son, and Bradford was working for Welch. He was looking for dirt on Townsend, wasn't he?" Before Erin could answer, Stern graced her with a reassuring smile. "Please don't take this the wrong way—I'm aware that you are a successful transgender woman, which explains why Bradford volunteered to meet with you. To him, you represented the road not traveled. Tell me, did he gather the courage to talk to you about himself?"

Erin hesitated, wondering if she was breaching the attorney-client privilege by answering a question posed by someone who claimed to be Montgomery's best friend. But who was she kidding? If she was ever pressed in court, what they had discussed wasn't covered by the privilege. Montgomery wasn't seeking legal advice. He was looking for dirt on Townsend and perhaps a kindred spirit in Erin.

"He did, didn't he? That's why you're hesitating. You're afraid of outing him," Stern continued, her voice now barely above a whisper. "You are all too aware of the consequences of being outed," she added with a knowing look.

"Chardonnay," the waiter said as he put the wineglass down in front of Erin. "And a vodka gimlet for you," he stated, placing the glass in front of Stern. "Enjoy, ladies," he added with a smile as he walked off.

Stern picked up her glass and held it out. "To Bradford."

"To Bradford," Erin replied, tapping her glass gently against Stern's.

Stern took a generous sip of her drink and lowered her glass, wrapping her fingers gently around its stem. "Allow me to spare you the angst of deciding what you should and shouldn't divulge," Stern said with a look of self-satisfaction. "In my old line of work, I learned how to size people up very quickly. Almost everyone who's lying or trying to hide something has a tell. I got really good at picking up the tells." A small grin took root in the corner of her mouth. "I've been watching you—no tells. Hopefully, my instincts are still good."

Rachel took another sip from her drink before continuing.

"In case you haven't guessed, like you, I'm also a trans woman," she said. "And to respond to your statement about not seeing me at his funeral, I was there. I went in boy mode, which I sometimes do for a variety of reasons. I did it for the funeral because I was actually with Brad's ex-wife, who wanted to attend. I saw you there, but given my quandary over your motives, and who I was with, I chose not to reveal myself."

Erin studied Stern's face, trying to picture what Stern looked like in "boy mode," without the makeup and wig. "But if you didn't know who I was, or what my motives were, why did you approach me at the funeral home?"

"Touché," she replied. "I like your skepticism," she said, swirling the contents of her glass. "I saw you at the wake in the afternoon with a gentleman. Obviously, you were together, but you didn't appear to be a couple—at least not in a romantic way. After Arnold Welch paid his respects, your friend attempted to talk to him. I couldn't hear what he was saying, but I could see your friend's reaction to Welch's bodyguard putting his hand on his chest, and that reaction suggested someone who is not used to being stopped. Now I suppose that could suggest many things, but to me it suggested law enforcement. Then, when you came back to the wake that night, I wanted to see if you too were law enforcement investigating Bradford's death, because I want to know who killed him."

Erin looked into her wineglass. "His name is Duane Swisher—seven years in the FBI. He's my law partner and best friend. I'd trust him with my life."

Rachel took a tissue from her purse and wiped the corner of her eye. "Bradford and I met in Provincetown in 1976 at an event called Fantasia Fair. Are you familiar with it?"

"I am," Erin replied. "I've never been, but I know it's an event in P-town for trans folks."

Stern nodded. "Yes, and 1976 was the second year it was held. You probably weren't even born yet."

"I would have been five," Erin allowed with a shrug.

"As you might imagine, things were very different back then. For most people in my generation, we didn't know there were other people like us. We grew up scared of being found out and feeling tremendous guilt and self-loathing. Almost nobody was out and open about who they were. And God forbid you were discovered—you'd lose your job, your friends, and your family. The main reason it was held in P-town was because it was one of the few places in the country where it was safe for gay and trans people to go." She snorted, "Not to mention you weren't likely to run into anyone you knew from your day job in P-town in October."

Stern hesitated, suddenly wistful. "We didn't call ourselves transgender back then. Most of us considered ourselves crossdressers or transvestites, having convinced ourselves that we weren't transsexuals—those brave souls who had surgery and lived as women. We just needed to get in touch with our feminine side from time to time. Of course, over the years, many of us came to accept our true selves."

She shook her head. "I was there with my wife, Marjorie, who knew about my hobby," she said, putting air quotes around "hobby." "I was lucky because Marj was pretty accepting of me. Anyway, the second day we were there, Marj and I were having breakfast, and we overheard the couple at the table next to us talking about New Jersey. Marj, who was a very outgoing and confident woman, struck up a conversation, and that couple turned out to be Brad and his wife, Patty. Although at the time, it was Jackie and her wife, Patty—Jacqueline being the name Brad used while *en femme*, his given mid-

dle name being John. Then, taking the 'ford' from Bradford, he
went by Jacqueline Ford."

"Excuse me, ladies," the waiter interrupted. "Blackened mahi-
mahi," he said, placing the dish in front of Rachel. "And seared
scallops for you, madam," he stated to Erin. "Can I get you anything else? Another drink?"

"No, thank you," they replied simultaneously.

"Bon appétit," he said, heading off.

Over dinner, Rachel recounted that when she met Montgomery, her name was Richard Stern. She was working for the
IRS at its Newark office and lived in Roselle Park. Montgomery,
who came from a very well-to-do family, was living in Maplewood
and working at an investment bank in New York City. Being new
to Fantasia Fair, Rachel and Jackie hung out, while their wives attended a number of events that were designed specifically for the
spouses. When the Fair was over, they all stayed in touch, and
they'd get together socially three or four times a year, before
heading up to P-town in October. That lasted until the summer of
1980, when Montgomery told Stern that he wasn't going to Fantasia Fair anymore because his wife had grown tired of his crossdressing. In an effort to save his marriage, he had gotten rid of all
his women's clothes—"a purge," as it was known—and gone back
into the closet. He also told Stern he felt it was best if they didn't
see each other anymore because Stern would be a constant reminder of what he had given up. Stern had offered not to talk
about that part of his life, and they could just be friends as guys,
but Montgomery had declined.

It remained that way until 2000, the year Marjorie passed away
from breast cancer. Following her death, Montgomery sent Stern
a sympathy card, with a note indicating that he had made a generous gift to the American Cancer Society in Marjorie's name. By
then, Patty and Brad had divorced. Brad had started his own financial services business and was doing very well. Stern had retired from the IRS after twenty-five years to take care of Marj.
After his divorce, Montgomery had resumed crossdressing, and
now that he was free to be Jackie, the two had resumed their
friendship.

"Coffee or dessert?" the waiter inquired as he cleared away their plates.

"Thank you. I'll have an espresso with a sambuca on the side," Rachel replied.

"And a decaf cappuccino for me, please," Erin responded.

Tears were glistening in the corner of Stern's eyes now. "After Marj's death, I started taking hormones and spending more and more time in Rachel mode. So much so that it was becoming awkward for me, trying to sneak in and out of my house without my neighbors seeing me. That's when Jackie suggested we buy a house together down here. Well, we found the house that I now live in, but when it came time to buy it, she insisted she was going to buy it, which she did. A few months later, she handed me the deed to the house, having transferred it from her name to mine. Even though I told her it wasn't necessary, it was her way of trying to make up to me for pausing our friendship twenty years earlier. She told me she had more money than she could ever spend and wanted me to be able to keep everything I got from the sale of my home. I went full-time—now you call it transitioned—in 2002, and formally changed my name to Rachel."

Their waiter returned with their drinks. Stern took the small lemon peel that came with her expresso, twisted it, and dropped it into the cup. She took a small sip and then carefully poured in some of the sambuca.

"Do you know anyone who would have been blackmailing Brad?" Erin asked.

Stern's face contorted. "Blackmail? No—why?"

"When I was being questioned at the prosecutor's office, they showed me pictures of Brad presenting as Jackie that were found near his body. Some of them appeared to be older—probably as far back as the Fantasia Fair days—while others, of him on his deck in Avalon, were more recent, taken with a telephoto lens. They accused me of trying to blackmail him."

"No. Absolutely not," Stern said, shaking her head emphatically. "I'm sure if someone was trying to blackmail him, he would have told me. He had just spent three days in Jackie mode. He was in great spirits when he left here." Stern squinted, confusion taking over her face. "I guess I'm not shocked there's some old photos. There were always people taking pictures at those events that they'd put in a newsletter and mail out if you were on the mailing list. There was no Internet, so in the beginning, it was no big deal. Later on, the photography policy became stricter. But more recent photos—that's surprising."

"They were surveillance photos taken from the dunes. Brad had no idea anyone was watching."

Erin glanced over Stern's shoulder to the mirrored wall behind her. Standing in the doorway between the restaurant and the bar area was a casually dressed man staring in their direction.

"Do you recognize the man in the doorway?" Erin asked, her voice barely above a whisper.

Stern looked up to see who Erin was referring to. "No, but as soon as I looked up, he turned and left."

"Shit," Erin mumbled.

"What's wrong?" Stern asked.

Fear gripped Erin like a vise. "I'm wondering if that guy is following me."

"Just because he was standing in the doorway, looking in our direction? Isn't that a little paranoid?"

Erin's eyes latched onto Stern's. "It's not paranoia if they're really out to get you," she said, unable to stop thinking of the body count of those who had been killed for nothing more than trying to help her and Duane defend their clients. "Regardless, a healthy dose of paranoia may serve you well too," she said to Stern. "Remember, your best friend wound up dead minutes after meeting with me. I don't want you to get in the crosshairs."

CHAPTER 11

Wednesday, June 10, 2009, 9:45 a.m.

WILL TOWNSEND HELD THE PHONE AWAY FROM HIS EAR, IMPA-tiently waiting for the senate president to stop droning on about Townsend's news conference. Of course, he knew that the legislation he'd be proposing would never pass the state senate and become law. He didn't need this asshole to tell him that.

As Townsend waited for the conversation to end, he watched Michael Gardner pace across the oriental carpet. It was only the second time in Townsend's forty-plus years of working with Gardner that he recalled seeing Gardner appear unnerved. The only other time was when they had served together in 'Nam. Townsend had sent Gardner out on what was supposed to be a cakewalk—lead a couple of platoons to a village, pick up some suspected Viet Cong, come back to base, and have a few beers. Instead, just outside the village, Gardner and his men were ambushed, losing five GIs. When the firefight was over, Gardner ordered the village burned to the ground. The final count of enemies killed was over seventy-five. Townsend had risked his own career to make sure that it was never reported that fifty were women and children.

When he was finally able to hang up, he looked at Gardner. "What the fuck is wrong with you? You're pacing back and forth like a caged tiger."

Gardner stopped. "We need to discuss an urgent situation," he responded tersely.

"I'm listening," Townsend replied.

"I fucked up," Gardner responded.

"Fucked up? Michael, what the hell are you talking about?"

Gardner laid out what had happened with Montgomery's phone and the fact that it was part of Stern's phone plan—meaning there'd be a bill, a record of the calls, and enough for a good cell-phone expert to place him in Avalon.

"I also have information that McCabe may have met with Stern last night in Asbury," Gardner added.

Townsend rubbed the back of his neck. "Damn it, Michael, I wish you had checked with me before you had Montgomery taken out."

"There was no time. I didn't get the information he was meeting with McCabe until Friday of Memorial Day weekend. You were out campaigning. They met, and I had no idea if McCabe had passed along damaging information. You pay me to fix things—I fixed it."

"Okay. So how do you intend to fix this? It sounds like this Stern character is a potential risk to you."

Gardner slowly inhaled. "Stern's transgender. Retired from the IRS. No children. Only relative is a sister-in-law who lives in Phoenix. Easiest solution is to make sure we get her and the house at the same time. Since there don't appear to be any close relatives, once she is taken care of, no one will be looking at the cell-phone records. If the house is also destroyed, there will be nowhere for Verizon to mail the bills. Based on this, no one should be able to make a connection between Montgomery and Stern."

"But even if you take care of Stern, won't the prosecutor's office still be able to get the bills?" Townsend asked.

"No reason for them to even look," Gardner replied. "Remember, the only reason I know Montgomery's cell is on Stern's bill is because I have the phone. With Stern gone, no one else should be looking to make the connection."

Townsend cocked his head to the side. "Isn't that a little iffy? Shouldn't you be certain about these things?"

Gardner's face was impassive. "Given the need to take care of this immediately, I've had to rush my intel a little bit, but I'm satisfied that the solution works."

"Your plan?"

"I've been in touch with Tony; he's set to go tonight."

"You know I don't trust him."

"I'm aware. This will be his last job for us."

"Fine. We don't need any more fuckups."

Gardner stiffened but said nothing.

"Anything new with McCabe?" Townsend asked.

"I'm told by my source in the prosecutor's office that there may be DNA evidence on the envelope containing the photographs." Before Townsend could say anything, Gardner held up his hand. "I suspect it's Montgomery's. One thing I can assure you, it's not mine."

"Good," Townsend replied, with a tinge of derision. "By the way, you'll be happy to know that Corliss tells me that since the press conference with Mallory, I'm back up to a six-point lead over Welch. Tomorrow I'll be holding a press conference with Harvey Bottoms, the executive director of the ALDA, who is going to endorse me. Milo is confident that, once that happens, Welch will be toast," Townsend said, basking in the turn of his fortunes.

"That's good," Gardner replied. "I'm glad you followed my advice."

Townsend tensed, unhappy with Gardner's insolence. "I suggest you fix the Stern situation before you take any victory laps."

"It will be taken care of tonight," Gardner replied.

"Let's hope so," Townsend said, folding his arms across his chest. "Let's fucking hope so."

"The Torch." Tony Rizzo sometimes joked that his moniker made him sound like a comic-book superhero. And although he possessed no superpowers, he was well known in certain circles for being able to do magical things with fire. He had no qualms about how he earned his keep; still, tonight's job made him uneasy. The way Gardner wanted it done did not require his talents. He was an artist. He liked to study his subject and carefully select how he would use his palette of accelerants, but Gardner insisted it had to be tonight. All Gardner cared about was that the occupants not be able to escape and that the structure be totally destroyed. This job was like asking Michelangelo to paint the bathroom.

Heathen, Tony thought. He hated working for people who had no appreciation for the beauty of what he did. The only saving grace was that Pete Benson was helping out. Without Pete, he would never have been able to pull this off in twenty-four hours.

Gardner had faxed him some pictures and a layout that showed what the house was like in 2002, the last time it was on the market. The frame was old, having been built in the 1920s, but from the records he found at the buildings department, Tony had been able to determine that a lot of work had been done to the interior since its sale. Fortunately, the basement still consisted of the original wooden beams and joists. Pete had been able to get in posing as a worker from New Jersey Natural Gas, there to check the meter. Once in the basement, he had been able to take some pictures and managed to unlatch the cellar door that led to the backyard. Assuming no one had checked, it would provide Tony with easy access.

He checked his watch. Pete had been watching the front of the house since the owner had returned, looking a little tipsy, around nine. Around eleven, a guy had left, but the target was still there, hopefully sound asleep.

He picked up the two-way radio. "All good?"

"Yeah, nothing's changed," Pete responded.

"All right, give me fifteen. I'm going in through the cellar door. I'll radio you when I'm back to the car."

Tony checked his gloves to make sure they were secure, then reached behind the front seat and grabbed the two three-gallon containers filled with chlordane, his accelerant of choice. It was highly flammable, odorless, and colorless. Even though Gardner didn't seem to care that the fire inspectors would know it was arson, Tony didn't want to use gasoline, as its odor alone might wake those sleeping before he was finished.

When he got to the cellar door, he put the containers down and removed a can of WD-40 from his jacket pocket. After taking care to spray each of the hinges, he gently turned the handle, relieved when the door slowly opened without a sound. Taking a penlight out of his back pocket, he picked up the jugs and made his way into the basement.

Pete had told him that halfway across was a pull cord for a ceiling light. With the room now partially illuminated, he found a cellar window and propped it open, ensuring the fire would have oxygen to breathe. Then he sprayed the ceiling beams and joists with the chlordane, hoping they'd burn enough to cause the floor above to collapse and bring the rest of the house crashing down, making it much harder for investigators. From there he made his way over to the steps. They were old, meaning they'd burn quickly, but they'd also creak, so he gingerly made his way silently up the stairs.

The first floor consisted of the living room, dining room, kitchen, and a screened-in back porch. The bedrooms were on the second and third floors, but luckily the stairs leading up were carpeted. He climbed to the second floor, pouring copious amounts of the chlordane around the closed bedroom doors, the hallway and the staircase leading to the third floor. He then headed back to the first floor, covering the steps, and doused the back porch, kitchen, and living room, pouring liberal amounts around the front door to block any escape. But as he slowly made his way down to the basement, coating the stairs as he went, he was suddenly met by the overpowering smell of gasoline.

What the fuck? Where is that coming from?

When he got to the bottom, the basement floor was covered in gas. Standing in the frame of the cellar door was Pete, holding a lighter, the flame already dancing. For a split second, the tableau made no sense. It was like walking into the room and everyone yelling, "Surprise!" That momentary feeling of confusion before you realized your friends were throwing you a surprise party.

And then reality set in. This was no party.

"Pete, what the fuck are you doing?" Tony yelled, making a mad dash for the cellar door, but he had only gone a few steps when Pete lit the rag sticking out of a bottle and threw it a few feet from where Tony was.

As the bottle shattered, the entire room was suddenly ablaze. Tony screamed and made one last effort to get to the door, but the last thing he saw as he and the room were engulfed in flames was the cellar door closing.

It was him or me, Pete reasoned as he headed down the Garden State Parkway, haunted by Tony's screams—screams that Pete knew would stay with him for the remainder of his days. But Gardner had made it clear that this was Tony's last job, and Gardner always got what he wanted.

But even Pete's desire for self-preservation failed to assuage his conscience. He hadn't known Tony well, but they had done a few jobs together and shared a few beers. Tony was a decent guy. And Pete had just killed him. No, not just killed him—burned him to death like a fucking lobster in a pot.

After Pete had closed the cellar door, he had made his way to the car on Sixth and had driven around the block, past the house. Already the glow from the fire inside could be seen in the windows, one of which exploded as he drove by. He had quickly turned down a side street and then had headed up Sixth Avenue, anxious to get out of town as quickly as possible. But even now, as he drove down the Parkway, he knew a piece of his soul remained in Asbury—a piece he could never get back.

He suddenly felt nauseous, and he wasn't sure if it was because he had just burned Tony alive or because his clothes reeked of gasoline. He should have been more careful with the gas, but what did he know about starting a fire? That had been Tony's job.

His phone ringing startled him.

"Where are you?" Gardner asked.

"On the Parkway, heading to meet Moss in AC."

"You were supposed to call me. Did everything go according to plan?"

"Yes," he replied, trying to ignore the screams echoing through his head. "Tony is dead, and no one made it out of the house."

"Good. Very good. As promised, Moss will have the bonus. Well done."

"Thank you," Pete replied, unable to shake the image of himself as Judas Iscariot collecting his thirty pieces of silver.

"Just lay low until I contact you. I'll be in touch in a few days to follow up once we're sure of the results."

It was a little after four in the morning when Pete arrived in Atlantic City and parked next to an abandoned lot on Rhode Island Avenue. He called the number he had been given, then walked one block over to Vermont Avenue, where Moss was waiting.

Pete had only met Moss once, but he was a tough man to forget. He was built like a sumo wrestler, with a scar that ran across his face—a reminder of an encounter with a razor blade during his time in Northern State Prison.

"Hey," Pete called.

"Yo," came the reply, resonating like the E string on a double bass. Moss ambled toward him. "Jesus, man. You pumping gas or shit? You smell like a fucking refinery."

"Sorry," Pete offered. "I spilled some gas on my pants."

"Spilled some on your pants? I don't know, dude, it smells like you're using gasoline as a fucking aftershave." Moss shook his head. "Don't you go lighting up a fucking cigarette, or we'll all blow the fuck up!" His laugh rolled out like thunder. "Seriously, man, you are going to fucking stink up the car. Kev ain't going to be too fucking happy," he added with a nod to the car idling at the curb.

"Look, I'm really sorry, but can we just get the hell out of here so I can get home and shower?"

"Sure, dude. But before we get in the car, boss man gave me something to give to you. Not that I don't trust Kev, but I don't want to be handing out cash if he ain't getting any. Know what I mean?"

Moss handed Pete an envelope. Even in the dark, as he peered in the envelope, Pete could make out the hundred-dollar bills wrapped in a rubber band.

"He also asked me to give you this," Moss said, causing Pete to look up. When he did, he was staring into the suppressor of a Sig P250.

"Wh—"

Moss pulled the trigger before Pete could verbalize his last thought.

He took a pair of gloves out of his pocket, put them on, reached down, and took the envelope out of Pete's hand.

"Thank you," he said to Pete's still-twitching body. Following Gardner's instructions to make it look like a robbery, he removed Pete's watch and riffled through Pete's pockets for his wallet. He took some small bills and a credit card, probably stolen, and threw the wallet next to Pete's now-lifeless body.

Moss quickly made his way back to the car.

"Drive," he commanded, cramming himself back into the passenger seat.

CHAPTER 12

Thursday, June 11, 2009, 7:30 a.m.

ERIN WAS IN THE MIDDLE OF PUTTING ON HER MAKEUP WHEN THE phone rang, so she let the call go to voice mail. After Mark's recorded greeting, she heard Swish's voice: "Erin, if you're there, pick up." She scurried out of the bathroom and grabbed the phone.

"Hey, what's up?" she answered.

"You have anything on your calendar for today?" he asked.

"No. The plea conference in the Morris case was adjourned, so I'm free. What's going on?"

"I'm not sure. I just got a call from someone I worked with when I was with the FBI telling me about a fire in Asbury Park, and well . . . ah, listen, E, I think the house might be Stern's."

"Why is someone at the FBI calling you about a fire in Asbury Park?" Erin paused, trying to connect the dots, when a wave of fear suddenly washed over her. "Wait. Is Stern okay?"

She held her breath, waiting for Swish to respond.

"Don't know. The house was totally destroyed, and the fire department can't search because it's still burning. As to how the FBI's involved, my suggestion is we meet in Asbury to see what we can find out, and I'll explain everything to you."

"Shit," Erin mumbled under her breath. "Okay. I just need to throw on some clothes. I'll see you there in about an hour."

"Sounds good," he replied.

An hour later, they stood down the street from the smoldering remains of 538 Seventh Avenue. From their vantage point, they could see that the roof had collapsed; several stray beams jutted at cross purposes into the sky, foreboding, like the crosses on Calvary. The front wall had caved in, leaving the floors that had been attached pitched at a steep angle. And although the rear and side walls remained upright, they were charred beyond recognition. A number of pumper trucks continued to pour water onto the pile of debris that only twelve hours earlier had been a gorgeous Victorian home.

They mingled with the crowd of onlookers, trying to pick up whatever information they could. Most were from the surrounding neighborhood, awakened at 3:15 a.m. by the wail of the sirens. The fire had been so intense that it melted the vinyl siding on the neighboring houses and forced the evacuation of the two houses that abutted the rear of the property. Word on the street was that the fire department had removed two bodies from the ruins, but there was no information on who they were or if there were any other additional victims.

The tears slowly slalomed down Erin's cheeks, and her legs wobbled, barely supporting her. Duane reached out and wrapped his arm around her back, providing some needed physical and emotional support. What had she been thinking? She should never have met publicly with Stern, not after what happened to Montgomery. She was the kiss of death.

"You okay?" Duane asked, giving her arm a gentle squeeze.

"No," was all that she could give voice to.

"Maybe . . ." He stopped.

"Maybe what?" she said.

"I don't know. Maybe she got out," he suggested.

She turned her attention back to the partial skeleton of the house, watching the gray smoke rise off the remains and float away on the breeze toward the ocean.

"Yeah," she whispered. "Maybe."

They stood in silence, watching a group of firefighters pointing and gesturing toward the building's remains. Standing with them was a group of men whose badges and guns were visible, marking them as plainclothes police officers. Scattered in among the fire trucks were a number of Asbury Park police cars with lights flashing, as well as a few unmarked vehicles.

"Lots of cops," she finally said.

"A fire of this size, with apparent loss of life, I'm sure there'll be arson investigators taking a look."

It wasn't like Erin hadn't considered that the fire was intentionally set—in fact, it was the first thing she thought. But she had held out hope that it wasn't—maybe an electrical fire, anything other than a scenario in which, two days after having dinner with Erin, someone torched Rachel Stern's home, and now she was dead.

"Let's take a walk," she said, giving his arm a tug. "I can't keep staring at this."

They picked their way through the crowd and turned down Park Avenue, making their way to Sunset Lake, where they found a bench facing the water.

"You were going to tell me how the FBI's involved," she said. "They generally don't do fire investigations."

"Here's what I was told. When I was with the FBI, I was assigned to the counterterrorism unit, and I spent a few years with the Joint Terrorism Task Force, or JTTF, as it's called. The JTTF includes folks from state, county, and local law enforcement, as well as agents from other federal agencies. Although I worked primarily out of the Newark office, there's a resident agency office in Red Bank, and I spent plenty of time there. I was with the JTTF for four of my seven years at the agency, and I got to know a lot of folks, some of whom are still there. One of those people, who works out of the Red Bank office, called me this morning."

"Why?" she asked.

"When you had dinner with Stern, she told you she worked for the IRS and retired in 1998," he said.

"Yeah, her wife had cancer."

"Well, what she didn't tell you was that she was not just some pencil-pusher checking tax returns. She was a special agent and spent the last five years of her career assigned to the JTTF, working out of the Red Bank office."

"Wait, did you know her?"

"No. She left in 1998. I came to the JTTF in 1999. Also, when she was there, her name was Richard Stern. I may have seen her name on some old reports, but we never had any dealings."

"What's this have to do with this morning?" Erin asked.

"Evidently, I'm not the only one who still has contacts on the job. Before she had dinner with you the other night, Stern made a call to a friend asking if they could give her some background on you and me."

"What would the feds have on me?"

Duane snorted. "A lot. You're a lawyer who has represented some unsavory characters, including some reputed organized-crime types. You're my partner, and we know there are people at the DOJ who think I leaked information to the press. Not to mention, we had some cases that the feds were interested in, including the Parsons case." He gave her a lopsided grin. "Yeah, they have a file on you. Nowhere near as thick as mine, but you're in there, my friend."

"Whatever. I'm still not following."

"Well, apparently Stern was a little leery of meeting you because you had shown up out of the blue at Bradford's funeral. Given that Stern had been checking on you only days earlier . . ."

Erin couldn't help but give Swish a hard stare. "You're not saying the FBI thinks I had something to do with the fire, are you?"

"They just want to talk to you."

"What?!" she said. "Are you shitting me?"

"E, try to see it from their perspective. They have a former agent whose best friend is killed and who is skittish about meeting with you. And then a couple of days later, her house burns down . . . well, you get the picture."

She took a deep breath and sighed. "I don't believe this," she said, resting her head in her hands.

"Hey, don't get upset. This isn't like dealing with the Cape May Prosecutor's Office. You just need to explain why you met Stern."

"Oh, sure, these are the feds." Her words were covered in sarcasm. "Let me guess, they're from the government and they're here to help. Nothing but consummate professionals who won't rush to judgment . . . says the man who was railroaded out of the FBI. Somehow, I don't feel very reassured."

"We know you had nothing to do with the fire," he offered.

"And we know I had nothing to do with Montgomery's death," she fired back, her voice getting louder. "That doesn't seem to stop people from accusing me of things." She tilted her head back and looked up at the cloud-covered sky. "Oh, sweet Jesus," she mumbled, "Stern is dead, and her only mistake was having dinner with me."

She suddenly sat upright. "The man in the mirror."

"What?" Duane said.

"When we were having dinner, there was a guy watching us from the entrance who I spotted in the mirrored wall. I asked Stern if she recognized him, but she said as soon as she looked in his direction, he went back into the bar."

"Do you think you could recognize him if you saw him again?" Duane asked.

Erin thought for a moment. "Probably not. I mean, I literally saw him for about two seconds in a mirror."

Duane's phone ringing broke her train of thought. When he looked at the display, he held a finger to his lips.

"What's up, Lou?" he asked. "Yeah, we're together in Asbury at the scene of the fire." He listened, occasionally nodding his head. "Okay, let me talk to her, and I'll give you a call back."

He clicked END and looked at her.

"Let me guess," she said. "Your buddies at the FBI would like to talk with me."

"Yeah."

"And tell me again why I should talk to them?"

He hesitated. "I worked with these people, E. I trust them. These aren't the folks from the DOJ who tried to jam me up. I haven't gotten the sense they think you're involved."

She closed her eyes. "I can't dance with them like I did with the prosecutor's office. Nothing Stern and I talked about is privileged."

"But don't forget, she transitioned, and they all know about her situation."

"Do I have a choice?" she asked, resignation in her voice.

"Sure. You can say no."

"You know you'd be telling any other client to remain silent and refuse to talk to them, don't you?"

"You're not any other client," he said with a wink that conveyed his confidence in her. "E, neither of us are really sure what's going on here, but we have a good hunch. Sometimes you hold your cards close to the vest, and sometimes you lay everything on the table."

She glanced down as if she were looking at actual playing cards fanned out in her hand. "Okay," she said. "But I want you to know that all I've got is a pair of twos."

"Let's hope deuces are wild," he replied.

For the first time all morning, she allowed herself a weak smile. "Okay. Let's head back to my condo, and I'll make us some coffee, and we can discuss how to play things with the feds."

"Sounds like a plan," he said.

"You know, this is getting old," Erin said to Swish, as she looked around the interview room, trying to find the cameras.

He leaned in. "You know we're being recorded now, don't you?" he whispered into her ear.

"That would be illegal," she said loudly. "It would be an infringement on my Sixth Amendment right to counsel."

Duane sat there shaking his head. "Is there a reason you're acting this way?"

"Yeah, because I'm sick and tired of being investigated for things I didn't do."

She wasn't sure why she wanted to play it this way, but when they had discussed how to handle the interview, she decided she wanted to be aggressive, maybe overly so, and do the talking.

Several minutes later, two men entered the room and introduced themselves. The first was FBI Special Agent Enrique Arroyo, the second IRS Special Agent Matt Chronicle. Erin hoped it didn't show on her face, but when Arroyo introduced himself, she almost did a double take. Erin was a huge soccer fan, having played since she was five years old, and all she could think was that Cesc Fàbregas, the captain of Arsenal, her favorite soccer team, had just walked into the room. Arroyo could have been Fàbregas's doppelganger. He had dark brown hair, narrow-set brown eyes, and thick eyebrows. His thin face and square jaw gave him the rugged look that would play well on a daytime soap opera.

Chronicle, on the other hand, looked more like a middle-aged accountant than a special agent, with a slight paunch, a comb-over, and a disheveled air before he even sat down. But Erin had learned long ago to never underestimate an adversary.

"Ms. McCabe," Chronicle began, "you are not in custody, you are free to leave, and you are not obligated to answer any of our questions. However, since you are a criminal defense attorney of some note, I presume you understand that under Title Eighteen, Section One Thousand One of the United States Code, it is a crime to knowingly and willfully make a false or fraudulent statement to a federal agent, such as myself or Agent Arroyo. Do you understand that, Ms. McCabe?"

"I do, Agent Chronicle."

"Do you know why we asked to speak with you?"

"I don't," she replied.

"Do you know a person by the name of Rachel Stern?"

"I do. And I'm trying to find out if—did she survive the fire?" Erin asked.

"I take it from your response that you're aware her home burned to the ground this morning?"

"I am. Can you please answer my question? Do you know if she's alive?" she asked, hearing the mix of desperation and frustration in her own voice.

"Ms. McCabe, let's try my questions first. Then we'll see what answers I can provide you."

"Or maybe we'll end the interview," Erin replied defiantly.

Chronicle inhaled as if he was trying to maintain his professionalism. "Ms. McCabe, try answering my questions, and then I will try to answer yours to the best of my ability. Fair?"

"Go ahead," Erin said, allowing her displeasure to be front and center.

"How did you meet Ms. Stern?"

"We met very briefly for the first time at the wake of Bradford Montgomery, and we met a second time for dinner two nights ago at the Tides in Asbury Park."

Chronicle then questioned her about the conversation, with enough detail that it was almost as if he was looking at a transcript.

"You also met with Bradford Montgomery the day he was murdered, correct?" he asked.

"I did," Erin replied.

Chronicle fixed his eyes on Erin. "It would appear that you're a dangerous person to meet with."

Erin's eyes flashed. "If you want to accuse me of something, Agent Chronicle, at least have the balls to do it. I don't take kindly to snide innuendos."

"Ms. McCabe," Agent Arroyo said softly.

"Stop," Erin barked. "Listen, handsome, I don't need your good cop, bad cop bullshit. I came in because I'm interested in finding out who killed Bradford Montgomery and what happened to Rachel as much, if not more, than you are. So if you want to talk, let's talk. But if you're going to accuse me of somehow being involved in what happened to Montgomery, or Ms. Stern, that's bullshit, and we're done. Your call. You tell me how you want to play this."

Chronicle tapped his pen on the table a few times. "What can you tell us about your meeting with Montgomery?"

"Not a lot. He consulted with me as an attorney, so the privilege applies to our conversation."

"Do you have any thoughts on why Montgomery was killed?" Arroyo asked.

"I do," she responded. "While I cannot divulge my conversations with Mr. Montgomery, when I had dinner with Ms. Stern, she told me that Mr. Montgomery had indicated he had a meeting to try and get information on Senator William Townsend to help the Welch campaign."

"Was that the meeting with you?"

"I presume so."

"Do you have any information on Townsend?" Chronicle interjected.

"Yes. But before you ask me what it is, you should know that there is a nondisclosure agreement that prevents me from revealing anything."

"You know that we could subpoena you to a grand jury and require you to disclose it," Arroyo suggested.

"You could, but under the nondisclosure agreement, I'd have to give notice to various parties in order to allow them to object, which would kind of defeat any desired secrecy."

"There's a much easier route," Duane offered.

"What's that, Mr. Swisher?" Arroyo replied.

"I can get you the exact dates, but about two years ago, before there was a nondisclosure agreement, I spoke with folks in the U.S. Attorney's Office about what we suspected."

"What happened as a result?" Arroyo asked.

"As far as I know, nothing," Duane replied. "Candidly, most of what we had then, and have now, is speculation, but you could check with your people to see if they did anything with what I told them."

Arroyo turned back to her. "Do you have any thoughts on why someone would want to kill Ms. Stern?"

Erin bit her lip. "None. She told me that Montgomery was her best friend, but other than that, I don't have a clue. The only thing I've come up with is that someone saw us having dinner and thought she was trying to get the same information from me that Montgomery was looking for."

"It must be some pretty damning information, if your theory is correct," Arroyo said.

"You know what's ironic, Agent Arroyo? As Duane told you, the information we had was mostly speculation. Nevertheless, it's all there for a good investigator or journalist to work on and see if they could put it all together—but money, power, and violence can buy a lot of silence," Erin said with an air of resignation.

Chronicle opened a folder and slid a picture across the table to Erin.

She picked up the picture, a mugshot. As soon as she studied it, she whipped her head to Duane. "This could be the guy," she said. "The guy in the mirror."

Chronicle looked bewildered. "I'm afraid I don't follow you, Ms. McCabe."

Erin explained about the person she had seen at the Tides. "Honestly, I couldn't put my hand on the Bible and swear this is the guy, but he certainly could be. Who is he?" she asked, handing the picture to Swish.

"His name was Peter Benson."

"Was?" she asked.

"His body was discovered this morning in Atlantic City, smelling of gasoline," Chronicle replied. "He's suspected of starting the fire at Ms. Stern's home. He was shot at point-blank range—looks like he was executed."

"Shit," Erin muttered to herself.

There was a light rap on the door, causing Chronicle to stand and crack open the door. Erin could hear a few whispered words, then Chronicle excused himself and left.

Two minutes later, Chronicle returned, this time with another individual. The man was tall, with short gray hair that formed a horseshoe around his otherwise bald head. He had on black pants, a white polo shirt, and a lavender V-neck sweater.

He took a seat opposite her. He looked familiar, but Erin was struggling to place him. Then he spoke.

"Hello, Erin," he said.

Erin's eyes went wide. "Rachel?" she said. "Oh my God—Rachel, you're alive!

CHAPTER 13

Thursday, June 11, 2009, 1:15 p.m.

RACHEL INSISTED THAT SHE DIDN'T WANT TO TALK TO ERIN AND Duane in the interrogation room, so, clutching their cups of the warmed-over dirty water the FBI passed off as coffee, they found an unused office free of any recording devices.

"I don't know what to say," Erin began. "I'm amazed and thrilled you're alive. I thought for sure you were dead. We saw the house. How? How'd you get out?"

Rachel pursed her lips and looked down at her lap. "I wasn't there when it started," she responded slowly, as if each word cut her as she said them. "I assume Julius—he's my tenant—and his girlfriend, Liza, were there."

She stopped to compose herself. "We're sorry, Rachel," Erin said. "We don't need to talk about this now."

Rachel looked up, her eyes glistening with fresh tears. "No. We do need to talk."

"All right," Erin offered reassuringly.

"When we had dinner, I told you I occasionally went out in boy mode, as I did for Brad's funeral . . . and as I did last night."

She stopped, closed her eyes, and drew in a deep breath before continuing. "I discovered a long time ago that I'm bisexual, and after Marjorie passed away, in around 2001, I began to explore my feelings toward men. At that point, I was still living as Richard, so I started going to some of the gay bars in the area. Around the same time, I started taking hormones in anticipation of transitioning. After I went full-time, I found that most of the lesbians I tried to date didn't want me because I still had a penis, and with gay men, I don't know, I guess I looked more like an ugly woman than a drag queen—and forget about straight men. After a couple freaked out on me when I told them I was trans, that was enough for me. About a year after I went full-time, I had some serious medical issues. As a result, I had to stop taking hormones, and my doctor strongly suggested that I not have gender-affirming surgery. So even though I was living full-time as Rachel, I'd occasionally go to the gay bars in what I call guy drag. That's the reason I'm dressed this way now," she said, gesturing with her hands. "I just found it was easier to hook up with a guy who saw me as a guy. That's what I did last night." She took a sip from her coffee and winced. "God, I forgot how awful this stuff is.

"Last night, I had a few drinks at the Tides and then went home," she finally said. "I was going to go to bed, but I was so depressed, thinking about what happened to Brad, I just didn't want to be alone. So around 11:00 p.m., I changed into guy drag and walked down the street to Georgie's. I never thought . . ."

Rachel put her fist up to her mouth, trying to quell the emotions that were attempting to burst into full display. The room fell silent, the what-ifs not lost on any of them.

"Sorry," Rachel said, taking time to regain her composure.

"You want a glass of water or something other than this horrid coffee?" Erin asked.

"No. I'll be okay," Rachel replied, before continuing. "Around midnight, I met a guy, Ron. We went back to his place. He lives over on Fifth Avenue, within walking distance of Georgie's. Sometime after three a.m., we heard all the sirens and fire trucks, but I didn't think anything about it. It's Asbury, there's always shit going on at all hours. But when he drove me home in the morning, everything was blocked off. Ron was nice enough to park one block over and walk with me. As soon as we got to Seventh, I let out a scream, because I could see it was my house. We got as close as we could, but . . ."

She looked down as if looking for a purse, then, as if a light bulb had suddenly gone on, reached into her pocket and took out a handkerchief.

"At that point, I didn't know what to do or who I could trust, so I reached out to one of my former colleagues, and they suggested I come in. Ron drove me on his way to work." She shot a sheepish look at Erin. "Erin, despite what Duane was told, I hadn't spoken to anyone here about you before we had dinner. All of that was a ruse to get you to come here." Rachel shrugged, her face betraying a combination of resignation and contrition. "After what happened, I was worried that I had been wrong to trust you. I had to see you again and hear how you reacted to being interrogated."

"Guess I passed," Erin said.

"Yeah," Stern replied with a pained smile.

"Who knows you're alive?" Duane asked.

"Besides the two of you, Chronicle, Arroyo, and two other agents here."

"Anyone from Asbury PD?" Duane said.

"No. Not that I'm aware of," she replied.

"Um, what about Ron?" Erin asked.

"He only knows me by my first name, Richard," Rachel answered sheepishly.

"Good," Duane said. "Right now, the fewer people who know you're alive, the better." He stopped, seemingly lost in thought. "Any children or family who are going to panic when they get the news about the fire?"

"No children," she replied. "I have a sister-in-law in Phoenix. Retired teacher. We get along okay. We talk about once a month."

"I feel a little awkward asking this," Duane said, "but do you have a will?"

"Yeah," Rachel replied, followed by a small sigh. "Unfortunately, like everything else I owned, it's in the house. It's in a fireproof box, but God knows if they'll even be able to find it in the rubble."

"Did a lawyer prepare it for you?"

"Yeah. Ron Donahue, he's here in town—I'm sorry, I mean Asbury."

"Who was named executor?"

Rachel tilted her head. "I'm not dead. Why all the questions about my estate plan?"

"By the looks of the house, the only way they're going to identify the deceased is through dental records, which could take some time. Assuming it was arson, someone clearly wants you dead. In which case, it may be a good thing for people to think you are dead for a while—hopefully, it'll keep you safe, while we try to figure out who's behind this and why. That's why I'm trying to figure out who has reason to start looking into your personal affairs."

"Well, the executor was Brad. But the contingent executor is my friend Evelyn Ketchum. She was a good friend of Marjorie's and knew about my life as Rachel. Her husband died suddenly from a heart attack about a year after Marjorie passed away. We get together about once a month, sometimes to have dinner, other times to see a movie or a show. Besides Brad . . ." she stopped. "Well, with Brad gone, she is my closest friend."

"It sounds like Evelyn will be the one who will be trying to find out if you're okay. Does she live local?"

"Old Bridge. Yeah, once she hears about a fire in Asbury, she'll be calling me. And when she learns the address, she'll be down here in a heartbeat."

"Which reminds me," Erin said, "don't answer your phone—in fact, turn it off. We need to get you a prepaid one just in case whoever is behind the arson tries to call your number to see what happens."

"Good point," Rachel replied.

"You trust Evelyn enough to let her in on the fact that you're alive?" Duane asked.

"Yes," Rachel replied without hesitation. "If I can't trust her, there's no one I can trust."

"Okay," Duane said. "Let's figure out how we let her know and where you can stay for the time being."

"I'm sure Evelyn would let me stay with her," Rachel offered.

Erin shook her head. "I'm not sure that's a good idea. Not

because I don't trust her, but because I don't want to underestimate the folks who are trying to kill you. I wouldn't want to put Evelyn's life in jeopardy."

"What do you suggest then?" Rachel asked.

"Who's the executor of Brad's estate?"

"I am, and I have ninety days from my appointment to select a financial institution to be co-executor. I went up to the surrogate in Newark on Monday and was appointed."

"Okay, here's what I was thinking—let me know if you think this works," Erin said.

"Can I ask you a stupid question?" Mark said that night as they shared a glass of wine after dinner. "Don't you ever get involved in any 'normal' criminal cases? You know, the kind where no one's trying to kill you or the people around you?"

"All the time," she said with a smirk, "but no one ever cares about those cases."

"You think Rachel will be safe?" he asked.

"I think so. Right now, everyone thinks she's dead. Assuming no one at the JTTF is working both sides of the fence, she should be okay for now. And even after the victims are identified, only Swish and I know where she is. We didn't even let the folks from the JTTF in on that secret."

"Why? Aren't they the good guys?"

"They are," she replied. "But if Townsend is behind this, as we suspect, he has tentacles that reach all over the place. Meaning, the fewer people who know, the better the chance Rachel has of staying safe."

"Won't she go stir-crazy hiding out?"

Erin shrugged. "I understand from Duane, who took her to where she's staying, that it's an amazing place. Plus, she's not afraid to go out in what she calls 'guy drag.' She'll be okay."

"How's she going to manage in terms of basic necessities?" Mark asked.

"I gave her the info on my Amazon account and one of my credit cards so she could order stuff without leaving a trail that can be traced back to her."

Mark gave her a quizzical look.

"I trust her," Erin said. "Besides, my card has a five-thousand-dollar limit. I won't go broke." She took a sip of her wine. "Her friend Evelyn is going to go see the lawyer who drew up her will, and hopefully they can start the process of filing an insurance claim for the house and her car. After all, whether it's her or her estate, there's valid insurance claims. The house did burn to the ground, so whether it's Rachel or her estate, someone is entitled to file a claim."

Mark took a sip of his wine, and a worried look spread across his face. "If Townsend is trying to prevent the people from Welch's campaign from getting the dirt that you and Swish know, why hasn't he come directly after both of you? After all, don't the two of you pose the biggest risk?" Mark asked.

She nodded in agreement. "I honestly don't know. Maybe it's just that we've lived up to the agreement for three years."

"Yeah, but up until now, no one's been offering you a lot of money to talk. I'm really worried that he's going to come after you," Mark said.

Erin shrugged. "I know what you're saying makes sense, but he clearly hasn't come after us, and I don't know why. It feels like there's something else involved, but I don't know what it is."

"Just be careful, please," Mark implored. "You have prosecutors investigating you, crazy politicians who are hell-bent on revenge, and now a woman you barely know has your credit card."

"Yeah, I know," she said. "But I'm honestly more worried about who else might be in danger because of me—like you—than I am for myself."

"We've been through that already. Don't go there again," he said.

She gave him a knowing smile. "Fine. How about we talk about something else I'm worried about—Saturday night."

"Saturday night? Your high school reunion?" he asked. "Really?"

"Yeah."

"Don't go," he suggested.

"I feel like I have to."

"Why?"

"Because if I don't, I feel like it's admitting that I'm embarrassed about being trans."

"Why would you think that? I skipped my reunion last year for no particular reason other than I didn't feel the need to see people who, for the most part, I hadn't seen in twenty years."

She knew Mark was right. It wasn't like she had any burning desire to see people who, for the most part, she hadn't seen in twenty years. But the memory of Bobby Mason haunted her. She wanted—no, she needed—to go because of him.

In high school, Bobby had it all—the boy most likely. He was movie-star handsome, valedictorian of the class, starting shortstop for three years on the baseball team, and every high school girl's fantasy. He had gone to Yale undergrad and then gotten into UPenn Medical School. During law school, Erin was living in Philadelphia and happened to run into him as they were both getting off a train at 30th Street Station. They hadn't been particularly close in high school, but the randomness of seeing a familiar face in an unfamiliar setting seemed to draw them together in that moment. As they talked, he had suddenly paused. "I'm sorry," he had said, turning to a guy standing next to him. "I'm so rude," he had continued. "Ian, this is my boyfriend, Greg. Greg, this is a friend of mine from high school, Ian McCabe." And with that introduction, he had come out to her as gay. They had continued to chat warmly for another ten minutes, and she was mildly embarrassed that she didn't have the courage to come out to him, but at that point in her life, Lauren was the only one who knew about her, and she honestly thought she'd never come out to anyone else. As they parted, they had exchanged phone numbers, with a promise to get together. But they hadn't. Two years after she saw him, she learned Bobby had died of AIDS. The most popular kid in her class had died alone; his family having disowned him after he was diagnosed.

Thinking about Bobby made her wonder if her former classmates had evolved since high school. All-boys Catholic high schools in the 1980s sometimes seemed like they were modeled on *Lord of the Flies*. Bullying and homophobia, while perhaps not de rigueur, were part of the culture. She wondered if Bobby knew he was gay in high school and, if he did, whether it would've made a difference if he had come out? Bobby was so damn popular; if the guys had known he was gay, would any of them have been less homophobic? Probably not, she realized. No, the more likely result would have been that he would have become an outcast.

"I guess this probably sounds a little crazy to you, but I suspect the majority of the guys I went to school with don't know anyone who's trans. Meaning, if I go, I feel like I have the opportunity to put a human face on the issue for them. Maybe that's all people need to be a little more understanding."

Mark wrapped his arm around her and pulled her in close. "It's not your responsibility to educate people on what it means to be transgender," he said softly.

"I know that," she said, allowing herself to fold into him. "But I have an opportunity a lot of trans folks don't, and I feel like I need to be out and proud of who I am."

"I told you I'd go with you," Mark said.

"I know. But I don't know how people will react to me. I'd be really upset if someone gave you grief about being with me."

"I can take care of myself," he replied.

"It's not you I worry about—it's me."

"I don't follow you."

"I'm finally confident in who I am, but if I see you mocked . . . I don't know. I just don't want to deal with all the angst and self-doubt again."

He bent over and gave her a warm kiss. "Let's see if I can boost your confidence," he said, as they stretched out on the couch.

CHAPTER 14

Saturday, June 13, 2009, 6:30 p.m.

HAVING DECIDED TO GO TO THE REUNION, SHE WAS DETERMINED to look her best. *The invitation said semi-formal, so damn it, let it rip,* she thought. She went to the salon to have Kim style her hair and get her nails done. She wore her black sheath dress that clung to her in all the right places, with a pair of black, open-toe pumps. And if Mark was any barometer of how she looked, she was doing well, because she almost didn't get out the door.

When she walked in, the registration table was manned by Scott Donaldson, who had been the senior class president, Troy Graham, who had been class secretary, and a woman Troy introduced as his wife, Amy. Erin's warm smile was met by their quizzical looks, she assumed because they were trying to determine why this single woman was at the check-in table.

"Hi, Scott. Hi, Troy. Nice to see you both again, and nice to meet you, Amy." Erin paused, her moment of truth at hand. "Um, I'm Erin McCabe," she stated, hoping they would realize who she was without more of an explanation.

Scott jumped up from the table, came around to where she was standing, and gave her a hug. "Erin, it's so great to see you again. Look at you," he said, taking a step back. "You look amazing. I was hoping you'd come. I've seen so much about you in the newspapers over the last three years. Oh my God, girl—you're a rock star."

"Thanks, Scott. It's great to see you too. But I am definitely not a rock star."

"Let's talk later," Scott offered, giving her a kiss on the cheek.

Troy turned to his wife, who had the box of lanyards with the name tags, and told her to look for McCabe. After thumbing through them, she looked perplexed, "There's only an Ian Mc-Cabe," she said.

Troy chuckled, looked up at Erin, snatched the name tag from his wife, and handed it to Erin. "Yeah, Ian's in the running for 'most changed since graduation.'"

The tag bore a copy of her senior yearbook picture, with the name IAN MCCABE boldly displayed above the photo.

Anxious to avoid a scene, she picked up one of the sticky tags they had on the table for spouses or significant others, the ones that said, HELLO. MY NAME IS, and wrote ERIN MCCABE, then defiantly placed it under her "official" name tag that she then hung around her neck.

"Thanks," she sighed.

Erin took a deep breath, held her clutch tightly, and walked into the dining room, where the Cardinal O'Hara Class of 1989 awaited. Looking around, she struggled to find someone she recognized; she wasn't the only one who had changed in twenty years. People were talking in small groups, laughing; several guys seemed to be holding forth about their high school exploits.

She made her way to one of the bars in the corner of the room and ordered a chardonnay. As the bartender poured her wine, she continued to scan the room, hoping to spot some of the guys from the soccer team. She figured that if anyone would accept her, her best chance might be with some of her former teammates.

Soccer had been Erin's entrée into the male world. She'd played varsity for four years and had been selected as all-county her senior year. She had continued to play after high school and was a regular starter on her college team. Even now, at the ripe old age of thirty-seven, she still played in a women's league on weekends.

Finally, she spotted Reggie Dixon, who had been the starting goalie. Dixon was a hard guy to miss. Somewhere around six-foot-two, he still looked rock-solid and was now sporting dreadlocks pulled back with a hair tie. She placed a tip in the jar, took her wine, and headed in Dixon's direction. She had always liked Dixon; he was outgoing, funny, and absolutely fearless on the soccer pitch. He used to wear a T-shirt to practice that had a picture of Jesus wearing goalie gloves that said, JESUS SAVES—BUT HAS HE EVER STOPPED A PK? She still remembered the day Father Sherman came up and told him to take it off because it was sacrilegious. Practice stopped, everyone turning to watch what was going to happen. They had a huge game the next day, and the T-shirt was Dixon's good-luck charm. Dixon had turned toward Father Sherman and said, "Jesus saves, right, Father?" Father Sherman agreed. "Did he ever stop a penalty kick?" Dixon asked. "Don't be ridiculous," Sherman replied. "Of course not." Dixon had clapped his goalie gloves together a few times and said, "Well then, leave us be, because tomorrow, me and Jesus might have to save a PK, and we need our practice."

He wore the shirt, but for disobeying Father Sherman, he got a week of detention. When every player on the team showed up to help him serve it, nothing further was said about the shirt for the rest of the season.

Dixon was talking to Steve Taylor, who had played defense, and Jake Richards, who had played up top as a striker. She could see Dixon trying to read her name tag as she approached. As she neared, she watched his eyes grow wide, and then a smile stretched across his face.

"Hi, Dix," she said.

"Damn, McCabe," he said, "if you had the moves you just displayed walking across the floor when you played in the midfield, you would have been all-state on top of all-county. Good thing I saw you in the newspaper a couple of times, because there's no way I would have put two and two together." He wrapped his long arms around her in a warm embrace. When he let her go, she looked at Taylor and Richards.

"Hi, guys. Good to see you again," she said with an apprehensive grin.

Taylor looked momentarily lost. "Ian?"

"Yeah," she replied, "but my name is Erin now."

Richards looked her up and down. "Great. Donaldson's a fag. Mason's a dead fag, and you're a trannie. What a fucking class," he said with a scowl, then nodded in the direction of Dixon and Taylor. "Catch you guys later."

Dixon stood there, watching Richards go. "Don't pay any attention to him, McCabe. He's still fucking pissed you made all-county and he didn't," Dixon said with a full-throated laugh.

Over the course of the night, she forced herself to mingle. Some of the guys seemed to know about her situation and were okay, others were completely baffled, and a few, like Richards, were obnoxious. She sought out Scott Donaldson because she wanted to hear more about how he was doing. Turned out he was a chemist at a pharmaceutical company, and he and his partner, John, who he had been with for over ten years, had just had a civil-union ceremony. John hadn't come to the reunion for basically the same reason Erin hadn't let Mark come—Scott didn't expect a warm welcome from their former classmates and didn't want John to have to deal with their bullshit. Erin found herself getting emotional when she mentioned having run into Bobby Mason years earlier and what a loss his death had been. Scott had given her a sad smile and proceeded to describe how he and Bobby had both known in high school that they were gay but hadn't come out for fear of what would happen, both in school and with their families. During the summer between their junior and senior years of college, they had reconnected and enjoyed a brief fling. Scott had been devastated when he learned Bobby had AIDS and had seen him in the hospital several weeks before he died. Unfortunately, Scott explained, being a gay man in the 1990s meant that, if you were lucky enough to survive, you lost a lot of friends to AIDS. Erin gave him a hug and told him that seeing him again had made her decision to come all worthwhile.

Around ten, she was at the table, chatting with Dixon, when Richards and Troy Graham approached.

"You have a lot of fucking nerve," Richards spit out.

She looked up, taken aback by his outburst. "I'm afraid I have no idea what you're talking about, Jake."

"You know damn well what I'm talking about, you fucking perv," he fired back, his voice rising above the din. "Our wives," he said, nodding toward Troy, "were in the ladies' room when you went in there, no doubt to get your jollies watching real women. I ought to beat the shit out of you," he suggested, clenching his fist.

"I saw you in the newspaper spouting off on all your transgender bullshit," Troy added. "What a bunch of crap."

"Just wait," Jake continued. "Once Senator Townsend gets elected governor, he'll deal with you and all your freak friends. Until then, leave the fucking ladies' room to women."

She could sense the noise in the room starting to fade as folks' attention was suddenly drawn to what was going on.

"Jake, I happen to be a woman," she offered, knowing it was unlikely to have any impact.

"Who the fuck are you kidding? I changed in the same locker room as you for four years. You're no more a woman than Troy is."

She couldn't help but grin as a rejoinder ran through her head.

"What the fuck is so funny?" Jake shouted.

"Nothing is funny about your words or your attitude, Jake. They're narrow-minded and small—just like other things about you."

"You little fuck," Jake said, as he moved toward her.

Dixon shot out of his chair, blocking his path toward Erin.

Dixon's eyes danced between Graham and Richards. "I think you and Troy had both better take a walk," Dixon said. "This conversation is over."

"Why are you all chummy with him?" Richards said, gesturing at Erin. "How'd you feel if your wife suddenly saw him in the ladies' room?"

"Just go back to your table, Jake," Dixon replied calmly.

"Fucking freak," he mumbled, staring at Erin, before turning and heading back to his table.

Dixon watched them go before returning to his seat.

"Thanks, Dix," Erin said.

"No worries," he replied, then gave her a conspiratorial grin. "I almost choked when you mentioned things about Jake being small."

"Now what made you think I was referencing anything in particular?" Erin asked, a false sense of innocence on display.

"Maybe because he had just said he changed in the same locker room with you for four years," Dixon chuckled.

"You sure you're okay?" Taylor asked.

"Yeah. Thanks," Erin said, touched by Taylor's concern.

Taylor shook his head. "Erin, I'll be the first to admit, I don't know what it's like for you, but seems to me, if you're happy, why should I care? You only have one life, and you might as well live it to the fullest and enjoy it."

"Thanks, Steve. I appreciate that," Erin replied.

"Do you get that kind of abuse often?" Steve's wife asked.

Erin shrugged. "Yeah, it happens, but only when someone knows I'm trans. Most of the time, I just blend in."

She cuddled up against Mark on the couch, resting her head on his shoulder. "Are you glad you went?" Mark asked.

"Not sure 'glad' is the word I'd use. How about I'm satisfied I made the right decision to go," she shifted her head slightly so she could see his face, "and to not take you."

"Ouch."

"I told you it had nothing to do with you. It would've just been harder to deal with the likes of Graham and Richards if you were there."

"Maybe if I had been there, they would have left you alone. Bullies rarely want to pick on someone their own size."

She smiled at him, his desire to protect her reassuring. Yet, there was something she found ill-fitting about her need for protection. Vulnerability was not something she recalled feeling prior to her transition. But now it was a part of her, whether she wanted it to be or not.

"Maybe," she replied. "Fortunately, Dix stepped in before it got out of hand."

He gave her a hug. "Doesn't sound like you changed any hearts and minds on how your classmates feel about trans people."

"I don't know. There are some people whose opinions are never going to change, and they're always the loudest ones in the crowd. But maybe there are others who may be a little more open," she said.

Her thoughts returned to Bobby, and she now felt less sanguine that had he come out in high school, it would've made a difference in how the guys acted; "queer" and "faggot" would still have been the pejoratives of choice. No, from what she saw tonight, nothing would have changed, except for Bobby.

Why did it matter who he loved? He was still brilliant, handsome, a great athlete, and a nice guy. But the reality was, as long as everyone thought he was straight, he was the most popular guy in the school. Had they known he was gay, he likely would have fallen from grace. It was sad and ironic, she thought, that Bobby's fate ultimately rested on who he loved. He remained popular in high school by keeping his sexual orientation hidden, but ultimately, he died from a disease that had become an epidemic because politicians thought it only infected gay men, so they didn't give a shit.

"You okay?" Mark asked.

"I don't know," she replied. "It's just really hard to hold on to the hope that someday who you are or who you love won't matter to anyone. People just have so much hate."

He pulled her close and kissed the top of her head. "I hear you," he said softly.

She hugged him tighter, silently chiding herself for ignoring that Mark had also been ostracized and mocked, including by his own family, simply because of the person he loved—her.

CHAPTER 15

Sunday, June 14, 2009, 10:00 a.m.

WITH EVERYTHING GOING ON, ERIN AND HER MOM HADN'T found time during the week to meet for breakfast, so Erin had suggested that she would swing by for breakfast after her parents went to Mass and take them to see Patrick and Brennan's soccer game.

Back when she'd lived alone in Cranford, she had her Sunday routine down to a science: walk into town to buy the Sunday *New York Times* and the *Star-Ledger*, head back and brew herself a fresh cup of coffee, usually a Costa Rican blend, check her emails, then stretch out on the couch and read the papers. Following her leisurely start, she'd usually go out for a long run. But since she had moved in with Mark, her Sunday routine had changed. They tended to sleep in—or, perhaps more accurately, they stayed in bed later—and Mark had the papers delivered. And her long runs had gotten a tad shorter. Only her devotion to grinding and making her own coffee had remained unchanged.

But today Erin had headed out early and stopped at O'Johnnie's Variety Store to pick up the papers to take to her parents' house. After she grabbed the *Times* and *Ledger* from the paper rack, a headline on the *Post-Dispatch* caught her attention—MURDERED FINANCIAL ADVISER'S SECRET LIFE WAS A DRAG!

She reached down and picked up the paper. There, to her surprise, was one of the pictures that Detective Lonza had showed her of a much younger Bradford Montgomery dressed as a woman. Based on what Rachel had told her, it looked like it had been taken at Fantasia Fair.

She bought the papers, including two copies of the *Post-Dispatch*. Once back in her car, she called Duane.

"Hey. How'd the reunion go?" he answered casually.

She hesitated. "About what I expected—a mixed bag. Think root canal, but with Novocain. We can talk about it tomorrow."

"Okay." Duane cleared his throat. "What's up?"

"I picked up an extra copy, so you don't have to run out and buy one, but the front page of the *Post-Dispatch* has a photo of Montgomery in drag."

"What? Why would the prosecutor's office leak those photos?"

"Not sure they did. This photo looks like the older ones, which, based on my conversations with Rachel, were probably taken in the late seventies at a trans event up on Cape Cod."

"Still, why is that photo in the paper now?" Duane asked.

"The article talks about the fact that Montgomery was a high-ranking official in Welch's campaign, which, after the paper sent the photo to the campaign, had no comment."

"Meaning you think Townsend is behind this?"

"That's my guess," Erin replied. "After all, the primary is Tuesday."

"Damn," Duane said.

"I'm heading to my mom and dad's for breakfast, then I'm going to take them to see Patrick and Brennan's soccer game, but if you have time, check online to see if any of the South Jersey or Philadelphia papers are running the story."

"Will do," Duane said. "Enjoy the game."

As she put her BlackBerry back in her purse, she pulled out a burner phone she had purchased several months earlier in connection with the Ann Parsons case and checked it, finding a missed call from an unknown number. She hit the number to dial it.

"Hello."

"Rachel, it's Erin. You called. Is everything okay?"

"Yeah. Well, actually, I don't know. I have no idea what it means, but I got a call from Chronicle just a little while ago. He wanted to let me know the fire department discovered another body in the rubble. In the basement. It was so badly burned that at first they weren't sure it was human. He said it looked like the person was doused in gasoline and set on fire."

Erin leaned back in her seat. "You have any idea who it could be?"

"None. None at all. Other than Julius and his girlfriend, there was no one else in the house when I left. Chronicle said that Asbury PD is speculating it may have been an unrelated murder victim whose body they wanted incinerated, or someone involved in setting the fire who didn't make it out."

"I guess that's possible," Erin interjected. "But I thought they found the guy who started the fire in Atlantic City."

"All I can tell you is that, based on Chronicle's description, it's going to take a while to ID whoever it is."

"You okay?" Erin asked.

"Yeah. A bit confused, but okay."

Erin hesitated. "Unfortunately, I think I'm only going to add to your confusion."

"Why? What's going on?" Rachel asked.

"On the front page of the *Post-Dispatch* is an article about Brad's murder and . . . well, the article has a picture of Brad dressed as a woman—one of the ones I told you I was shown that look like they were from the Fantasia Fair days."

"What?" Stern screamed. "How could they have gotten those pictures?"

"Not sure how they got them—whether it's a leak at the CMPO, or someone tipped them off there to find them."

"But why? He's dead. Why are they doing this to him now?"

"Duane and I think it's aimed at embarrassing Welch's campaign."

"Oh God, poor Brad," Rachel sobbed. "He tried so hard to keep that part of his life secret. Those bastards!"

After Erin finished her call with Rachel, she quickly called Swish back to let him know about the discovery of the third body, before heading off to her parents.

* * *

"Hi, Mom. Hi, Dad," she called out as she let herself in.

She'd only made it halfway across the living room when her mother came into view, wiping her hands on her apron.

"Hello, dear," her mother said, giving her a peck on the cheek. "Nice to see you," she said.

"Good to see you too," Erin replied, giving her mother a one-armed hug.

"Come have a cup of coffee while I make breakfast."

"Thanks," Erin replied, even though she dreaded her mom's coffee. Her parents drank their coffee so strong that Erin could fill it halfway with milk and the mixture was still the color of dark chocolate.

As they walked into the kitchen, Pat looked up from the *Sunday Herald*.

"Hi, Dad," Erin said, putting the *Times* and the *Ledger* next to his coffee cup. "How's everything?"

"Peachy," her father replied, not even attempting to hide that things were far from it.

"You want your eggs scrambled or over easy?" her mom asked.

"Ah, over easy, please," Erin replied, raising an eyebrow. "Is everything okay?" she asked, looking back and forth between her parents.

"Of course," her mother responded, taking the eggs out of the carton.

"No," her father replied tersely.

"Pat," her mother remonstrated. "Not now."

"Wait. What's going on?" Erin asked.

Her father looked at her. "Really? What's going on? You, you're what's going on," he said. "I'm trying to get with the program, I really am. I call you Erin. I usually use the pronouns you want me to use. But I don't understand why you have to rub this in my face. Every time I turn around, I see or hear about you and transgender this or transgender that. Frankly, I'm tired of all the transgender stuff. Today at Mass, two guys I was in the Fathers' Club with came up to me and said they heard my 'daughter' made quite the impression at the reunion last night. Why couldn't you just skip the reunion—you know, maybe cut me a little slack? Do you have any idea how embarrassing this is for me?"

Erin stood in stunned silence; each accusation her father hurled at her stung like a fresh lash from a whip and, in the process, ripped open scars that she thought had healed. Erin truly believed her dad loved her, but now, for the first time in almost two years, her belief that he had finally accepted her as a woman was shattered. She wasn't his daughter; she was an embarrassment.

She heard her mother's voice, but it sounded as if it was coming through a tunnel, far away.

"Patrick McCabe, that's uncalled for. You apologize this instant."

"For what, Peg? I didn't do anything. She did," he said, pointing at Erin. "She's the one in the newspapers; she's the one giving interviews," he continued, hammering the "she" each time he said it. "She's the one that showed up at her high school reunion—an all-boys high school, I might add—looking like some . . . some . . ." His voice trailed off, as if catching himself before putting words to what he was thinking.

For a split second, time seemed to stop, the three of them frozen in place. Her mother at the stove, spatula in hand, her mouth agape; her father staring at her, his face flush with anger; and Erin, hot tears running down her cheeks, trying desperately to hold her emotions in check.

"I should go," Erin finally managed to mumble, a catch in her voice.

Her father sighed. "No," he said, shaking his head. "I . . . I should have kept my mouth shut," he offered with an air of resignation. Then, rising from the table, he walked into the den, closing the door behind him.

Her mother turned off the burner and laid the spatula on the counter. "Have some coffee, dear," she said, walking past Erin and into the den.

Erin dropped down onto a kitchen chair. *Why? Why is it so hard*

for people to accept who I am? An embarrassment—I am an embarrass-
ment. She rested her head on her palms, her mind dancing from
thought to thought. After everything that happened last night,
now she had to deal with this.

Lost in her thoughts, Erin was startled when her mother
wrapped her arms around her. "I'm sorry," she whispered.

Erin quickly used the back of her hand to brush the tears away.

"It's okay," Erin said. "Not your fault," she quickly added.

"I know it's hard, but give your dad time, he's getting better."

Erin winced. Why did anyone need to get better? Why wasn't
she good enough just the way she was?

"You said over easy, right?" her mother asked, heading back toward the stove.

"Nothing for me. I'll just make myself some coffee," Erin said,
heading to the cabinet for a mug.

Her mother put the spatula down and turned back with a
pained smile. "I know how you feel about my coffee. Why don't
we skip breakfast here and you can stop at Dunkin' Donuts along
the way and pick up some coffee and donuts? You could even
grab some munchkins for the boys to have after the game. Just
give me five minutes to change."

"Sure, but what about Dad? Isn't he going to have breakfast
and come with us?"

"Not today," her mother replied, heading up the stairs to her
bedroom.

Erin and her mom rode in silence until after Erin had stopped
and picked up their coffee and donuts.

"I thought you were upset with your father, not me," her
mother said, breaking the silence.

"I'm not upset with you . . . I'm not upset with anyone," Erin
replied.

"Oh, stop it, of course you're upset," her mother replied with
her usual bluntness. "And I understand why. I know how much
you want your father to accept you, and when he doesn't, it makes
you feel like you've let him down. But you can't take the fact that

he struggles sometimes as a reflection on you. It's just that . . . well, he's not used to having a daughter."

"No, Mom," Erin said, still feeling raw. "If I had been assigned female at birth, Dad would be fine with me. It's not that I'm a woman that bothers him; it's the fact that I'm trans, and he and most of his friends don't see me as a woman—that's why he struggles. You heard him, I'm an embarrassment. What I'll never be is a woman."

Erin glanced over at her mom, who was chewing on her lower lip, her face a mixture of sadness and resolve. "I'm sorry," Erin said softly. "The reunion last night was a bit awkward, and I guess I just wasn't prepared for Dad to pile on."

"Erin, honey, your dad wasn't piling on. He . . . well, after Mass, he took some ribbing from Brian Graham, Troy's dad. That's all."

Erin snorted. "Well, I guess the apple didn't fall far from the tree. Troy was one of the guys who gave me grief last night. What'd his dad have to say?"

"I don't want to upset you even more," her mom said softly.

"You can tell me," Erin said. "Maybe it'll help me understand things a little bit better from Dad's perspective."

Her mother seemed to hesitate. "As we were leaving church, we saw Brian and Betty talking to some folks, so we walked over to say hello. We exchanged some small talk, and then Mr. Graham said, 'I understand your son—oh, I'm sorry, your daughter—went to the reunion last night. Troy told me Ian was the prettiest graduate there and looked fetching in his black dress and heels.' At that point, Betty said, 'Brian, that's enough,' and asked me how Sean and the grandkids were doing. But, of course, by then, the other couples were sharing a laugh, and your father looked like he wanted the ground to open and swallow him."

Erin squeezed the steering wheel tightly, trying to tamp down her urge to say something about the Grahams.

"I'm sorry, honey," her mother said. "I know I should have said something in your defense, but I was afraid it would only make matters worse for your father."

"It's okay," Erin replied, as the window of guilt slowly opened, allowing the chilly winds of self-doubt to sweep across her psyche.

Erin and Peg stood on the sideline along with Sean and Liz, watching Patrick and Brennan's game.

Erin adored her nephews. Patrick, now fourteen, a freshman in high school, and twelve-year-old Brennan, in seventh grade, were two of the best players on their travel soccer team, the Princeton Cobras.

The game was a nail-biter. With just ten minutes left to go in the semifinals of the U-14 Boys State Cup game, the Cobras, despite having dominated most of the game, were down 2–3 to the Jersey Knights. The winner would go on to the finals next weekend at Fort Dix; for the losing team, the season was over.

As she stood there, it wasn't lost on Erin what a huge role her nephews had played in reuniting the family after she transitioned. When she had come out, Erin had been confident that Sean, who was one of the most sought-after orthopedic surgeons in the state, would understand. And yet, after she'd had facial surgery and started living as Erin, Sean had stopped communicating with her. He had told their mother that he needed to protect Patrick and Brennan; because the boys had been so close to their Uncle Ian, he wasn't sure how they'd react to the news their uncle was now their Aunt Erin. Erin had been devastated. Protect the boys from her? As if being near her was somehow going to impact the boys' sexual orientation or gender identity?

About two years after she had transitioned, Erin had gotten an email from her nephews inviting her to their soccer game—an invitation that came without Sean's knowledge. Once Sean had witnessed his sons' love for their aunt, and how comfortable they were with her, things had started to get better.

"Everything okay?" Liz asked. "You're unusually quiet, and your mom has spent most of the afternoon talking to your brother. What's up?"

Erin loved Liz like a sister. When Sean wasn't talking to Erin, Liz had quietly prodded him to be more understanding. Not to mention the fact that she had ignored the boys' secret communication with their aunt in order to allow their scheme to play out.

"I don't want to distract you from the game," Erin said.

"I'm a mother of two boys. I'm an expert in multitasking," Liz replied with a laugh.

Erin quickly explained what had happened when she had gotten to her parents' that morning.

"I don't know, Liz. Sometimes I feel like I take one step forward and two steps back with my dad. It hurts to know that I'm an embarrassment to him."

"I'm sorry, Erin," Liz said. "I don't know what it is, but the relationship between fathers and their children, especially sons, sometimes seems like a minefield that both sides are trying to safely navigate without a map. I'm not sure I know the right way to put this into words without . . . well, without offending you. But on some level, your dad still sees you, and relates to you, as his son."

"Trust me. I know that."

Liz pursed her lips. "But that doesn't mean he doesn't love you."

"He sure has a funny way of showing it," Erin replied.

"I think you're confusing two things—his love for you and pleasing him." Liz held up her hand when Erin went to respond. "When I watch Patrick and Brennan, they have such a different relationship with Sean than they do with me. Even though he doesn't push them, they try so hard to please him. I think they know intuitively that they'll always have my love. But it's almost like they feel they could lose Sean's if they disappoint him; of course, they won't, and he tells them that all the time, but they want him to be so proud of them. And on some level, I think that's what you're going through with your dad. You're still trying to please him, to make him proud of you, but the one thing he wants—his son—you can't give him because that's not who you are. I'm sure it's hard for you, but try to be patient with him and trust that he loves you."

"I'm trying, Liz, I really am. But you're right, it is hard sometimes. It's hard to remember that he didn't talk to me for over two years after I transitioned—didn't even want to see me. This morning he told me I embarrassed him. I mean, let's face it, I'm a disappointment to him. And I don't think there's any way I can ever fix that."

"I'm not sure 'disappointment' is fair," Liz countered. "I agree he doesn't understand you, but he does love you. Don't give up on him."

"I'm not giving up on him. I just worry he's given up on me."

The sudden screams from the Cobras' fans drew their attention back to the field. The Cobras were on the attack. Patrick, who played outside midfielder, had made a pass to one of the forwards, and then made a run toward the goal. The forward had spotted Patrick's run and had threaded a pass back through the Knights' defense. Patrick cut into the box, received the perfectly weighted pass, and fired a shot into the top corner of the goal. As the ball hit the net, the Cobras fans started screaming and jumping up and down. But the joy quickly subsided when the ref conferred with his linesman on the sidelines. After several seconds, the ref blew his whistle, then held his arm straight up in the air.

"What's going on?" Peg asked.

Erin turned to her mom. "Apparently, the player Patrick passed the ball to was in an offside position when Patrick made the pass, even though he was onside when he received the pass."

"Offside, onside—what's that mean in English?" her mom asked.

"It means the goal doesn't count, and the score is still two–three."

"Oh no!"

The sidelines were a cacophony of emotions—whoops and screams of joy from the Knights' fans as they realized the goal had been disallowed, groans and muted cursing from the Cobras' contingent.

The loss of the tying goal seemed to deflate the Cobras, and although they mounted a few attacks in the closing minutes, the Knights defended desperately, knocking the ball out of bounds every chance they could to waste as much time as possible. When the final whistle sounded, the Knights danced around the field celebrating, while the Cobras trudged through the final hand-shake, then slumped toward the sideline, despondent.

Liz and Sean stepped forward and gave each of them a hug. Peg then followed suit, but Erin hung back, watching it all.

Finally, their eyes caught hers.

"Tough loss, but you guys played a great game," Erin said.

"Was Timmy really offsides, Aunt Erin? Coach thought it was a bad call," Brennan asked.

"Honestly, Bren, I couldn't tell from my angle, but over and back is always a tough call. He certainly was onside when he got the pass; the question is, was he offside when the pass was made. Regardless, I thought the refs did a really good job all game."

The six of them slowly began their trek to the parking lot, Erin and her nephews trailing several yards behind the others.

"Just doesn't seem fair," Patrick said.

"What isn't fair?" Erin asked.

"We outplayed them most of the game, and yet we lost."

Erin nodded knowingly. "Yeah, soccer can be a cruel game. The best team doesn't always win."

"See, it's not fair," Patrick snapped.

"Really?" Erin said. "Of all the teams that you beat this season, did you always think you guys were the best team?"

Patrick hesitated. "Well . . ."

"We weren't better than Colonia," Brennan chimed in. "And we beat them two–nil."

"We played really hard that game," Patrick responded.

"Yeah, and we got lucky too," Brennan countered. "Remember, my first shot hit off the defender's leg and changed directions, so the goalie never had a chance."

"I was at that game, and both of you are right," Erin added. "You played really hard, and you got a bit lucky—and sometimes that happens, like it did today for the Knights. Just because things didn't go the way you wanted, don't get too down on yourselves. Think more long-term."

"What's that mean?" Patrick asked.

"It means that, as important as this game was to you today, it just isn't that important in the grand scheme of things. I can guarantee that when you try out for varsity or apply to college, no one is ever going to ask how your travel team did in the U-14 State Cup—never! So as disappointing as today is, try to keep it in perspective. Things are easy when you win. What's important is how you handle things when they don't go the way you hoped. Don't give up; don't stop trying."

"Good advice."

Erin looked up to see her mother.

"I agree with your Aunt Erin. You guys had a great game. So, don't give up, and don't stop trying." Peg caught Erin looking and winked. "It's good advice for all of us to follow."

CHAPTER 16

Monday, June 15, 2009, 9:00 a.m.

"WHAT DO YOU MAKE OF THE THIRD BODY?" ERIN ASKED Duane as they sat across from each other in the conference room.

"I'm leaning toward Asbury PD's theory that the person was one of the arsonists. The question is why didn't they get out?" He rubbed his lip with his forefinger. "Add to that the fact that another potential arsonist winds up murdered in AC, and it sure begins to look like whoever is behind this didn't want anyone around who could name names."

"Well, we sure know from past experience that's consistent with Townsend's MO," she replied. "That, plus the leaked pictures of Montgomery, is enough to convince me that he's behind all of this."

"Assuming you're right, there's a piece we're missing," Duane said.

"What?"

"If this is all just to stop people from learning what we know, he would have come after us, but he hasn't. Why? That's the part we're missing."

Erin shook her head. "You're right. But I don't know."

The intercom on the phone in the center of the conference table buzzed.

"Erin," Cheryl said, "there's an attorney on the phone by the name of Logan Stevens; they said it's an emergency, and they need to speak with you."

Erin looked to Duane, who shrugged. Didn't ring a bell for her either.

"All right. Is it Mr. or Ms. Stevens?" Erin asked.

"I asked," Cheryl replied, "and they said neither."

"Okay. Put them through," Erin responded, grinning as she saw Duane react to the "neither."

Erin hit the hands-free button.

"Erin McCabe," she answered.

"Ms. McCabe, my name is Logan Stevens, and I'm an attorney in New Brunswick. I'm calling because I desperately need a criminal defense attorney for a client of mine."

"Please call me Erin. And, just so you know, I have you on a speakerphone with my partner, Duane Swisher. May we call you Logan?"

"I don't see why not. It's my fucking name. And, just so you know, I'm genderqueer, and my pronouns are they, them, theirs."

"Thanks," Erin replied. "So why do you think I'm the lawyer your client needs?"

"Because there aren't a fucking lot of attorneys who are trans and doing criminal defense work. And even though being trans isn't absolutely necessary, it sure as hell won't hurt."

"Fair enough. What's the case about?" Erin asked.

"I do mostly family law. And because I'm genderqueer, I work a lot with LGBTQ clients, and I do a fair amount of name changes for trans folks. A few months ago, I was retained by the mom of an eleven-year-old trans girl to change her daughter's name. Mom and Dad are divorced. Dad, a fellow by the name of Paul Costello, has been absent from the child's life almost all of her eleven years, but as required, we gave him notice of the name change. Mom didn't expect he'd respond—but respond he did. On June 4th, not only did I get served with an objection to the name change, but I received an Order to Show Cause filed by the American Liberty Defense Alliance, who's now representing him."

"Wait," Erin interrupted. "Is this the case that Senator Townsend talked about at his news conference?"

"Yep. That's my case," Stevens replied.

"Okay, so what happened?" Erin asked.

"The Order to Show Cause sought to immediately remove custody of the child from my client based on child abuse. Last Monday, we had an emergent hearing, and the judge agreed, ordering that, until the final hearing, he was giving sole custody to the dad."

"What was the alleged child abuse?" Duane asked.

"Allowing her child to live in accordance with her gender identity," Stevens replied.

"What!" Erin screamed. "How's that possible?"

"You know Judge Curruzi?"

"No," Erin replied. "I don't do any family law."

"Well, if you did, you'd know how it's possible."

"Okay, but I'm confused. You said you need a criminal attorney."

"My client, the mom, Michelle Costello, picked her daughter up at school on Thursday and then disappeared. There's a warrant out for her arrest. She's facing a criminal contempt charge from Judge Curruzi, and on top of that, the Middlesex County Prosecutor's Office has issued a criminal complaint charging her with interference with custody, a second-degree crime."

"Ouch," Erin replied.

"Do you have time to meet with me today, so I can fill you in on the details and see if you'd be interested in taking the case?"

Erin hesitated. "Ah, just so you know, Logan, I'm under a criminal investigation. I don't think anything will come of it, but I wouldn't want you to be surprised."

"I don't give a shit, as long as you're still trans and still a criminal defense attorney. I can be at your office around one. Does that work for you?"

Erin looked up at Swish, who nodded. "Sure. That works. See you then."

After they hung up, Duane gave Erin a sidelong glance. "What's 'genderqueer' mean, and why does Logan use they, them and theirs as pronouns—those are plurals, aren't they?"

"I'm not sure I'm the best one to explain this," Erin began, "but most people view gender in terms of their being two choices—male or female."

"Isn't that all there is?"

"No, not really," Erin said. "Look, I understand your confusion. I always saw the world as being binary—I was just in the wrong part of the binary. But even for people who fit in the binary, there's a spectrum. Some guys are more masculine, some women more feminine, but they still identify as either male or female. Someone who's genderqueer doesn't fit in either box. Their gender identity is neither male nor female. Just like I knew my gender identity was female, someone like Logan knows their gender identity is none of the above. Since they aren't either male or female, neither set of pronouns works. That's why they use they, them, theirs."

"Damn," Duane said. "And I thought I was finally getting good with the trans shit, and now I have to learn a whole new set of rules."

Erin laughed. "No, not a new set of rules. The same rule—just accept people as they are."

Logan Stevens arrived promptly at one.

They were about the same height as Erin, but with a stocky build. Their skin was light brown, and their short afro was cut in a high fade style. They wore a men's navy-blue suit, with a white shirt, and a red-and-blue striped tie.

"Hi, Logan, I'm Erin. Nice to meet you."

"Nice to meet you too."

"Come on in. I'll introduce you to Duane. And by the way, he was getting pretty proud of the fact that he finally learned to navigate the terminology around my being trans, but genderqueer is all new to him. So please forgive him if he screws up," Erin said with an apologetic grin.

"Yeah. I understand that no one gets me," Logan replied.

Once Erin had done the introductions, she and Logan settled into the chairs in front of Duane's desk.

"Thank you for seeing me on such short notice," Logan began.

"No worries," Erin responded. "Let's go over things again," she said, grabbing a legal pad and a pen, taking notes as Logan recapped what they had told them over the phone.

"By the way, what's Hannah's dead name, address, and date of birth?" Erin asked.

"Her what?" Duane interjected.

Erin smiled at Duane. "Dead name. The name they were given at birth or had prior to transitioning. You know, like Ian," she said, referring to her own dead name.

"Nicholas," Logan replied, opening a file they had brought. "Address is 1222 Barron Avenue, Woodbridge. Date of birth is April 22nd, 1998."

"Thanks. Didn't mean to interrupt. You were saying."

"I represented Michelle when she got divorced. At the time, I was a brand spanking new associate at the firm of Palmer & Holden in Woodbridge, and they gave me Michelle's divorce to handle because it was basically a no-brainer—even I couldn't fuck it up. Father wasn't contesting custody, and they had worked out the child support issue amicably. It went through with no problem." Their expression grew dark. "But about five months ago, Michelle came to see me about an issue she was having with the school principal giving Hannah a hard time over her transitioning. I wrote a nastygram, threatening to sue them under the Law Against Discrimination, and after that, the principal pretty much got with the program. While I was doing that, Michelle asked me if I could handle a name change application for Hannah. Like I told you, I do a lot of name changes, and knowing the father's lack of interest, I figured, even though it was a trans kid, everything would be okay."

"You still at the same firm?" Duane asked.

"Nah, I left Palmer about six years ago and opened up my own shop. They had a hard time dealing with me when they thought I was a lesbian; when I came out as genderqueer, they basically suggested I take all my queer clients elsewhere."

"Sorry," Erin said.

"Don't be," they said. "It's all good. Actually, it's the best fucking thing that happened to me personally and professionally. I never fit in there. I'm a biracial, pansexual, genderqueer person who was trying to fit my mostly Black ass into a very conservative environment. Now I don't have to worry about what the very uptight, white, cisgender partners are thinking about my very queer clients. The only thing I miss is watching their heads explode when they saw some of my clients."

"What's happening with the name change?" Duane asked.

"As I mentioned, first I received an objection from the ALDA on behalf of Costello. Then I got this crazy-ass Order to Show Cause filed on his behalf, claiming that Michelle was trying to turn his son into a girl and it constituted child abuse. It was supported by affidavits from Costello, who hasn't seen his kid in three years, and some psychologist who's never even spoken to Hannah. I filed affidavits from Michelle, her therapist, and the psychologist Hannah has been seeing, all stating this was what Hannah wanted, not what Michelle wanted. Even though it was Judge Curruzi, I couldn't imagine he'd take away custody based on the bullshit they submitted. Unfortunately, I underestimated Curruzi's stupidity, transphobia, or both. He granted the temporary restraining order, holding that there was sufficient credible evidence that Michelle was 'forcing' Hannah—except in his decision he kept using Hannah's dead name—to become a girl against 'his' will and ordered that temporary custody be transferred to Paul until a plenary hearing could be held."

"That's crazy," Erin said.

"You got that right," Logan replied. "Anyway, as you might imagine, both Michelle and Hannah, who wasn't even allowed in the courtroom, let alone to testify, flipped the fuck out. To her credit, Michelle convinced Hannah that this was only temporary and we'd get it reversed. That was last Monday. On Thursday, Michelle waited for Hannah to get out of school, picked her up, and they disappeared." Logan stopped. "Listen, I need your assurances that the next part will remain confidential."

"Of course," Erin said. "You're consulting with us for representation for Michelle."

"Yeah, but what if I have an idea of where they are?"

"That could become a little more problematic," Duane suggested. "Depends on whether some judge considers the whereabouts of a fugitive client to be privileged or not. Could go either way."

"Doesn't matter. I wouldn't give it up no matter what happened. Someone would have to stick a crowbar up my ass to pry it out of me," Logan replied, a defiant sneer gracing their face.

"My suggestion," Erin said, "is that for now, let's skip what you know about their whereabouts. We don't need to know, and if we do, I prefer to find it out from the client. Do you have a copy of the criminal complaint?"

Logan took a green form out of their file and handed it to Erin, who took a look at the charges.

"Swish, hand me the statute book with 2C:13-4 in it," she said.

Duane pulled out a book from his credenza and handed it to Erin. She flipped through until she found what she was looking for and began to read.

"Shit," she mumbled.

"What?" Duane asked.

"The statute provides an affirmative defense to the person taking the child, but only if, as soon as practical, but no later than within twenty-four hours, the parent taking the child gives notice to the police, the county prosecutor, and the Division of Youth and Family Services where the child is located."

"Guess that ship has sailed," Duane replied.

"There is something else you should be aware of," Logan offered.

"What's that?" Erin asked.

"After Michelle took Hannah, she called me to let me know what she'd done and why. Apparently, on Wednesday, at the recommendation of the ALDA, her ex took Hannah to some quack who practices conversion therapy."

"What's conversion therapy?" Duane asked.

"It's bullshit, is what it is," Logan spit out.

Erin nodded. "In essence, it's an effort to try and turn gay people straight or trans people cis."

"Does it work?" he asked.

"No!" Erin and Logan yelled in unison.

"Think of it this way," Erin continued. "Imagine if I suggested that you go to therapy to make you gay or trans. Would you believe that was possible?"

"No. That's crazy," he replied.

"Exactly," Erin said.

"Hannah called Michelle on Wednesday night and was distraught. Michelle could barely understand her between her sobs. When Michelle finally got Hannah to calm down, Hannah told her about the conversion-therapy session. Apparently, the 'therapy' consisted of calling her names like 'queer' and 'trannie' and telling 'him' all 'he' had to do was look between 'his' legs to know 'he' was a boy. Then they said God made him a boy, cut off her hair, and complimented her on how she looked like a boy again. Of course, throughout the whole session they only used her dead name. Michelle said Hannah was so distraught she was afraid Hannah was going to commit suicide. Naturally, she did what any mother would do to protect her child. The next day, she went and got her at school, and they took off."

Erin sighed. "Let me ask this. Does Michelle have money to pay not only for you, but for us as well?"

For the first time since they met, Logan's brash demeanor seemed to melt like ice cream on a hot summer's day.

"Well . . . not exactly," their tone apologetic. "When she came to me for the name change, I charged her seven hundred and fifty dollars. Of course, when her ex filed the Order to Show Cause, we talked briefly about the fact that I would need an additional retainer, but when the shit hit the fan and Curruzi granted the Order to Show Cause—well, we didn't talk too much about fees."

"I sense there's more that you're not telling us," Erin said.

"Michelle's a school nurse at Woodbridge High School. As soon as the school learns there's criminal charges pending against her, she'll be placed on unpaid administrative leave and could face tenure charges seeking to terminate her. I know she's had issues with her family over Hannah. So, I don't think she can count on any financial support from them. She owns a modest home, with a mortgage . . . well, you get the picture."

"Yeah, we get the picture," Duane said.

Erin looked across the desk at her partner, hoping her expression conveyed the message. With a sigh, Duane placed his hand over his mouth and closed his eyes.

"Sure," he said.

Logan looked from one to the other. "Sorry. Did I miss something?" they asked.

Duane chuckled. "My partner just gave me the 'I don't care if there's no money, I want to take this case' look."

"And you agreed?" Logan asked, surprised.

He looked at Erin with a rueful grin. "We've done pretty well financially over the last few years, and sometimes you just have to pay it forward."

Erin's eyes conveyed her gratitude. "Thanks," she said, then turned back to Logan. "This is where it starts to get a little complicated. Unless you have a power of attorney for Michelle . . ."

"I don't," Logan replied.

"I didn't think you would. Anyway, without a POA you can't retain me to represent her. For that, I need to speak with Michelle. I know you said she called you, but now that it's known that she's a fugitive, I'm sure Middlesex County has or will get a warrant to track and listen in to her cell phone. You know what kind of phone she has?"

"No, not a clue."

Erin thought for a moment. "Let's assume, for purposes of argument, Michelle and Hannah are not where they were when she talked to you Thursday evening. The next time you communicate, don't ask her where she is. You need to watch your own behind. The more law enforcement thinks you know, the greater the likelihood they will haul you before a grand jury or, worse, charge you with aiding and abetting. Michelle doesn't need you locked up for refusing to answer questions. She needs you trying to get Curruzi's order reversed. Even though you're her attorney, you'll have to walk a fine line between providing legal advice and aiding and abetting a fugitive. Remember, the attorney-client privilege doesn't apply to aiding someone in the commission of a crime."

"Great," Logan replied sarcastically. "What do you suggest?"

"How savvy do you think Michelle is?" Erin asked.

"What do you mean?"

"Do you think she'll know the police can track and listen to her calls?"

"Shit no," Logan replied. "I didn't know that. I'm sure she doesn't have a clue."

"Okay, then here's my recommendation," Erin began. "Text her and tell her to find a pay phone to call you on your office line. When she calls, make sure you say you're her attorney. I doubt law enforcement is up on your office phone, but even if they are, at least you create a legal issue with them listening in. Tell her to turn off her cell phone because they can track her through her phone, move to a new location, and buy a prepaid phone. Then I'm going to give you a number for one that I have. Tell Michelle to call me on that number, and I'll talk to her about representing her."

Logan scratched their head. "Man, this is a lot of cloak-and-dagger shit."

"Yeah, well, don't be surprised if the cops come knocking on your door and demanding to know where Michelle is," Duane said.

"Like I said, they'd have to pry it out of me," Logan responded, their tone once again defiant.

"That's good," Erin said, "but it's even better if you don't know where she is. That'll keep you out of the crosshairs." Erin paused. "You may also want to pick up a prepaid phone."

"Assuming she retains you, any thoughts on how to get her out of this mess?" Logan asked.

"Not sure," Erin replied. "Even if it doesn't technically fit within the statutory defense, we may have to let the police, the prosecutor's office, and DYFS know that they're safe and see if we can discuss a resolution."

"Why?" Logan asked. "If Michelle's fucked for saving her kid's life, I don't want to sell her out."

"Let me ask you a practical question," Duane chimed in. "Your client . . . maybe our client too," he added with a smirk in Erin's direction, "is a school nurse who has limited financial resources. Right now, every law-enforcement agency in New Jersey has received a situational awareness alert with a description of her, her car, her license plate, and Hannah. Realistically, how long do you think she can avoid being discovered and arrested? Another day? A couple of days? A week? Two? She doesn't know what she's doing. She's going to make a mistake and get caught. Really, it's not a matter of if, it's just a matter of time."

"There's another factor to consider," Erin said, picking up Duane's thread. "Even if she's technically committed the offense, we want her to be seen in the best possible light. Here's a mom doing everything she can to protect her daughter. That's how we want the public, the press, the judge, and, if we're lucky, even the prosecutor's office to see her. That'll potentially help us with a plea bargain, with sentencing, and, if we have to try the case, with jury nullification."

"Jury nullification—what the hell is that?"

"In simple terms," Erin began, "it's when a defense lawyer can get the jury to the point where they don't care that the defendant committed the crime, they just aren't going to convict them. Whether it's because they like the client, think the law is stupid, or think the prosecutor is a jerk—doesn't matter. If we get the right jury, who hears what the conversion therapist did to Hannah, who knows?"

Logan's skepticism was apparent. "Does that really happen?" they asked.

"Sometimes," Erin replied, trying not to convey how much of a long shot it was.

"What do you think?" Erin asked Duane after Logan left.

Duane folded his arms across his chest and leaned back in his desk chair. "What do I think? I think you're walking yourself into a hornet's nest, that's what I think. Assuming Michelle retains us, the minute you reach out to the prosecutor's office, you're going to get slapped with a grand-jury subpoena. You know that, right?"

"Yeah, I kind of assume I will," she said offhandedly.

Duane leaned forward. "E, look. Trust me, I get why you want to take this case. But you know that when the prosecutor's office serves you with a subpoena to testify before the grand jury as to what you know about where Michelle and Hannah are, you're going to have to move to quash it. Meaning, because we're representing Michelle, we're going to have to get another lawyer to represent you to handle the motion. It's one thing to take on Michelle's case pro bono; it's another thing to take a case that's going to cost us money because we have to hire a lawyer."

Erin gave him a weak smile. There was a reason Swish managed the business side of their partnership; he actually thought about how they were going to pay the bills. "I hear you," she said. "And I know you're right." She sighed. "You know Ryan Farley?"

"Only by name. He's in Jersey City, right?"

"Yeah. He and I were in a case together when I worked for the PD—good guy, good lawyer," she replied. "I know he had a case that went to the New Jersey Supreme Court involving a prosecutor subpoenaing a lawyer to a grand jury to testify about his client's whereabouts. I figure I'd give Ryan a call and see if he's available in case I need him."

"Okay, but—"

"Swish," she said, interrupting him. "If I need to retain Ryan, I'll pay out of my pocket."

Duane stroked his goatee, his brown eyes taking her in, and slowly his expression changed from the guy paying the bills to the one who understood Erin's need to tilt at windmills.

"Thanks," he said, "but we're partners, and we're in this together."

CHAPTER 17

Monday, June 15, 2009, 3:00 p.m.

Erin was startled by the unfamiliar ringtone of the burner phone buried beneath the clutter on her desk.

"Erin McCabe," she answered, still a bit breathless from knocking everything aside in her hunt.

"How can I be sure this is Ms. McCabe?" a woman's voice on the other end asked.

"I presume Logan Stevens, your current lawyer, gave you this number to call and told you it was my number?"

"They did, but I don't know how I can be sure it's not the police trying to trap me?"

Erin thought for a moment, admiring Michelle's paranoia and trying to come up with something to convince her. "Have you investigated Lupron for Hannah?" Erin finally asked.

"Um . . ."

"Do you think a member of law enforcement would know that Lupron is used to delay puberty in trans kids?"

"No," the voice on the other end responded, but the doubt lingered.

"Michelle, this is Erin. Please trust me."

"Okay," Michelle responded hesitantly.

"Did you purchase a prepaid phone?" Erin asked.

There was a long pause. "No. I didn't know where to get one."

"Are you on a pay phone?" Erin asked.

"No. I used all my change calling Logan and someone else," Michelle replied.

Erin closed her eyes and took a deep breath. "Okay. Michelle, you're calling me about me representing you on the criminal charges, correct?" she asked, knowing that her statement should cause anyone from law enforcement who might be listening to stop because it was an attorney-client conversation, even if she also knew they wouldn't. At least she knew it would probably be inadmissible.

"Yes," Michelle replied weakly.

"Good, then listen to me. Because you are a fugitive, the police are looking for you. I want to talk to you about how we handle your situation. But the police can track your location based on you using your cell phone or even just by having your cell phone on," Erin said, hoping that Michelle would get the message. "So go to a Best Buy or a drug store—a chain one—and ask for what's called a prepaid phone. They'll know what you want. Once you charge it up, call me back at this number. And Michelle, keep in mind the police may also be tracking your credit-card transactions and bank activity."

"Okay," she responded. "I'm trying, Ms. McCabe."

"I'm sure you are," Erin replied. "Go get the phone and call me, and we'll talk through how we handle things."

"Okay. Thank you."

The call disconnected, leaving Erin staring off into space, a feeling deep in her gut telling her this was going to turn into a shit show. She had heard mothers describe how they flew into mama-bear mode to protect their kids. That's all Michelle had done—tried to protect her trans child from folks who refused to believe that an eleven-year-old knew who she was.

Erin could sympathize with Hannah. Erin had known she was a girl ever since she first had conscious memory—three, four years old, whenever it was. She remembered going to bed at night and praying that when she woke up, everyone would see her for the girl she was, but that never happened. Afraid that people would hate her if she told them the truth, she forced herself to be the boy everyone else saw. Then she found soccer. It allowed her to hide among the guys because she didn't have to be big and strong to be good. And suddenly there was a way to fit into a world where she felt terribly out of place. In high school, she had met Lauren and fallen in love. At that point in her life, having hidden who she was from everyone, she was determined to be a guy's guy, and she became convinced that her love for Lauren would keep the feelings of being a woman at bay.

Well, we know how well that worked out, she thought.

Now, damn it, she had to find a way to help Michelle, a mother who had listened when her child had the courage to say, "Mom, I'm a girl, not a boy." But how? Michelle was scared and on the run, trying to hide in an electronic world where hiding was almost impossible, especially for someone who had no clue as to what they were doing.

"You got a minute?" Duane asked from the doorway.

"Sure. Come on in. What's up?"

"I just got a call from Agent Arroyo," he said, dropping down into a chair.

"How is Cesc Fàbregas?" she asked.

Duane seemed confused. "Who?"

"Sorry, my own little fantasy. What's going on?"

"The medical examiner identified Julius Hayser from his dental records."

"Okay. No surprise there."

"Apparently, they had also secured Rachel's dental records and now know that neither of the other two corpses are her."

"Oh shit," Erin said, bolting upright in her chair. "You don't think Asbury or the prosecutor's office is going to think Rachel set the fire, do you?"

"No worries. Arroyo and Chronicle are already on it. They've set up a meeting tomorrow with some of the top brass in Asbury PD and the prosecutor's office to let them know that Rachel is alive and they've confirmed her alibi."

"They going to tell them that Rachel thinks the second body might be Hayser's girlfriend?" Erin asked.

"Yeah, they're just going to try to keep the lid on public disclosure as long as they can," he said.

"Unfortunately, the clock is now ticking," Erin said. "They're not going to be able to keep the identity of the deceased quiet forever. After all, she probably has a family who is worried since they haven't heard from her."

"There's still an unidentified body that apparently is going to be very hard to ID," Duane offered.

"Probably not going to fly," Erin responded. "Once the identity of the first two are made public, whoever's behind this is likely going to know who the third body is—remember, if our theory is right, it's one of their own."

"Good point," Duane said. "Let's hope Chronicle can buy some more time. After all, Rachel is a former colleague."

"Yeah, let's hope," Erin agreed. "By the way," she continued, since they were sharing bad news, "I heard from Michelle."

"Um, you don't sound real happy about it," Swish replied.

She proceeded to explain to him what had happened.

"This isn't making me feel warm and fuzzy about how this is going to go down," he said.

"Join the crowd," she added.

"Mom, turn off your phone."

"What?"

"Mom, the lawyer was just telling you that they can trace you, even if you just have your phone on. Turn it off."

Michelle glanced over at her daughter in the passenger's seat and was struck by how much of a disconnect she felt at seeing Hannah with her hair cut short, even though it made her look the way she did back when she was Nicholas. Hannah was her daughter, and it pained her to see what they had done to her.

"Okay," she said, handing her phone to her daughter. "Turn it off for me. You're right; it does sound like every cop in New Jersey is going to be looking for us."

They had left the friend's house where they had been staying in Freehold and were now heading north to her ex-brother-in-law's house in Hackettstown. After she had finished talking with Logan, she'd realized she was going to need a different place to stay, so she had called Gary from a pay phone and asked if they could stay at the studio apartment he had above his garage in Hackettstown. She was relieved when he said yes, and even more relieved when he told her that the key she had from when she stayed there twelve years ago would still work. Gary and his partner, Alex, were staying at their place in Sea Girt for a couple of weeks, so she and Hannah would have the whole house to themselves.

"Are we gonna be okay, Mom?"

Michelle hated to lie but knew that her daughter was sitting on a precipice; she worried that if she let Hannah think for a moment she'd have to go back to her father, Hannah would topple over the edge, and Michelle would lose her forever.

"Yes, hon. Between Logan and this new lawyer, they're going to work it out. Everything's going to be fine; we just have to stay out of sight for a while." When she glanced over, Hannah was staring out her side window. "Are you okay?"

Hannah wiped her eye. "I guess," she said, before falling silent.

"I'm sorry all this is happening to you," Michelle said, trying hard not to get emotional.

"I just don't know why he suddenly says he cares about me, Mom. My whole life, I've almost never seen him, but now he wants to tell me what to do."

"I don't understand it either, hon. It certainly isn't like your father to want to be involved," Michelle said.

"Dad said that the people who were helping him told him that I was too young to know what I was doing and that this was all your fault. He said he knew he hadn't been a good father, and had he been around, I wouldn't want to do this. He told me he was trying to make it up to me." Hannah hesitated. "I guess it didn't help that I started screaming at him that he was ruining my life and things were much better when I didn't see him," her tone showing no evidence of remorse.

Michelle allowed herself a small smile of satisfaction, proud of her daughter's defiance.

"Why don't people think I know who I am?"

"I don't know, hon. Maybe it's because you're young, or maybe because people are afraid of people who are different from them."

"You know what's funny," Hannah said. "When I went back to school after Dad had all my hair cut, most of the kids were really nice, even the boys. I guess some of their parents saw stuff about me in the newspaper and what was happening between you and Dad, and they must have said things about me. But the kids felt bad for me because they know I'm a girl."

"Does it bother you that people know about you and that you're transgender?" Michelle asked.

Hannah looked over. "No. I guess not. I just wish people could accept that even though my body is a little different from other girls, I'm still a girl."

"I wish they could too, hon," Michelle said.

They rode for several minutes saying nothing, both seemingly lost in their thoughts. "Do you think we can trust Uncle Gary?" Hannah asked, finally breaking the silence.

"I do. Uncle Gary has always been there for you, and for me too. Even after your father left, and we got divorced, your Uncle Gary has always stayed in touch with us."

"But he's Dad's brother."

"That's true, but they rarely see each other—maybe once in the last five years, and that was at their father's funeral. After your Uncle Gary came out, your father's family wouldn't have anything to do with him. I know your father talks to him from time to time, but he didn't come to Uncle Gary and Uncle Alex's civil-union ceremony two years ago. Your Uncle Gary's a good man—so yes, Hannah, I trust him."

"Do you remember how to get to his house?" Hannah asked.

Michelle had to smile. "Yes," she replied. "You don't know this, but I actually lived in the apartment above Uncle Gary's garage for a few months before you were born. Your father and I had an argument, and I just needed a place to stay. I guess I lived there for about three months, so I got to know my way around Hackettstown fairly well."

"What was your argument about?" Hannah asked.

"Oh, I don't even remember. We hadn't been married that long, so it was probably about money," she lied.

"Was it about me?" Hannah said.

Michelle felt as though her heart was going to burst. "How could we argue over you? You weren't even born yet."

"I don't know. It seems like I've brought nothing but trouble to your life," Hannah answered, her head bowed.

"Don't you ever say that. You are the best thing that has ever happened in my life, and I cherish every moment we're together."

"I'm just afraid that they're going to arrest you and send me back to my father."

"That's why we have the lawyers, honey. To work things out for us. It'll be okay," Michelle said, even though she had no idea how they were going to get out of this mess.

She could feel Hannah's stare as she drove.

"I won't go back," Hannah said, turning her head away. "I won't," she whispered, as she stared out the window.

Hannah's desperation scared Michelle. They needed to get to Gary's, where hopefully they would be safe, at least for a while. They needed time—time to allow Logan and this new lawyer to fix things.

Michelle turned her focus back to the road. The daylight was both her friend and her enemy. True, she had lived in Hackettstown for three months, but driving during the day helped her recognize the landmarks as she went. She knew finding Gary's house was difficult under the best of circumstances. The road he lived off of climbed up the side of a mountain, and with no streetlights, finding it at night was a shot in the dark—literally. Of course, the daylight came with its own set of risks. She was terrified that some cop on the lookout for a 2002 blue Camry would spot her and pull her over. She'd wind up in jail, and Hannah would wind up back with her father—or worse.

Fortunately, traffic was heavy as she headed out Interstate 287, and she could hide between the eighteen-wheelers. But downtown Hackettstown would be trickier, especially since she also had to find a store to buy a prepaid cell phone. She remembered there was a Staples and a Home Depot on the outskirts of town. Hopefully, they'd have what the attorney had told her to buy.

If they could just get to Gary's, they should be safe for a while. Gary's house had a driveway that ran through the woods for several hundred yards; there was no chance that they'd be seen once there. Now she just had to get them there.

"Call me crazy, but I don't think sitting there staring at the phone is going to make it ring," Mark said, looking over at Erin from the dining room table, where he was doing lesson plans on his laptop.

Erin shot him a dirty look. It was nine p.m., and the fact that she hadn't heard from Michelle was worrying her.

"You never know," she said.

As if on cue, the phone rang. She stuck her tongue out at him, jumped off the couch, and answered on her way to the bedroom.

"Michelle, are you okay?"

"Yes. I'm sorry, Ms. McCabe, it's just been a long day, and then I had to find a place to get the phone and wait for it to charge."

"Call me Erin," she began. "I'm just glad to hear from you. I was beginning to get worried."

Erin closed the bedroom door behind her as she slowly explained to Michelle the seriousness of the situation Michelle was in, and how she and Duane hoped to handle it.

CHAPTER 18

Tuesday, June 16, 2009, 9:00 a.m.

GARDNER DIALED THE NUMBER AND WAITED.

"Lonza."

"Lieutenant," Gardner responded. "Just checking in to see if there's anything new in the Montgomery case."

"Good timing on your part," Lonza replied. "We just got the DNA back on the handprint on the envelope that had the pictures in it, and it wasn't all Montgomery's. They ran it through CODIS, the FBI DNA database, but no hits. Yesterday they delivered the glass McCabe drank out of at Montgomery's house to the state police lab to determine if the other DNA on the envelope is hers."

"How long will that take?"

"Anywhere from a week to a month," Lonza responded. "But we've asked them to expedite it."

"Thank you, Lieutenant. I'll check back in a week or so to see where we are."

"Sure. I'll be here," Lonza replied.

Garner disconnected and dialed another number, this one belonging to an acquaintance from his days at the NSA, Walter Johnson, who had opened up his own investigative firm in New Jersey.

"Hello?"

"Were you able to find out anything?" Gardner asked.

"Why the fuck do you block your number when you're calling me?"

"I trust you, Walter. I just don't trust the folks at your cellphone service provider."

There was a small snort. "You can take the spook out of the agency, but you can't take the agency out of the spook. Anyway, I do have something for you. Next of kin haven't been notified, though, so this isn't official yet."

"Understood."

"Okay. The fire was definitely arson, and three bodies were removed from the home and taken to the morgue. There's a positive ID on Julius Hayser, a tenant in the building. No ID yet on bodies two and three. They thought the second body, which was found with Hayser, was the owner, a woman by the name of Stern, but dental records show it wasn't. They now think it may have been Hayser's girlfriend."

Gardner closed his eyes and rubbed his hand across his forehead. *Fucking A. How is this possible?* He took a few deep breaths to compose himself. "Are they finished looking for bodies?"

"That's the impression I got. You want me to go back and double-check?"

"Yes."

"Will do. Anything else?"

"Not for now. I appreciate your help."

Gardner clicked END and disconnected. "Fuck!" he spit out. She had to be there. What the fuck was going on? Benson had told him she was there. "I swear to God," he said out loud to no one, "if you weren't fucking dead, I'd kill you."

He began pacing, trying to decide next steps. Stern's house was gone, which meant that mail would be held at the post office until she surfaced. But where the fuck was she if she wasn't in the house when it burned down? He glanced at his watch—nine thirty a.m. He had to head to Townsend's campaign headquarters.

"Fuck," he muttered. He didn't need this now. If she wasn't dead, he had to find her and finish the job, before any of her mail made it into her hands. He took out his phone and punched in the numbers. "Crossman, it's Farmer."

"Jesus, Farmer. I don't hear from you for months, now twice in a couple of weeks. What's up?"

"How much for tracking someone's banking and credit transactions in real time?"

"Two grand a day."

"You're a fucking thief, you know that?"

"Thanks—coming from you, I'll take that as a compliment."

"I need a max of ten days. Make it a thousand a day, and I'll get you ten grand now. If you get me what I need on day one, you keep the change."

"You call me a thief, and then you want discount rates? You got balls, Farmer."

"Crossman, you'd be doing life at a supermax if it weren't for me. I could've ratted you out back when you were still with the NSA for running your little business on the side, but I didn't."

There was a long silence.

"Who?" Crossman finally asked.

"Same one as before, Rachel Stern. Oh, and check on a Richard Stern too."

"You want me to keep tabs on two people for this price?"

"Same person," Gardener said. "Different names, same social security number."

Crossman chuckled. "You know some strange folks, Farmer."

"We have a deal?"

"Yeah. As soon as I have the money, I'll go live on Stern. But, Farmer, we're even—no more deals after this."

"Sure," Gardner replied. "Just make sure I get what I need."

It was a little after eleven when Duane walked into Erin's office, fresh from handling the arraignment of a new client charged with being a drug distributor for selling three ounces of pot to an undercover cop.

"Did Michelle retain us?" he asked, settling into the chair opposite her desk and taking a sip from his coffee.

"She did," Erin replied. "We finally connected around nine last night."

"How's she doing?"

"She's scared. Hannah was in another room, so Michelle was free to talk. Basically, she's terrified that if Hannah has to go back to her father and goes through any more sessions of conversion therapy, she's going to try and take her own life. And, of course, Michelle now realizes that by fleeing with Hannah, she not only has put her custody case in jeopardy, but she could wind up in jail. Let's just say she's not in a real good place right now."

"Speaking of places, are they safe?" Duane asked.

Erin winced and rested her forehead in her hand. "Yeah, sounds that way."

Duane's eyes widened. "E, what's going on? My highly trained skills from when I was an FBI agent tell me there's more there to unpack," he said sarcastically.

"Oh yeah, there's definitely more to unpack," she replied. "Unfortunately, she inadvertently told me where they are—well, not technically where they are, but even little ol' me, who is not a highly trained former FBI agent, could find them in about five minutes with access to the Internet."

"Shit," Duane replied. "Um, stupid question—how was it inadvertent?"

"Like you, I wanted to know if she and Hannah were safe, so I just asked. Well, let's just say, in answering the question, she referenced having called someone; they were using that person's house."

"Got it. Next question—you connect with the prosecutor's office?"

"Yeah," Erin replied, trying to keep the foreboding out of her voice.

"Afraid to ask—how'd it go?"

"My guess is that the grand-jury subpoena will be here tomorrow," Erin replied.

Duane sat back. "That bad?"

"Yeah. I spoke with an assistant prosecutor by the name of John Beasley. Not sure what was worse, his misogyny or his transphobia.

After telling him I was representing Michelle and was calling in a good-faith effort to comply with the affirmative defense under the statute, he went off on me. Called Michelle a child abuser, hell-bent on turning her child into a pervert, and said that, once she was apprehended, he was going to prosecute her to the fullest extent of the law. For some reason, he seemed to think Hannah— although that's not the name he used—had a close relationship with her father—again, not the pronoun he used—and that Michelle was trying to destroy that relationship."

"Gonna be a shit show, isn't it?" Duane said, shaking his head. "What makes you think a subpoena is coming?" he asked.

"He demanded to know where my client was. When I told him that was privileged, he laughed and said, 'We'll see how privileged it is when you're facing going to jail.'" Erin shrugged. "Not sure why it seems like everyone I deal with these days wants to put me in jail."

"How do you want to handle this?" Duane asked.

"I have a call scheduled with Ryan at four. You available?"

"Actually, I told Cori I'd go with her to the pediatrician for the kids' checkups. You want me to let her know I can't make it?"

"Absolutely not!" Erin responded. "I can fill you in tomorrow."

"Thanks," Duane replied.

"No worries," Erin said, her smile warm and genuine, which she hoped hid the tinge of jealousy. Swish and Corrine had two children—Austin, who was now four, and their baby, Alysha, who was four months old. If there was one regret Erin had about her transition, it was losing the opportunity to have children of her own. As foolish as it seemed now, Erin had hoped that she and Lauren would stay together after she transitioned. She had even banked her sperm before she started taking hormones, deluding herself with the hope that the fact that they could still have children together would convince Lauren their relationship could be saved. It hadn't.

If she and Mark ultimately got married, there was the possibility of adoption. She knew a number of gay and lesbian couples who had adopted, but she was trans, and she had never really explored how that impacted her rights. Then there were Mark's feelings about having a family. She had consciously avoided the subject, more over her own insecurities than based on anything he had said or done.

"You okay?" Duane asked.

"Yeah, just wondering how this is going to play out," she lied.

Around three, Duane stuck his head in her office.

"I'm going to take off. Give me a call later, and you can let me know what Ryan thinks."

"Erin," Cheryl's voice on the office intercom interrupted before she could respond. "There are two detectives from the Middlesex County Prosecutor's Office with something for you. Do you want me to send them back?"

"No. I'll come out and say hello." She looked at Duane. "Guess they're serious."

She and Duane walked out to the reception area together. Two men were in reception, and one of them was holding an envelope.

"Can I help you?" Erin asked.

"Are you Erin McCabe?" the shorter of the two inquired.

"I am," she replied.

"Ms. McCabe, I'm Detective Cornish, and this is Detective Lewis," he said as they both flashed their credentials.

"Can I see those, please?" Duane said, stepping forward.

"And who are you?" Cornish said with a bit of an attitude.

"Ms. McCabe's attorney," Duane replied, his own attitude on full display.

"I never go anywhere without him," Erin quipped, hoping to tone down the tension.

The two detectives looked at each other, and then Cornish handed his credentials to Duane, who took a pad off of the reception desk and copied down the information. He handed the credentials back to Cornish and then extended his hand to Lewis, who handed over his.

"Thank you, gentlemen," Duane said when he was finished.

"Ms. McCabe, this is a subpoena for documents and for your appearance before the Middlesex County Grand Jury next Tuesday at ten thirty. Sign here acknowledging that you have received the subpoena."

Erin took the document from Cornish, read it, and then handed it to Duane. After he read it and gave her the nod, she walked over to the reception desk, took a pen from Cheryl, signed the acknowledgment of service, and handed it back to Cornish.

He smirked. "Thank you, Ms. McCabe. Have a nice day."

"Give my love to Assistant Prosecutor Beasley," she replied, causing Cornish to look back over his shoulder.

After they had left, Erin looked at Swish. "Well, that was fun."

"Give my love to Assistant Prosecutor Beasley," he mimicked, causing Cheryl to snicker.

"Hey, at least I didn't tell him to go eff himself. I'm getting better."

"You're incorrigible," he said, rubbing the bridge of his nose.

"Get out of here," Erin said. "I don't want to be responsible for your babies being late for their appointment. I'll call you around five thirty to let you know what Ryan thinks."

"You seem more worried about being served with a grand-jury subpoena today than being the target of a murder investigation," Mark said, as Erin explained her day while they finished dinner.

"I am," Erin said, taking a sip of water.

"Why?" Mark asked, perplexed that, unlike her almost cavalier attitude of a few weeks ago, she now seemed apprehensive and distracted.

Erin shrugged. "I understand that murder is an incredibly serious charge, but I know I had nothing to do with it. And even though the system doesn't always work, I don't think they could ever prove to a jury there's a case against me." She paused, her face scrunching. "The grand-jury subpoena, on the other hand . . . well, that's tricky because each day that my client keeps her child away from the father makes it an ongoing crime. The attorney-client privilege protects information a client tells me about a past crime; it doesn't necessarily apply to continuing criminal conduct. Meaning if I don't tell the grand jury where she is, I could be held in contempt."

"That doesn't sound good. What's the punishment for that?" Mark asked.

"It can be a fine for each day I refuse to tell them, or I could be imprisoned until I tell them where she is, or until the judge is convinced that, despite sitting in jail, I'm never going to tell—or, of course, until my client is caught," Erin said. "The purpose is basically to coerce me into talking."

"Oh, that's like what they do when teachers go on strike. After the judge orders them to go back to work, they put some teachers in jail for a few hours, and then everyone goes back to the negotiating table. So, once they put you in jail for a few hours, you'll have to tell them where she is, right?" Mark asked.

Erin took another sip of her water but didn't say anything.

"Right?" Mark repeated.

"Honestly, I don't know the answer to that," she finally said.

"Okay, I'm confused. Why would you risk going to jail?" he asked, puzzled by her uncertainty. "I'm not saying your client's a bad person, but she did break the law."

"It's not that simple, hon," she replied. "There's stuff I can't share with you, but the child's life could be in danger. I'm not sure I could live with myself if our client was arrested based on my information and then something happened to her daughter."

"But she's going to be with her father. It's not like they're putting her into foster care. Why would he be a threat?"

Erin shook her head, and her tone turned more assertive. "You've read what was in the paper. The father is accusing our client of trying to turn her into a girl against her will. Trans kids whose parents reject them or refuse to allow them to be their true selves or, worse still, put them through conversion therapy, attempt suicide at rates four times that of non-trans kids. The numbers are scary. I'm not worried about her father hurting her. I'm worried about her harming herself because he'll force her to live as a boy."

"Okay, I get that. It sounds like the dad might be a bit of a jerk, but you can't protect every trans kid whose parents won't accept them. And we both know that, sooner or later, mom and the kid are going to be located, whether you tell them or not. E, this isn't your battle to fight—there's the mom, the dad, the kid, a judge— let them sort it out. I don't want you to go to jail over something that you can't change."

"You're right. I can't change it, and I can't protect every trans kid," she responded, a fire in her eyes. "But I don't have to be an- other cog in the wheel that grinds this child to a pulp. And maybe if I fight back, and refuse to cooperate, I can help save her." She looked down at her unfinished dinner, her ire seemingly spent. "And maybe," she said softly, "it will give her and other trans kids hope that people are willing to fight for them."

An awkward silence enveloped them, and Mark felt a growing sense of frustration. He wanted to be supportive, but sometimes it seemed that she was so wrapped up in trans causes or trans clients that everything she did seemed to be viewed through a transgender perspective—a perspective that he found hard to understand.

"Why are you making your life so difficult?" he finally asked.

"I don't know what you mean," Erin replied. "I'm just trying to do my job as a lawyer."

"Yeah, but we both know you probably wouldn't have taken this case if the kid wasn't trans. I mean, you're quoted in the news- paper as a trans woman; you went to your reunion because you had to show the trans flag; everything you do seems trans-focused. Why can't you allow yourself to just be a normal woman?"

As soon as the words left his mouth, he wanted them back.

Erin drew in a deep breath and fell silent.

"I'm sorry. That didn't come out the way I meant it," he said quickly.

She stood and picked up her water. "I'm going to watch the pri- mary results," she said, walking out of the living room.

Shit. You're an idiot. He moved to the couch, trying to collect his thoughts. He loved her, and the truth was he didn't think of her as a trans woman. She was a woman—a beautiful, intelligent woman. But he had just told her she wasn't a normal woman. Shit!

When he walked into the bedroom, Erin was lying on the bed, her head turned to the side, the television off.

He headed over to the bed and sat down on the edge. "Erin, I am so sorry. I know what I said made it sound like you're not normal. I swear that's not what I meant. Please believe me."

"It's all right," she mumbled.

"No, it's not," he replied.

She rolled over so she was looking up at him. "Honest, I understand what you were trying to say—if I'd just stop drawing attention to the fact that I'm trans, I could have a 'normal' life, whatever that is."

"I just meant maybe life would be easier for you. That's all I was trying to say," he offered weakly.

"I get it," she said, her voice barely above a whisper. "I certainly know my dad feels that way. And honestly, there are times when that sounds really good to me too. Trust me, I get tired of being me sometimes too." She stopped, her blue eyes conveying both her sadness and her resolve. "But, as much as there are times when I wish I could just fade into the woodwork and disappear, I can't, Mark. I just can't. Honestly, until three years ago, when I was outed in every newspaper in the state by Senator Townsend because I defended the woman who killed his son, I never expected I'd be out and open about who I am. But here I am."

She pushed herself up into a sitting position, with her back leaning up against the headboard. "I'm sorry. I know I don't make things easy for you. But if I don't defend people like me, who will?" She gave him a small, rueful smile. "I know you catch a lot of grief because of me. Christ, your brothers and mother don't talk to you because we're dating. So, I'd understand if you want to call time on us."

Mark got up from the edge of the bed and walked around to the other side before stretching out next to her. He took her hand.

"In my AP American Lit class, we're doing Fitzgerald. He once wrote about Zelda, 'I fell in love with her courage, her sincerity, and her flaming self-respect. And it's these things I'd believe in, even if the whole world indulged in wild suspicions that she wasn't all she should be.'" He squeezed her hand. "I don't have Fitzgerald's flair for words, but I know a good quote when I see one," he said with a grin. "That's how I feel about you. I don't care what the rest of the world thinks. I know who you are, and that's why I love you. I'm not worried about me. I just worry about you sometimes and all the crap you have to deal with. I hope you can forgive me for letting my mouth get ahead of my brain."

She put her head on his chest. "Thanks. Not sure I have Zelda's flaming self-respect, but thank you." They lay there in silence. Finally, she looked up at him. "Also, you do know that Zelda was institutionalized in a mental hospital and considered a failure, right?"

He snorted. "Yes, but opinions about her talents have changed, and her novel is now respected on its own terms."

She rolled over, reached for the remote, and looked back over her shoulder at him. "Being appreciated after you're dead is so overrated," she said with a smirk.

She turned on the television and selected News12 NJ.

"To recap, the winner of the Republican primary is State Senator William Townsend. A few weeks ago, it looked like political newcomer and Tea Party favorite Arnold Welch had a shot at an upset, but at the end of the day, Senator Townsend's fund-raising superiority and name recognition were just too much for Welch to overcome. It looks like Senator Townsend will cruise to victory with a comfortable margin. On the Democratic side, while the race hasn't been called yet, former State Attorney General Henry Nestor has a four-point lead on Assemblywoman Marie Honick."

"Shit," Erin mumbled, turning the television off.

In Senator Townsend's fifth-floor suite at the Lafayette Hotel, the party was in full swing. His campaign team had opened a few bottles of champagne, and his campaign manager, Milo Corliss, was on his second round of toasts. Even Townsend's wife, Sheila, who rarely ventured out in public since the death of their son, Will, had gone onstage with him. Tonight was for celebrating. Tomorrow, the campaign against Henry Nestor would start in earnest.

Michael Gardner stood in the far corner, not partaking in the celebration. The first report from Crossman had only added to his confusion. In the days since the fire, there had been absolutely no activity on any of Stern's credit cards, bank accounts, or cell phone. There were only two possibilities—she was dead, and they hadn't found her body yet, in which case, game, set, match. Or she had gone underground. That was the assumption he had to work on. That's also what his gut told him—Rachel Stern was somewhere out there, and at some point, he'd have to let Townsend know.

Assuming she was alive, what she had learned from her years at the JTTF would make his hunt a little more difficult. But he was resourceful—he'd find her. His dilemma was to do so before she realized she held the keys to McCabe's defense and his demise.

CHAPTER 19

Tuesday, June 23, 2009, 2:00 p.m.

ERIN HAD NEVER BEEN INSIDE THE GRAND-JURY ROOM, IT BEING THE sole province of the prosecutor's office. As she was led in, the first thing that struck her was that the cold, windowless room was smaller than she had imagined. It also seemed crowded. There was the clerk, Assistant Prosecutor John Beasley, another assistant prosecutor whose name Erin didn't catch, and the twenty-three ordinary citizens who reported there once a week for twenty weeks, whose task was to hear the evidence presented by the prosecutor and determine if there was probable cause to believe a crime had been committed—in this case, whether Michelle had committed the crime of interfering with custody. If twelve of the twenty-three found probable cause, the grand jury would return an indictment.

Walking to the witness chair, Erin recalled the old bromide among the criminal defense bar that a good prosecutor could get a grand jury to indict a ham sandwich. Now she understood why—this was Beasley's fiefdom.

Just as Ryan Farley had predicted, earlier that morning, Judge Zachery Douglas had made short shrift of the motion Farley had filed on Erin's behalf to quash the grand-jury subpoena in its entirety. The subpoena had called for Erin to produce all documents she had concerning Michelle and Hannah, but other than the notes Erin had taken when she had met with Logan Stevens, Erin had no documents. Douglas had reviewed Erin's notes in chambers, ruled them privileged, and granted that part of the motion. Douglas had then moved on quickly to the second part of the motion, which sought to prevent Erin from having to testify before the grand jury. Farley's argument was that since Erin was Michelle's lawyer, she couldn't be compelled to testify because any information Erin had was protected by the attorney-client privilege. Douglas, who had lowered his reading glasses to the tip of his nose, peered over the top of the rims. "Mr. Farley, how can I know whether or not the answers are privileged until I hear what the questions are?" Douglas had then ordered Erin to appear before the grand jury and stated that if she invoked the privilege, he would deal with the issue on a question-by-question basis.

Erin remained standing as the clerk administered the oath. When she finished, the clerk asked Erin for her name and address and told her to be seated. With that, Erin settled into the seat in the front of the room, twenty-three sets of eyes focused on her.

"How are you employed, Ms. McCabe?" Beasley began.

"I'm a partner in the law firm of McCabe & Swisher in Cranford, New Jersey."

"Are you familiar with an individual by the name of Michelle Costello?" he asked.

"I am."

"Is she a client of your firm?"

"She is."

"When did she retain you?"

"Monday, June 15, 2009," Erin replied.

"How did she retain you?"

"We had a telephone conversation, and during that call, she advised me that she wanted to retain me to represent her."

"What telephone number did Ms. Costello call you from?"

"Respectfully, Mr. Beasley," Erin said as politely as she could, knowing that Judge Douglas, and probably an appellate court, would get a copy of the transcript, "I refuse to answer that question as that information is protected by the attorney-client privilege."

Despite knowing that Erin intended to invoke the privilege, Beasley seemed surprised by her response and took a few seconds before he continued.

"When you spoke with Ms. Costello, where was she located?"

"I refuse to answer that question as that information is protected by the attorney-client privilege," Erin replied.

Beasley then asked if Michelle was in New Jersey and if Nicholas was with Michelle, which Erin again refused to answer.

Thirty minutes later, Erin was back in Douglas's courtroom, sitting at the counsel table next to Ryan, once again finding it terribly strange to be the client in this tableau and not the lawyer. Duane and Logan were sitting in the first row behind the railing, there to lend whatever moral support they could.

Douglas placed his glasses on the top of his head. "Mr. Farley, correct me if I'm wrong, but as I understand Assistant Prosecutor Beasley's representations, Ms. McCabe has refused to answer questions regarding if she knows where Ms. Costello is located; whether Ms. Costello is still in the state of New Jersey; and whether her child is with her. Do I have that correct?"

Ryan rose to his feet. He was wiry in build and noted for his handlebar mustache, which over time had morphed in color from brown to gray, befitting his sixty-five years.

"Yes, Your Honor, you are correct," Farley replied.

Douglas rested his elbows on the bench. "Do you also agree that Subsection E of the statute for the offense of interfering with custody states that 'the offenses enumerated in this section are continuous in nature and continue for so long as the child is concealed or detained'?"

"I agree that's what the statute says, Judge."

"Well then, Mr. Farley," Douglas continued, squinting and rubbing the bridge of his nose, "if this is a continuing crime, doesn't it fall within the crime-fraud exception to the attorney-client privilege? In other words, Ms. McCabe isn't entitled to help her client commit an ongoing crime by shielding her client's whereabouts."

"Judge, I would bring to the court's attention the case *In the Matter of Joseph L. Nackson, Esq.*, in which the New Jersey Supreme

Court held that, in a case involving the crime of bail jumping—a continuing offense, similar to the present situation—the client was entitled to seek advice from counsel and that the privilege did apply. The court stated that even undeserving people, such as bail jumpers, are entitled to consult with counsel to learn their rights, and those conversations, and the client's location, can remain privileged. I believe that is precisely the situation Ms. McCabe finds herself in. Whatever her client is alleged to have done, she is presumed innocent and is entitled to discuss her situation with a lawyer—in this case, Ms. McCabe."

Beasley stood. "May I respond, Your Honor?"

"No, there's no need," Douglas replied. "I've heard enough. Mr. Farley, while I agree with you that Ms. Costello is entitled to consult with counsel to learn what her rights are, where I disagree is that I don't believe she is entitled to hide her whereabouts under the cloak of attorney-client privilege. I believe that if Ms. McCabe knows the whereabouts of Ms. Costello, she is obligated to reveal that to the grand jury, as I find Ms. Costello's location is not a privileged communication. So I am ordering Ms. McCabe to answer the questions set forth by Assistant Prosecutor Beasley at the start of this hearing." Douglas paused, looking down at a book he had open on his bench. "Let me see if we can move this along. Ms. McCabe, you've heard my ruling. If I send you back before the grand jury, are you going to answer the questions I've ordered you to answer?"

Erin rose to her feet, Ryan following suit and standing next to her.

"Judge, I mean this most respectfully, but I do not agree with Your Honor's ruling, and I believe the attorney-client privilege does obligate me to refuse to answer the questions proposed by Mr. Beasley," Erin said. "So, no, Your Honor, I will not answer the questions."

Douglas nodded. "I see. Ms. McCabe, I remind you that your refusal to answer will be contemptuous, and I will hold you in civil contempt. Do you understand that?"

"I do, Your Honor."

"Do you understand that I will remand you to the custody of

the Middlesex County Sheriff to be incarcerated until such time that you purge yourself of contempt by answering the questions?"

"I understand you have the power to do so," she replied.

"Ms. McCabe, not only do I have the power to do so, I am telling you I will do it. Do you understand that?"

Erin drew in a deep breath and stood as straight as she could. "I do, Your Honor."

"Are you still refusing to follow my order and answer the questions?"

Out of the corner of her eye, Erin could see two sheriff's officers moving into place off to her right. She momentarily closed her eyes.

"I am, Your Honor."

"Ms. McCabe. I find you in contempt of court for your refusal to answer the questions after being ordered to do so, and I hereby remand you to the custody of the Middlesex County Sheriff until such time as you agree to comply with the court's order."

The sheriff's officers began moving toward Erin.

"Your Honor, may I respectfully request a stay of Ms. McCabe's incarceration to allow me time to file an emergent appeal of your ruling?" Ryan said. "I believe, based on *Nackson*, that we have made a sufficient showing that Ms. McCabe's position is not only being made in good faith, but we have reason to believe that Your Honor's ruling on the privilege could be reversed on appeal."

Beasley was suddenly on his feet. "Judge, I object to any stay. We are dealing with an eleven-year-old boy who was taken against his will by a mother trying to turn him into a girl. Every moment that goes by when we don't know where the defendant and her child are is another moment in which the defendant can abuse her child. We all know that Ms. McCabe, who is a transgendered herself, will do everything she can to help this abuser turn her child into a freak. Not only would I ask that Ms. McCabe be incarcerated immediately, I ask that you impose a substantial monetary fine for every day she refuses to answer these critical questions."

Erin stiffened with anger, only to suddenly feel Ryan's hand on her arm. When she looked at him, he gently shook his head no. She was the client, and he didn't want her to say a word.

Ryan turned back toward the bench. "Judge—"

"Mr. Farley," Douglas said, cutting Ryan off. "It's two thirty p.m. I will stay my order until the close of business tomorrow to allow you time to apply to the Appellate Division for a stay. If a stay is not granted by then, I want Ms. McCabe in my courtroom at eight thirty on Thursday morning to surrender to the sheriff's officers." Douglas paused, giving Beasley a long, icy stare. "In response to Assistant Prosecutor Beasley's argument, I will note, for the record, that I am not involved in the underlying custody case. Accordingly, I will refrain from commenting on the underlying facts, except to say that Assistant Prosecutor Beasley's comments on the record about the status of a minor child will be stricken from the public record. If and when we need to deal with how the child's status plays into this case, we will determine how best to handle it on the record. Moreover, to the extent Mr. Beasley implies that transgender individuals are freaks, those comments are totally inappropriate. Additionally, while I do not know Ms. McCabe, and to the best of my knowledge she has never appeared before me prior to this, I find that she has been respectful throughout these proceedings. I agree with Mr. Farley and find for the record that Ms. McCabe is acting in good faith. I have no reason to doubt that her position is based on her sincere belief that she is upholding her obligation as an attorney to her client. I do not envy Ms. McCabe the position she finds herself in. I'm sure it has not been a pleasant experience. I give her, and Mr. Farley, credit for handling the proceedings in keeping with the highest standards of professional responsibility. In this case, unlike most cases where an attorney disagrees with a judge's decision, there are severe personal consequences for Ms. McCabe. Under those circumstances, I find it appropriate to grant a short stay to allow for appellate review. I will enter the appropriate orders. Thank you, counsel. We're adjourned."

"Thank you, Your Honor," Ryan replied.

* * *

Back at their office, Erin called Mark to let him know she'd be working late, and why. Then she called her mom to not only forewarn her that she might wind up in the papers again tomorrow, but that there was also a chance she could wind up in jail.

After calming her mother down, she headed to the conference room, where Duane and Logan were on a conference call assisting Ryan, who was at his office, prepare the necessary papers to file in the Appellate Division first thing in the morning, seeking an emergency stay of the contempt order—a stay that was Erin's only hope to remain out of jail.

It wasn't like the thought she might wind up in jail hadn't occurred to her—it had been front and center since Michelle had inadvertently opened the door to where she and Hannah were staying. It was just that now it felt real. Standing in the courtroom today and watching the sheriff's officers moving into position, ready to take her into custody, left her a little shaken. She had watched that scene play out numerous times after the jury returned a guilty verdict or on sentencing day, when the sheriff's officers swooped in, cuffed her client, and led them out to the holding cell to await being transported to the jail. But this time, they were there for her, and it did not exactly make her feel warm and fuzzy. The irony that it was happening for this, and not Lonza's threat, wasn't lost on her either.

She had hated the impotence of being the client when they were in the courtroom, but she soon found herself immersed in strategizing with Swish, Ryan, and Logan—a team that gave her confidence they could ultimately prevail. Ryan was someone she had long admired for his courtroom skills, but over the last week, she had come to appreciate his talent as a legal tactician. As for Swish, having worked with him for over six years, she already knew that he was a much better writer than she was, and as he explained his suggested changes to the first draft of the brief, she could only admire his legal dexterity. And as she watched and listened to Logan, Erin found herself appreciating that beneath Logan's brash exterior was a gifted attorney who more than held their own with Swish and Ryan.

It was just after nine when they were all satisfied with the final draft of the brief. Ryan was going to have his office hand-deliver it first thing in the morning to Judge Gena Short, who was the appellate judge hearing emergent applications, and to Assistant Prosecutor Beasley. After Logan left, Erin and Duane sat alone in their conference room.

"I guess we should make some contingency plans in case I wind up a guest of Middlesex County," Erin said.

"Stay positive," Duane replied. "I'll be very surprised if the Appellate Division doesn't issue a temporary stay. I really think we have a good argument."

Gardner picked up his burner, saw the number, and answered. "Specs?"

"Yeah. What ya need?"

"I have a job for you. I need someone to pay a visit to an attorney in Asbury. The lawyer's name is Donahue . . . Ronald Donahue," Gardner said. "He does real estate, wills, estates—that kind of shit. He just filed an insurance claim on a house that burned down in Asbury, and I need to know who his client is. Based on the background information I've gotten on him, he seems like kind of a nebbish."

"How do you want it handled?"

"With him, no rough stuff, be subtle. Someone posing as a fraud investigator from the New Jersey Attorney General's Office should work. Given his line of work, he won't know any AG investigators." Gardner laughed. "Besides, even if he wanted to check, it's impossible to get any information with one call to the AG's office."

Gardner then went over the information they'd need to pull off the ruse.

"What about if we get the name you're looking for?" Specs asked.

"Call me, and we'll talk. If we locate Donahue's client, I'm counting on them to lead me to someone else. Someone I need to find as soon as possible."

"It sounds like you might want someone who's not afraid to get their hands dirty."

"If we find who I'm looking for, that will certainly be the case. But for now, just get me the information."

"Okay. I know a guy who'll be good. I'll put him together with a dancer who works at my club. She'll be perfect since she wants to get into acting," he said with a chuckle.

"I don't care. Just get me what I need," Gardner insisted.

"Consider it done."

Things were finally starting to fall into place, Gardner thought after he hung up. Up until now, he had hit a dead end. Even his sources in the intelligence community, who had connections to the Joint Terrorism Task Force that Stern used to be a part of, had no information on her whereabouts. But this morning, Crossman had finally gotten a hit of sorts. An insurance claim had been filed by Donahue on behalf of Stern or, alternatively, on behalf of Stern's estate to cover the cost of Asbury Park demolishing the house. As much as there were times when he despised Crossman, taking the initiative to check on Stern's insurance policies to see if there were claims reflected one of the reasons he relied on him—he had his tentacles everywhere and was the best at what he did.

Yeah, he thought, things were looking up.

CHAPTER 20

Wednesday, June 24, 2009, 9:00 a.m.

"**M**R. DONAHUE, THERE ARE TWO INVESTIGATORS FROM THE Attorney General's Office who would like to speak with you."

Ron looked down at the phone on his desk. "What line are they on, Joan?"

"Oh, I'm sorry. They're here—out front, not on the phone."

Ron was puzzled. Why would investigators from the Attorney General's Office want to speak with him? He did some wills and real estate closings, nothing very controversial. "Okay. I'll be right out."

Waiting in his reception area were a man and woman who looked like they had just stepped out of a recruiting advertisement for the FBI. The man looked to be in his late thirties; he was tall, well-built, with short hair and the look of someone whose hemorrhoids were bothering him. The woman was also tall, but younger and model thin. Her blond hair was pulled back in a high ponytail, and the unbuttoned top three buttons of her powder-blue blouse placed her ample cleavage on full display. She flashed a smile so sensuous and inviting it almost gave Ron an erection.

"Investigator John Jones from the Insurance Fraud Division of the New Jersey Attorney General's Office, and this is my partner, Investigator Eve Lee," the man said, closing the credentials as quickly as he had opened them. Ms. Lee also opened a set of credentials, but Ron saw nothing other than her chest.

"Nice to meet you," Ron stammered. "How can I help you?"

Jones glanced in the direction of Joan. "Is there somewhere we can speak privately, Mr. Donahue? This involves a confidential investigation."

"Of course. Follow me," Ron said, leading the way back to his office.

"Mr. Donahue, we are investigating an arson and potential insurance fraud claim involving the house at 538 Seventh Avenue in Asbury Park, which is owned by Rachel Stern," Jones said. "Are you familiar with the insurance claim?"

"Yes," Ron answered tentatively.

"Have you met with Ms. Stern concerning this claim?"

"Well, no. Ms. Stern hasn't been seen since the night of the fire. It's my understanding she's presumed to have perished in the fire."

"And exactly where does your understanding come from, Mr. Donahue?"

"Well, from her friend, who is the executor of Ms. Stern's estate."

"And what's her name, Mr. Donahue?"

Ron hesitated. Evelyn Ketchum had asked him not to use her name; that's why he had filed the claim personally.

"I'm not sure I'm at liberty to provide that information. To the extent she is my client, she asked that her name be kept confidential."

"Mr. Donahue, I can assure you that Ms. Stern did not die in the fire, and that is why we are investigating. At this point, we believe you are unwittingly involved in a scheme by Ms. Stern to fake her death, burn down her house, and collect the insurance proceeds. Unfortunately for Ms. Stern and anyone involved in this scheme with her, three people died in that fire. So, while we are investigating the fraud aspect, other law-enforcement agencies are investigating Ms. Stern and whoever else may be involved for murder. Like I said, right now we believe you are merely a pawn, but if you have something to hide and want to lawyer up, we can come back with a grand-jury subpoena. Totally up to you, Mr. Donahue."

Ron could feel the sweat running from his armpits down his sides and soaking his shirt. Jesus, how was any of this possible? He didn't know Rachel well—he had just helped her with the leases for her tenants and had done her will; she always seemed decent enough. When Evelyn had come to him and explained that Rachel was missing and Asbury was demanding to be paid to demolish the home, he had offered to help. But insurance fraud and murder—no, there was no way he was getting sucked into anything like that.

"The name of the woman who contacted me is Evelyn Ketchum, and if you wait a minute, I'll get you her contact information." As he brought up the Outlook contact and hit *print,* he attempted to plead his case. "Listen, all I did was file a claim. I don't know anything about fraud or murder. I have no idea about anything else. I swear."

When he handed the printout to Investigator Jones, his hand was noticeably shaking.

"Thank you, Mr. Donahue," Investigator Lee purred. "We appreciate your cooperation."

"You don't believe I had anything to do with this, do you?" Ron asked, hating the quiver in his voice.

"No. We think you've been used by some pretty devious individuals," Jones said. "As Investigator Lee said, we appreciate your help. I would strongly suggest that you not speak to anyone about our visit, especially Ms. Ketchum. Obviously, this investigation is ongoing, so your assistance in keeping this conversation and our investigation under wraps will certainly go a long way to convincing us that you are nothing but an innocent dupe."

Jones and Lee rose from their chairs.

"We'll be in touch," Jones said, his tone slightly menacing.

With that, they turned and walked out of his office.

Ron felt like he was going to throw up. He placed his arms on the desk and laid his head on his arms. *Oh my God, what have I gotten myself involved in?*

* * *

Erin was sitting in Duane's office, discussing the merits of the appeal, when Cheryl buzzed to let them know Ryan was on the line.

"I'm calling with some news that, if I'm reading the tea leaves correctly, is good for us," Ryan said. "I received a call from Judge Short's chambers, advising me that she was going to hear the oral argument on our application for a stay this afternoon at two thirty."

"Why do you see that as good news?" Erin asked.

"My experience is that when they know they're going to deny a stay, you just get a one-page order faxed back with a box checked 'denied.' When they want to hear from you, it means they're leaning your way but want to make sure."

"Do they ever just fax back a one-page order granting the stay?" Duane asked.

"Not in this type of case. This involves delaying a grand-jury investigation. They don't usually do that."

"Got it. Where's Judge Short located—the Hughes Justice Complex?" Erin asked, referring to the building in Trenton that housed much of the judiciary's infrastructure, including the New Jersey Supreme Court and some of the appellate courts.

"Yeah," Ryan replied.

"Okay, I'll meet you there around two in case you want to go over anything before the argument," Erin said.

"See you then," Ryan replied.

"I'm going with you," Duane said with a look that indicated he didn't want an argument.

"You don't have to. Even if we lose, I'm not going to jail today."

"Moral support," he replied. "Besides, if we lose and we have to run to the Supreme Court to try and get the stay there, Ryan might need some help."

"Jesus, you're an optimist," she replied sarcastically.

"Just covering the bases, my friend. Just covering the bases," he said with a smile.

* * *

Investigator Jones rang the front doorbell. When the door finally opened, Jones was greeted by a woman who fit the description of Evelyn Ketchum.

"Good afternoon, ma'am," he began in a tone befitting a social worker. "My name is Investigator Jones with the New Jersey Attorney General's Office," he said, flashing his credentials. "I work with the Major Crimes Division, and we're investigating the attempt to murder Rachel Stern. I'm looking for"—he looked down at a pad in his hand—"an Evelyn Ketchum. Would you know Ms. Ketchum?"

"Yes. I'm Evelyn Ketchum. How can I help you?"

"Nice to meet you, Ms. Ketchum. As I said, we're investigating the fire at Ms. Stern's home and trying to determine why someone tried to kill her. We're aware that, in order to protect herself, Ms. Stern has gone into hiding, but we believe she may be in danger, and we need to reach her. We were given your name by her attorney, Ron Donahue, as someone who may know how to do that. I will tell you that Mr. Donahue was initially very reluctant, but when we showed him the evidence behind our concern, he agreed to share your contact information."

"I'm surprised that Ron didn't call to ask me first," Evelyn replied, eyeing Investigator Jones warily.

"We asked him not to, ma'am. As I said, this investigation is moving very quickly." He turned and pointed to the car. "My partner, Investigator Lee, is making calls right now because we believe there is a terrorist network seeking revenge for an investigation Ms. Stern was involved in when she worked for the Joint Terrorism Task Force."

"Oh my," Ketchum said, her eyes opening wide.

Jones sensed that the reference to the JTTF had the desired effect of causing Ketchum to lower her guard.

"Ms. Ketchum, do you know where Ms. Stern is. I'm not asking you to tell me, I'm just trying to find out if you know?"

"Honestly, Investigator, I don't know. Rachel told me it was for my own protection."

"Smart woman," Jones said. "I'd expect no less from a trained agent." He looked up, as if thinking. "Let me ask you this: Do you have a way to contact Rachel in the case of an emergency? Trust me, this is an emergency."

She hesitated. "Yes. I have a phone number."

"Can you call her for me and let her know she's in danger?" he asked.

"Of course. Let me get my phone. It's in my purse."

She turned and headed back into her living room. As she did, Stevens slowly walked into the house.

"Here it is," she said, retrieving the phone from the depths of her purse. She held the phone up in front of her face and scrolled through her contacts until she found the number. She hit CALL and turned her back to Jones. As she did, he slowly made his way across the room so that he was only feet behind her. He parted his jacket and removed the gun from its holster.

"Hello, Rachel. It's Evelyn."

He placed the gun so the suppressor was within inches of the back of her head and pulled the trigger twice in quick succession. Evelyn crumbled to the floor, the phone bouncing on the carpet as she fell.

Jones walked over to where Evelyn was lying, spasms causing her body to jerk. He fired two more shots into her temple. He then walked over and retrieved the phone.

"Evelyn? Evelyn, are you there? Evelyn, what was that noise?" came the increasingly frantic questions. "Evelyn, are you all right? Please say something."

He said nothing, leaving the line connected, hoping that would make it easier to pinpoint Stern's location through cell-tower data.

When Stern finally hung up, he calmly walked out to the car and slid into the driver's seat, handing his faux partner the phone.

"Copy down the number from the last call that was just made."

"Wow, she gave you her phone!" Lee exclaimed.

"I can be quite charming and persuasive when I need to be," he said with a leering grin as he admired her breasts.

Gardner stood in the rear of Townsend's office as Corliss finished giving Townsend his afternoon report and going over his campaign schedule for tomorrow. After Corliss left, Gardner moved forward toward Townsend's desk.

"You look dour this afternoon. The campaign is humming, polls are looking good—what's wrong?" Townsend asked.

"Stern is alive," he replied, his voice devoid of emotion.

"What?" he shouted, pounding his fist on the desk. "How is that possible? You assured me everyone in the house perished," he said, his jaw tightening, his tone menacing.

"I don't know. There were only three bodies recovered—her tenant, his girlfriend, and Tony. This afternoon, we were able to confirm that she's alive. We are in the process of trying to do a cell-tower analysis, but I'm concerned she'll be gone before we can pinpoint her location."

"What's this mean?" Townsend demanded, clenching and unclenching his fists.

"Assuming that at some point Stern discovers the phone records, they will corroborate that someone communicated with Montgomery while they were talking on the beach, in line with McCabe's story. And they would also learn the number of the burner I was using, and an expert would be able to determine it was used in Avalon at around the time of the murder. However, in order for someone to put me in the area, they'd have to know my cell-phone number and get a warrant to do a cell-tower search on my phone."

Townsend leaned back in his chair and folded his arms across his chest. "This is your fuckup, Michael. You own this, not me. I remind you that I had nothing to do with your decision to take out Montgomery. You understand me?"

"Perfectly," Gardner replied. "However, it's in neither of our interests for this to blow up."

"What's that supposed to mean?" Townsend said, rising from his chair, his palms resting on the desktop, his face contorted with anger. "Are you threatening me?"

"You know me better than that. I simply meant it would not be helpful to your campaign to have your personal lawyer arrested for murder."

Townsend slowly sat down. "Whatever you need to do to find her—do it. Then eliminate her."

CHAPTER 21

Erin, Duane, and Logan were sitting in the empty court-room waiting for the argument to begin. Being somewhat super-stitious, Erin had worn her lucky outfit—a navy-blue business suit over a white silk blouse and beige high heels. Ryan and Beasley were already sitting at their respective counsel tables reviewing their notes for the oral argument.

As they waited, Erin's burner phone vibrated. She took a quick glance at the phone's display and saw it was Rachel, calling from her prepaid phone. A wave of concern ran through Erin. She and Rachel had agreed that a call at any time other than their two daily agreed check-ins was to be considered an emergency.

Knowing that speaking on a cell phone in a courtroom was strictly forbidden, she hit the ANSWER button, then whispered, "Hold on." She nudged Duane and then motioned with a nod to head outside the courtroom. As she squeezed past Logan, she said, "We have to take this. We'll be in the hallway. Please come get us if the judge comes out."

"Sorry, Rachel," she said as soon as she could talk. "Swish and I are in court, trying to keep me out of jail. What's going on?"

"I think something happened to Evelyn. She called me, and then I heard two muffled pops, and she dropped the phone. Then I heard two more pops. I kept calling her name, but there was no response. Erin, I've fired a gun with a suppressor on it," she said, clearly distraught. "It sounded like that."

Erin let out a breath. "Okay, let's hope you're wrong, but I'll have Duane call Chronicle."

"If they have her phone, they may be able to use the cell-tower data to get a fix on my location," Rachel said. "If my phone pinged off any towers in the Short Hills area, it wouldn't be hard to figure out I'm at Brad's."

"Agreed. Let's go to Plan B. I gave you the keys to my place. Call a cab from Brad's landline. Then take the train to my place. When you get off, I'm only about a ten-minute walk from the station. Lie low there for the time being, until we can figure out what's going on. Call me on this phone from my landline when you get there. And get a new prepaid in case yours is compromised."

Logan opened the courtroom door. "The judge is coming onto the bench."

Erin nodded. "Rachel, I have to go. I'm in a bit of a jam. Duane will explain." She handed the phone to Duane and made it back into the courtroom just as Judges Gena Short and Angelo Vantuno took the bench.

"Good afternoon, counsel. Thank you for appearing on such short notice. As you know, generally an application for an emergent stay is heard by one judge. But this is a very important issue, with an attorney facing incarceration for contempt, and since Judge Vantuno, who sits on the same appellate panel as I do, was in his chambers today, we decided to hear the arguments together. Can we have the appearances of counsel for the record, please."

"Assistant Prosecutor John Beasley for the State."

"Ryan Farley from the Law Offices of Ryan Farley, on behalf of Erin McCabe, Your Honors."

Judge Short proceeded to outline the issues that were before the court and periodically asked each attorney if they agreed with the facts, which they did.

Since Erin was the appellant, Ryan argued first and went over most of the same points he had argued in front of Judge Douglas.

Beasley, who hadn't had much opportunity to argue in front of Douglas, unloaded, calling Michelle dangerous and a child abuser who was keeping her child from a loving and caring father, and painting Erin as an aider and abettor in committing child abuse.

Judge Vantuno chewed on the frame of his glasses, seeming to nod in agreement with Beasley's argument. "Mr. Beasley," he finally interrupted, "I recognize you are handling the criminal case, and not the custody matter, so I will forgive you some lapses in your factual presentation. However, while the custody matter is not before us, counsel for the appellant did provide us with some of the pleading filed by the father in the custody action, in which he freely admits that he had not seen his child in over three years. Again, I don't think it's appropriate for us to take sides in a matter not before us, and I recognize the father's parenting skills may not necessarily be a defense for Ms. Costello, but I do think you are painting a somewhat inaccurate picture of the facts. Nonetheless, the sole issue we have to decide is whether the questions you want Ms. McCabe to answer are protected by the attorney-client privilege or not. Whether Ms. McCabe's client is a saint or a sinner doesn't necessarily resolve the privilege question."

"Respectfully, Your Honor, I disagree. Locating Ms. McCabe's client may literally be a matter of life and death, and we should not allow Ms. McCabe to assist in the perversion of this child by shielding her client's whereabouts. If this case involved a child molester who had kidnapped the child and was torturing him, I dare say this court would not countenance an attorney shielding the molester's location. And while I realize the facts of this case may not appear as egregious as the hypothetical I just provided, if you were to hold that Ms. McCabe is not obligated to answer questions in this case, I don't see how the court could distinguish the hypothetical situation I presented from the present case."

"Mr. Beasley," Judge Short interjected, "until Judge Curruzi ordered custody changed, the child has been in the sole custody of the mother since birth. Frankly, I'm not sure I understand Judge

Curruzi's rationale, but whether we agree with him or not, that issue is not before us. What we'd like you to focus on is the privilege issue and why this matter isn't governed by *In the Matter of Nackson*, as suggested by Mr. Farley."

"Your Honor, *Nackson* was a bail-jumping case, in which the underlying charge was a drug-possession charge involving marijuana. As I've noted, this is a child-abuse case."

"Mr. Beasley, it's not a child-abuse case," Judge Vantuno interrupted, frustration creeping into his tone. "It's an interference with a custody case involving a mother who had sole custody of the child since birth, until that abruptly changed on an Order to Show Cause. Can we agree on that?"

"Yes, Your Honor," Beasley replied begrudgingly.

"So, if I understand your answer to Judge Short's question, what you're saying is the nature of the offense dictates whether or not there's an attorney-client privilege?" Vantuno asked.

"Yes, Your Honor, precisely. This is not a marijuana bail-jumping case. This is a heinous crime in which the defendant's location should not be protected. However, unlike the hypothetical, this is a real case, with real-life consequences."

"Thank you, Mr. Beasley," Judge Short said.

"Mr. Farley, let me ask you, what about the prosecutor's hypothetical?" Judge Short asked. "Does the nature of the crime impact how we should apply the privilege? Doesn't *Nackson* require us to weigh the potential harm that might result from shielding the information from disclosure?"

Rising from his seat, Ryan rebuttoned his suit jacket. "It does, and that's precisely why the information on the custody action is so critically important. This case is not like the hypothetical posed by Assistant Prosecutor Beasley. This involves the child's mother, who, as both you and Judge Vantuno have pointed out, has had sole custody of the child since the child was born. To compare this situation to hiding a child molester is totally inappropriate."

Short and Vantuno looked at each other and nodded. "All right, we're going to take a ten-minute recess, and we'll come back with our decision."

Everyone stood as the judges left the bench. As soon as they were gone, Erin turned around and saw Duane standing in the back of the courtroom, his normally stoic demeanor replaced by the look of someone who knew bad news was coming.

"Anything?" she mouthed.

He shook his head.

"Nothing?" Erin asked Duane as soon as they were in the hallway.

"No. I got hold of Chronicle and explained the situation. He was going to call Old Bridge PD and ask them to do a welfare check. I gave Chronicle my cell. Nothing so far."

Erin saw the puzzled looks on Ryan's and Logan's faces. "Sorry, but we have a bit of a situation going on with one of our other cases."

"What'd you think?" Erin asked, trying to refocus on her case.

"I think we're in good shape," Ryan said.

Logan shrugged. "Judge Vantuno worries me a bit."

"I agree," Erin said. "Although they did sound singularly unimpressed with Judge Curruzi."

"Most people are," Logan responded. "Unfortunately, he has tenure, and they have nowhere to put him. For some reason, the powers that be think he can do the least damage in the Family Part. I can never figure out why they put bad, clueless judges in Family. They can destroy people's lives there, and the good judges are left trying to clean up the messes."

A clerk stuck her head outside the courtroom door. "Counsel, the judge is coming back on the bench."

Back inside, Erin felt her stomach doing somersaults. The thought of going to jail was singularly unappealing. Judge Short entered from the side and took her seat.

"Be seated, everyone," she said, then looked down at her yellow legal pad. "This is the *Matter of Erin B. McCabe, Esq.* I will issue a short, written decision later today, but as counsel will see when they get the opinion, we agree with the state that the nature of the offense is a critical factor in weighing the applicability of the privilege."

Oh shit, Erin thought, closing her eyes and holding her breath.

"However," Short continued, "Judge Vantuno and I agree that the issues presented by this application are weighty and deserving of full briefing and oral argument. Accordingly, my chambers will fax Judge Douglas our order staying his contempt order. Again, while we recognize that the issues in the custody matter will still not be before us, we feel it is appropriate for us to review all pleadings in the custody matter, and we may well invite counsel for the parties in the custody action to participate as amicus on this appeal. In the meantime, we are going to preserve the status quo, and we don't believe it is appropriate for Ms. McCabe to be held in civil contempt and incarcerated while this appeal is pending. Thank you, counsel, for your excellent work on short notice."

As Short left the bench, Erin let out a sigh of relief. Both Logan and Duane leaned over and hugged her.

Beasley threw his notes in his satchel, shot Erin a look of disdain, and quickly left.

Erin walked up to where Ryan was packing his briefcase and gave him a hug. "Thanks," she said. "I know there's still a long way to go, but based on what Judge Short said, I'm liking our chances."

"Me too," Ryan said. "But you're right—the proof is in the pudding. We lived to fight another day, which is sometimes all we can do in this business."

As they rode down in the elevator, Erin texted Mark that they had won. She almost suggested they go out to dinner but held off because she was still waiting for news about Evelyn. Depending on what Duane found out, even with the win, she might be in no mood to celebrate.

Walking out of the Justice Complex into the sunlight, Erin drew in a deep breath of the warm summer air. As they descended the steps, there appeared to be a television crew filming from the sidewalk.

Great, Erin thought. *More press. My dad will be thrilled.*

"McCabe!" a voice called out.

Thinking it was a reporter wanting a comment, she ignored it, ready to push past to the parking lot. But then several Trenton police officers approached from the side of the courthouse.

"Erin McCabe!" the voice called out again.

This time she turned and saw Detective Adam Lonza, a self-satisfied look pasted on his face.

What the hell is he doing here?

Lonza quickly walked toward her, closing to within a few feet. "Erin McCabe, I hereby place you under arrest for the murder of Bradford Montgomery."

"What the hell are you talking about?" Duane said, instinctively taking a step forward in an effort to come between Erin and Lonza.

"Don't get involved, Swisher, or I'll have you arrested for interference. You're her lawyer, so here's the arrest warrant," he said with a sneer, shoving a piece of paper toward Duane. "Bail has been set at a million dollars, and her first appearance is tomorrow at two before Superior Court Judge Samuel Connors."

Duane quickly snatched the paper, read it, and looked at Erin.

Lonza then handed Duane two other forms. "These are search warrants for Ms. McCabe's cell phone and her condo in Bradley Beach, which also allows us to seize all cell phones and computers on her person or at the residence. The search warrant for Bradley Beach is being executed as we speak." Turning back to Erin, a self-satisfied smirk spread across his face. "Officer," Lonza said to one of the uniformed officers, "take her purse, please."

Erin bit down on her lip, trying to quell the emotions that were whirling around inside her like someone had turned on a blender. She refused to give Lonza the satisfaction of seeing her get emotional. *Fuck him,* she thought. Taking her purse from her shoulder, she had a momentary sense of panic—her burner. Then she remembered she had given it to Swish to finish the call with Rachel.

He still had it.

She slid her purse off her shoulder and handed it to the officer.

"You don't know how much joy this gives me," Lonza said. "Put your hands behind your back."

She desperately wanted to call him an arrogant asshole, but the advice Swish had given her the last time came flooding back. "When you're the client, and not the lawyer, you keep your mouth shut."

With a look of disdain, she placed her hands behind her back. After the cuffs clicked on her wrists, he adjusted them, and she was sure he made them a little tighter than they had to be on purpose.

"Call Mark and my mom," Erin said quietly to Duane.

"Will do," he said, his face a mix of anger, concern, and helplessness.

Then, with the TV crew filming, Lonza led her by the arm to a waiting unmarked car, where Detective Carter waited by the opened door.

Through the back-seat window, she took one last look at Duane, Ryan, and Logan, who were standing on the sidewalk, staring in disbelief, as the car pulled away from the curb headed to the Cape May County jail.

CHAPTER 22

Lonza and Carter escorted Erin into the Cape May County Correctional Facility, one on either side. They walked her up to the bulletproof glass enclosure, where a corrections officer who looked to be in his forties was filling out paperwork. From his name tag she could see that his last name was Grasso.

"Hey, Lonz, what ya got?" Grasso asked when he looked up from his paperwork.

"Erin McCabe—charged with murder, first degree," he said, sliding some paperwork to Grasso through an opening in the glass.

Grasso looked Erin up and down. "Guess it's those sweet, innocent-looking ones you have to watch out for."

"She isn't sweet, she isn't innocent, and she isn't a she," Lonza replied.

"What are you talking about?" Grasso asked.

"Trannie, my friend. My suggestion—lock him up with the guys and give them all a treat."

"Ah. Well, wherever she . . . he goes is above my pay grade. I just send them to Classification," Grasso replied, then he looked at Erin. "You got a pussy, sweetness?"

Erin glared and said nothing.

"Oh, it's in the paperwork, but I guess I should have told you; he's an attorney," Lonza said.

Grasso looked at Lonza, his face reflecting his unhappiness with just getting this information. "Fuck, I don't need a fucking lawsuit. Listen," he said, addressing Erin, "you want to be searched by a male or female CO?"

"Female," Erin replied.

"They're going to be doing a full-body-cavity strip search, so I don't want any of my female officers to get any surprises. Your lower body—one orifice to search, or two?"

"Two," she spit out.

"You're not going to put him with the women, are you?" Lonza asked.

"I told you, Lonz—above my pay grade."

"Is Sergeant Caruso on duty?" Lonza asked.

"Yeah, but he left word not to disturb him. A superior officer tells me not to disturb him, I don't disturb him."

"Blame me," Lonza responded.

Grasso looked at Lonza like he had two heads. "Blame you? You'll be out of here in five minutes. I gotta work with the guy until he retires. I'm not bothering him."

Lonza rubbed his jaw. "All right, just make sure he knows Mc-Cabe's here, and make sure he knows I'm the one who brought him in."

"Will do," Grasso said, reaching for his radio. "Grasso at the front desk. Williams, I have an inmate for you to do an intake on." He listened for a moment. "Lonz, what's bail?"

"A million, no ten percent."

Grasso let out a low whistle. "Yeah, Williams, she'll definitely be spending the night—murder, first-degree, million cash bail."

Five minutes later, Corrections Office Lillian Williams arrived where Lonza was waiting with Erin. Williams, a solidly built Black woman, was several inches taller than Erin. She took the paperwork from Grasso and looked through it.

"You can remove your cuffs, Detective Lonza," she said, her tone less than cordial. "I got her from here."

Lonza unlocked his handcuffs. "All yours," he said. "And by the way, he isn't a she—born a guy."

"Whatever. I just do my job. I don't care if she's a Martian."

When Erin's hands were free of the handcuffs, she rubbed her wrists, trying to get some circulation back into her hands.

"Put your hands in front of you, miss," Williams said.

When Erin did as she was instructed, Williams took a pair of cuffs off her belt and placed them loosely on Erin's wrists.

"Hey, McCabe, you haven't said anything to me in four hours," Lonza said, taking a parting shot. "Not the sassy smart-ass you were the last time I saw you, huh? I told you I was going to put your ass in jail—and here you are. What ya gotta say for yourself now?"

She turned and scowled. "The same thing I said to you the last time I saw you."

"Oh yeah, what was that?" he asked.

Erin hesitated, Duane's admonition still fresh in her head. *Oh, what the hell.*

"Go fuck yourself," she said.

Williams quickly moved to Erin's side, grabbed her arm, and said, "Let's go.

"A word of advice," Williams said when they were farther down the corridor, "you mouth off to a CO the way you just did to Lonza, and you're going to have problems. You keep your mouth shut, and if you're asked a question, it's 'yes, sir,' 'no, sir,' 'yes, ma'am,' or 'no ma'am.' Got it?"

"Yes, ma'am," Erin replied without hesitation.

Williams chuckled. "I like folks who learn quickly. Who'd you murder?"

Erin looked at Williams. "No one."

"Good. You learn quickly, and you're smart. I saw on your paperwork you're a lawyer and this is your first time being charged, so don't get out of line, and don't trust anyone. Everyone here, from the warden down to the inmates, is out for themselves. If you don't forget that, you'll be okay."

She steered Erin into a holding cell.

"I'll be back as soon as the nurse is ready for you," she said. "She'll do a medical intake, part of which is a physical exam, including a full-body search. If you're hiding anything, now's the time to tell me. When we're done, you'll shower, and we'll give you a jumpsuit. You'll be able to keep your underwear and bra, unless it's an underwire—is it?"

"No, ma'am," Erin replied.

Williams smiled. "What kind of law do you do?"

"Criminal defense," Erin replied.

"Ain't that a fuck," Williams replied. "Word gets out around here that we got a criminal defense lawyer on premises, and you're going to be one popular lady."

The next afternoon, Erin was sitting alone in a holding cell on the second floor of the Cape May County Courthouse. She was tired, angry, and more than a little scared. So much had happened after they won in court yesterday that everything just seemed to be a blur. She felt like she had eaten some strange hallucinogenic mushroom and what was happening to her had to be some mind-altered trip—it couldn't be real.

But it was real. She was in jail, cut off. She didn't even know what had happened to Evelyn and Rachel.

She heard voices down at the far end of the corridor, and shortly thereafter, the imposing figure of Duane Abraham Swisher sauntered down the hallway. She wanted to jump up and hug him, but there was the little matter of the handcuffs and iron bars in the way. She also knew, from many visits to holding cells when she was on the other side of the bars, that physical contact between a lawyer and a prisoner was forbidden.

As Swish neared, she stood. She felt a lump in her throat, but she was determined not to cry—she couldn't do that to Swish. Over the last six years, they had been through a lot together, personally and professionally, and knowing him as she did, she knew he had to be going through his own emotional hell over her current situation, so she was determined to be strong for him.

"Hey," she said, when he stopped in front of the cell. "Fancy meeting you here."

He gave her a weak grin. "Yeah, I just happened to be in the neighborhood, so I thought I'd stop by and say hello," he replied, his face betraying his concern.

"How's Evelyn?" she asked before he could say anything else.

There was no need for Duane to respond. His normal poker face told her everything she needed to know.

"She's dead, isn't she?" Erin said.

He nodded.

"Shit." She hesitated, trying to digest the news. "How?"

"From what Chronicle told me, four gunshots to the head. Two in the back, then whoever it was doubled-tapped her in the temple. It was a professional execution."

Erin hung her head. The news that Evelyn was dead wasn't totally unexpected, but the manner took her breath away. "Is Rachel okay?" Erin asked hurriedly after regaining her composure.

"Yeah—pretty shaken up, and obviously distraught over her friend's death, but she's safe. Just so you know, because Lonza said they were searching Bradley Beach, we didn't go with Plan B."

"Where is she then?" Erin asked.

"Logan's," Duane said with a self-satisfied smile. "When Logan overheard what was going on, they offered to help. We can always go back to Plan B or C when things settle down."

Erin looked at the floor of her holding cell. "I don't get it. Why kill Evelyn? She didn't even know where Rachel was."

"Chronicle thinks it was for two reasons. One, when the Homicide detectives searched Evelyn's home as part of their crime-scene investigation, they didn't find a cell phone, and we know she had one. So, the murderer took it to try and locate Rachel. And, second, to send a message to Rachel that they're going to find her."

"But why? What are we missing, Swish? They haven't come after us. Which means Rachel knows or has something that's getting people killed." Erin leaned her head against the bars. "This sucks. Rachel and Michelle are both in hiding, and I'm totally worthless because I'm sitting here in jail." She met his eyes. "I'm sorry. I know this is all falling on you."

"Don't go there," he said. "I'll be fine. Are they treating you okay?" he asked, changing the subject.

She nodded. "Yeah, the usual snide comments, but I'm still in classification, so I'm not in the general population yet."

"They putting you with the women?" he asked.

She chewed on her lower lip. "I won't know for sure until I'm out of classification, but I think so. They did a PREA eval on me," she said, referring to the Prison Rape Elimination Act, the federal law designed to prevent sexual assaults in correctional facilities, "plus a full-body-cavity search, so they know my anatomy pretty well. Based on what I could glean, they put me down as female for PREA."

He looked down at his shoes, and she could tell from the pained expression on his face what he was thinking.

"Swish," she said, "I've done this long enough to know the drill. Let's face it, as much as you want to, there's nothing you can do for me today. All there is right now is a criminal complaint, so they'll hold me over for grand jury. You'll ask for a reduction in the bail. Whoever the AP is will tell the judge that all hell will break loose if I'm out on bail, and the judge will tell you to do a bail motion. Translation, I'm a guest here for at least the next week, maybe longer."

"There's another option," Duane said. "I drove down here with Mark and your parents, and with your brother's help, they're working with Hamburg Bail Bonds to post bail."

"No!" Erin said. "Absolutely not. My bail is a million dollars. That means to post a bond, they'll have to pay Hamburg the ten-percent premium—so a hundred thousand dollars they'll never get back. Plus, they'll have to post collateral worth over a million, which likely means my mom and dad and Mark putting up their homes. No. Please, please don't let them do that, Swish."

"But they're terrified that something will happen to you in here," he explained.

Erin shared their fear, but knew she had to swallow it in front of Swish; otherwise, he and her family would redouble their efforts to get her out on bail.

"I understand. But hopefully I can barter my jailhouse legal services to keep myself safe. Let's see where we are after you make the bail motion. Please, Swish. A hundred grand is way too much money to piss away. I can survive for a few weeks. Tell them to wait."

"They won't be happy," Swish replied.

"Won't be the first time I upset folks. Speaking of which, did my perp walk make the news?"

Swish's face contorted like someone was holding putrid meat under his nose. "Yeah. You made the eleven o'clock news last night. Sorry."

"My dad say anything?"

"No. He's been very quiet. If it's any consolation, it happened too late to make this morning's papers."

Erin nodded, anticipating what tomorrow's headlines would bring and feeling bad that she was only adding to her dad's embarrassment.

"Since this hasn't been to the grand jury yet, what do you think about asking for a probable-cause hearing?" Swish asked, changing the subject. "I mean, I for one would sure as hell like to know what happened in the last month that resulted in you being charged."

Erin thought for a moment. It wasn't like she hadn't asked herself the same question several hundred times over the last twenty-three hours. "Let's see what they say when you ask to lower my bail. If we don't find out then, it might be worth a shot."

A woman entered the hallway. "Counsel, the judge will be going out on the bench shortly. Please have a seat at the counsel table. The sheriff's officers will bring your client in."

"Wish my parents and Mark weren't here to see me like this," she said, gesturing to her orange jumpsuit.

"They're here to support you. They won't give a shit what you look like," he replied but then pretended to study her. "Although I have to admit, the orange does clash with your red hair."

She gave him a wide grin. "Thanks. You really know how to boost a girl's morale."

He turned both palms up as if to say, "What do you want from me?"

"See you inside, big guy," she said, giving him a thumbs-up.

He nodded and made his way down the hallway to the entrance to the courtroom.

A few minutes later, two burley sheriff's officers appeared at the cell.

"Okay, step back from the cell door," one commanded.

When Erin did, they stepped inside, one on either side, and escorted her down the hallway and into the courtroom.

As soon as they entered the courtroom, she spotted her parents and Mark sitting in the first row behind Duane. Her mom gasped when she saw Erin but recovered quickly and gave a small wave. Erin gave her parents a small smile, pursed her lips, and simulated a kiss. As they escorted Erin to her seat next to Swish, she could see that her mom's eyes were red and swollen from crying. Her dad appeared stoic, but Erin was both surprised and happy he had come, even if it was only as moral support for her mom. Mark looked like he could be a lawyer. He was dressed in a suit, with a white shirt and tie, and his usual stubble was gone—his face as clean-shaven as she had ever seen it. He also looked like he hadn't slept, the strain of Erin's situation written on his face. She simulated a kiss for him too.

Erin glanced across the room. Lonza was sitting at the counsel table with a gentleman she didn't recognize, but who she knew from experience had to be the assistant prosecutor.

If being interrogated as a suspect was strange, being in court as a defendant was like an out-of-body experience. In a few minutes, the judge would enter the courtroom, and Swish would enter his appearance as the attorney representing her—she was the defendant; she was the one facing thirty years to life. He would drive back to their office, while she would be led out in handcuffs. If she ever got out of this nightmare, she knew she'd never see the process the same way again. There were no "routine" court appearances when you were the one staring down incarceration. For the defendant, at every single turn, something could happen, good or bad, that would forever change the trajectory of their life. And all of it, or nearly all of it, was in the hands of someone else—your lawyer, the prosecutor, the judge, the jury. Until now, even when she spent sleepless nights worrying about a case or a client, she spent it in her own bed, in her own home, not in some cold and distant cell. Now, she was about to learn what it was like to entrust your life to someone else. Not a welcome thought.

But as she looked at Swish's determined face, she knew there was no one else she trusted her life with more than him.

"All rise," the court clerk intoned.

As everyone stood, Judge Samuel Connors came out of his chambers and bounded up the three steps to his chair. "Be seated," he said, before he even sat down.

Neither Erin nor Duane was familiar with Connors. He appeared young for a judge, maybe early forties. Around five foot five or six, with a handsome face and a full head of brown hair, he reminded her of Tom Cruise.

"Appearances, please," Connors said.

"Assistant Prosecutor Thomas Pendergast for the State, Your Honor."

As Swish rose, she had to overcome the ingrained response of standing and stating her name for the record.

"Duane Swisher from the law firm of McCabe and Swisher for the defendant, Erin McCabe, Your Honor."

"Thank you, counsel, and welcome, Mr. Swisher. I don't believe we've had the pleasure of meeting before."

"We have not, Your Honor. Thank you."

"All right. This matter is before me for a first appearance on a criminal complaint charging Ms. McCabe with murder, a first-degree crime. This matter has not been presented to a grand jury yet, so I will not take a plea at this point and will simply refer the matter to the Cape May County Prosecutor's Office for further proceedings. Any applications, Mr. Swisher?"

Duane stood. "Thank you, Your Honor. As you can see from the complaint, bail was set at one million dollars, no ten percent. I would represent to the court that Ms. McCabe is my law partner and has been for the last six years. We have known each other far longer, going back to when we were in college, albeit different ones. Ms. McCabe is an outstanding attorney with an excellent reputation both inside and outside the courtroom. She has never been charged with any offense of any kind prior to these charges. She lives in Clark, New Jersey, with her boyfriend, Mark Simpson, who is seated behind me, next to Patrick and Margaret McCabe, Erin's parents. Ms. McCabe has been a lawyer in this state for almost twelve years. She has roots here; she has a career here; she has family and friends here. She is not a flight risk. She is going to stay and defend herself against these outrageous charges and clear her name and reputation. Based on this, Judge, I would most respectfully request that bail be reduced to one hundred thousand dollars."

"Thank you, Mr. Swisher. Mr. Pendergast, does the State have a position?"

"Absolutely, Judge," Pendergast said, standing. "We vigorously oppose this application. As Your Honor noted, Ms. McCabe is charged with murder, which is a crime of the first degree, meaning if the defendant is convicted, she is facing a minimum sentence of thirty years imprisonment without the possibility of parole and a maximum sentence of life imprisonment without the opportunity for parole. Based on the proof my office has accumulated, we believe the evidence of guilt is overwhelming, and given the circumstances of the crime, we will be seeking the maximum sentence. We will be able to establish that the defendant was with the victim within the time that the medical examiner has determined was the time of death. Her fingerprints and DNA were found inside the victim's home, and, most important, we have established that the defendant's DNA was on an envelope found with the victim's body, with his hand resting on the envelope. In that envelope were pictures we believe the defendant was trying to use to blackmail the victim. Given this overwhelming evidence of the defendant's guilt, we believe she has both the financial means and the motivation to flee. Accordingly, we dispute counsel's assertion that the defendant is not a risk of flight. Given what she is facing, we believe the only way to assure her appearance is to keep her in custody, and we would like to see the court increase her bail to two million dollars."

Duane jumped out of his seat. "Judge, that's outrageous—"

"Mr. Swisher, allow me to interrupt," Connors said. "I'm not going to increase the defendant's bail. However, at this point, I'm not going to reduce it either. I'm going to have pretrial services do a report, and I'll ask you to do a formal motion, which I will hear on short notice once I get the report. I remind both of you that the sole purpose of bail is to ensure the defendant's appearance at trial, so the only issue I will concern myself with is the risk of flight. Although I have never met the defendant, I am well aware of Ms. McCabe and her reputation as a criminal defense attorney. Based on Mr. Swisher's description of Ms. McCabe, which I have no reason to doubt, it certainly does appear that she has roots in her community, and so I remind the prosecutor's office that, while likelihood of conviction is something I can weigh in determining flight risk, it is not the end all and be all of my determination. Mr. Swisher, get your motion filed, and once I get the report, I will get everyone back here to hear it. Anything else, counsel?"

"Judge, may I have a few minutes with my client?" Duane asked.

Connors looked over at the officers standing at the side of the counsel table. One of them pointed to his wristwatch, causing Connors to look at his own.

"Mr. Swisher, I know that the sheriff's officers are anxious to get Ms. McCabe back to the jail before three, when the afternoon count begins, but . . ." Connors looked down at his watch again. "I'll give you ten minutes in the holding area. That's the best I can do."

"Thank you, Your Honor," Duane replied.

CHAPTER 23

Thursday, June 25, 2009, 2:40 p.m.

"Is SHE OKAY?" PEG ASKED AS SOON AS DUANE JOINED THEM IN the hallway outside the courtroom.

"Yeah, she's okay, Peg. Erin's pretty resilient."

Peg wanted to believe him, but the sight of Erin in handcuffs and the orange prison jumpsuit had been unnerving. Pat wrapped his arm around her shoulder and gave her a small hug.

"What are we doing about bail?" Mark asked.

"I know none of you are going to like this, but Erin wants to wait because she doesn't want you to lose a hundred thousand dollars paying the bail bondsman to bail her out."

"But we all agreed," Mark said. "We want her out."

"I agree," Pat chimed in.

"Erin's adamant," Duane responded.

"I'm confused, Duane. How does waiting help?" Peg asked.

Duane explained that if he could get her bail reduced with the bail motion, it would cost them a lot less.

"Swish, money isn't the issue—her safety is," Mark offered in response.

"I hear you, Mark, but she made me promise I would not let you bail her out until after the motion."

"Are they going to put her in jail with the men?" Peg asked, wiping her eyes with the tissue she was holding, shuddering to think what might happen to Erin if she was in the male lockup. "I know that's what they did to your client Sharise."

"Erin doesn't think so, Peg. Remember, Erin's had gender-affirming surgery, and Sharise hadn't."

"So she'll be in with the women?" Pat asked.

"Yeah, hopefully. And if she's not, we can always have the bondsman bail her out then," Duane said reassuringly.

"Don't worry. I'll come up with the money if I have to," Mark replied.

Peg gave Mark a warm smile, touched by his concern for Erin.

"I can't say I'm happy about this, but I've created enough problems. I don't want Erin angry with me for ignoring what she wants," Pat said.

Peg gave her husband a gentle squeeze. "I'm sure she'll be happy to let you make it up to her once she's out."

"Duane, can I ask a question?" Peg asked.

"Of course."

"When the prosecutor person was talking, he said that they had evidence that Erin was trying to blackmail Mr. Montgomery with pictures of him that were in an envelope. What kind of pictures are they talking about? And why do they think Erin was blackmailing him?"

Duane rubbed his chin. "The pictures were of him dressed as a woman."

"Yeah, I saw one of those in the *Post-Dispatch*," Pat said, rolling his eyes.

Peg gave her husband a menacing stare. "Don't you start going backwards on me, Patrick McCabe."

Peg turned her attention back to Duane. "I didn't see the picture Pat is referring to. Are you saying Mr. Montgomery was transgender?" Peg asked.

"Yeah, Peg. From what he told Erin, he was. But he was dealing with these issues over thirty years ago when attitudes were much different. And given his circumstance, both personally and in terms of his career, he never transitioned."

"Oh," Peg said. She stared straight ahead, but a small sigh seeped out. "Based on what I've seen, I don't know that things have improved much in thirty years."

"Swish, what does it mean that the prosecutor said Erin's DNA was on the envelope? That sounded significant," Mark asked.

"It is. Erin and I were trying to figure out what had changed that caused them to arrest her. Now we know. The envelope he referred to contained the pictures of Montgomery. When they interrogated Erin about a month ago, they showed her the photos, and she told them she had never seen them before."

"If she never saw them, how did her DNA get on the envelope?" Mark asked.

"Not sure yet," Duane replied. "And of course, we've yet to see the results of the DNA tests. Pendergast wouldn't be the first assistant prosecutor to stretch the truth. But, based on my experience, there's at least one possible explanation that is totally consistent with Erin never having touched the envelope."

"I just can't believe this is happening," Peg said with a sigh. "I'm worried about her," she said, then looked at Mark and Pat. "We're all worried," she said. Noticing the concern etched on Duane's face, she reached out and took his hand. "Including you," she said, gently squeezing his hand.

Gordon Paterson wasn't surprised to see the private cell-phone number of William Townsend pop up on his display shortly after McCabe's initial appearance had concluded.

"First Assistant Prosecutor Paterson," he answered.

"You keep this up, and it will be Prosecutor Paterson," the voice on the other end said with a good-natured laugh. "Gordon, Will Townsend here. Congratulations. You told me the other day you expected an arrest shortly, but this was even faster than I expected. Simply unbelievable that it turns out it was McCabe."

"Thank you, sir. But . . . well, sir, we're still analyzing what we seized yesterday from her person and condo. We did not locate the murder weapon."

"I see. But obviously you had enough to charge her."

"Yes, of course. Her DNA is on a key piece of evidence, but

there are still some holes we need to plug. But I can assure you, sir, that I am confident in the case we're building."

"Excellent, Gordon. As I told you when we met, this case is a career maker for you."

"I haven't forgotten sir."

Later, Gordon sat across the conference-room table from Lonza, Carter, and Pendergast. "The search warrant turn up anything?"

"Not yet," Lonza replied. "The lab is still looking at all the knives. Unfortunately, it looks like McCabe ran a few of the sharper ones through the dishwasher."

"Were there just knives in the dishwasher?" Gordon asked expectedly.

"Um, no. There were several dishes, silverware, water glasses, and wineglasses too."

Gordon shook his head. "So, what are we going to argue to the jury? That McCabe threw a dinner party and washed the dishes to cover up washing the blood off the murder weapon? Give me a break, Adam. That boat doesn't float. Anything on the computers?"

"The folks in Computer Crimes are still reviewing."

"Anything in her emails?"

"Nothing in her personal ones, and the warrant requires that any work emails need a judge's review to ensure we're not invading the attorney-client privilege with her other clients," Lonza replied.

"What about her phone—phone log, text messages? Anything?" Gordon asked.

"Nothing yet," Lonza said, his lips twisting.

Gordon stood, took a few steps back, and leaned against the conference-room wall. "Look, folks, I understand that there's enough here to get a grand jury to indict McCabe, but assuming this case goes to trial with what we have now, her lawyer will have a field day exploiting what we don't have." He turned his focus to Lonza and Carter. "Let's figure out how we shore up the case and plug the holes. What can we do in terms of your ongoing investigation?"

"We probably should've done search warrants on her apartment in Cranford and her law office," Lonza replied.

Gordon took a step forward and rested his hands on the back of his chair. "Leave aside her law office. Why didn't we hit her apartment?"

The room fell silent.

"Anyone?" Gordon finally inquired, his tone indicating his growing frustration.

"Not sure why," Carter offered. "Just when we got the DNA back, we wanted to move quickly."

Gordon returned to his seat and grabbed a yellow legal pad sitting on the table. "She's in custody, so let's take our time and make sure we get it right this time," he said. "We need a warrant for her apartment," he continued as he wrote on the legal pad.

"Tom, have someone do some research on what we'll need to get a warrant on her law office. That might be a stretch. What else?" he asked.

"What about her boyfriend?" Lonza asked.

"What about him?" Gordon replied.

"Swisher said in court this afternoon that she lives in Clark with her boyfriend. I think we should search his place too. Not only could there be something there, but we squeeze her by dragging him into the investigation."

"I like that," Pendergast chimed in. "Let's turn up the heat."

They spent the next thirty minutes going over what records they should search for and what other leads they could follow up on. When they were done, Gordon put his pen down on the legal pad. "All right, we have our work cut out. Let's see what we can turn up." He slowly stood. "Also, as we're doing all of this, there's one other thing I don't want you to ignore." They all looked at him. "The possibility that McCabe's innocent," he said, taking his legal pad and walking out of the room.

CHAPTER 24

Friday, June 26, 2009, 8:30 a.m.

DUANE WAS EXHAUSTED. IT WAS ONLY EIGHT THIRTY IN THE MORNing, and even after his third cup of coffee, he was still dragging. The last two days had been killers. The trip down and back to Cape May, coupled with the stress of representing his partner and best friend, who was sitting in jail, had worn him down. To top everything off, Alysha, who had spoiled them by sleeping four or five hours at a clip, decided this was the week she was going to be up every two hours. Cori, who was breastfeeding, bore the brunt of that, but it had still left Duane feeling more than a little sleep-deprived.

Yesterday, as news began to break about Erin's arrest, he had spent most of the morning reaching out to Erin's clients, adversaries, and judges, explaining the need for time to sort things out. Then he had worked every person he knew to try to find someone close to Arnold Welch, hoping that Welch, or someone in his campaign, would have information that could help exculpate Erin.

This morning the shit had truly hit the fan as Erin's arrest was on the front page of every newspaper in New Jersey, New York City, and Philadelphia. The main office phone hadn't stopped ringing since he'd arrived at around eight. Since Cheryl didn't start until nine, he was just letting everything go to voice mail.

Duane was startled when his phone intercom buzzed. "Duane?"

"Cheryl, what are you doing here?" he asked, glancing at his watch.

"Um, I saw today's paper, and I thought it might be a little hectic."

"Thanks," he replied, appreciative of her dedication.

"There's a Marilyn Atkins on the line for you," Cheryl said.

He thought for a moment, running the name through his mental Rolodex. "Name doesn't ring a bell. Did she say who she was?" he asked, expecting that she was a reporter or secretary to a judge.

"The administrative assistant for Arnold Welch. Do you want me to take a message?"

"No!" Duane screamed. "I'm sorry, Cheryl. I didn't mean to startle you," he said apologetically, sure his reaction had shocked her. "Put her through, please."

Two and a half hours later, Duane sat in the reception area of Welch Logistics, Inc. Around 11:15, a woman came out, introduced herself, and asked Duane to follow her. She led him down a hallway, which was lined with artwork worthy of a museum, to the corner office belonging to Arnold Welch. There was a large mahogany desk at one end and a twelve-person mahogany conference-room table at the other. There was a computer with two monitors and a forty-eight-inch television set to CNBC with the sound muted. And at the center of it all was the man himself. He wore a blue-pinstripe suit, and the cuffs of his starched white shirt were monogrammed with his initials.

"Thank you for contacting me," Duane said.

"Please have a seat," Welch said, leading the way to the conference-room table. "I heard from several people that you've been trying to reach me, and when I saw the papers this morning, I understood why," Welch said, tugging on the cuffs of his shirt. "How can I help you, Mr. Swisher?"

"I'm trying to find out what you know about Bradford's meeting with Erin on Memorial Day, and if you have any idea as to who may have killed him?"

"So you're telling me that Ms. McCabe is innocent?" Welch asked, his tone flippant.

"Yes," Duane said, his expression growing darker. "But I suspect you knew that already."

"I remember you confronting me at Brad's wake," Welch countered, displaying a more aggressive tack.

"And I remember you refusing to talk to me and putting one of your bodyguards in my face," Duane fired back, the bodyguard's hand on his chest still vivid.

"It was at a wake, damn it, and I was in the middle of a primary election," Welch said defiantly. "A wake of someone whom I knew very well . . ." he added, before lowering his voice to a whisper, "and someone I believe was killed because of me."

Duane tilted his head, processing Welch's admission, and quickly reassessed his approach. *More flies with honey*, he thought. "You're right. I apologize. And I'm sorry for your loss." He let the silence ferment for a few seconds. "Why do you think Brad was killed because of you?"

Welch raised his eyes, taking Duane in. "Because I was the one who asked him to meet with your partner."

"Why him? He was a financial adviser. Why not send someone who was doing opposition research?"

Arnold slowly rose and walked to the glass wall. "I assume Ms. McCabe told you—Brad was transgender. Obviously, unlike Ms. McCabe, he never transitioned because he never felt he could afford the personal and professional costs. And if you're wondering how I knew, it's because he told me."

Welch stopped and stared out the window. "You're also probably wondering why Brad would tell me, of all people, an extremely socially conservative person, not known for being accepting of minorities and LGBT people, especially since Brad had lived his entire life in the closet," Welch said.

"I am," Duane answered.

"I don't have children, Mr. Swisher, and so I've always been very close to my sister and brother-in-law and their three children.

They have . . . had three boys. My sister and brother-in-law are not as conservative as I am—few people are," he added as an aside. "But certainly, they're not liberals—mainstream Republicans, I guess is the best description. Well, about four years ago, they told me that their youngest child was transgender. Candidly, I had no idea what that even meant. So, when they told me that Brian was going to start living as Brittany, I flipped out. I accused them of being crazy . . ." he stopped. "Look, I said a lot of things, which nearly destroyed my relationship with them. I refused to see them for over two years.

"At some point, my mother, who was in her eighties, told me she wanted me to take her out to dinner for her birthday at her favorite restaurant, which, of course, I did. When we arrived, my sister and her family were already there, including Brittany." He gave a small snort. "I honestly didn't recognize this lovely four-teen-year-old girl as my nephew. She was smiling and laughing and just so happy. Not long after that, I told Brad about what had happened and how upset and confused I was. I mean, I was still upset with my sister, but at the same time, I couldn't dispute how genuinely happy my niece seemed. That's when Brad told me about himself and how much he had struggled, knowing he could never be who he knew he was. I was stunned. I'd known Brad for twenty-plus years! He was a brilliant businessman. I just couldn't believe it." Welch took a deep breath and slowly exhaled. "Well, to make this already long story short, I'm still not sure I understand it, but when I see my niece now, she is a beautiful, fun-loving young woman and just a joy to be with."

"And that's why you didn't say anything during the campaign when Townsend joined forces with the ALDA attacking trans peo-ple or when the papers ran the picture of Montgomery," Duane said, filling in the blanks.

Welch nodded. "Anyway, when Brad offered to meet with Mc-Cabe personally, I agreed, thinking he might have a better chance of connecting with her, never thinking for a moment there was any danger."

"Have you shared this with the prosecutor's office?" Duane asked.

"No. No one has asked to speak to me," Welch replied.

"They have telephones, you know. You can call them," Duane said.

"Thank you for the advice, Mr. Swisher," Welch responded coldly.

"Look, Mr. Welch, you called and agreed to meet with me. I presume it's because you know Erin didn't kill Mr. Montgomery, and you'd like to see whoever really did kill him brought to justice. If you're not willing to help, why am I here?"

"You ask me what you want, Mr. Swisher, and we'll go from there. But no one is going to tell me what to do. Clear?" Welch responded.

"Perfectly clear," Duane replied. "Who on your team knew they were meeting?"

"I don't believe it was a leak, if that's what you're getting at. Unfortunately, it's much worse," he said, rubbing his hands together. "I ran my gubernatorial campaign on a shoestring because, in the beginning, I didn't think I had a chance. It was mostly self-financed, and we didn't have the most sophisticated IT resources. Despite allegations to the contrary, Welch Logistics, which has an incredibly sophisticated computer and data operation, was not involved in any way in my campaign. However, after the results of the primary last week, I had Welch's CTO and some of his staff look at the campaign's computer network, basically to secure it in case I ran again in the future. When they did, they discovered we had been hacked at the end of March, right around the time that I started to cut into Townsend's lead."

"Have you gone to the FBI with this?" Duane asked.

"Mr. Swisher, I'm not going to disclose what we've done."

"I am a former FBI agent, and hacking is a federal crime. They would certainly want to know."

Welch looked skeptically at Duane. "I don't know if I knew you were in the FBI."

"Okay—now I've just told you. I hope you've reported it."

"Mr. Swisher, as I said before, I don't like to be told what to do."

"Did your CTO tell you what the hackers had access to?" Duane continued.

"Unfortunately, everything—emails, itineraries, internal financial records, public filings, internal polling—literally everything. And, specifically, emails in which we discussed what we could offer to get information from your partner."

"Do you know if Brad had more than one cell phone?" Duane asked.

"He did," Welch replied. "At one point, the campaign purchased prepaid phones for a number of people." He studied Duane. "Let's just say my campaign had contacts with what some people would call fringe elements; we call them allies, but it was better if there were no records of our communications—plausible deniability, as they say. When I offered one to Brad, he declined, telling me he already had a second cell he used with his transgender friends. He told me not to worry; it wasn't in his name and couldn't be traced back to him. He provided me with the number, and we used it when we needed to."

Duane tried not to show his excitement. "Do you have the number?"

Welch walked over to his desk and retrieved his cell phone and gave Duane the number.

"Thank you," Duane said. "Do you have any thoughts on who killed Brad?"

Welch gave a small laugh. "No, Mr. Swisher. Unfortunately, I don't. But I think it's safe to assume that it was someone who thought the information you and Ms. McCabe possess concerning Townsend was worth killing for. If there's nothing else, Mr. Swisher, I must take care of other matters."

Duane stood and shook his hand.

"Thank you for your time," he said. "You've been very helpful."

Finally, all the pieces fit, Duane thought, making his way to his car. Now he had to figure out how to play it to get Erin out of jail, and at the same time not endanger Rachel any more than she already was.

Damn it, Gardner thought. Whether it was dumb luck or her skill as a former agent, Stern had managed to stay one step ahead of him. Other than the insurance claim, Crossman had come up with nothing, meaning she was adroit enough to function off the grid—no banks, no credit cards, no phone—or at least no phone that he had the number for.

The only lead he had was from the information from Ketchum's phone. The cell-tower tracking analysis showed that Ketchum's call to Stern had been relayed through a cell-phone tower near Millburn. When he saw that, he immediately realized that Stern had been hiding out at Montgomery's home in Short Hills. Armed with that, Walter Johnson had been able to find out that a cab had picked up a male passenger at Montgomery's address the same day Ketchum was killed and taken him to the Short Hills train station. Gardner had been initially confused, then all the tumblers fell into place. Stern was hiding dressed as a guy. It also explained why Benson may have missed Stern the night of the fire—she had gone out as a guy. *Fuck!*

If he had still been at NSA, he would have been able to track where she had gone from Short Hills. But without the sophisticated resources that law enforcement had to view security cameras at Penn Station, in either Newark or New York, Stern's most likely destinations, it was back to square one. The only thing he had going in his favor was that as long as Stern was on the run, she wouldn't be collecting her mail.

His burner vibrated. He pulled it out of his pocket, checked the display, and answered. "Yes, Lieutenant," Gardner answered.

"I finally spoke to my buddy who's a sergeant over at the jail. They classified her as female for housing purposes, but the good news is she's going into maximum security. He told me that, because of overcrowding, McCabe will be in a cell with two other inmates, both of them charged with murder. When he found out where McCabe was going, we talked, and he pulled out one of McCabe's cellmates and spoke to her about how if she could get McCabe to confess to her, her cooperation would go a long way in helping her with her case. He said she's smart, and he's confident she got the message."

"A confession would be nice," Gardner responded.

"True," Lonza replied, "especially when we have the first assistant who's in charge of the case telling us to make sure we don't overlook any evidence that McCabe is innocent."

"I'm sure he's just being cautious," Gardner responded, masking his concern that perhaps Paterson was not as beholden to Townsend as it appeared. "Are you aware of any evidence exculpating McCabe?" he asked expectedly.

"No."

"I assume you'll let me know if you hear anything to the contrary."

"Of course," Lonza replied.

"By the way," Lonza continued, "my buddy at the jail said the second inmate that McCabe is housed with is a psychopath who might go after McCabe when she finds out McCabe is trans," he said with a small laugh. "Obviously, given my position, I can't hope for that, but shit does happen, especially among accused murderers."

"So true," Gardner responded. "All any of us want is justice for Mr. Montgomery." He paused. "Of course, justice takes many forms."

After Gardner disconnected, he weighed his options. He was no closer to finding Stern, and although the investigation of McCabe was going better than he had expected, Paterson's reference to evidence of her innocence was a storm cloud that couldn't be ignored.

He needed to find a solution, and quickly; time was not his ally. To his dismay, the solution of eliminating Stern had proven elusive, and he had to face the reality that if he couldn't find Stern, he needed a different fix. Perhaps the answer was simply to eliminate McCabe. She was the prime suspect in Montgomery's murder. She was under arrest and locked up with two murder suspects. If she died, the investigation into Montgomery's murder would likely die with her. Lonza's information on a deranged cell-mate, who was already facing murder charges, offered an unex-pected opportunity. It was clean and straightforward, and one that he found more appealing the more he thought about it. If it went well, he'd have good news for Townsend. If it didn't, no one would be the wiser.

CHAPTER 25

Friday, June 26, 2009, 2:30 p.m.

THE CAPE MAY COUNTY CORRECTIONAL CENTER WAS ALMOST FORTY years old, and it wasn't wearing its age well. It was overcrowded, insect-infested, and it was too hot in the summer and too cold in the winter. Erin had been assigned to a cell that had been designed to house two inmates, but she was now the third.

As the corrections officer escorted Erin inside, she pointed to a temporary bed they had installed right next to the toilet. "That's for you, McCabe. Just make sure your cellmates piss in the toilet and not on your head," she said with a laugh.

She turned to the other two women in the cell. "You two be nice to the new girl," the CO said. "And in her case, she really is a new girl. Isn't that right, Ian?" she snickered.

After she left, Erin sat on the edge of her bunk, trying to collect her thoughts.

"What's your name?" the woman on the top bunk asked.

Erin looked up at the woman. She was Black, appeared to be in her forties, with a round face, her hair tightly braided. "McCabe," she said. "Erin McCabe."

"What did the CO mean, you being a new girl, McCabe? Why'd she call you Ian?" the woman on the bottom bunk chimed in.

Erin said nothing.

"Yo, princess. I asked you a question," Bottom Bunk said.

Erin glanced across the cell. It was hard for Erin to gauge the woman's size because of the way she was positioned on the bunk. But she looked to be in her thirties, white, thin, her brown hair a mangled mess of tangles. "I don't know. Maybe you should ask her," Erin replied, eyeing her cellmate warily.

"Well, I am asking you, bitch. What's your story?"

"Knock it off, Anita," Top Bunk said. "Just give her a break." She looked down at Erin. "This your first time in jail?"

Erin turned her attention to the woman in the top bunk. "Yeah, it is," she said.

"I'm Sylvia," Top Bunk said. "She's Anita. Welcome to hell."

Anita stood up and took a step toward Erin's bunk. "Look, bitch. I ain't all nice and friendly like Syl here. When I ask you a question, I expect an answer. We understand each other?" she demanded, standing in front of Erin and clenching and unclenching her fists.

"I'm not looking for any problems, okay?" Erin replied.

"Well, maybe you ain't looking, but you already found it," Anita said, her voice rising. "Answer me!"

Erin studied her, trying to prepare herself. She had taken Krav Maga classes for three years now, starting after her apartment had been broken into several times. Over the years, she had become good enough to earn her green belt, but right now she didn't need any trouble.

"I think she was referring to the fact that I'm transgender."

"You're what?" Anita said, her face twisted into a mask of confusion.

"She's trans, you idiot," Sylvia said with a snort. "Based on what the CO said, I'm guessing she was born a guy."

Anita continued to look like she was having a hard time processing the information. "You got a dick?"

"No," Erin replied. "I'm the same as you."

"Ain't nobody the same as Anita," Sylvia chuckled. "Thank God."

Anita turned toward her cellmate. "You shut the fuck up." With one final glare at Erin, she slid back into her bunk. "This place isn't bad enough, now I gotta room with some guy without a dick," she mumbled to herself.

* * *

Duane sat in his office, plotting out next steps. He had just gotten off the phone with Ben Silver, one of the best criminal defense attorneys in the business, who had represented him during the leak investigation. Duane had reached out to see if Ben knew anyone at the Cape May County Prosecutor's Office whom he could trust with evidence that could exculpate Erin. Ben had recommended that he try to connect with First Assistant Prosecutor Gordon Paterson. Ben had represented his father, Ray Paterson, who was an assemblyman from Cape May. According to Ben, Ray had been one of the first politicians arrested as part of a federal investigation, Operation Jersey Sting, for allegedly taking bribes. Shortly after his arrest, he died of what was ruled an accidental overdose of sleeping medication and alcohol.

He was about to call Rachel to discuss his meeting with Welch when the burner sitting on his desk suddenly sprung to life.

"Hello, Michelle," he said, recognizing her burner number on the display.

"Duane, I just saw the news. They said Erin's in jail for murder. Oh my God, what's this mean?"

Duane kicked himself for allowing Michelle's situation to slip out of his focus. He should have called her. Now he found himself thinking out loud. "Try to stay calm, Michelle," he said, immediately realizing that it probably wasn't the right thing to say. "I'm working on getting Erin out on bail, but, in the meantime, I'm still working with Logan on your case, and Logan has filed an appeal of Judge Curruzi's order," he offered, inwardly cringing at how hollow that sounded. "Once Erin gets out, hopefully we'll be able to resolve your situation."

"But Erin was the one who told me that we needed to come up with a plan because, sooner or later, I'd get caught."

"I know, and I agree. But let me focus on Erin, and then we'll have time to help you and Hannah."

"Duane, she's charged with murder!" panic creeping into her tone. "How will she be able to focus on anything other than her own case?"

"Michelle, please believe me when I tell you, Erin is completely innocent. I'm hopeful that, by this time next week, she'll be out on bail. In the meantime, I'll check with Logan and see what's happening on their end in terms of the custody issues."

There was a long silence. "I'm scared, Duane," she finally said. "I don't know how much longer I can go on like this."

"Just a little longer, Michelle. Try and hang on a little longer."

"Okay," she replied, without conviction.

"Is Hannah okay?"

"Yeah. She's just happy she can be herself again. But . . ."

Duane could hear her sobbing softly in the background. "I'm sorry, Michelle. I know how scared and worried you are. Try and stay strong for Hannah."

After their call ended, he felt like shit. All he had to offer her were empty platitudes—"stay strong," "hang in there," "just a little longer . . ." The truth was, he had little else in his arsenal. Even if Erin weren't in jail, the only options right now were for Michelle to stay on the run or work out the terms of her surrender, knowing that Hannah would be returned to her father. It was a Hobson's choice. Their only real hope was that the Appellate Division would reverse Judge Curruzi's issuance of the order changing custody. Logan was confident, but the case was complicated by Michelle's taking Hannah and fleeing. And, even on an expedited appeal, a decision wouldn't come down for weeks.

After mulling the situation, he called Rachel to fill her in.

"I met with Welch today."

"Duane, I know he was a friend of Brad's, but I don't trust him."

"I hear you, but let me tell you what he told me, and then we can sort through it." Swish told her about the fact that Welch had known Brad was trans and that's why he had asked Brad to meet with Erin. "Rachel, are you aware that Brad had a cell phone other than his work cell?"

"Sure. He was so paranoid about being outed that he had a second cell phone for the Jackie part of his life."

"Did he have it with him over Memorial Day weekend?"

"Yeah. He called me when he got to Avalon on Sunday night."

"There's no record of him having another phone."

"That's because it was a second phone on my plan, so no one would see his bill. I paid for it every month as part of my bill."

Duane sighed. "That's why they're trying to kill you."

"Because I paid Brad's phone bill?" she asked, incredulous.

"No, not for paying the bill—to prevent anyone from seeing the bill. Erin told the detectives that Brad received two calls and a text while they were on the beach. However, they only found his business phone, and when they went through the call log, there was no record of the calls or text. Welch also told me that his campaign servers were hacked. It's likely whoever killed Brad had that number because Welch had it."

"Shit," Rachel said, almost to herself.

"Who's your carrier?" Swish asked.

"Verizon."

"We need to get your phone bill. We may also still be able to get a copy of the text message from Verizon. Have you gone to paperless billing?" Duane asked.

"No. I still get it in the mail."

"Of course," he replied, the final piece of the puzzle dropping into place. "Burn down your house with you in it, and no one ever gets your bill, or, if they do, they have no way of knowing Brad's phone is on it."

"Do you want me to have Chronicle get it?"

"No. Without an active investigation, he can't. And while I don't have any reason to believe there are any leaks at the task force, there's no sense in exposing you. If I need to, I'll get it through a subpoena. This could be it, Rachel. At the very least, hopefully I can get them to reduce Erin's bail."

"But you told me her DNA was on the envelope. How do you get around that?"

"That's the easy part. Trust me," he said.

"How's Erin doing?" she asked.

"I don't know. She was in classification, so I haven't spoken to her since yesterday."

"You know that, with a murder charge, they'll put her in max security, don't you?"

"Well aware," he replied.

"I'm not trying to worry you, Duane, but those women can play rough in there."

"Don't underestimate Erin. She's pretty tough," he said, hoping he was right.

Duane punched in Paterson's number.

"Paterson," the voice said.

Duane was momentarily surprised, expecting that at three p.m. on a Friday in the summer, the call would go to voice mail.

"First Assistant Paterson, my name is Duane Swisher. I represent Erin McCabe."

"Good afternoon, Mr. Swisher. Please call me Gordon. What can I do for you?"

"I'm reaching out on the recommendation of Ben Silver. He had the honor of representing your father," Duane said.

"I remember Mr. Silver. An excellent lawyer. My dad thought very highly of him," Paterson replied.

"He suggested I should reach out to you because I have information to share concerning the case against Er—sorry, my client, Erin McCabe, and I'd like to set up a meeting as soon as possible to discuss the information with you."

"Any reason you're calling me as opposed to AP Pendergast, who you dealt with at the initial appearance?"

"I don't know Mr. Pendergast, and Ben told me I could trust you."

Duane waited, unsure what his next move would be if Paterson said no.

"How's Monday at 11:30?" Paterson proposed.

Because they were maximum security, Erin and her cellmates weren't allowed to work in the jail's kitchen or laundry. That meant the routine was fairly simple. At six a.m., a CO came on the PA system and woke everyone up. Roll call was at six fifteen, breakfast came at seven, and other than the one hour they got out in the exercise yard, a break for lunch, dinner, and two other roll calls, she either spent the rest of her time in the dayroom watching the ten other women in max argue over what to put on the television, playing cards, or lying on her bunk. This morning, Erin had gotten lucky and snagged a paperback that was left on the book cart. With Anita watching television in the common room, she actually might get a chance to read.

"What are you in for?" Sylvia asked from her top bunk.

Erin looked up. "Don't want to talk about it."

"Come on, McCabe, open up a bit."

"No thanks," Erin replied.

"Geez, you're a scared little mouse, aren't you?"

Erin studied Sylvia and, in that moment, made a decision. "Yeah, I'm scared, but I'm not a little mouse. I'm a criminal defense attorney who's seen far too many jailhouse conversations come back to haunt a client."

Sylvia shot up and dangled her legs over the side of the bunk. "Wait. You're a fucking criminal defense lawyer?"

"Yeah."

"What the fuck." Sylvia stared at her. "Are you a new lawyer? You ever try any cases?"

Erin nodded. "I've been a lawyer for almost twelve years, and yes, I've tried cases."

Sylvia reached under her pillow and pulled out a file folder. Then she slid off her bunk. "Can you look at this for me? I've got a lawyer that my sister hired. He's okay, but he never seems to have time for my case. He said he's got to file all these motions, but he wasn't really optimistic. He said if we lost, he could work out a plea, or if I went to trial, I'd probably be found guilty and sentenced to life. I don't know what to make of this stuff. Could you just read it?"

Once again, Erin had a new appreciation for what it was like for a client, sitting in a jail, trying to understand what was happening, and totally dependent on their lawyer.

Erin reached out her hand. "Let me take a look."

An hour later, Erin put the papers back in the folder. "Here," she said, handing the file back to Sylvia. "I noticed from the phone records you have one of the new iPhones."

"Yeah. I worked at an AT&T store and thought they were cool."

"Look, I'm not your lawyer, but I wrote down some notes for you for the next time you talk to your lawyer. I suggest you ask him about filing a motion to suppress the search of your iPhone. The search warrant allowed them to look at your emails and text messages. But it looks like they used your Safari searches of the web, your maps, and photos to show you planning and then following the person you're alleged to have killed."

"What does that mean in English?" Sylvia asked.

"It means that if they went beyond what they were legally entitled to search for on your phone and used that evidence to indict you, you may be able to get the evidence thrown out," Erin suggested.

Sylvia stared at Erin. "Why are you helping me? You understand that I'm charged with murdering my ex-boyfriend?"

"I saw that," Erin said. "But I also saw in there that you had a restraining order against him because he beat you up several times, but that didn't stop him from continuing to threaten to kill you, including the day he died."

Sylvia cupped her finger over her mouth. "You think this motion has a shot?"

Erin's eyes smiled. "Yeah, I do. Besides, what do you have to lose?"

"Thank you," Sylvia said.

"By the way," Erin said, holding a piece of paper. "I did keep one thing you had in the file. I guess you forgot it was in there."

Sylvia's eyes went wide. "I need that back," she demanded.

Erin's look hardened. "Who gave this to you?"

"You trying to get me killed? Give that to me," Sylvia said, lunging at the document.

Despite the fact that Sylvia was almost four inches taller and weighed thirty pounds more, Erin was easily able to block Sylvia's outstretched arm using her Krav Maga training.

Sylvia took a step back, eyeing Erin and breathing heavily. "I don't want to hurt you," she said, her tone not as menacing as her words. "You just don't understand how things work in here. If I don't do what they want, my life will become a living hell."

"So, instead, you sell me out. Is that it? Tell your attorney I told you what I had done and see if he could get you a decent plea if you testified against me? And all you had to do was repeat everything they had written down for you. Nice," Erin said, glaring at Sylvia.

"I won't do it. Just give me the paper. If they find out you have it, I could wind up dead," Sylvia pleaded.

"Okay, you two," a guard said from behind Erin. "Time to go out in the yard and get some fresh air."

Erin quickly folded the paper and stuck it in her jumpsuit pocket. The two of them were then led out into the exercise yard with the other women held in max security.

The yard was about sixty feet by sixty feet and surrounded on three sides by a fifteen-foot-high fence topped with razor wire. The fourth side was the back of the jail. Across the road was the Cape May County Veterans Cemetery. After a number of complaints from families of those being buried that they were unnerved by the sight of the inmates standing at the fence, the warden had agreed not to allow prisoners in the yard when there was an actual burial going on. No funeral today, so here they were.

Realizing she hadn't gone for a run in over a week, Erin began walking the perimeter. She had been a runner since college. She had started so she'd be in shape for soccer season, but over time, running had morphed from a way to stay in shape to a form of therapy. Initially, after her marriage fell apart and she was dealing with her estrangement from her father and brother, she ran just to try to keep from falling apart. Once she had met Mark, going for a run had become something they enjoyed doing together.

As she slowly walked the yard, her emotions overtook her. She missed Mark, her mom, her family, Swish, everything she took for granted just five days ago. She could now see them for what they were—the most important things in her life.

As she was completing her second loop, she spotted Sylvia and two other inmates standing in her path. Sylvia's face was clouded by rage, and her hands were balled into tight fists.

"Just give me what I want, and we won't have any problems," Sylvia said, taking a step toward Erin.

Suddenly, Sylvia's expression changed.

"Behind you!" Sylvia screamed.

Erin wasn't sure why, probably just dumb luck, but in the nanosecond that she had to decide whether to turn around and probably be jumped by Sylvia and her friends, or stay still and confront her, she turned. Less than ten feet away and running at her with a shiv was Anita.

Erin quickly stepped to the side, chopped down on Anita's outstretched arm with her left hand, pivoted, and then caught Anita under the jaw with the palm of her right hand, snapping her head back and causing her to fall backward. As Anita's head cracked against the concrete yard, Erin quickly spun around to try to defend herself against Sylvia, but Sylvia hadn't moved since she had shouted.

Sylvia slowly approached where Anita lay unconscious on the ground.

"Shit, girl," she said, her eyes wide and a look of approval on her face. "Bet they didn't teach you that in law school."

Suddenly, sirens went off. Over the loudspeaker came the shout of "Code 23, exercise yard!"

Sylvia pursed her lips. "Get ready, girl, because any second a whole lot of shit's gonna fall on you."

Erin realized that because she was directly involved in an altercation, she was probably going to be searched. *Damn it,* she thought. She quickly reached into the pocket of her jumpsuit and crushed the paper she had taken from Sylvia. Grabbing Sylvia's hand, she squeezed the paper into her hand. Sylvia looked at Erin, then at her hand, and then quickly moved away, fading into the crowd of gawking inmates.

What followed was pandemonium as six officers came running out of the building, several blowing whistles. Erin took several steps back from Anita's body, thinking they'd want room to examine her fallen attacker. But as Erin turned toward the onrushing officers, hoping to explain what had happened, two officers tackled her to the ground, one launching himself into her chest, the other around her legs.

Being alone had never bothered Erin, but there was something disorienting about being in an eight-by-ten-foot, cinder-block cell with no windows, a solid metal door, and only two slides—one they could put a food tray through, and one the guard could open to check on you. She had a bunk, a toilet, and a small sink, and that was it.

She wrapped herself in the blanket—she was cold, even though it was summer. She had no idea if it was day or night.

After they tackled her, things were a bit of a blur. She couldn't remember how many of them were all over her. Someone had called her a trannie fuck, and she remembered other things that had happened while she was on the ground, officers kicking, punching, grabbing, and groping her. They had dragged her out of the yard and thrown her into disciplinary detention for assault-ing another prisoner. Once in the cell, she had lain on the bunk and fallen asleep, or maybe she passed out. Now, as she tried to orient herself, she realized she was sore all over. She rubbed her bottom lip, feeling the swelling, trying to recall exactly how that had happened—she couldn't. She ran her finger along her teeth and was relieved to feel that they all seemed to be intact.

She wasn't sure how long she lay there. There was no way to compute time; time just was. Suddenly, the slide on the front of her cell slid open. "McCabe, breakfast."

She dragged herself out of bed, her head throbbing, her rib cage screaming.

"Bon appétit," the prisoner on the other side said as she pushed the tray through.

Erin shuffled back to her bunk with the tray. She tried what she assumed was coffee. It was horrible, but she sipped it as if it was a thirty-dollar-a-pound Kona Roast, trying to savor every drop. Then she turned her head sideways so she could rest it on the cool cinder blocks, hoping that would ease her pounding headache. All she could picture was Anita lying on the ground.

Her own reactions had been instinctual, born of three years of self-defense classes. She tried to tell them what had happened; all she had done was defend herself—Anita had a shiv. But here she sat. And what if Anita was dead? What then? She was sitting in jail for a death she had nothing to do with, but now she might stay here for one she was responsible for.

Suddenly, she felt like she was adrift on a boat rolling on the ocean waves. The room began spinning. Nausea gripped her. She stumbled toward the toilet in the corner of the room and began to vomit. She continued to retch even after there was nothing left in her stomach, draped over the toilet, gagging and heaving.

CHAPTER 26

Monday, June 29, 2009, 11:00 a.m.

D UANE HAD GOTTEN TO AVALON EARLY, SO HE DECIDED TO WALK around town. He wasn't sure why Paterson had set up the meeting at Avalon PD as opposed to the prosecutor's office, but if it was for secrecy, Duane was going to ruin it—he was the only Black face in town.

When he walked up to the security booth, the officer behind the glass eyed him suspiciously. Duane, always weary of reaching into the breast pocket of his jacket anywhere near a police officer, already had taken out his driver's license and credentials as a former FBI agent, and he slid them through the opening in the glass.

"Duane Swisher to see Detective Carter and First Assistant Gordon Paterson," he said before he was asked.

A few minutes after the desk officer had made a call, Detective Carter opened a door and waved Duane over. "Hello, Mr. Swisher," she said. "Follow me."

They went up a flight of stairs and entered an open area that had approximately a half dozen cubicles spaced out; on the left side were several offices. She followed a path straight back through the cubicles and opened a door to what was a decent-size conference room.

Once inside the conference room, Duane was greeted by an

average-looking man in his mid-forties. He wore a navy-blue sport coat with gray slacks. His shirt was slightly frayed around the collar, and his striped tie looked like a present from a holiday or a birthday long past.

"Gordon Paterson," he said, walking forward toward Duane.

"Duane Swisher," he replied, shaking Paterson's outstretched hand.

"Have a seat, Duane," Paterson offered, pointing to the table. "You said you had some information you wanted to discuss concerning your client. What's going on?"

Carter had a legal pad in front of her ready to take notes. It suddenly dawned on Duane that this was a conference room, not an interrogation room—no cameras, no recording devices, at least no obvious ones.

"Detective Carter, I'm sure you'll recall that, when my client and I came down to speak with you and Detective Lonza over a month ago, one of the things you believed linked her to the crime was her telling Lonza that, while they were standing on the beach, Montgomery received a call he didn't answer, then what Erin believed was a text message, and then a call he did answer. Detective Lonza confronted my client over the fact that his cell phone was in his house and there were no calls or text messages between six and nine thirty p.m."

"I recall that," Carter replied.

Duane then shared with them the information he had discovered on Montgomery's second cell phone, the efforts to eliminate Rachel, and the information he had received from Welch. He filled them in on the fact that the people who torched Rachel's house were both murdered and that Rachel's closest friend had been murdered as someone continued to hunt for her. As he spoke, he watched Carter furiously taking notes. Paterson, on the other hand, was sitting back in his chair, his brow knitted, seemingly nonplussed by what Duane was telling them.

"Assuming this is all verifiable," Carter said, "it doesn't necessarily exculpate your client. There's still the fact that her DNA was found on the envelope with the photos."

"Obviously, I haven't seen the crime-scene photographs yet, but eventually I will, so let me pose a question. When Mr. Montgomery's body was discovered, was his right hand resting on the envelope?" Duane asked.

Carter looked to Paterson, whose face betrayed his confusion.

"It was," Paterson responded.

"There's your answer," Duane replied. "Memorial Day was the first time Erin met Mr. Montgomery. What would you expect would be the last thing they would do before she left?"

"Shake hands?" Carter said, more of a question than a statement.

"Exactly. Erin and Montgomery shook hands, she left, he walked back, met his killer, and the last thing he touched with his right hand was the envelope. It's called secondary DNA transfer. When Erin shook hands with him, she left traces of her DNA on his hand. When his hand came to rest on the envelope, he transferred her DNA from his hand to the envelope."

"Sounds pretty tenuous to me," Carter replied.

"It's really not," Duane replied. "When I was with the FBI, we had a case where we found DNA at the crime scene, leading us to identify a suspect. However, when we tracked down our prime suspect, it turned out he was in the hospital at the time the crime was committed. So how did his DNA get at the crime scene, you ask?" Duane posed the question with a mischievous grin. "The same EMTs who had transported him to the hospital had answered the call to respond to our crime scene to treat the victim. Not sure what that says about the hygiene of the EMTs involved, but based on the hospital records, there was no way our suspect could have committed the crime. Same thing applies here. But don't take my word for it. Contact any DNA expert you want, and they'll confirm it happens."

There was a long stretch during which no one said anything. Finally, Paterson folded his hands on the table and leaned forward. "If it wasn't your client who killed Mr. Montgomery, perhaps she had a role in setting this whole thing up. It seems odd that Montgomery meets with your client, surveillance doesn't pick anyone else up in the area, and he winds up dead."

"I suggest you speak with Arnold Welch," Duane said.

"And why would we want to do that?" Paterson replied.

"Because he'll tell you he sent Montgomery to meet with Erin in an attempt to get information on William Townsend. He will also tell you his campaign email server was hacked, and it's possible others were aware of the meeting."

"Are you suggesting that someone acting on behalf of Senator Townsend could somehow be behind the death of Mr. Montgomery?" Paterson asked.

"That's precisely what I'm suggesting, Gordon."

Paterson leaned back in his chair.

"Mr. Swisher," Carter began, "even if we put any credence into your wild theory that someone tied to a candidate for governor is somehow responsible for a whole series of murders, there's no way we could ever connect Senator Townsend to these crimes. All you have at this point is rank speculation."

Duane's head nodded slightly. "Detective, it's not my job to convict anyone. That's your job. And," he said, gesturing toward Paterson, "your job as a prosecutor is to see that justice is done. Not to hold an innocent woman because you can't prove someone else committed the crime. I've just poked a large enough hole in your case against my partner to drive a goddamn bus through. I honestly have no dog in the fight of who actually did kill Montgomery, but you asked me, and I told you, yes, I think Townsend is behind it. And if you want my advice, I'd send the photos that were taken of Montgomery when he was in Avalon out to a lab for a machine identification code analysis. If you can identify the printer they were printed on, you may be able to track down the owner of the printer and, from there, find out who asked to have the photos printed."

"Duane," Paterson said slowly, a troubled look covering his face, "give Detective Carter and me a few minutes."

It was almost twenty minutes before they returned.

"We need time to investigate the information you've provided," Paterson said, as he retook his seat. "We'll obviously need some time to subpoena the phone records and interview Mr. Welch. During that time, we simply can't release your client." He quickly held up his hand to stop Duane. "However, if you make a motion to lower Ms. McCabe's bail to $250,000, with a ten percent cash alternative, we will not oppose it."

"Thank you," Duane said, knowing that what Paterson was offering was the opportunity to post $25,000 cash bail. Since they wouldn't need a bail bondsman, if the charges were ultimately dropped, the $25,000 would be returned to whoever posted it.

"Before you thank me, there's one complicating factor," Paterson said, taking a deep breath. "We received word that your client is currently in disciplinary detention for assaulting an inmate. Apparently, the other inmate is hospitalized, and I don't know her condition. Your client is scheduled for a disciplinary hearing at two thirty today. When we're finished here, I'm going to go over and personally look at the video of the incident. Obviously, I have no authority over the jail, but I want to see for myself what happened, determine if it impacts our position on bail, and find out if the Sheriff's Office intends to file criminal charges."

Duane ran his hand over the top of his head. *Damn it, we should have bailed her out on Thursday.* "Okay. I'm heading over to the jail now. Hopefully, I can see my client before the hearing. Maybe we can connect after you see the videos and I see Erin."

"Sure," Paterson replied. He took out a business card, scribbled a number on the back, and handed it to Duane. "Call me on my cell."

Duane had visited any number of clients in jail, but up until now, none had been in disciplinary detention. Because of Erin's status, they wouldn't be meeting in one of the rooms set aside for attorney-client meetings, but in a special secure portion of D-wing.

Once there, Duane was placed in a chain-link enclosure separated in halves by a chain-link wall. All he could think of was that it looked like a diving cage. On his half was a chair and a small shelf on which he could place a legal pad and take notes.

After about five minutes, two officers emerged from the control room, one male, one female, the latter carrying shackles and a waist belt. They walked across the room to one of the eight cells and made a signal back to the control room; Duane could hear the sound of the door being electronically unlocked. As the male officer stood in the doorway, the female officer proceeded inside. Several minutes later, the officer escorted Erin out.

Erin was shackled at her ankles and her wrists, a thick chain running between them and secured in front, with her hands handcuffed to the waist belt.

Duane was in shock as he watched her shuffle forward. Even from the enclosure, he could make out the dark bruises on Erin's cheeks and under her eyes. Her lips were swollen, and her face had several small cuts.

Once Erin was in the enclosure, the female officer took out a second pair of handcuffs and connected Erin to an eyebolt secured to a small metal shelf on Erin's side of the enclosure. The officer then locked Erin in and took up a position at a desk, approximately twenty feet away but with a clear view of them both.

"Hey, big guy. Nice to see you," Erin said, although because of her swollen lips the words came out sounding more like, "Heh, mig guy. Nite ta see ya."

Duane tried desperately to swallow his emotions. Up close, the swelling on Erin's face was sickening, and he was momentarily at a loss as to what to say.

"I've never seen a Black man turn green before, but if you're feeling as sick as you look, please don't vomit on me. I already have enough problems," Erin said with what looked to be a small lopsided grin.

"I'm sorry, E. What the hell happened?"

"Long story," Erin replied. "At this point, I'm more concerned about whether I'm going to be charged with a different murder."

"Murder?" he said, forcing himself to keep his voice down. "What are you talking about?"

Erin explained what had happened in the exercise yard and her last view of Anita.

"Wait. I thought you were assaulted by other inmates. Who did this to you?"

"Correction officers. I don't know their names."

"Jesus, E, it sounds like an open-and-shut case of self-defense. Why are they treating you like this?"

"Just lucky, I guess," she offered, shrugging. "Anything new on your end?"

"Yeah," Swish replied. "I actually was coming to see you with what I think is great news."

He walked her through everything that had happened over the last few days, including his just-concluded meeting with Paterson.

Erin sighed. "Yeah, that is good stuff. You do good work, counselor. As long as they don't try to screw me by charging me with what happened with Anita, I may have a shot of getting out of here."

"What do you mean by 'a shot'? We'll bail you out the minute the bail is reduced."

"Unfortunately, there's one other wrinkle. One of my cellmates was given a script of my jailhouse confession to memorize. She's charged with murder, and ratting me out via her attorney may be her 'get out of jail free' card."

"Fuck," Swish said.

"My sentiments exactly," Erin said.

"Five minutes, counsel!" the officer shouted from the desk.

"Swish, listen. Let's see what happens when you speak with Paterson," Erin said. "As long as I'm in disciplinary detention, I can't have visitors other than you. If I'm not going to be charged for what happened with Anita, the worst that can happen is fourteen more days in solitary. Honestly, as disorienting as it is, it may be the safest place for me right now." She looked down the hallway at the guard. "And just so you know," she said in a whisper, "a friendly nurse took some photos with her phone."

"Good to know. But nothing else is going to happen," he said. He looked at his watch. "I'll be back tomorrow around this time with a certification for the bail motion. I'll also update you on what I find out from Paterson."

"Sounds like a plan," she said, her eyes showing her gratitude.

"Please take care of yourself," Swish said, as he fought back his emotions.

"Doing my best, big guy. Doing my best."

As he was being escorted up the catwalk, Duane turned back to see the two guards escorting a shuffling Erin back to her cell. There was a small part of him that wondered if she'd ever get out of jail.

He called Paterson from the jail parking lot. At least this way, if there was more bad news, he wouldn't drive off the road.

"Gordon, it's Duane. I've just seen Erin. Any news?"

"I suspect the incident will not affect your bail motion."

"Good." He paused. "Does that also mean Erin is not going to be charged by your office with any other offenses?"

"No, not necessarily. It just means the other inmate is expected to recover. So, if there are charges . . ." Paterson hesitated. "Let's just say the bail we discussed would be appropriate on those charges as well."

Duane was a boiling cauldron of emotions—thrilled his worst fears wouldn't be realized and he'd be able to get Erin out on bail, but furious with what had happened to her, and with Paterson's evasiveness. "Gordon, based on my conversation with my client, the situation with the other inmate is a clear case of self-defense. Did you view the video?"

"I did."

"What's it show?"

"Duane, I really can't go into that now."

"Why? If Erin gets charged, I'll get to see it."

"I'm sorry, Duane. If there are other charges, you'll be able to see it. If there aren't other charges, then the video is irrelevant."

Duane took a deep breath, trying to keep his anger in check, knowing that he didn't want to say anything that would cause Paterson to change his position.

"Let me ask you this: Does the video show what happened to Erin after the other inmate was on the ground?"

His question was met by silence. It lasted so long, he finally said, "Gordon are you still there?"

"Yes, I'm here. And yes, the video shows everything."

"Thank you," Duane said. "I'll deliver a formal letter for the preservation of the video to the facility, the county and your office tomorrow."

Paterson paced his office. After the meeting, he had told Carter not to share the new information Swisher provided with anyone. He had to thread the needle on this. As much as he wanted to be the prosecutor, if it blew up, not only would he have no shot at the top spot, but his career might be over.

He walked back to his desk chair and sat down, turning so he was facing his credenza. There were the pictures of his wife, Marian, and daughters, Gwen and Abigail—God, he didn't want to make their lives more difficult. Next to them was a picture of his mom and dad, taken at his wedding fourteen years ago, eight years before his dad died.

He reached over and picked it up. "All I ever wanted was for you to be proud of me. I hope I don't fuck this up," he whispered to the picture, as if his father could hear him.

Then he spun around, unlocked his top desk drawer, and took out a flip phone. He scrolled his contacts and hit the number.

"Hi," the voice on the other end said. "How'd the meeting with Swisher go?"

"That's why I'm calling," he replied.

CHAPTER 27

Thursday, July 2, 2009, 10:00 a.m.

DUANE WALKED AROUND THE CONFERENCE-ROOM TABLE AND greeted everyone. He had met Erin's brother, Sean, and her sister-in-law, Liz, on several occasions years ago but hadn't seen them since Erin had transitioned. He knew Mark well because they were teammates in an adult basketball league, Mark having played college ball as an undergraduate at NYU.

When he got to Peg, he wrapped his arms around her in a huge hug. Then he looked at Pat. Duane had been pleasantly surprised when Pat had showed up for the initial appearance, but knowing how strained things had been between Erin and her father because of previous press coverage, Duane was concerned that the continuous reporting on Erin's arrest, including the *Post-Dispatch*'s article with the titillating headline IT TAKES ONE TO KILL ONE, which discussed her transgender status at length, may have once again stoked Pat's unhappiness. Instead, as Pat grasped Duane's hand with both of his, his face conveyed sadness and concern, not anger.

"I have some disappointing news," he said. "The bail motion is not going to be heard this afternoon, because, since the Fourth is Saturday, tomorrow is a state holiday."

His news was met with a collective sigh of disappointment and, in Peg's case, a very emotional, "Oh no."

"But I have been assured by the judge's staff that it will happen Monday."

"Duane, when you called on Tuesday after you filed the motion, you were confident that the prosecutor's office wasn't going to oppose it, and you thought the judge would grant it. Has any of that changed?" Mark asked.

"No. As far as I know, nothing has changed, and I fully expect that we'll be able to bail Erin out on Monday. The prosecutor's office didn't request the delay. It's simply because of the court's schedule."

"Duane, I have a certified check for twenty-five thousand dollars for you to take now," Sean said.

"You don't have to do that," Mark interjected. "I have the money to post for her."

Sean gave Mark a sad smile. "Let me take care of this. It's my small way to try and make amends for the way I treated my sister after her transition. And from what Duane explained, it's not like I'm being that magnanimous. Assuming she doesn't jump bail, we'll get our money back," he said with a half grin. "Seriously, we got this."

"Thanks," Mark said.

"There's something else I need to let you know about, but I wanted to wait until we could get together in person." Duane looked at the five concerned faces on the other side of the table. "Erin is being held in solitary confinement. It's actually called disciplinary detention, but we all know it as solitary."

"Why?" Peg squeaked, her hand covering her mouth.

Duane proceeded to fill them in on what had happened in the exercise yard, hastening to add that the prosecutor's office had confirmed they would not be filing any additional charges. Despite that, Erin had been given the maximum of fifteen days in disciplinary detention.

"There's one other thing," Duane continued. "When you see Erin, I don't want you to be surprised. She got beat up pretty badly by the corrections officers following what happened."

"Oh my God, no!" Peg cried.

Pat put his arm around his wife and pulled her close.

"Is she going to be okay?" he asked.

"Yeah. I think so, Pat," Duane responded. "She's sore, bruised, and a little shaken up, but the prison medical staff didn't see any permanent injuries."

"How can they get away with that?" Liz asked.

"Maybe they won't," Duane said firmly, "but that's a battle for another day. Right now, the most important thing we can do is get Erin out of there as soon as possible."

"Do you think they're ultimately going to dismiss the charges?" Mark asked.

"Yeah, based on the information from Welch and Stern, I'm very confident the charges will be dropped."

"And then I hope you sue the bastards for her," Pat spit out.

Liz and Sean looked at each other, pleasantly surprised by his strident tone in support of Erin.

After Swish had answered all their questions, it was agreed that Mark would be there at the bail hearing to bring Erin home. Peg originally wanted to go, but Pat gave her a gentle nudge.

"Let Mark bring her home. We'll see Erin after she gets some rest."

After they left the office, Peg, Pat, Liz, and Sean stopped to have lunch at the Rustic Mill Diner.

"I think Duane knows more than he's telling us," Peg said to no one in particular.

"What makes you say that, Mom?" Sean asked.

"I don't know—mother's intuition."

"I agree," Liz chimed in. "If he's warning us about what she's going to look like when she gets out, which is more than a week after it happened, it must have been bad."

"I feel guilty that I didn't go to the bail bondsman the day after she was arrested," Sean added.

"Sean, I don't care how well you're doing financially, a hundred thousand dollars is a lot of money," Peg said. "Plus, that's not what Erin wanted."

"If something happens to her, I'll never forgive myself," Pat said.

They all paused and looked at him.

He looked at each of them in turn and took a deep breath. "I know what you're all thinking—it's about time. I get it. I should have learned my lesson three years ago when she was shot, but even after that, I couldn't get with the program." He paused and took a deep breath. "Look, I'll be honest, I still don't understand her being transgender and what that means, but instead of accepting her and letting her be herself, I acted like she had to live life on my terms." He glanced over at Peg. "Go ahead, you can say it."

"Say what?" Peg asked.

"I told you so. You've been telling me this for the last five years and that I'm an idiot."

For the first time all morning, Peg wore a small smile. "Patrick McCabe, I never said you were an idiot. Pigheaded and a little backward with regard to your views on certain things might be a better description," she said, leaning into him and giving him a playful hug. "I'm sure your daughter will be more than happy to allow you to make it up to her."

It was around 1:30 p.m. when Swish walked out to the reception desk. "Cheryl, I don't think anything is going to happen for the rest of the day. Why don't you take off and start your weekend a little early?"

"Thanks," she said, but then seemed to hesitate. "Is Erin going to be okay? I know her family seemed pretty upset when they left, and Mark looked like he was ready to strangle someone. I'm worried about her."

"I think we're all worried about her," Swish replied. "But Erin's a pretty tough cookie. And we should be getting her out on Monday. So yeah, I think she'll be okay."

The sound of the phone ringing brought an end to their conversation. "Good afternoon, McCabe and Swisher," Cheryl answered.

"Hold on a moment. Let me see if he's available." She placed the call on hold and looked up at him. "It's Logan," she said.

"Hey, Logan. What's up?" he said when he picked up the call in his office.

"Swish, listen, we may have a little problem with Michelle."

"What's going on?" he asked.

"She called me to let me know that they're going to have to find a new place come Monday morning. Apparently, wherever they are, the owner will be returning on Monday, and she thinks it's best if they're not there when he arrives."

"Okay. I feel bad. I spoke with Michelle the other day, but with everything that's happened to Erin, I really haven't focused on her situation," Swish said. "When I spoke to her last week, all I had to offer were a lot of empty clichés."

Logan gave a small snort. "To be fair, Swish, your partner's in jail, and this really wasn't your baby. We both know you're involved because Erin wanted to take the case."

"True. But Michelle is a client of the firm, which means that, while Erin's been out of commission, Michelle is my responsibility. I did reach out to Assistant Prosecutor Beasley to see if we could reach some accommodation if Michelle surrendered, but he basically told me to pound salt and then made fun of the fact that Erin was already in jail. It was a good thing I couldn't reach him through the phone. Anything new on your appeal of Curruzi's decision?"

"Just got the opposition brief. My reply is due on the thirteenth, and they've scheduled oral argument for July 30th."

"Wow," Duane replied. "They're really fast-tracking it."

"Yeah. Definitely a good sign," Logan replied.

"Getting back to Michelle, did she indicate if she had another place to go?" Swish asked.

"She said she was still working on it—and, um, maybe I gave her some suggestions."

"Logan, please be careful. I'm having a hard enough time getting my partner out of jail. I don't want you locked up for aiding and abetting or harboring a fugitive."

"I hear you, Swish."

He paused, realizing their response wasn't reassuring. "After

Erin gets out and has a few days to recuperate, the three of us should get together and figure out what the next steps are for Michelle and Hannah. They can't stay on the run forever," Swish said.

"Sounds good," Logan replied. "And by the way, speaking of people on the run, Rachel thinks that, in light of . . . well, let's just say in light of other things, she's going to move on to Plan C, whatever that is. I told her it would be okay to stay, but I think she's insisting that on Monday I take her to the train station."

"Lots of people moving on Monday. Guess I shouldn't ask if Rachel's decision to move is related to anything else?"

"Yeah. You probably shouldn't," Logan replied.

"I thought you'd want to know that there's something going on," Lonza said.

"What do you mean?" Gardner asked, still disappointed by the news he had received earlier in the week that the psychotic cellmate's attempt to take out McCabe had failed.

"McCabe's lawyer filed a motion to reduce her bail, and our office hasn't filed any opposition. The AP said he was directed by the first assistant not to oppose the motion, and that the first assistant told him that he'd personally be handling the bail hearing on Monday."

"What did her lawyer ask bail to be reduced to?" Gardner asked.

"Two hundred and fifty thousand, with a ten percent cash alternative—meaning, she puts up twenty-five grand, and she's out."

Gardner tried to piece together what this meant. "Have there been any developments in the case—new evidence or anything like that?"

"That's just it. As far as I know, nothing's changed since we picked her up last week," Lonza said.

"When will the motion be heard?" Gardner asked.

"Monday," Lonza replied.

"Thank you. I appreciate the heads-up. I'll be in touch."

He disconnected and stood staring at the wall. With McCabe locked up in disciplinary detention, there was no way to get to her. The doors to those cells were under 24/7 video surveillance. If she was bailed out on Monday, she'd never go back into the general population. *Damn it!* He needed to shift gears yet again. If he couldn't eliminate McCabe, he needed to go back and redouble his efforts to find Stern.

He picked up his burner and dialed Walter Johnson.

"If it's a blocked number, it must be Michael Gardner," Johnson answered.

"Walter, I know you sent some people last weekend to stake out the two addresses I gave you, and it didn't appear anyone was living at either, but I need you to send a couple of people back to double-check to see if a person I'm looking for is staying in either of those places. The person's name is Rachel Stern, but they're transgender, and apparently, they sometimes go back to their former appearance as Richard Stern. Richard was a special agent for the IRS. I'll send you a photo from his credentials, and I'll send you a copy of Rachel's driver's license."

"I'm assuming that if my people don't see anyone, this time you want them to check inside?"

Gardner thought for a moment. "The Bradley Beach condo might be tough to get into. Not only is it summer, but it's Fourth of July weekend. There's bound to be a lot of people around, so it's probably too risky to try to get inside. Maybe try a fake food delivery, and if no one answers, just observe. My guess is she isn't there. Too much going on at the shore this time of year and too close to where she lived in Asbury. But in Cranford, if they don't see anyone, tell them to check it out discreetly."

"No worries. I have a good team to send to Cranford. They've been working together for years. One of them is the best B&E guy I know. He could break into Fort Knox," Walter offered.

"Good. Let me know by the end of the weekend."

CHAPTER 28

Friday, July 3, 2009, 6:30 a.m.

WILL TOWNSEND'S HAIR WAS STILL WET FROM THE SHOWER when he opened the door for Gardner. He was annoyed by the intrusion—even though he was up every day at 4:45 to do his exercise regimen, he usually didn't have a meeting before 7:30 at the earliest.

"Coffee's on the counter," he offered, taking a seat on a stool at the marble-topped center island. "What's so damn important that it couldn't wait until Sunday?"

Gardner poured coffee into a mug and took a seat opposite Townsend. "McCabe's bail will be reduced on Monday, and as a result, she will be released on bail," he replied. "And your boy, First Assistant Prosecutor Paterson, is not doing anything to stop it."

"Where does your information come from?" Townsend demanded.

"Will, you're not the only one with sources inside the prosecutor's office. My source is the lead detective on the case."

"Does he know why they're allowing her bail to be reduced?" Townsend asked.

"No. He's as confused as I am. He's not aware of any new evidence."

"I'll reach out to Paterson later," Townsend replied, wondering what the hell Paterson was up to and troubled by the fact that he hadn't been kept in the loop.

"Anything else?" he asked.

"I learned earlier this week that she's in solitary for knocking out another inmate. I was also told that, in subduing her, the guards gave her a beating."

Townsend snorted. "She knocked out another inmate? Sounds like we underestimated the bitch."

"There is one piece of good news. Hopefully one of her cellmates is going to testify that McCabe confessed that she murdered Montgomery."

"Well, at least that's encouraging." Townsend shook his head. "Let me talk to Paterson and see what the hell is going on with the bail. He better have a good explanation." Townsend poured himself some more coffee. "Where are we with Stern?" he asked.

"We haven't been able to find her. I have multiple efforts underway."

Townsend pushed himself away from the counter and walked over to the kitchen window. "I don't like this, Michael."

"Trust me, I don't like it either. Remember, it's my neck that she could put in the noose," Gardner replied.

"Right," Townsend replied. "But as you so graciously reminded me the last time we spoke, it wouldn't be very helpful to my campaign to have my personal attorney under investigation for murdering one of my opponent's campaign-finance people," he replied, not trying to mask his irritation. "What a fucking shit show."

"Assuming McCabe gets out, I'm hoping she'll lead us to Stern," Gardner said.

Townsend retook his seat on the stool, his eyes locked on Gardner. "Michael, you and I have been through a lot together, and, other than in 'Nam, you've never failed me. And even there, I understand why you did what you did. Right now, I am riding the coattails of Jim Rogers, one of the most popular Republican governors in New Jersey history. That means this race is mine— unless I fuck it up, or someone fucks it up for me. And I'm not going to fuck it up. You know my game plan. Other than the Muslim bastard in the White House right now and H. W., every president since Gerald Ford was a governor. Don't fuck this up on me, Michael. Do whatever you have to do to fix this."

"Understood," Gardner replied.

After Gardner left, Townsend checked his campaign schedule. His first event was in Toms River at noon. If Paterson could meet with him this morning, he could make it in time. He took out his BlackBerry and texted Paterson.

Sorry to bother you on a legal holiday. Need to meet with you asap. Let me know if ur available this morning to meet in AC.

He headed into the bedroom to get dressed, picking out a casual collared shirt, a summer-weight sport coat that he could always take off and carry during the parade, and a pair of khakis. When he was dressed, he heard his phone chime.

I can be there by 8:45 if that works for you. Same place?

Townsend looked at his watch.

Perfect—yes, same place, he replied, smiling to himself that, at least based on Paterson's quick response, he was still on board and looking to become prosecutor.

When he arrived, Paterson was waiting in the hallway outside Townsend's office suite—another good sign, Townsend thought.

"Good morning, Gordon. Have you been waiting long?

"No, sir . . . uh, Will. Just got here."

Townsend took out his keys and unlocked the door. "Sorry, no staff today. Thanks for coming on such short notice, and on a holiday no less."

"No problem. I was heading into the office anyway. With most people off, it's a good day to catch up on paperwork."

"I like your dedication," Townsend said, giving Paterson a slight nod. "You continue to impress me, Gordon. Can I offer you some coffee?"

"No, thank you. I'm good."

Townsend led the way through the empty office to the conference room and flicked on the lights. "Sit. I'm sure you're wondering why I asked to meet."

"Actually, I suspect I know why—the McCabe bail motion."

Townsend tilted his head, surprised by Paterson's head-on approach. "Indeed. What's going on? Based on what I read in the papers, sounds like you have her dead to rights. Her DNA was found on some evidence, if I remember correctly."

"You're correct, Will. There is a lot of circumstantial evidence that points to McCabe as the murderer. But . . ." he hesitated. "Well candidly, we don't have the smoking gun or, in this case, the bloody knife, to seal the deal. We're concerned we don't have enough to prove the case beyond a reasonable doubt."

"Okay, but how is letting her out on bail going to help?" Townsend asked.

"First of all, we keep Judge Connors happy. He took pains at the initial appearance to emphasize bail was only to ensure her appearance, and he certainly telegraphed that he thought the current bail was too high. Second, we're still looking for the murder weapon. We're working on getting warrants for a house in Clark, where she apparently is spending most of her time with her boyfriend, her apartment in Cranford, and her law office. Her cell phone's GPS tracking information on the day after the murder is consistent with her going to her office or her apartment."

"Let me interrupt," Townsend said, "Shouldn't you have done all of that already? Don't you think the knife is long gone? Thrown into the ocean or a dumpster somewhere?"

"You're right. We made a mistake when we arrested her by only asking for a search warrant for her condo in Bradley Beach. I'm not going to throw anyone on my team under the bus; after all, I did assume responsibility for the case. Let me just say that I should have been more diligent in questioning my team on what needed to be done. So I agree; these searches should have been done when she was arrested, which now makes the knife a long shot but, in my opinion, worth it. More important, our search is going to encompass anything that might show she had access to this kind of knife. According to the ME, the knife was a stiletto, with approximately a six-inch blade, so it's a bit unusual. We're also going to do a warrant for her credit-card receipts to see if they show records of any purchases from a sporting goods store, an Army/Navy store, or any place that might sell this kind of knife. If we can find proof that she had that kind of knife, it strengthens our case immensely. Needless to say, if we find the knife, it's a home run."

"Gordon, I truly appreciate you sharing all of this with me. It certainly sounds like you know exactly what you're doing. When do you think you'll be executing the additional search warrants?"

"I want to have my team thoroughly examine what we've already seized. My guess is about two weeks." Gordon smiled and held up his hand. "I suspect you're going to say, 'Why so long?'"

Townsend nodded.

"Several reasons, but the primary one is that we want to hit everything simultaneously, including her law office. That's going to require coming up with procedures to satisfy the judge issuing the warrant that we're taking all the necessary steps to protect the attorney-client privilege as it relates to her firm's other clients. It can be a painstaking process."

"Thank you, Gordon. I appreciate your candor," Townsend said. "I hate to cut this short, but I have to run to a campaign event. A few more months and I'll be governor-elect, and you'll be well on your way to being the prosecutor."

Townsend stood and offered his hand. Gordon jumped out of his seat, clasped Townsend's hand with both of his, and gave a firm shake.

"Thank you, Will. You know that's my dream."

After Will let Paterson out of the office, he took out his phone and hit the number 6 in his stored numbers.

"Yes," Gardner's voice answered.

"I just met with Paterson. He gave me some good information I'd like to exploit. Let's meet on Monday."

Erin looked up from her bunk as Corrections Officer Lillian Williams entered her cell, holding sheets of paper.

"Whatcha writing, McCabe, *War and Peace?* According to the logbook, these ten will make seventy sheets of paper you've gotten so far."

Erin offered a small grin. Williams was one of the officers who treated the inmates with respect. On Monday night, when Williams had first come to check on her, Erin was already feeling the effects of isolation. Between her injuries—physical *and* emotional—and staring at the same four walls, she was quickly becoming disoriented. Fifteen minutes later, Williams was back with ten sheets of blank paper and a flexible pen that couldn't be used as a weapon. "Here's the paper and pen you asked for," Williams had said. Erin had stared blankly, having no recollection of asking for either item. Then Williams said under her breath, "You have to do something, or you'll go stir-crazy. Write a legal brief, write a letter, write something—exercise your mind."

After Williams left that first night, Erin had forced herself to stand. Everything still ached—her face from being punched, her ribs from being kicked, her arms from having them yanked behind her so they could put cuffs on her—but even worse were the invisible wounds, the ones left by the gropes, the taunts, and the threats. Williams was right; if she didn't do something, she'd start to unravel. But what to write?

Now, five days later, Erin was still writing—letters to activist groups concerning Michelle and her daughter, and the horrors of conversion therapy; letters to allies of the LGBTQ community to garner support for legislation banning conversion therapy for minors; letters railing against Senator Townsend and his use of trans children as a political issue; and letters to Mark, her mom, Sean, Liz, and the boys, just in case something happened to her.

Taking the new sheets of paper from Williams, Erin gave her a small smile. "Officer Williams, this is for you," Erin said, handing her a folded sheet of paper. "I wanted you to know you made a difference, and I'm not sure how I would have gotten through without your advice. Thank you."

Williams took the note. "You know I have to turn this in, don't you?"

"I figured as much," Erin replied. "That's why I wrote it, hoping that people will read it."

"You make it sound like I won't be seeing you after tonight," Williams said.

"You're off the next two nights, and I have a bail hearing on Monday. So who knows? But in case I do get out, I just wanted to say thank you."

Williams slowly nodded. "Well then, good luck. I hope you get out." When she reached the door, she looked back over her shoulder. "And, McCabe, don't come back."

After Erin heard the door lock slide into place, she took a clean sheet of paper and began to write the one letter she had struggled with all week, trying to find the words to convey what she wanted to say.

> *Dear Dad: How can I say all the things I want to say without causing you any more pain than I've already caused you? Let me start with the easy part—despite our ups and downs, I love you. I know you struggle with who I am. And I'm sure there's times when you wonder why I had to follow the road I'm on. It's so hard to explain to someone what it's like to be me; there are times when I don't understand it myself. But I didn't decide one day to be a woman. I didn't decide anything. This is just who I am and who I've always been. And after thirty years of trying to live up to everyone else's expectations in the hope of keeping them happy, I just couldn't do it anymore.* ~~At one point things were so bad I almost ended it all. But Lauren convinced me to get help.~~

No, he didn't need to know about her thinking about suicide, she thought, crossing out that part, deciding she'd make this a draft and rewrite it.

> *So here I am, and as hard as it may be for you to understand, for the first time in my life, I'm happy with who I am . . .*

CHAPTER 29

Sunday, July 5, 2009, 2:30 a.m.

THE POUNDING ON THE DOOR STARTLED MICHELLE. BLEARY-EYED, she glanced at the clock on the nightstand—two thirty a.m. What the hell was that noise?

She stumbled out of bed and grabbed her robe. As she started down the stairs, the pounding grew louder, until suddenly the front door flew open, literally ripped off its hinges, and a figure, dressed all in black, holding an assault rifle, came through the doorway. Michelle's screams echoed throughout the house as she turned and ran back up the stairs.

"Police!" a voice bellowed at her back.

As Michelle reached the top of the stairs, Hannah was coming out of her room, a puzzled look on her sleepy face. "Mom, wh—"

"Freeze! Police!" this time barked by multiple voices.

Michelle wrapped Hannah in her arms and turned to look back down the stairs. Four figures in black were assembled at the base, with their weapons pointed at her and Hannah.

"Let the child go," yelled the figure closest to the steps, his command rolling up the stairs like thunder through a valley. "Now! Let him go!"

Michelle and Hannah collapsed to the floor, huddled together in a single mass of intertwined limbs. With her arms clutching her daughter, Michelle could feel Hannah shaking in terror.

"Mom," Hannah whimpered.

The sound of boots pounding up the stairs drowned out Hannah's small voice. Suddenly, a hand grasped Michelle's hair and yanked her away from Hannah. As her head jerked back, an arm reached across her neck and hoisted her off her daughter.

"Mooooom!" Hannah screamed, as she was pried from her mother's arms.

"Don't move," one of the figures demanded, pointing the barrel of his rifle in Michelle's face.

"Don't worry, Nicholas, you're safe now," a man announced.

"Mom! Help me!" Hannah cried.

Two of the men flipped Michelle on her stomach, and then a third knelt on her upper back, while the other two each grabbed an arm and yanked them behind her back, placing handcuffs on her wrists.

"You have the right to remain silent!" one of them screamed at her. "Anything you say can and will be used against you."

Michelle was hysterical. As they dragged her to her feet, she saw two men carrying Hannah out the door, her arms outstretched, shrieking for Michelle.

"Please, let me speak to my daughter," Michelle sputtered between her sobs.

"You don't have a daughter, bitch," one of the officers taunted. "And you'll probably never see your son again—at least not without bars separating you."

CHAPTER 30

Monday, July 6, 2009, 7:30 a.m.

TOWNSEND SAT BEHIND THE DESK IN HIS SPACIOUS TOMS RIVER office not even trying to hide his frustration with Gardner's inability to resolve the Montgomery debacle. It was time for him to reassert control and end the mess Gardner had created. He was running for governor, damn it; he didn't need these distractions. He needed this to be over—now.

"I take it you were satisfied with Paterson's explanation," Gardner asked.

Townsend snorted. "I don't trust anyone, although what he said made sense. Plus, I think he's still desperate to be prosecutor—that alone should keep him in line." Townsend interlaced his fingers and cracked his knuckles. "The good news is that what they're planning next offers us an opportunity to seal McCabe's fate."

"How so?" Gardner replied.

"Did you have McCabe's places in Bradley Beach and Cranford checked out?"

"Yeah. At the condo in Bradley Beach, the only one they saw was the guy McCabe lives with. Probably went there in anticipation of having to drive to Cape May for the bail hearing. In Cranford, no one's there. The report I got back is that, by the look of the place, no one's lived there for several months. They also put a tracking device on McCabe's car at her law office. I should have the receiver on the tracking device this afternoon."

"Good. One of the reasons they're letting her out is they also want to follow her. But from our perspective, what's important is that Paterson admitted they screwed up and never got a search warrant for her office, her apartment in Cranford, or the boy-friend's house in Clark."

"Okay. How's that help?"

"I want you to get the knife into her place in Cranford."

Gardner moved his head from side to side, his eyes narrowing. "That's risky," he responded.

"Why is it riskier than any of the other shit you've done? Jesus Christ, you had Stern's house torched!"

Gardner let out a small laugh. "In case you haven't noticed, there's no one left to talk about that mission. Other than my fuckup with Montgomery's phone, I've been very careful about making sure nothing can be traced back to me, which means nothing can be traced back to you."

A pretty big fuckup, Townsend thought but did not give voice to. "So how's this any different from torching the house? Find some-one, then make sure they remain silent—permanently."

"Because to make sure the job is done right, I'd have to give the knife to someone I know and trust—an acquaintance—and I don't necessarily want to eliminate an acquaintance," Gardner replied. "Besides, at this point, you've ruined McCabe's reputa-tion. The first thing that comes up when you search her are the articles about Montgomery. No matter what happens, her career is history. Let me focus on finding Stern. She, he, whoever the fuck they are—they're our Achilles' heel. You focus on becoming governor, and I'll focus on making sure Stern is eliminated. Let the prosecutor's office deal with McCabe."

Townsend sneered. "I don't need you to tell me what to focus on, Michael," he replied, annoyed with Gardner's insolence. "If I didn't have to deal with this shit, maybe I could focus on running for governor."

"Will, assuming her cellmate comes forward with her jailhouse confession, your boy should have enough to convict her—assuming Stern is silenced."

"No, Michael. I want this done my way," he said, his voice rising. "I want the case against her to be airtight. I want her to suffer every day knowing she's spending the rest of her life in prison for a crime she didn't commit, and I want her to know I'm responsible for her misery." He took a breath, trying to calm himself before continuing.

"We have time. Paterson said he wouldn't be applying for the warrant for about two weeks. Just make sure your source lets you know when that's going to happen. Then when I tell you to go, I want you ready to go. Understood?" Townsend said.

Gardner took a deep breath. "Understood."

At 9:35 a.m., the door that led from the holding cells to the courtroom opened, and three sheriff's officers shepherded Erin and two other women, who were chained to one another, into the courtroom and directed them to sit in the jury box. Several minutes later, Judge Collins took the bench and looked down at a printout of his cases. He quickly handled those of the two other inmates with Erin, both of whom were there for their initial appearances.

"The next matter on my list is a bail application in *State v. McCabe*," Judge Collins announced. But before Duane had even reached the table designated for defense counsel, Collins added, "I'm going to take a five-minute recess, and I'll see counsel on the McCabe matter in chambers."

Collins was standing behind his desk as they walked in. "Gordon, good to see you," Collins said. "And Mr. Swisher, nice to meet you. Please, both of you, have a seat."

"I asked to speak with you privately because I have Mr. Swisher's bail motion, and I see no opposition from the State. Gordon, I just want to make sure that your office is not taking any position on this motion? Do I have that right?"

"Yes, Your Honor. We do not oppose the motion."

"I see," Collins responded. "Well, that makes my job a little easier. I'm not going to make either of you do a dog-and-pony show for the record. When we go out, I'm going to say I've reviewed the motion, ask the State if they have any opposition, and when you tell me there's no opposition, I will grant the motion." Collins again shifted his focus back to Duane. "When we're done, wait outside in the hallway. I'll have my clerk bring you out several copies of the executed order, so you can get Ms. McCabe out as soon as possible."

"Thank you, Judge."

Following the hearing, it had taken another hour before the paperwork was processed and the jail was notified that Erin could be released. Mark and Duane had both driven from the courthouse to the jail, and Mark delivered some casual clothes for Erin to the front desk, knowing that when she was locked up, she had been dressed in a skirt and heels.

"It'll take about thirty to forty-five minutes to get her processed," the officer at the front desk explained to Mark and Duane.

"Thanks," Mark replied.

"Let's wait outside," Duane suggested.

They took a seat on a bench under a portico that covered the visitors' entrance to the jail. It was a sunny summer day, and even though it was only noon, it was already getting steamy.

"I hate to do this to you," Duane said, "but I need to speak to Erin for about ten minutes before you head home."

"Everything okay?" Mark asked.

"Not really. One of our clients was arrested over the weekend, and I want Erin to know. The case means a lot to her, and there's an arraignment on Wednesday."

"The case with the mom who took her transgender child and disappeared?"

"That's the one," Duane replied.

Mark nodded. "Yeah, she'll want to know," he said, with a hint of resignation. "And she'll want to be there Wednesday."

Duane gave him a funny look. "You're probably right, but I'll see if I can get her to take a week off. She needs it."

"I agree she needs some time off, but she'll be there," Mark said.

"I'll try," Duane said.

Mark looked at his friend. "Good luck with that," he replied with a chuckle.

After Duane headed off to make some calls, Mark tried to calm his fears. His palms were sweating, and he kept rubbing them on the back of his pants leg. From his vantage point in the gallery, he could see how bruised Erin's face was. But as concerning as the bruises were, he worried more about the wounds he couldn't see. She had been in custody for almost two weeks, most of it spent in solitary confinement. Would she be carrying emotional scars as well? After his "normal woman" comment, he worried that he'd say the wrong thing, and he didn't want to screw up again.

And then, there she was—walking down the hallway, escorted by a female corrections officer. As he watched, a crooked smile slowly began to spread across her face, and her eyes, which only moments earlier had appeared blank, suddenly seemed to fill with relief, and then joy.

Erin wanted to run to Mark, but she knew from helping bail out clients that she had to sign out.

"Have a good day, Ms. McCabe," the officer said when Erin handed her back the pen.

"You too," Erin replied.

As soon as she crossed the threshold to freedom, she put the bag on the floor and threw her arms around Mark, kissing him.

"God, it's good to see you," Mark said when they finally broke their embrace.

"It's wonderful to see you too," she replied, tearing up.

He picked up the bag, and they walked out the door into the warm summer air. She closed her eyes and sucked in a deep breath—*God, that feels good.* She had not taken a breath of fresh air since she was locked up in solitary over a week ago. When she opened her eyes, Swish was running toward her, only to hesitate at the last moment.

"Can I give you a hug?" he asked.

"How about if I hug you, big guy?" she offered, conscious of how tender her ribs and shoulders still were.

He leaned over, and she put her arms around his neck.

"Thanks," she said.

"It's great to see you, E."

"It's great to be seen," she replied with a small grin.

The three of them stood there talking. Occasionally, she'd catch one of them staring at her face, which she had yet to get a good look at, but if it was as bruised as some of the other parts of her body, it couldn't be a pretty sight.

"Look, I know both of you probably want to get on the road, but can I talk to you for a few minutes before you go?" Swish asked her.

"I'll go start the car," Mark volunteered.

"What's going on?" Erin asked.

"Michelle was arrested Sunday morning. I brought you copies of today's papers so you could see the coverage. It's pretty one-sided, and I'm sure you won't be surprised that several papers have connected Michelle's case to Townsend and Mallory's news conference. Even though they didn't use Hannah's name, the articles effectively out her as trans."

"Shit," Erin mumbled.

"Michelle was indicted on second-degree interference with custody. She's being arraigned Wednesday morning at nine before Judge Douglas in New Brunswick."

"How'd they find her?"

"Based on what Michelle told Logan, Michelle had turned on her cell phone to see if she had missed calls, and she had missed several from her mother. Worried, she called back. Needless to say, based on that, the authorities picked up her location."

"Was she still at the ex-brother-in-law's?"

"Yeah," Swish replied. "I spoke with Assistant Prosecutor Beasley and told him that no one was to interrogate her without her lawyer being present, and when Logan spoke to Michelle, they reminded her not to speak with anyone. On my way back to the office, I'm going to stop and visit with her."

Erin chewed on her lip and looked up at the sky. "I'm not sure

I can drive yet, but I can have Mark drop me off at the office on Wednesday, if you can pick me up."

"E, what are you talking about? I'll cover the arraignment. I just wanted to let you know what's going on," Swish said. "You need to take some time off to rest and recover."

"Swish, I just sat alone in a room for a week. All I did was rest—and try not to lose my mind. I need to be there for Michelle." She hesitated. "I need to be there for me."

He stood quietly, studying her. Finally, he said, "I'll pick you up at Mark's at seven thirty."

"Thanks," she said. "There are a couple of other things you can do for me."

"What's that?" he asked.

"When you visit with Michelle, I want you to talk to her about strategy. You and I both know that, legally, she's got no defense to the charge. If we sit back and wait, our only hope is to convince a jury to find her not guilty because they're offended by the charges against her—always a risky approach."

"Agreed," Swish said.

"More important, that would take time—a year or longer to get to trial. After months of conversion therapy, Hannah could be scarred for life, or worse, have taken her own life." She stopped, trying to imagine the trauma an eleven-year-old would suffer from repeatedly being demeaned and told that they weren't normal.

"We need to go on the offense now, starting with getting Michelle out on bail," Erin said. "I realize that it's not without risks, and it requires us to make Hannah's plight front and center, so we need to make sure Michelle is okay with that. But I don't see another way to go. Especially since Hannah's already essentially been outed.

"While I was in solitary, I wrote some things down. You're a much better writer than I am, so maybe you can take my jailhouse gibberish, organize it and turn it into emails, which we need to get out to the media, LGBTQ organizations, and other allies. We have to galvanize public opinion behind Michelle. Essentially, we need to try and do jury nullification before the case even moves forward. We need to counteract the narrative that the prosecutor's office—and, from what you tell me, the press—are saying and win her case in the court of public opinion." She hesitated. "If you and Cheryl can get these out later this afternoon, maybe we can get a few people outside the courthouse Wednesday."

He rubbed his goatee. "You're right, it's risky, but I hear what you're saying about Hannah. After I meet with Michelle, I'll give you a call to let you know what she thinks." Swish leaned back against his car. "Where are your missives?"

"In the paper bag Mark has. They're all labeled as legal notes to you because jail officials aren't supposed to read or confiscate my communications with my attorney. They probably read them but couldn't make sense of what I was talking about. I hope you can."

They walked back to Mark's Jeep, and she retrieved her notes from the bag and handed him a bundle of papers.

"One last favor," she said. "Do you have the burner? They seized my cell phone, and I want to make some calls on the way home."

"I can do better than that. When I met with Paterson, since they had already extracted everything they needed, he gave me your phone." He took her BlackBerry out of his jacket pocket and handed it to her. "I charged it up on the way down this morning. You're good to go."

"Thanks," she said, giving him a peck on the cheek. "I'll talk to you later."

"You want to stop and get something to eat?" Mark asked when she got into his Wrangler.

"Not sure I want to be seen like this," she said, flipping down the visor and opening the mirror to take a closer look at her face. "Oh shit . . ."

Although most of the bruising was gone from her cheeks and she no longer had a fat lip, her face was still swollen, and the areas under her eyes were still discolored. At the sight of her wounded self, all the swirling emotions of the last thirteen days tore through her like a cyclone, ripping her apart. She covered her mouth with her hand, trying to muffle her sobs as Mark jumped out, came around, opened her door, and held her, allowing her tears to dampen his shirt.

When she finally composed herself, and with lunch no longer on the agenda, they headed for home. As they headed up the Parkway, the first thing she did was call her mom to let her know that she was out. They agreed to have breakfast on Thursday and that she and Mark would come over for dinner on Saturday. Erin just hoped her face would be healed by then so she could spare her mother and father seeing her battered and bruised.

When she finished talking to her mom, she told Mark everything that had happened over the last two weeks, including the fact that Sylvia still might testify against her.

"We're about twenty minutes away from Bradley Beach," he said as they passed the exit for Toms River. "You want to spend a couple of days of R&R at the condo?"

She winced, suddenly realizing she hadn't told him about Michelle's arraignment. "No," she said, "I need to get home. I have to be in court on Wednesday."

"On the case of the mom with the trans daughter?" he asked.

"Yeah," she replied, giving him a quizzical look.

He said nothing for the longest time. "Swish try to talk you out of going?"

"He did," she said.

He stole a glance, and she wasn't sure what she saw in his face—resignation, admiration, frustration . . . some mix of the three?

"Let's get you home so you can soak in the bath, and I'll make us some homemade soup," he offered, his voice soothing and genuine.

She cocked her head, a smile spreading across her swollen face.

"Sounds wonderful," she said. And for the first time since this odyssey had begun, she felt her body start to relax.

CHAPTER 31

As Erin watched the prisoners being led into the court-room, all she could think of were Joan Didion's words "Life changes fast. Life changes in the instant." In Erin's case, it wasn't exactly an instant, but it was fast. On Monday, she was the one in chains; now, forty-eight hours later, she was back on the outside looking in.

Logan, who was sitting on her right, poked her.

"Michelle's the second one in the chain gang," they whispered.

Erin studied the grim faces of the women waiting for the clerk to call their names, knowing exactly what they were feeling—the fear, the confusion, the helplessness.

The courtroom was packed, with still more people outside in the hallway. She and Swish had been shocked when they showed up at the courthouse; there was a long line to get through security, and everyone was heading to Judge Douglas's courtroom. The response was beyond Erin's wildest dreams. The crowd contained a number of LGBTQ activists, including Andi Christian, the executive director of NJ Equality. Even the press had turned out, photographers beginning to snap pictures as soon as Michelle entered the courtroom. All Erin could hope was that all this publicity she had stoked wouldn't result in a backlash against Michelle or Hannah.

"State versus Michelle Costello," the clerk called out, and Erin and Duane made their way up to the counsel table.

"Good morning, counsel," Judge Douglas said, removing his reading glasses and laying them on the bench in front of him. "Appearances, please."

"Assistant Prosecutor John Beasley for the State, Your Honor."

"Good morning, Your Honor. Erin McCabe and Duane Swisher for the defendant, Michelle Costello," Erin said.

"Nice to see you again, Ms. McCabe," he said in a tone indicating he was sincere.

"Thank you, Judge," she replied, fighting back the temptation to add something glib about her last visit to his courtroom.

"Let's do the easy part first," Douglas began. "I have before me Indictment 09-04-0802. Mr. Beasley, have you provided a copy of the indictment to counsel?"

"I have, Your Honor."

"Judge," Erin said, "I acknowledge receipt of a copy of the indictment, and on behalf of my client, I waive the reading of same and enter a plea of not guilty. As Your Honor is aware, I would like to be heard on the issue of bail."

Douglas picked up his reading glasses and slid them back on. "The record should reflect," he started, "that yesterday, I received a motion from defense counsel to reduce the defendant's bail, which is currently set at $500,000 cash. I also received a second motion from counsel seeking to allow them to produce documents in connection with the bail motion, under seal—in other words, shielded from public access—because the documents they want the court to consider involve medical and other confidential information concerning the defendant's minor child, whom counsel have referred to using the child's initials, H.C. Late yesterday afternoon, I received opposition to both motions from the prosecutor's office, including objecting to using 'H.C.' to refer to the minor, insisting it should be 'N.C.' Given the fact that I don't know that we can even argue the motion without discussing the potential confidential information, I'm going to grant the motion to seal the records, for the limited purpose of determining whether these records should even be considered as part of the bail motion."

Douglas looked up from his notes at the packed courtroom and removed his glasses. "Normally, I would clear the courtroom and hear the motions, but I am presented with two logistical issues. First, the record should reflect that the courtroom is full— standing room only. Second, there are two other inmates here with the defendant, so I need to have them removed as well. What I'm going to do is ask the sheriff's officers to unshackle the defendant from the other two inmates and have those inmates returned to the holding cell. Then I want Ms. Costello taken to my jury room, where I will hold a confidential hearing."

Ten minutes later, Erin, Duane, and Michelle sat on one side of the long conference table that was used by jurors when deliberating a verdict. Opposite them was Assistant Prosecutor Beasley, who appeared none too happy. Two officers hovered behind Michelle. A court reporter sat at the judge's side, pecking away on her stenotype machine; the judge's court clerk and his law clerk completed the entourage.

"Let me be blunt, counsel," Douglas said, taking time to fix both sides of the table with a look. "I woke up Monday morning to headlines claiming that the defendant is attempting to force the child to be a girl. If that wasn't bad enough, I woke up yesterday morning to headlines that the child is transgender and the father is trying to use conversion therapy to 'convert' the child back to being a boy. And then, this morning, both sides are screaming at each other in the press." Douglas looked around the room. "I've yet to see counsel quoted in any of these articles, and I'd better not, because I will issue a formal gag order if I have to. However, at this point, it seems like this case has taken on a political life of its own."

He turned to Erin. "Ms. McCabe, the reason I've agreed to hear this under seal is only because you have proffered that you wanted to present medical information and other confidential information as part of this hearing. That said, if you're going to just repeat what's already out there in the press, I may not keep it confidential. Please proceed."

Erin started to rise from her seat.

"You may remain seated, counsel," Douglas said, waving his hand.

"Thank you, Your Honor. As we know, the purpose of bail is to insure a defendant's presence in court. Obviously, the burden is heightened when a defendant is charged with a crime that involves flight. However, I'd posit to the court that the burden is met when there are extraordinary circumstances that account for the defendant's actions, and I will show that, even if the law doesn't approve of the conduct, human nature does."

Erin opened a manila folder in front of her and slid a set of photographs across the table to Beasley.

"Judge, for the record, I'm handing Mr. Beasley six photographs." She removed another set of photos from the folder. "Judge, with the court's permission, I will ask your clerk to mark them as exhibits D-1 through D-6 for purposes of this hearing."

"Any objection?" Douglas asked Beasley.

"Yes, Judge," Beasley responded instantly. "There's been no foundation laid for these photographs, and there's been no testimony authenticating the pictures. We don't know who took them or, for that matter, who the people are in the pictures."

Douglas turned his gaze back to Erin.

"Judge, for the limited purpose of authenticating the photographs, I am willing to have my client testify that she's the one who took the photographs and identify the individuals in the photographs."

Douglas turned his attention back to Beasley, who shrugged.

"For purposes of today's hearing, I'll stipulate," Beasley said, shaking his head.

"Proceed," Douglas said.

Erin waited until the clerk had marked the exhibits. "Judge, I'd ask you to look at exhibits D-1 and D-2. In those two photos, you see four happy, laughing young girls at a birthday party. One of those young girls is H.C. Since I presume Your Honor has never seen H.C. before, I suspect you won't be able to pick out which girl was assigned male at birth."

Douglas studied the photos, then looked up.

"I'd ask Your Honor to now look at what have been marked as exhibits D-3 and D-4, which are pictures of just H.C. at the same party, which happened to be her eleventh birthday back in April. Again, all you can see is a very happy young girl. "

Douglas looked at the exhibits, then picked up the first two exhibits, studying them against the new photos.

"Your Honor, in the final two pictures, which are marked exhibits D-5 and D-6, you'll see the same child looking quite despondent after custody was changed to her father and after her long brown hair had been cut off in an attempt to make her look like a boy."

Erin waited as Douglas spread the six photographs out on the table in front of him. When he finally looked up, she took it as her cue to continue.

"Judge, I'd also like to have marked the various certifications filed in the custody matter before Judge Curruzi. These include my client's certification, H.C.'s father's certification, the certification of Mary O'Connor, my client's therapist, and the certification of Dr. Marsha Bradshaw, the psychologist who has been treating H.C. for the last six months, who states that H.C. is transgender and has a female gender identity."

"Judge, again I have to object," Beasley interjected. "Counsel continues to refer to the child using female pronouns, using initials that don't represent *his* name, and raising issues irrelevant to whether the defendant is entitled to a reduction in bail."

"Mr. Beasley has a point. How is this relevant, Ms. McCabe?" Douglas asked.

"Judge, if I might be allowed to present one more certification, this one executed by Dr. Bradshaw yesterday, opining on her concern that, faced with having custody taken away from her mother and being given to her father, the rejection of her gender identity by her father, and the forced participation in reparative therapy, also known as conversion therapy, H.C. was, and remains, at an extremely high risk of suicide."

Erin inhaled, struggling to keep her emotions in check.

"When you put all of this together, Judge, you have a situation in which my client—who has raised H.C. by herself, with no help other than child support from H.C.'s father for eleven years—suddenly, and for no reason other than she is trying to be supportive of her transgender daughter, is stripped of custody of her child. Then, when she found that her child was expressing suicidal ideation, her reaction wasn't to commit a crime, it was to protect her child from imminent harm," Erin argued, fixing her gaze on Beasley.

Erin turned her attention back to the judge, knowing that what she was about to argue was the one part that Beasley would have a legitimate objection to because she was about to stray from the evidence to the personal.

"Judge, I suspect that I'm the only one in this room who understands what H.C. was and is going through. As a transgender woman, I can tell you it was and is incredibly hard for me—an adult—to be rejected by family and friends. For H.C., not only is she being rejected, she is literally being tortured in an effort to 'convert' her to being a boy. Judge, I ask you to please think about what that must be like for H.C. She is being mocked and ridiculed in an effort to *cure* her. H.C. doesn't need to be cured any more than I need to be cured. Like any child, she just needs to be loved. There is absolutely nothing wrong with H.C.—look at those pictures—she's a happy kid. What's wrong is people who want to use her as a pawn in an effort to advance their own political agenda and a legal system that, rather than protecting the child, forces a mother to do what she needs to do to save her child's life."

"Ms. McCabe," Douglas interrupted, "in terms of bail, given that custody of the child is still with the child's father—meaning, all the same conditions that existed when the defendant fled the first time will be in place again—why wouldn't your client do the exact same thing again in an effort to protect her child?"

Erin wanted to turn and give Swish a high five, because on their way to the courthouse, he had asked her the same question. Together they had worked out her response.

"Because the first time, my client had no idea that she might potentially be committing a serious crime, nor did she understand that there were other avenues available to her, through both the courts and the Division of Youth and Family Services. It was not my client's intention then, and it's not her intention now, to violate the law. I also remind the court that when I was before Your Honor in a very different role—as a witness subpoenaed to appear before the grand jury—it was because I contacted the prosecutor's office, as well as DYFS, to notify them of my representation, to inform them the child was safe, and to see if we could arrange for my client to surrender. The prosecutor's office's response was to subpoena me."

"Mr. Beasley, any response?" Douglas asked.

"Judge, as I said earlier, none of this is relevant," Beasley said dismissively, glaring at Erin. "The defendant has a history of flight—that's all that matters. She's now facing a second-degree crime, carrying with it a presumption of incarceration, which gives her even more incentive to flee. As to counsel's impassioned plea about an eleven-year-old child being rejected because no one but his mother accepts him for who he is . . . Please. He's eleven. He hasn't even gone through puberty yet. When I was eleven, I wanted to be an astronaut or a cowboy. When he's an adult, if he still has delusions that he's a woman—well then, I guess he'll be free to follow in counsel's footsteps. Until then, his father, with the help of the courts, has every right to keep him from making a colossal mistake. As for counsel contacting me, it was not in compliance with the statutory requirements, and, accordingly, my office acted appropriately. Accordingly, the State asks that bail be continued as $500,000 cash."

Douglas looked at Erin. "Any rebuttal?"

"Yes, Judge. If Your Honor reviews the reports of Dr. Bradshaw, you'll see that she emphasizes that studies have shown that forcing a transgender child who has gender dysphoria, as H.C. does, to go through the puberty in accordance with their sex assigned at birth puts that child at high risk for self-harm. That's not my opinion or even just Dr. Bradshaw's—that's the opinion of the medical community. As for an eleven-year-old's ability to know who she is, I again refer the court to Dr. Bradshaw's certification, where she lays out in detail her findings concerning H.C.'s awareness of exactly who she is. I would just add for the record that I knew from about the age of four that I was female, but unlike H.C., I lacked the courage to tell anyone how I felt, which is why I transitioned as an adult."

Douglas nodded slowly. "All right, give me a few minutes to review everything. When I'm finished, I'll put my decision on the record. I will note that I'm satisfied that the material Ms. McCabe requested to have filed under seal should remain confidential, and I will have them so marked. If the sheriff's officers would please escort the defendant back to the jury box, and if counsel would return to the courtroom, I will be out shortly with my decision."

Douglas motioned for Josh, his law clerk, to have a seat at the now-empty conference-room table. Douglas had been on the bench for fifteen years, and over time, his law clerks had ranged from outstanding to disasters. Josh was near the top. He was a bright guy who had already landed a job with one of the biggest firms in the state when his clerkship was over at the end of August.

"This is a tough one," Douglas said. "I know Beasley can be a bit obnoxious, but he's right—she has a history of flight, and that sets a pretty high bar. But damn, I could understand why a mom might panic and try to keep her child safe."

Douglas looked down at the photos in front of him, leafing through them one by one, struck by the joy in the child's face at the birthday party and the sadness in their eyes after custody was changed and their hair was cut. God, what was life like for him . . . her, he wondered.

Next, he picked up Bradshaw's most recent certification and reread it.

"I have to admit, I don't understand any of this transgender stuff," he said to his clerk. "You're younger than I am. Do you know anyone who's transgender?" Douglas asked.

"Yeah, I didn't know the person really well, but there was a kid I went to college with who transitioned. He was assigned female and transitioned to a guy. I know he took a lot of crap because his freshman year he had attended school as a girl, and he was gorgeous. Every straight guy on campus lusted after her—well, her then. When he came back after spring break, word began to make the rounds that he would be transitioning."

"Wait," Douglas said. "There are women who transition to men?"

"Yes, Judge. There's trans men, just as there's trans women like Ms. McCabe."

Douglas shook his head. "Like I said, this is all new to me. What happened with this person?"

"I think everyone was in shock, especially the guys who had tried to date him. When we graduated three years later, you would never have known that this guy with a full beard had been assigned female. Like I said, I didn't know him that well, but a month before graduation, he agreed to speak at an event about being accepting of those who are different from ourselves. He talked about how, as he was growing up, everyone told him how beautiful he was and how he had tried to suppress his feelings that he was male. And, eventually, it just got too much for him to handle. He shared that over spring break his freshman year, he tried to kill himself. That's when his parents finally realized they could have a dead daughter or a happy son."

Douglas looked down at the exhibits, drawn by the pain in the child's face after their hair was cut. "Josh, there's an old legal maximum. Tough cases make bad law. This is definitely a tough case."

Fifteen minutes later, Douglas and Josh walked out of the jury room, and Douglas slowly walked up the three steps to his bench. He folded his hands across his chest and let out a small sigh.

"I've heard the arguments of counsel and reviewed the papers filed in support of the motion to reduce the defendant's bail—

both those filed publicly and those filed under seal. This is a tough case because, as the prosecutor has pointed out, the defendant has a history of flight. I recognize a parent's desire to protect their child, but they must do so within the bounds of the law. I also recognize that there was a belated, albeit imperfect, attempt on behalf of the defendant to remedy the situation once counsel was retained. Finally, I must acknowledge on the public record that there have been numerous newspaper articles over the last several days that repeatedly reference the child's gender identity. As I told counsel privately, I am not happy that the child's personal information is in the public domain. However, since it is, I will simply note that I was provided certain information by defense counsel—which will appropriately remain under seal—that I find convinces me that the defendant had a reasonable belief that her child was in imminent danger. Since the application before me is for bail, and not the guilt or innocence of the defendant, I am satisfied that the defendant's prior flight should not be a barrier to her having a reasonable bail set, and I am likewise satisfied that her past behavior is unlikely to be repeated. Accordingly, I will grant the defendant's application to reduce bail, and I will set bail at fifty thousand."

There were some muffled "yeas" from the spectators in the courtroom, causing Douglas to bang his gavel and ask for quiet.

"I also want to caution counsel concerning statements to the media," he said, looking out on the packed courtroom. "I will be monitoring them, and as I indicated, I will not hesitate to impose a gag order if I feel it is needed."

Beasley immediately jumped to his feet. "Judge, I understand Your Honor has ruled, but I ask you to please reconsider your decision."

"Mr. Beasley, I have thought very hard about my decision, and I did not make it lightly. Accordingly, I will not reconsider. And if your next request is for a stay, the request is denied. I will be more than happy to sign the appropriate order if you'd like to take an appeal. Thank you all. We're in recess."

* * *

After Douglas left the bench, Erin made a quick dash to the jury box. Michelle looked stunned, as if still trying to process what had just happened.

"Hang in there," Erin said to Michelle before the officers could lead her out. "Unless the appellate court grants a stay, we should have you bailed out by this afternoon."

Michelle raised her shackled hands to her eyes and wiped away the tears. "Thank you," she said. "Thank you so much."

Erin made her way back to the counsel table and Duane and Logan.

"Great job," Logan said, sporting a huge grin.

"Thanks," Erin replied. "Now let's get her out so you can file an emergent appeal on the custody issue with the Appellate Division."

"Agreed," Duane said. "I'll give Hamburg Bail Bonds a call to get things rolling. Now all we need is someone to come up with the premium."

"How much will that be?" Logan asked.

"Five thousand," Duane replied.

"Assuming they accept credit cards, I got this."

Duane and Erin looked at each other.

"Are you sure?" Duane asked.

Logan chewed on their lower lip. "Yeah. I'm sure."

"Counsel, can we get a comment?"

Two reporters were hovering eagerly by the railing.

Erin gave them a self-satisfied look. "You heard the judge's admonition. All I will say is we are happy with the decision and look forward to vindicating our client at trial."

"What about the child being forced to be a girl? Do you have any comment?"

"No. We'll have no further comment," Erin replied.

Gordon called the cell number he'd been given.

"Hi," the voice on the other end answered. "Something important must be up if you're using the bat phone," she said with a small chuckle.

"Yeah, we have an interesting development."

"What's that?"

"I received a call from an attorney representing a Sylvia Walker, who's charged with murdering her boyfriend. The lawyer wants to come in and make a proffer on some information he says his client has about another inmate."

"Okay. How's a jailhouse snitch related to what we've been talking about?"

"Walker was in the same cell as McCabe," Paterson replied.

"Hmm. That does make it interesting. When are you meeting?"

"Friday at two."

"Jailhouse snitches are always a double-edged sword, but this could be interesting and potentially make things very complicated."

"Agreed. We'll talk on Friday."

CHAPTER 32

Thursday, July 9, 2009, 3:04 a.m.

THE SOUND OF THE PHONE RINGING ON THE NIGHT TABLE STARTLED Erin. Through her dream-laden eyes, she caught sight of the numbers on the digital alarm clock—3:04 a.m.

Shit, she thought, grasping for the phone, *nothing good happens at three a.m.*

"Hello," she said with equal parts fear and concern.

"Erin, it's Mom," Peg said, her voice filled with panic. "It's your father . . . I think . . . I think he's dead." Her voice dissolved into sobs.

Erin shot to a sitting position. "What's happening?"

"He's not moving," she moaned.

"Mom, did you call nine-one-one?"

"Yes," she stammered.

"I'm on my way. I'll be there in ten minutes. Did you call Sean?"

"No, he's too far . . ."

"Okay, I'll call him from the car. I'm coming."

When she looked up, Mark already had on a T-shirt and jeans and was standing near her side of the bed.

"What's going on?" he asked.

She jumped out of bed and quickly started throwing on clothes. "My mom said my dad's not moving. She thinks . . ." She couldn't finish. She quickly unplugged her BlackBerry from the charger, grabbed her purse, and took out her keys. "Oh shit," she said. "My car's at the office."

"Come on. I'm driving. You call your brother," Mark said, taking her by the arm and leading her out of the house.

As soon as they were in the car, she hit the number for Sean's landline.

"Hello," a very groggy-sounding Liz answered.

"Liz, I need Sean."

"Erin, is everything all right?"

"No!" she replied. She could hear Liz in the background, "It's Erin. Something's wrong."

"Hey, what's going on?" Sean said.

"Mom just called. She said Dad's not moving. Sean, she thinks . . . she thinks he's dead." The words seemed to catch in her throat, as if saying them out loud made them true. "She called nine-one-one, and Mark and I are on our way. We'll be there in ten minutes."

"All right, I'm leaving now. Call me on my cell when you get there. Maybe I can talk to the EMTs. At least get what hospital they're taking Dad to so I can reach out to whoever I know there, and I'll divert to wherever they're taking him."

Erin couldn't help but be struck by her brother's demeanor. He had found a different gear—he was in doctor mode now. All things were possible. For her, she was still trying to process her mother's words—"I think he's dead."

"Okay. I'll call you."

When they pulled up to the house, there was a police car and ambulance parked in front, the red and blue lights bouncing off the neighboring homes. Erin ran up the walk and through the open front door. Straight ahead down the hallway that separated the living room from the kitchen were several EMTs working on her father, prone on the kitchen floor. All she could see through the scrum of people were his feet and lower legs.

Out of the corner of her eye, she caught sight of her mother on the couch, clutching her robe as if it were about to fly off of her.

"Mom," Erin said, hurrying to her mother's side.

Her mother looked at her, her eyes confused, like she was still trying to process what was happening.

"He's not moving. I went to bed. He was sitting in the den watching the news. I woke up around three, and he wasn't in bed. When I came downstairs, he was lying on the kitchen floor." She looked up blankly. "Erin, I think he's dead."

"Okay, Mom. It's okay. The EMTs are working on him now," Erin said, trying to wrap her mother into a protective cocoon.

"Excuse me, ma'am, are you a relative?"

Erin looked up to see a Cranford police officer standing in the arched doorway to the dining room. He was holding a pen and a small pad.

"Yes. This is my mom, and . . ."

"Can I speak with you for a moment, please?" he asked gently.

"Sure."

Erin motioned for Mark to sit next to her mom, then went to join the officer.

"I'm sorry to bother you, ma'am, but your mom is understandably distraught, and I was wondering if I could get some basic information."

"Of course . . . but my dad—how's my dad?"

"They're working on him, ma'am."

From where Erin was standing, she could see two EMTs kneeling next to her father and one hovering nearby, but there was no gurney. They didn't appear frantic. Maybe it wasn't as bad as her mother thought. Or maybe . . .

"Your name, ma'am."

"Erin McCabe," she said.

"Are you Patrick's daughter?" he asked.

"Yes," she said, a sliver of guilt jabbing her.

He handed her a wallet. "This was in your dad's back pocket. The EMTs took it out when they laid him on his back to do CPR."

"Thank you," she said, clutching her father's thick black wallet.

"Can I get you dad's full name and date of birth?"

"Patrick Sean McCabe—date of birth is November 7, 1941."

"Do you happen to know his social security number?"

"No, I don't, but I'm sure I could find it somewhere."

"That's all right. We can get it later." He wrote down some

notes on his pad. "Do you know if your dad had any preexisting health issues—in particular, any cardiac issues?"

"Nothing that I'm aware of, but my mom would know better than me," Erin replied.

"If you could check with her, that would be helpful," he said.

The two EMTs who had been kneeling next to her dad were no longer concentrating on him. Instead, they were starting to pack up their medical gear. One beckoned the officer back over, calling him Joe.

"Excuse me," he said to Erin, and headed toward the kitchen.

He spoke for several seconds with one of the EMTs, and then they waved Erin over.

The EMT offered his hand, and Erin shook it.

"I'm very sorry, ma'am, but we tried everything. Unfortunately, your dad has passed away. He likely had a sudden cardiac arrest, and I suspect he had been gone for some time before we got here. If it's any consolation, it appears to have been very sudden. I'm fairly confident he didn't suffer at all."

She tried to process what he was saying through the euphemisms for death—*passed away*—*gone*. Her dad was dead. No, he couldn't be dead. It was her dad—he just couldn't be.

"I'm sorry, ma'am," Officer Joe was saying. "Do you know what funeral home your mom will want to use?"

"Ah, no. No, I don't know. We've never talked about it. I'll have to ask her."

"Okay. Well, just so you know, you should call the funeral home as soon as possible. They all have answering services and will arrange to pick up the . . . pick up your father."

"They're not going to take him to the hospital?" Erin asked.

"No, ma'am," Officer Joe said. "They've already spoken to the doctor, and based on the information provided, the doctor has pronounced your father dead. There's no reason to go to the hospital."

On some level, it made sense, but on some other level, some existential level, nothing did. Her dad was dead. We all die, but the fact that her father was dead was incomprehensible. She did her best to fight back the tears because once they started, she wasn't sure she could stop them, and somehow, she had to find the strength to go into the living room and tell her mom that her husband of forty-five years was . . . gone. He was dead.

"The only other question is whether your mom would like an autopsy performed," Officer Joe said.

"If we do, what happens?" Erin asked.

"We would have your father's body transported to the Union County Medical Examiner's Office for them to perform it."

"My brother, who's a doctor, is on his way, and I'd like him to be involved in the decision. Is that okay?"

"Sure, ma'am. Do you know when he'll be here?"

"No. I'll find out."

As the EMTs were finishing packing up their gear, they left a clear path to where she could see her dad. A half-empty bottle of beer sat on the kitchen table in front of the chair he must have been sitting in. Lying there on the floor, he looked like he was just sleeping. *Wake up, Dad. Oh, Dad, please wake up.*

She looked up at Officer Joe. "Thank you," she said, not knowing what she was thanking him for. Then she walked back through the dining room into the living room. Mark moved aside as soon as he saw her face, and she sat on the couch next to her mom.

"I'm sorry, Mom," she squeaked, throwing her arms around her mother. The tears running down their faces mixed together as they clung to each other.

After several minutes, her mother whispered, "You'd better call Sean and let him know."

Erin moved her face away and nodded. "We also need to decide if we want an autopsy and what funeral home you want to use," Erin said. "I thought we'd let Sean decide the autopsy issue. Is that okay?"

Her mom nodded.

"Do you know which funeral home you want to use?" she asked.

"Dad and I talked about using Dooley's; they're right here in town."

While her mind momentarily contemplated her parents having

a conversation like that, Erin looked over at Mark. "Could you get Dooley's number while I call Sean?"

"Sure," Mark replied.

She stayed close to her mom, figuring that Sean would want to talk to her, and punched in his number.

"Where are you? What's happening?" Sean answered.

"I'm at the house," she replied, struggling to find the words. "Um, Sean, Dad's . . . gone," she finally managed to say.

"Shit," he replied, then fell silent. The only noise Erin could hear was the background noise of his car on the highway. "Sorry. I guess I should have been expecting that, but . . . You al . . . Never mind. We'll talk when I get there."

"How far away are you?" Erin asked.

"About twenty minutes."

"The police want to know if we want an autopsy done, and I'd like you to make that call," she said.

"Okay. Is Mom there?"

"Yeah. Here she is," Erin said, handing her phone to her mother.

While her mother talked to Sean and Mark talked to someone at Dooley's, the three EMTs and Officer Joe made their way into the living room.

"My brother's about twenty minutes away and is talking to my mom now about the autopsy."

"That's fine, ma'am. I'm going to be in my car doing some paperwork. Let me know what you decide."

After he left, Erin wandered into the kitchen. She leaned against the counter by the sink, looking across the linoleum floor at her father's body. His beer sat in the same spot his coffee cup had sat the last day they spoke. The day he asked her if she had any idea how embarrassing her being transgender was for him. The day he walked away and closed the door to avoid having to deal with her. And now he was gone. She could never make it right, never undo his embarrassment, no matter what she achieved.

She slowly slid down the cabinets until she was sitting on the floor. She pulled her knees up to her chest and folded over, her head buried in her arms. The cry came from somewhere inside her she didn't know existed. A place where she had stored all the pain and anger caused by the vitriol directed at her. A place where all the self-loathing and guilt resided, buried deep under her desire to be proud of who she was. A place that she had tried to hide as diligently as she had previously hidden her gender identity from the world and from those she thought loved her. A place where she stood naked and exposed, unable to deflect the scorn of those who judged her and mocked her for who she was.

"Erin. Erin, I'm here," Mark whispered sitting next to her on the floor and pulling her convulsing body into his.

"I embarrassed him!" she wailed. "I've been in the papers every day . . . every day for weeks. He hated seeing me in the papers. Oh my God. It's my fault." Her head bounced up against Mark's chest as she sobbed. "I'm so sorry, Dad," she moaned.

Mark put his arms under her and lifted her up so she was standing. "Please stop. Please don't beat yourself up. It's not your fault. It's no one's fault." He helped her up and steered her gently back into the living room, where he guided her back to the couch. He crouched in front of her. "Don't do this to yourself. Your dad loved you."

"No. No, he loved me before. Not now."

"Erin, honey. Mark's right," Peg said, moving next to her daughter. "Sean and Liz will tell you. The Friday before you got out of jail, your dad told us how foolish he had acted."

"I wanted so much for him to be proud of me. And all I'll ever have is the image of him closing the door on me in disgust," Erin sighed.

Peg pulled Erin close and gently stroked her hair. "Your dad had his flaws, but he was a good man who loved you very much. I know there were times he struggled, but he always, always loved you."

Erin looked up at her mom. "I'm sorry. I'm supposed to be the one comforting you, not the other way around."

Her mother kissed the top of her head. "I think we're supposed to comfort each other. Don't worry, you'll get your turn. It just hasn't sunk in yet for me. When it does, I know you'll be there for me." Peg pulled back a little from Erin. "Honey, your face is bruised. Is that from when you were in jail?"

It took Erin a few seconds to realize she had no makeup on, so unlike when she had gone to court, the bruises were still dramatically visible.

"Yeah," was all she managed to say.

She closed her eyes and held her mother a little tighter, taking small comfort in knowing that, if this had happened a week ago, she would've been alone, sitting in solitary, with this horrible news.

CHAPTER 33

"WHY ARE YOU SHOVING THE OBITUARY SECTION OF THE *Ledger* under my nose?" Townsend growled.

"Middle of the page, Patrick S. McCabe," Gardner responded.

"A relative of McCabe's?" Townsend said.

"Her father," Gardner replied.

"Yeah, okay," Townsend said dismissively. "But I had no axe to grind with him. It's his fucking kid that I'd like to see in the obituary pages. Anything on Stern?"

"Nothing. But the father's death also explains why the car hasn't moved. She's probably with the boyfriend," Gardner said. "I also heard from my friendly detective in the prosecutor's office that his office is going to be applying for search warrants for McCabe's apartment in Cranford and the boyfriend's house in Clark on Wednesday."

"That means we need to get the knife in her apartment by Tuesday night at the latest," Townsend said, folding his arms across his chest and letting out a deep breath.

"I still don't like it, Will. We can get her without the knife," Gardner offered.

Townsend glanced down at the obituary and pretended not to hear him. "Visitors are welcome on Sunday at Dooley's Funeral Home, with a funeral Mass at St. Michael's on Monday at ten," he read aloud. "This is perfect. She'll definitely be with the boyfriend on Sunday night. Get your people to put the knife in her place then. She goes back to jail, and I pound on Henry Nestor for supporting these crazy fucks." He smiled at Gardner. "It's a win-win, Michael. She gets to bury her father before going to jail, and I get to bury her by sending her to jail for the rest of her life."

Gardner strolled into Harold's Deli, pulled out a chair, and sat down at the table. He was growing tired of Townsend's refusal to listen, but he had allowed his anger and frustration to dissipate on the ride up. Now was the time to be businesslike.

"To what do I owe the pleasure of actually being in your company?" Walter Johnson asked.

"I have something that needs to be discussed in-person—plus, I like the pastrami here."

"I swear, Michael, you're more secretive now than when you were at the agency."

"Whatever," Gardner replied. "One can never be too careful."

"What's up?" Johnson asked.

"The two people you sent into the apartment in Cranford, you told me they're good, correct?" Gardner asked.

"Yes. I told you the B&E guy is the best I've seen. He's spotless. No signs of forced entry, no prints—nobody better," Johnson replied.

"How trustworthy are they?" Gardner asked.

"Michael, what kind of question is that? I wouldn't use anyone I couldn't trust a hundred percent. Why?"

Gardner hesitated, weighing his options, knowing he was potentially putting Walter's neck in a noose. "I need them to go back Sunday night, early Monday morning," he said, finally deciding that Townsend was still his ticket to the top. Hopefully, he'd be able to find a way to protect Walter, even if his hired help might be history.

"Okay, I should be able to arrange that. But you didn't need to meet with me for that. What's going on?" Walter asked.

"This time when they go in, I need something left behind." Gardner reached into his pants pocket and took out something wrapped in a napkin. He slid it across the table. "Inside the napkin is a plastic baggie. Inside that baggie is a knife. I assume there's a dresser in the bedroom. Put the knife in one of the drawers. Obviously, no fingerprints can be left on it. Last thing, it's a switchblade. I don't want it to be opened. It needs to be preserved just the way it is."

Johnson's face twisted. "Michael, do I want to know what I'm . . . what you're getting my guys involved in?"

"They're just making sure that justice is done. That's all. Same thing we used to do all the time when we worked for the government—helping to make sure the good guys prevail."

Johnson's look was skeptical, but he slid the napkin off the table and shoved it in his pants pocket.

"Here's payment for your prior services," Gardner said, putting an envelope on the table.

"Thank you, Michael. You understand that for this foray it will be double."

"Just make sure it gets done."

"We need to help out," Erin said to Mark, trying to will herself to move off the couch.

It had been a long day, and she was running on fumes. First thing in the morning, before they went to the funeral home, she, Sean, and their mom had written Pat's obituary. Then, joined by Mark and Liz, they had all gone to the funeral home to make the arrangements for the funeral—a process Erin had never been part of before. There were so many things to be taken care of—picking out a casket, selecting prayer cards, naming pallbearers, purchasing a cemetery plot, reviewing the list of readings and hymns the church had provided to select what they wanted at the funeral Mass, and finally discussing what everything would cost. After they left the funeral home, they went to the florist to pick out flowers and then finally to The Garden in Elizabeth, the restaurant where they decided to hold the repast. Sean and Liz had then headed off to the Union County Medical Examiner's Office, hopefully to get the preliminary findings on the cause of Pat's death, while she and Mark returned to her parents' home with her mom.

Somehow, despite the fact that she was thirty years older, once she got home, Peg found her second wind and busied herself with returning phone calls from various relatives and friends.

"What can we do?" Erin asked, walking into the kitchen where Duane and Corrine, who had come over around noon with cold cuts, salads, and bread and rolls, were busy getting everything ready.

Corrine looked up at the clock on the wall. "You could do me a huge favor by giving Alysha a bottle. I pumped earlier. Would you mind?"

"No," Erin said, heading over and picking Alysha up from her pack 'n' play.

"And, Mark, if you could check on Patrick, Brennan, and Austin down in the basement, that would be a help," Duane added.

Erin headed back into the living room with Alysha and her bottle and settled back onto the couch. Now almost five months old, Alysha smiled and cooed for Erin, then let loose a joyous giggle as Erin played peekaboo with her. Erin then cuddled her in her arms and let Alysha start sucking on the bottle. Erin marveled at how just the sound of Alysha laughing had offered a brief respite from the sadness and pain of her father's loss. Even amid her grief, she couldn't help but wonder what the joys of motherhood felt like—to hold your child, to watch them grow, to share their joys and sorrows. Perhaps, if she and Mark got married someday, they could adopt. Or maybe, she thought, her mind wandering to a darker place, because she was trans, they'd say she was unfit.

Erin had Alysha on her shoulder and was gently trying to coax a burp from her when Sean and Liz walked in. They both made a fuss over Alysha before Sean sat down next to Erin, as she resumed feeding Alysha.

"All indications are that Dad died of natural causes, probably sudden cardiac arrest. There's no way to determine exactly what happened, even with an autopsy, but the likely cause is an arrhythmia that caused his heart to stop."

"In a bizarre way, that's a relief," she said, biting on her lower lip when she felt tears gathering. "It doesn't make losing Dad any easier, but given all that's happened with me over the last few months, I was a little worried that maybe in an effort to exact revenge on me, someone had done something to Dad."

"No, nothing like that," Sean said. "And I know it will be small consolation for Mom, but she could have been sitting right next to Dad when this happened, and she wouldn't have been able to do anything to save him. In those kinds of situations, you really need a defibrillator to shock the heart back to beating."

"I hope it helps her to know that," Erin said. "She's been beating herself up pretty badly."

"Yeah, she has," Sean replied. "And from what Mom told us, she's not the only one."

Liz sat down on the other side of Erin, and both she and Sean explained what had happened exactly one week earlier at the diner.

"Thanks," Erin replied when they were finished. "I guess it helps to know that Dad wasn't angry with me when he died, I just wish my last memory of us together was different." She looked from one to the other, giving each a sad smile. "I'm okay. Go talk to Mom."

When Alysha finished her bottle, Erin placed her back on her shoulder and gently tapped her back. After a few seconds, Alysha gave a small "urp," and Erin took her off her shoulder and held her on her lap.

She was such a beautiful little girl—happy, content, and innocent. *How long, sweet girl, before you feel the sting of bias because of the color of your skin? How long before you're told you can't do something because you're a girl? How long before someone mocks you, hates you, discriminates against you—how long before the world shows its ugly side to you?* As Erin cradled Alysha in her arms, rocking her gently, her feelings of awe at this tiny human mixed with the realization that no one escapes the cruel reality of the world as they grow up. Just a small taste, she thought, of how easily the joys and worries of parenthood weave together.

CHAPTER 34

Acting U.S. Attorney Ed Champion looked around the room at the all-star team he had assembled—Assistant U.S. Attorney Mary Beth Ford, FBI Special Agent in Charge of the Newark Office Abhay Patel, Special Agent Gerard Pitts, and Special Agent in Charge of the JTTF Charles Russo. These folks were the best. And, depending on where this investigation led, he might need the best.

"I just need to say something before we begin," Champion said, looking around the room, trying to gauge everyone's reaction to the just-ended conference call with Gordon Paterson and Detective Carter. "That guy's got guts, because professionally, this cannot end well for him."

"Why do you say that?" Ford asked.

"Think about it," Champion replied. "Based on what he told us, his case against McCabe is falling apart, which is no doubt going to piss off Senator Townsend. Not to mention, if word gets back to Townsend that he's been working with us in investigating Townsend and Gardner, his only chance of escaping Townsend's political wrath will be to move as far north in New Jersey as possible, maybe Sussex County."

"Nah, too Republican," Patel said with a shrug.

"I guess his only hope is that we take Townsend down," Ford suggested.

Champion shook his head. "I'm afraid even that won't help him. Townsend has a lot of friends—no, I'm afraid Gordon has committed professional . . ." He stopped, suddenly aware that the word he was about to use was painfully inappropriate.

"Let me give you some backstory, because some of you know this, but others may not," Champion continued. "About eight years ago, when I was the lead AUSA on Operation Jersey Sting, Gordon Paterson's dad, Ray Paterson, was one of the first politicians we arrested. At the time, we believed that Paterson was nothing more than the Cape May County bagman for Senator Townsend, and our game plan was to try and flip him to get Townsend. Unfortunately, Paterson wound up dead—officially from an accidental overdose of sleeping pills and alcohol, but there were a lot of people, myself included, who felt he killed himself to spare his family either the ignominy of being indicted and convicted, or the wrath of Townsend if he cooperated."

"You're not suggesting—are you?" Ford asked.

"To be honest with you, I hadn't even thought about that possibility until right now," Champion replied, an ugly feeling growing in the pit of his stomach. And even though the circumstances were vastly different, the pressure that Townsend could bring to bear on Gordon was eerily similar. "But let's hope not," he added, more for himself than anyone else.

"Which brings me to my second point. Townsend has connections everywhere, including in the DOJ and this office. His personal attorney, Michael Gardner, has multiple ties within the intelligence communities from decades working for the CIA and NSA. Let me be blunt—we can't have any leaks. I trust each and every one of you, but no one outside of this group gets this info— no secretaries, no trusted aides, no one!" He looked around the table at each of them for added effect. "For reasons we'll go through, I'm concerned not only about the impact a leak could have on Paterson and Carter, but about a leak's impact on the safety of potential witnesses as well. Finally, I remind you that Senator Townsend is a candidate for governor. We need to make sure we stay out of the race."

Champion turned to Russo. "Charlie, fill Mary Beth and Gerry in on how and why the JTTF is involved."

Russo proceeded to explain who Rachel Stern was, her connection to Montgomery, the fire at her house, and her decision to go underground. He then told them about the murder of Evelyn Ketchum and that his team had developed leads on two people believed to be involved in the murder. His agents had also learned that the Atlantic City police had a person of interest in connection with the murder of one of the people believed to have torched Stern's home, but he had to call his guys off under orders from the Newark office.

Patel looked down the table at Russo. "Charlie, you and your team are owed an explanation as to why we shut you down, and this is a perfect example of why Ed is so concerned with secrecy.

"We believe there's a leak in Asbury PD. Shortly after your team got a lead from them on the ID of the woman who posed as an investigator from the AG's office, Woodbridge PD found the body of a woman matching her description in an abandoned industrial site in Keasbey, along the Raritan River. She was shot twice in the back of the head. Her name was Karen Lawrence—a twenty-four-year-old barmaid and aspiring actress."

"Shit," Russo mumbled.

"Charlie, I want to be clear. We don't think the JTTF has been compromised in any way, nor are we blaming your people for looking into the attempt to murder a former member of your team. I also want to add that, assuming this is the woman involved in the murder of Evelyn Ketchum, we're not sure how, or if, her murder is related to that. Preliminary indications are that she was sexually assaulted before she was murdered," he added, pursing his lips.

"Let me just second what Abhay said: we believe this leak came from Asbury, not us," Champion offered. "But this just drives home my point. Until we are certain, none of what we are discussing leaves this room." Champion gave a nod to Patel for him to continue.

"Charlie, based on the surveillance videos that your people got from Asbury, and additional ones near the site in Keasbey, we believe the second person impersonating an AG investigator is an individual by the name of Dylan Spencer. Given his link to both events, we like him for the murders of both Ketchum and Lawrence. But since we want to keep our interest in him under the radar, we had the Middlesex County Prosecutor's Office put out a situational awareness alert that he's wanted for questioning in connection with the Lawrence murder—no reference to Ketchum."

"Thanks," Russo replied. "I apologize, and maybe you want me out of the loop on this, but why did Paterson reach out to us in the first place?" Russo asked.

"Fair question, and no, we're not keeping anything from you. So let me make sure we're all on the same page," Champion replied.

"Paterson called me shortly after Bradford Montgomery was murdered. At that point, McCabe was the lead suspect in the murder, and while Paterson thought they had a good circumstantial case against her, he felt like the alleged motive—blackmail—didn't add up. He had also found it strange that within days of the murder, out of the blue, Townsend had asked to meet with him. Then, when they met, Townsend wound up talking to him about the case, while also seeming to dangle the prosecutor's job in front of him if he could nail McCabe. That's why he called me to see if we were aware of any connections between Townsend and Montgomery. Knowing what had occurred with his father and some other information I knew of, I reached out to Abhay to see what, if anything, else we had. Mary Beth and Gerry, why don't you share what you've been able to develop?"

Ford and Pitts then shared the information they'd learned from interviewing Welch and what their investigation had uncovered so far concerning the hack of Welch's campaign servers.

When they were finished, Champion looked down the table, taking in Russo's quizzical expression, and smiled to himself, satisfied that he had made the right decision to invite him to participate—a skeptic was good to have on the team.

"Charlie, you look like you have a question. What's on your mind?"

"Maybe it's me, but I seem to be missing something. I'm not trying to sound like a naysayer, but what Paterson told us in terms of Montgomery having a second phone, DNA transfer, and now McCabe's cellmate coming forward to say that a corrections officer fed her a script to testify against McCabe—all of that is great for McCabe in showing she didn't kill Montgomery, but how does any of it get tied to Townsend, and what's the federal crime that we're investigating?"

"The crime is easy," Champion replied. "RICO," he said, referring to the Racketeer Influenced Corrupt Organizations Act, a federal statute that made crimes that would normally only be violations of state law into federal crimes if they were committed as part of a criminal enterprise.

"What's the criminal enterprise?" Russo asked, his face contorted in thought.

"Townsend's campaign," Champion replied, causing Russo to raise an eyebrow. "As to how, or if, we can connect any of this to Townsend, that's a tougher question. Mary Beth, correct me if I'm wrong, but right now, all we have is a series of crimes that may be connected, with no evidence that actually connects them. Do I have that right?"

"You do," Ford replied. "Our belief is that everything is connected to Montgomery's murder, but so far, we haven't been able to link any of these pieces to anyone close to Townsend. We have the cell-phone records for Montgomery's second phone, and they do confirm what McCabe said when she was interviewed, that Montgomery received two calls and a text message shortly before his death. We're in the process of having cell-tower information run on those. As Gerry mentioned, we have the lab looking at the photos of Montgomery, and the Computer Crimes team is still trying to determine the source of the hack on the Welch campaign. Obviously, we'll see if Paterson can develop any information based on the inmate's proffer. But right now, we have nothing that connects Townsend to any of this."

"Look, folks," Champion said, "I don't have to tell you that Townsend is one of the most powerful pols in New Jersey, so we need to move carefully. As Ralph Waldo Emerson once said,

'When you strike at a king, you must kill him.' And in fairness to Townsend, as Mary Beth said, we still have nothing yet that ties him to any of this. In light of the fact that he's a candidate for governor, the DOJ's policy against making anything public within sixty days of a pending election is going to come into play in a little over a month. After that, we'll need to hold off until after the election to do anything. The bottom line is that I don't want our office's integrity attacked for investigating the Republican candidate for governor with claims we're trying to get the Democrat elected. If he's involved in this, we'll go after him. But right now, we've got nothing concrete—translation, we tread lightly."

CHAPTER 35

Monday, July 13, 2009, 2:30 p.m.

ERIN UNDERSTOOD THAT THE RITUALS SURROUNDING WAKES, FU-
nerals, and burials were supposed to be for the benefit of the sur-
vivors, but for her, the stares and snide comments from some of
her dad's friends and colleagues, and some of her own relatives,
had stung. Not only was she seen as the transgender child who
had caused her father a fair amount of consternation, she was an
accused murderer. After her arrest, the press had been relentless,
and many of the accompanying stories had prominently featured
her backstory as a transgender woman, as well as photographs
of her, with some of the more salacious articles displaying photos
of her before and after she transitioned, with multiple references
to her dead name.

Still, there had been some moments that had given her solace.
Mark's sister, Molly, and her wife, Robin, had been with them
throughout. Erin's ex-wife, Lauren, had come to the wake and funeral, which had touched Erin deeply. Logan and Michelle had
stopped by to pay their respects and deliver the good news that
the Appellate Division had granted Michelle's emergent application for supervised visitation with Hannah while the case was on
appeal.

And Mark . . . Mark had been her rock. He had never left her
side, not even when she was emotionally beating herself up over

the strains in her relationship with her father. Not even when his own relationships were strained by the fact that neither his brothers nor his mom had so much as called to extend their condolences.

Now, as she and Mark lingered with her mom and the last remaining people leaving the repast at The Garden, Erin knew that tomorrow her life would need to return to some semblance of normal. Somehow, the world hadn't stopped when her dad had died; people still went to work or the beach; they laughed and had fun. Their lives went on unchanged and unaffected by the devastation in hers, just as her life was unaffected by the losses in theirs. The world didn't stop for anyone.

As she exited the restaurant, Erin noticed Detective Sergeant Ed Kluska from the Union County Prosecutor's Office Homicide Unit standing on the sidewalk near the parking lot. Kluska was a hard guy to miss. At six feet two and close to 260 pounds, his physique made him imposing, even when he didn't want to be. That plus his bushy biker beard and shaved head gave him a well-earned reputation as a no-nonsense detective. Only months earlier, Kluska had figured prominently in the Ann Parsons case that Erin and Duane had handled.

At first, she thought he had stopped by to pay his respects, but then Erin saw another Homicide detective, Eve Dotson, standing nearby.

"Excuse me, Mom," she said. "I just have to say hello to someone. Swish!" Erin called out to get his attention.

Duane did a double take on seeing Kluska but joined her as they headed over.

"My condolences, Erin," Kluska said.

"Thank you, Ed. I appreciate your stopping by," Erin replied.

"Actually, I'm here on business. I know the timing sucks, but would you mind if we went inside to discuss something. It'll just take a few minutes."

"Okay. Let me just let my mom know."

By the time Erin made it inside the restaurant, the staff was busy cleaning up. Kluska and Dotson were sitting at a table in the back corner with Duane.

"I presume you don't know what happened at your apartment in Cranford last night," Kluska asked after Erin sat down.

"No," Erin responded with a mixture of confusion and trepidation.

"Someone was killed there last night," Kluska said apologetically.

Erin sucked in a breath and stiffened. "In my apartment! Oh my God, no. Not Rachel."

"I'm sorry," Kluska said, placing his hand on Erin's arm. "No, it wasn't Rachel Stern who was killed. It was a person who broke into your apartment."

"Wait? What? Someone broke into my apartment, but Rachel's okay?" Erin asked.

"Yes. Yeah, she's fine. Well, a little shaken, but physically she's fine."

"What happened?" Duane asked.

"About three o'clock this morning, Stern was awakened by a sound. She told us that, based on what she's been through, she slept with a gun under the pillow. Apparently, whoever had broken in didn't think there was anyone living there, because when they got to the bedroom, they flicked on the light. Stern yelled for them to freeze, but instead the person lunged at her, and she shot him. She immediately called nine-one-one, and the police and EMTs were there in minutes. He died a few hours ago without regaining consciousness."

Erin tried to process what it all meant—was it a random break-in, or had they been able to track Rachel to Erin's place?

"I'm assuming you knew Rachel was there?" Kluska asked.

"Yeah. Of course," Erin replied.

"Okay, good. We'll do an investigation, but it certainly looks like an open-and-shut case of self-defense. As a retired law-enforcement officer in good standing, she's allowed to have a weapon, and from what she told us, when she yelled at the intruder to freeze, he lunged at her. We also found a knife next to his body."

"He had a knife?" Erin asked.

"Yeah. It's some kind of stiletto switchblade."

Erin looked at Duane, who nodded.

"Ed, I assume you know about my situation."

"Christ, McCabe," he said, falling back into his normal detective mode, "you've been in every goddamn newspaper in the state. Of course, I know what's going on. And off the record, knowing you, I don't think there's a chance in hell you did it."

"Thanks, Ed," she said with a weak smile. "Anyway, the victim in that case was stabbed with a knife, which was never recovered. It's probably a long shot, but I believe the people who are actually responsible for the murder would do anything possible to frame me—including planting the murder weapon in my apartment."

"Interesting," Kluska said, stroking his bushy beard. "No harm in having it tested by our Forensics Unit. If it was a setup, there's probably blood on it, and we can see if the DNA matches the guy you're accused of murdering."

"Thanks," Erin replied. "Any information on the guy who broke in?"

"We have some leads, but I can't share anything at this point. Active investigation—you know the drill. I can tell you that Cranford PD believes others may have been involved and are actively looking."

"Where's Rachel?" Erin asked, panic bubbling to the surface.

"A friend by the name of Logan picked her up."

Erin exhaled in relief. "Thanks."

Kluska stole a glance at Dotson. "Dotson, do me a favor. Go start the car and run the AC on high so it's nice and cool."

Dotson gave him a quizzical look but stood up and offered her condolences before heading out to the parking lot.

"I'm telling you this because, based on the Parsons case, I know I can trust you." He looked around the room conspiratorially. "After we questioned Stern, she reached out to some folks at the JTTF, who sent two agents to talk to us and Cranford PD. Any idea why the feds seem really interested in this?"

"Honestly, other than the fact that Stern is a former member of the JTTF, not a clue. Unless . . ." Erin stopped and exchanged a glance with Duane.

"Unless?" Kluska said.

"Three years ago we talked to the feds about our suspicions concerning Will Townsend," Duane said.

"Wait? Will Townsend, as in state senator, candidate for governor Will Townsend?"

"Yeah, that would be the one," Duane said with a twisted grin. "Anyway, we still have our suspicions about Townsend."

"Will fucking Townsend." Kluska let out a low whistle. "Jesus, you two get involved in some crazy shit."

"True. But we don't go looking for it; it just seems to find us," Erin replied.

"Well, if you do learn anything you can share, I'd appreciate a heads-up. I'm sure it won't come as any surprise to you—especially you, Swisher—but the feds never tell us shit. They could arrest six people in connection with the break-in at your place, and I'll find out about it when I see it in the paper." Kluska stopped, momentarily looking at a loss for words. "Look, McCabe, I am sorry about your dad and . . . well, about all the shit you've been through lately. You ever need anything, you call me. I owe you one."

Erin was touched. Kluska wasn't someone known for displaying any emotion other than anger or annoyance. "Thanks, Ed. I appreciate it. My dad and I had had a bit of a tough go of it since I transitioned, but he was a good man, and I'm really going to miss him. In terms of the other stuff, let us know about the knife, and if we hear anything, we'll pass it along."

"Everything okay?" Mark asked when she climbed into his Jeep five minutes later.

"Yeah," she said. "Someone broke into my apartment in Cranford."

"What?" Mark exploded.

"He's dead," Erin replied, then sighed. "It's a long story. I'll explain it to you on the way to my mom's."

"I don't fucking believe it," Townsend fumed. "None of this would have happened if you hadn't gone rogue and killed Montgomery."

Gardner, who was no longer in the mood to be the whipping boy, fired back. "Need I remind you, Will, that you might not be the Republican nominee if I hadn't. And I'll also remind you that I'm not the one who wanted to plant the knife in the apartment in the first place."

They stood, separated by the desk in Townsend's office, glaring at each other, two bulls ready to lock horns.

"Who the fuck do you think you're talking to, you ungrateful fuck? If it wasn't for me, you would have wound up just like Lieutenant Calley, court-martialed and imprisoned for killing Vietnamese women and children. I saved your fucking ass!" Townsend screamed.

"And I've saved you enough times to have repaid the debt."

"I decide when the debt is repaid," Townsend spit out. "Remember, you work for me, not the other way around."

Gardner tried to swallow the fury raging inside him. As much as he wanted to lash out, he couldn't afford to sever his ties; he still needed Townsend to succeed. That, and if things really went sideways, Townsend's connections could save his skin.

"Got it," he finally said.

"Enough of this fucking bullshit," Townsend grumbled as he grabbed the bottle of scotch off his credenza and filled his glass. "How bad is it?" he asked, plopping down behind his desk.

Gardner pulled out one of the chairs in front of the desk and took a seat. "I think it's safe to assume the police have the knife. Johnson wasn't exactly sure what happened. One of his guys waited in the car, while the other guy headed inside to plant the knife. As was their usual practice, the two of them stayed in communication with burner phones. According to the guy in the car, everything seemed to be going according to plan, when he suddenly heard a voice scream out and what sounded like a gunshot. At that point, he decided he had better take off before the police arrived. Johnson later learned his guy inside had been shot and killed."

"I thought they had told you no one was there," Townsend asked.

"They had. As to who was there—my best guess is Stern."

"Jesus. Can this get any more fucked up?" Townsend said, downing his scotch. "Who knows of your involvement?"

"Just Johnson. I gave him the knife."

"You need to eliminate him," Townsend said, matter-of-factly.

"He's solid," Gardner replied. "I told you before, we've worked together for a long time, inside and outside of government."

"Michael, there's no one who's solid when their neck is on the line. He's a weak link."

"There's no one who can connect you to any of this," Gardner responded.

"That's not true," Townsend replied. "You can."

Gardner's eyes narrowed. "What are you implying, Will?"

"I'm not implying anything—I'm being pretty fucking explicit. I want your friend eliminated, and then you may want to think about taking a vacation somewhere until this shit dies down. Let's be realistic here, Michael. If someone was killed trying to plant the knife in McCabe's apartment, it won't take Clarence Darrow to show she didn't kill Montgomery. I don't care how deep in my pocket the prosecutor is, there's no way McCabe's going down for murder. Which means they'll start looking for another suspect. With Stern still alive, how long before they find the cell-phone records? Face facts, Michael, you're vulnerable. And if you're vulnerable, I'm vulnerable. Stop worrying about your dear old friend, whoever the fuck he is, and start taking care of the person who brought you to the dance—me!"

No point in arguing, Gardner decided. Townsend was wrong. There was another way. He didn't need to eliminate Walter, just the person who could connect Walter to the knife. Walter was too valuable a resource. People like that didn't grow on trees. But Townsend wouldn't understand that because he'd long ago given up getting his hands dirty.

Why the fuck should he, when he has idiots like me at his beck and call?

Gardner waited until he was miles away from Townsend's house before hitting Johnson's number. To his surprise and annoyance, no one answered. Michael pulled into a convenience-store parking lot. He took out his burner, made sure the number was blocked, and typed, **Need another pastrami sandwich asap. Let me know when ur available.**

He hit SEND and walked into the store to get a cup of coffee. Walter would understand the situation. Death came for us all sooner or later. Gardner would just have to speed up the process for Walter's compadre.

"Hello?"

"Vic, it's Will Townsend."

"Will Townsend. To what do I owe the honor?" Victor Marion replied.

"I need a favor," Townsend said.

There was a long silence.

"Last time I did you a favor, your fucking lawyer sold me down the river, and I wound up doing five years at South Woods State Prison," Vic said.

"That's actually why I'm calling."

"About Gardner? You know I hate that motherfucker, don't you?"

"I'm well aware of your feelings about Michael. Do you know where the White House Diner is in Moorestown?"

"Yeah."

"Meet me there tomorrow morning at six thirty, and we'll talk."

"I don't know what the fuck you have in mind, but I won't work with that bastard again. I'd rather see him dead."

"I'm counting on that," Townsend replied.

CHAPTER 36

Tuesday, July 14, 2009, 5:30 p.m.

Hannah sat on the couch in the therapist's office, trying to stay calm and remain focused.

"So, Nicholas, how are we today?" the therapist asked, stroking his scruffy beard.

She thought about not responding but knew from her previous "sessions" that silence was fruitless. "I told you last week, and the first time I was here, when you cut my hair, that my name is Hannah."

"I have your records right in front of me, and it says your name is Nicholas. Why do you keep saying your name is Hannah?"

"Because that's my name."

"Hannah's a girl's name. You're not a girl, Nick; you're a boy."

"No, I'm not."

"Really. Let me ask you, Nick, do you have a penis or vagina?"

Hannah blushed. "I have a penis," she said softly.

"Of course, you do, Nick. And the reason you have a penis is because you're a boy. And like all boys, you have a penis."

"Please stop. I don't know why I was born with a penis. I'm a girl."

"Who sexually abused you, Nick?"

What? Hannah thought. "No one abused me."

"I know you father's brother, your Uncle Gary, is gay. Did he abuse you when you were younger?"

"No!" Hannah screamed. "That's a terrible thing to say. My Uncle Gary's always been very nice to me."

"Maybe he played with your penis when you were young; is that why you don't want to have a penis? Is that what happened? Think hard, Nicholas. Didn't your Uncle Gary abuse you? Or maybe it was the person he lives with, Alex. Did Alex abuse you?"

"No! No one abused me. Stop saying that."

"Nicholas, it's very normal for people who were abused, especially at a young age, to block it out. It's a defense mechanism. I'm certain that's what happened to you, and to try and compensate for being abused, you've convinced yourself that you're a girl. Think hard, Nick. Who abused you?"

Why did he keep telling her she'd been abused? She'd never been abused. "Please stop. You're confusing me."

"You're confused because you're a victim of abuse. That's what happens. Your mind plays tricks on you to protect you from remembering. Maybe it was one of your mother's boyfriends. Is that who it was?"

"No. My mother doesn't have a boyfriend."

"Oh, I see. Does your mother have a girlfriend?"

"No."

"Maybe it's your mother who's abusing you."

"What? My mom's never hurt me in any way."

"Did your mother always want a daughter? Is that it? You're just trying to give your mother what she wants."

"No. My mom loved me when I was Nicholas, and she loves me now."

"Does she force you to dress like a girl?"

"No. No, no, no—please. It's not my mom. I wasn't abused. I'm a girl. I don't know why I was born with a penis. Please stop."

"Do you want to have sex with boys? Is that it?"

"No. I don't know. I don't even think about sex."

"Doesn't the thought of having sex with another boy excite you?"

"No. Yuck."

"Oh, you're attracted to girls then?"

"No," Hannah said. "I don't know. I told you, I don't think about it."

"Do you hate your father?"

"I don't . . ." she stopped. How could she hate a man she hardly knew? The few times he had tried to talk to her about things, he didn't seem mean, just clueless. "I hate what my father is doing to me."

"Did you know that I once thought I was gay?"

"What?"

"It's true. When I was young, I got involved in a homosexual lifestyle, but fortunately, my family didn't give up on me, and I found God. Now, through the power of prayer, I'm happily married to a woman. God can save you as well, Nicholas. Trust in God, and you will accept that you are a boy."

She stared at him. *He's so strange,* she thought. *Why would I want God to make me a boy?*

"Don't you see, just like my family, your dad is trying to save you. Your father loves you," he said.

"I don't need to be saved. I need him to get out of my life. I didn't see him for eleven years, and now he's ruining my life."

"So you feel abandoned by your father. The one male figure in your life deserted you."

"I never knew my father. But there were other men in my life."

"Please don't tell me you're talking about your Uncle Gary and that Alex fellow. They're not normal men."

"They've always been good to me."

"I'm sure they have because they're trying to seduce you into their queer lifestyle."

"They're not like that."

"Nick, you're so young and naïve. All gays are like that. They can't reproduce, so they seduce."

She couldn't take this much longer. "You're wrong," she said, her voice cracking.

"You know your father has signed you up for a special camp starting Saturday, don't you?"

"Camp? No. What are you talking about? I don't want to go to camp."

"It will help you enjoy all the things that boys love, like sports and camping. You'll be with some boys like yourself, who are confused, but you'll be with other boys and young men who will teach you how to be a man and show you how the power of prayer can rid you of your confusion."

Her stomach churned. There was no way she could do this. "I already like sports," she said, trying to strike a defiant tone, but knowing she fell short.

"Then you must be a boy."

"Lots of girls like sports. Almost all the girls who are my friends play sports."

"Oh, Nick. You have so much to learn. They're probably all lesbians. That's why they like sports."

"Lesbians? What's wrong with you?"

Thirty minutes later she walked out to the parking lot, where her father was waiting in his car.

"How'd it go?" he asked.

She glared at him. "It's horrible, okay? He tells me all the time I was abused—maybe by Uncle Gary or Uncle Alex—you know, your 'queer' brother and his boyfriend. I guess the only reason you're not a suspect is because you never saw me. Although you abandoning me is also a likely cause of my 'confusion,'" she said. "Why are you doing this to me? Just get out of my life like you were for the first eleven years." She suddenly started to sob and turned toward the window. "See what a little girl I am—I cry all the time."

"I'm sorry, Nick. I'm not trying to hurt you. I just don't want to see you ruin your life."

She quickly spun around. "You, your crazy doctor and lawyers—you're the ones ruining my life! You're the ones trying to send my mom to jail, and now you're sending me to some camp to train me how to be a boy. Don't you understand? *I am not a boy*," she screamed. "I hate you!"

CHAPTER 37

Wednesday, July 15, 2009, 7:00 a.m.

TOWNSEND SAT AT THE KITCHEN ISLAND, HIS ARMS FOLDED ACROSS his chest, listening to Gardner.

"I'd been trying to reach Johnson since after you and I spoke Monday night. Then yesterday afternoon around two, I got a call from a guy I know from my days at the NSA. He told me that the word on the street is that Johnson had been picked up Monday night by the feds."

"The feds?" Townsend said.

"That was my reaction too."

"What's that mean? What do the feds have to do with this?"

"Not a fucking clue," Gardner responded. "The only good news that I can give you is that I haven't heard from Johnson. I suspect that if he was cooperating, they would have wired him and tried to have him call me or meet me."

Townsend tried not to show any emotion, but he was sure now that his instincts were good—Gardner had reached his "use by" date. This was a shit show, which made his decision easy. The fact that Gardner had brought this on himself erased any misgivings.

"As you suggested the other day, I agree it's time for me to disappear for a while."

Townsend took a sip from his coffee. "I take it that's the reason for the new look," he said, gesturing to Gardner's shaved head and the start of a goatee.

"Yeah. I did enough clandestine stuff when I was with the Company to know how to get lost and stay lost as long as I have to."

"When are you leaving?"

Gardner laughed. "Once I walk out the door, you won't see me again until we meet in hell."

Will rubbed his hands together, contemplating what Gardner had said. That was too soon. He needed more time. Then it struck him—a way to kill two birds with one stone.

"I need you to do one more job for me before you disappear."

Gardner gave him a quizzical look. "What's that?" he asked warily.

"I should have listened to you three years ago. Stern can't hurt me, but McCabe still could. I want you to take out McCabe before you disappear. You're the only one I can trust to do it. Plus, it'll give you the satisfaction of knowing you were right all along."

Gardner cupped his fist over his mouth. "I don't want to make the mistake of waiting too long to disappear."

"Look, you're going to disappear anyway, and you said it doesn't look like Johnson is cooperating. You leave now, or tonight, it shouldn't make a difference. This is really personal for me, Michael. If she's not going to rot in jail, I want her to rot six feet under."

"What about Swisher? Aren't you worried about him?"

"Nah. He's a disgraced ex-FBI guy. Plus, he's got a family. You eliminate McCabe, he'll keep his mouth shut."

Gardner studied Townsend. "Fine," he replied. "I realize that over the last few weeks, you and I haven't always seen eye to eye. Just remember that, if I need something down the road, I did this for you."

An hour later, Townsend made his way out to the limo waiting to take him to his first campaign stop of the day. "Here you go, Senator," the retired state trooper in charge of his security detail said, handing him a GPS monitoring device. "You're good to go."

As the limo rolled down the highway, Townsend made a call. "We're all set. Meet me at the Marriott on Route 1 in Princeton. I'll have what you need. And he's leaving town, so it has to be today."

Townsend sat back in his seat, a little surprised by the fact that he had no remorse. He and Gardner had been through a lot together. But Gardner knew where all the bodies were buried—literally. True, he had been a loyal soldier, but like any soldier, he was expendable. Time to move on.

His cell phone vibrated.

"Hello," he answered.

"Senator, Frank McDonald, returning your call."

"Frank, how the hell is my favorite attorney?"

"I'm doing well, Will. How about you? How's the campaign going?

"Really well. Thanks. Unfortunately, I may need some legal help, and that's why I'm reaching out."

"Sure, but I don't do any campaign stuff. You know me, strictly criminal defense."

"I'm well aware of your specialty, Frank. I'm reaching out because I have some concerns that my personal attorney may have gotten involved in some stuff he shouldn't have, and I want to have you in place in case someone tries to tie me into whatever he did."

"We talking about Michael?"

"We are."

"Okay. I know you're a very busy man. When and where do you want to meet?"

"I'm in Princeton this morning, New Brunswick for a luncheon, and I have a fundraiser in Millburn this evening. How about I meet you at your office in Roseland around three thirty. Does that work?"

McDonald chuckled. "For you, Will, I'll make it work. See you at three thirty."

Lonza strolled into the conference room at ten thirty, carrying a folder with the information for the search warrants on McCabe's office, her apartment in Cranford, and her boyfriend's house in Clark. Two steps into the room, he stopped dead in his tracks, his mood shifting from confidence to confusion to concern. Seated at the head of the conference table was Prosecutor

Musgraves; on her right was Gordon Paterson, and on Musgraves's left was Detective Carter. Farther down the table was Corrections Sergeant Leonard Caruso, his eyes downcast, staring at the table. Next to him was Tom Pendergast, who looked like he had been crying, and across the table from Pendergast sat Lonza's union representative, Detective Bob Andre.

"Have a seat," Paterson sat, pointing to the seat next to Andre.

What the fuck is going on? he wondered as he slowly sat down.

"I'm not going to beat around the bush, Adam. First thing you should know is that this discussion is being recorded. I also want you to know that you are the subject of a criminal investigation for official misconduct, a second-degree crime. Accordingly, you have the right to remain silent. Anything you say can and will be used against you in a court of law. You also have the right to counsel. If you cannot afford a lawyer, one will be appointed for you. Do you understand your rights?"

"Is this a joke?" Lonza said, glancing around the room, waiting for people to laugh. No one was laughing.

"Yeah. I understand my rights," he spit out. "What the hell is going on?"

Paterson nodded to Andre, who handed Lonza a waiver form and a pen. "Please initial each of your rights, and sign whether you're either waiving or not waiving your rights."

Lonza looked defiantly at Paterson. "I ain't waiving shit," he said, signing the form.

Paterson nodded again to Andre, who handed Lonza a second form.

"Detective Lonza, you've just been handed an Internal Affairs Complaint signed by Prosecutor Musgraves. The complaint charges you with various acts of misconduct and violations of the office policies and procedures. Detective Andre is present as your union representative."

"This is bullshit," Lonza said.

Andre leaned over. "Shut up and listen," he whispered to Lonza.

"I'm now going to have Detective Andre hand you another

form to sign. These are your Garrity warnings. You have already invoked your right to remain silent under the Fifth Amendment, which you have the absolute right to do. However, the prosecutor's office has decided to provide you with use immunity, meaning that anything you say as part of the Internal Affairs investigation will not be used against you in the criminal case. It also means that you do not have the right to refuse to answer questions as part of the IA probe. If you nonetheless refuse to answer questions, that will be grounds for us to terminate your employment."

Lonza felt like he'd been sucker punched. What the fuck was going on? Second degree—that meant mandatory jail time.

"You have an absolute right to a lawyer," Paterson continued. "However, since you have been provided use immunity for the Internal Affairs investigation, you are required to answer certain limited questions, under oath, subject to perjury. Do you understand that?"

Lonza looked at Andre. *What the fuck good are you? Why aren't you saying something?* "Yeah. Understood," he finally said.

"Before we question you, you should know that we have already gathered evidence against you," Paterson continued. "That includes the fact that you worked with Corrections Sergeant Caruso to try to persuade an inmate to provide a false confession against a suspect in a murder investigation. Additionally, Assistant Prosecutor Pendergast has disclosed conversations you've had with an individual outside of this agency concerning the same ongoing murder investigation, including providing that person with confidential material that is part of the investigation. And Detective Carter has provided us with a fax you sent to a particular individual, again providing that individual with confidential information."

Lonza looked from one to the other. He was truly fucked. What had gone wrong?

"Here's the deal, Detective. Corrections Sergeant Caruso is going to resign and cooperate against you, in return for not being prosecuted. AP Pendergast has agreed to resign and cooperate against you, in return for not being prosecuted. As for you, in return for your resignation, full cooperation, and your agreement that you will be barred from ever being involved in law enforcement in any capacity, anywhere in the country, we are willing to waive indicting you and, instead, file an accusation charging you with one count of hindering an investigation. We are also willing to consent to your admission into the Pretrial Intervention Program. Meaning, if you successfully complete the program, you'll have no criminal conviction, and the charges will be dismissed. This is a one-time offer. You are free to say no. However, if you do, we will take the matter to a grand jury, and we believe there is more than enough to indict you. Your call, Adam."

"What are you doing here?" Swish asked from the doorway to Erin's office.

"Last time I checked, I own half the place," Erin replied, motioning for him to come in. "Have a seat."

"Seriously, why are you here?" he asked, grabbing a seat in one of the three beige club chairs in front of her desk and laying a manila file folder on the desk. "After what you've been through, I didn't expect to see you for at least a couple of weeks."

"And after today, chances are you won't see me for a couple of weeks. But I needed to pick up my car, and so I thought it might be a good idea just to check on my other cases," Erin replied.

"E, everything's under control. Take some time for yourself."

She smiled. "Honest, Swish, I will. Mark and I spent all day yesterday at my mom's, helping her with things, and since Mark doesn't want to miss tonight's b-ball game, we're heading down to Bradley Beach tomorrow morning. He tells me the team captain gets really pissed when people don't show up for games," she said, her smile morphing into a playful grin.

"Knock it off. I didn't expect Mark to be at the game tonight. Just head down this afternoon."

"One thing I've learned about both my partner and my boyfriend is to never make either of them choose between me and a basketball game, because I'm pretty sure I finish second every time," she said with a smirk. "Seriously, I'm okay. Honestly, I don't think things have hit me yet—jail, the beating, my dad—everything's just a blur right now. But I have to come up next week to take my mom to the surrogate's office to probate my dad's will, and I've made an appointment to see my therapist to help me deal with a lot of things, but mostly with the guilt over how things ended with me and my dad."

Swish went to say something, but she continued. "I know what you're going to say. I know that by the day you met with everyone, my dad had really come around and had my back. And I'm really thankful to hear that, but there's a different reality that I need to weave into that narrative, a narrative that's darker than that positive one. Hopefully, I'll get there. But I know myself well enough to realize I'm going to need some professional help to do so."

"E, you've been through some crazy shit. Take as much time as you need. I can hold the fort until you feel comfortable coming back."

"Thanks, Swish. I can't thank you enough for everything. You and Corrine were so much help to everyone. I don't know how to thank both of you."

"No worries. That's what friends are for," he replied.

Erin came around the desk to give him a hug. "Thanks," she said, a small catch in her voice.

Afterward, he handed her the file folder.

"These came in last week while you were out," he said.

When she opened the folder, she immediately inhaled. There were ten color photos—five of her battered face, the other five of the bruises on her torso and arms, and finally a copy of the nurse's report concerning Erin's injuries. "Damn," Erin said, looking up at Swish. "They really kicked the shit out of me. Not sure how I managed to keep all my teeth."

"She wanted you sent to the hospital for an evaluation. She also indicated she thought you had a concussion."

"Yeah, I kind of reached the same conclusion. I was nauseous for a couple of days and really disoriented. Part of it was from being in solitary, but some of it was a head injury."

"Maybe you should get to a doctor now?"

"Sean did a quick physical. He suggested I get a CAT scan, but I haven't had time. Besides, I'd be dead by now if I had an epidural hematoma. And look who's talking. What was it, about six months ago you signed yourself out of the hospital after suffering a severe concussion?"

Swish shrugged. "Whatever. You know you have a lawsuit over what happened?"

"Yeah, I know," she said. "I have time to decide. But if I go ahead, my goal will be to try to force them to get rid of the abusive COs, not the money."

It was a little after five when Acting U.S. Attorney Ed Champion walked into the conference room where AUSA Mary Beth Ford and FBI Special Agent Gerard Pitts were already in place.

"I hear we have some developments. What's going on?"

Ford brought him up to date on what they had learned from Paterson and on the arrest of former NSA officer Walter Johnson, who had been implicated in the Cranford break-in. Pitts gave an update on the cell-tower data that placed Gardner in Avalon and said that the machine-identification-code analysis had led them to a photographer in Margate, who had tentatively identified Gardner as the person who had hired him to take the photos and the one he had given the photos to.

"The last pieces, Ed," Ford said, jumping back in, "are that Dylan Spencer, the person suspected of masquerading as an investigator from the state AG's office, and of taking part in the murders of Evelyn Ketchum and Karen Lawrence, was arrested in Philadelphia. So far, he isn't talking. Same goes for a suspect by the name of Travis Moss. He was picked up by Atlantic City PD and is being held in connection with the murder of Peter Benson, one of the people suspected of being involved in torching Rachel Stern's house."

Champion rubbed his mouth. "Looks like all roads lead to Gardner, but it'll be hard to get him to roll on Townsend." He stopped and sighed. "We have anything that connects Townsend directly to any of this shit?"

"Unfortunately, no, Ed. Even assuming we can get Gardner on some or all of this, I agree it'll be pretty hard to get him to cooperate against Townsend—and that's assuming Townsend knew what Gardner was doing."

"What's Paterson want to do?"

"Honestly, I think he's kind of hoping we make the first move," Ford said. "Let's face it, if or when he goes after Townsend's personal attorney for the murder of Montgomery, the shit is really going to hit the fan for him."

"Yeah, not an enviable position for him to be in," Champion said. "But even if we wanted to go first, we still don't have enough for a RICO. If we try and bring him in now, we won't have anything to scare him with."

"I agree," Ford said.

"All right. Let's do this," Champion said. "Tell Paterson we'll support him with whatever he wants to do, and we understand if he wants to hold off for now. Let him know what our dilemma is but that we're hoping something breaks in a few days or so."

"Got it," Ford said. "I'll let him know."

CHAPTER 38

Wednesday, July 15, 2009, 8:00 p.m.

NO JEEP, GARDNER THOUGHT AS HE DROVE BY THE HOUSE. MC-Cabe's car was out front, but he wasn't sure what it meant that the boyfriend's Jeep wasn't there. It could be they were out together or that she was home by herself. The latter would be the ideal scenario, but even if they were together, he could still ambush them when they got home.

He pulled over and parked several houses down. He didn't have too much time, but he figured he had enough to be patient—wait until dark and see what happens, he thought.

Setting her cup of tea on the night table, Erin propped up the pillows, stretched out on the bed, and cracked open *A Thousand Splendid Suns*. She had picked up the book over a year ago at a local bookstore, but with work and everything going on in her life, it had sat on her bookshelf. Now, with at least ten days at the shore looming, she had decided she wanted to get as far away from work as possible. No Grisham, Turow, or Scottoline this summer; she needed something different. And what could be further away from an American courtroom than the story of two Afghan women?

She hadn't read more than the first paragraph when her Black-Berry started beeping. *Damn*, she thought, as she fumbled for the blasted device. A quick glance at the display caused an immediate rush of concern.

"Michelle?" she answered.

"Oh, Erin, thank God you answered," Michelle said, her voice a mixture of breathless relief and terror. "I don't know what to do. I called Logan, but they didn't answer."

"What's wrong?" Erin asked.

"My ex just called. He had gone out to the grocery store, and when he got home, Hannah was gone. She left a note . . . she said . . . she said she couldn't take it anymore, and she was going to end her life. Oh God, I don't know what to do."

"Did Paul call nine-one-one?"

"I don't know. He said he was going out to search the neighborhood."

"Where does Paul live?"

"He's . . . in South Amboy. Bordentown Street."

"Are you home?"

"Yeah. I'm home."

"Okay, call nine-one-one. You'll connect to Woodbridge. Tell them that you're concerned that your child, who's staying with their father in South Amboy, may be suicidal and explain what you told me. They should be able to patch you through to South Amboy."

"All right . . . I guess."

"Michelle, do you have a landline?"

"Yes."

"What number will Paul call?"

"My cell."

"Then call nine-one-one on your landline. As soon as you hear back from Paul, call me on this number. In the meantime, I'm going to head toward South Amboy. If you don't hear back from Paul in ten minutes, call me."

"All right."

Erin jumped out of bed, threw on jeans and a top, grabbed her BlackBerry, along with a burner she had, threw them in her purse, and ran out the door to her car. As she headed to the Parkway, she called Mark, knowing that she'd have to leave a message because he was in the middle of his game.

"Hey, it's me," she said after the beep. "I'm on my way to South Amboy. Hannah left a note that she's going to commit suicide. I'm heading down to see if I can find her before she hurts herself. I'll check back later when I know more. Oh, and do me a favor and let Swish know what's going on. Thanks."

Before she could even put the phone down, it sprang back to life.

"Yes, Michelle," she answered.

"I spoke with nine-one-one, and even though they gave me a hard time over her name, they reached out to South Amboy for me. And Paul called back. There's no sign of her." Michelle's voice cracked. "There's more. Paul . . . he has a gun . . . it's missing."

"What?"

"Apparently, Paul kept a gun in his night-table drawer, and when he looked just now, it was gone," she said, as she began to sob. "Erin, it's worse, he said he always keeps his gun ready to fire, so all Hannah has to do is pull the trigger. There's no safety. Paul's beside himself."

"Shit," Erin mumbled under her breath. She hated handguns. Too many people did stupid things simply because they had a gun in their hand. *Stay calm*, she thought. "Michelle, think about it, if Hannah wanted to shoot herself, she could have done it at the house. My guess is that she took it just in case . . ." Erin let her voice trail off, not wanting to finish the sentence.

"I keep calling her cell, but she's not answering," Michelle said.

"Wait, Hannah has a cell phone?" Erin asked.

"Yes. I snuck her a burner. I wanted her to be able to call me so her father wouldn't know."

Erin grabbed her burner. "What's the number?" Erin asked and then punched in the numbers as Michelle called them out. Erin hit SEND, and the phone at the other end rang—a good sign, meaning it was at least turned on. After five rings, it went to voice mail. Erin figured it was worthless, but she left a message.

"Where would she be going if she wanted to hurt herself? There's a train that goes through South Amboy, right?"

"Yes, the North Jersey Coast Line. But I can't imagine her stepping in front of a train," Michelle said, her weeping growing more pronounced. "Maybe the bridge?" Michelle said between her sobs.

"The bridge?" Erin asked.

"Yeah, when we were driving from Freehold to Hackettstown and crossed the Raritan River, she said something about reading that someone had recently committed suicide by jumping from the bridge."

Erin tried to put herself into the head of an eleven-year-old. There were three bridges over the Raritan all within a quarter of a mile of each other—the Parkway, Route 9, and Route 35. Hannah would probably be smart enough to realize there was no way for her to walk on the Parkway, and even if she did, she'd quickly be reported by drivers passing by. But right next to it was the Route 9 bridge, and there was also the Victory Bridge that ran between Sayreville and Perth Amboy. Both were only about a mile and a half from South Amboy—a twenty- to thirty-minute walk—and an attractive venue for jumpers.

"Tell Paul to head to the bridge on Route 9. I'm going to head to the Victory Bridge."

"Okay," Michelle replied.

Erin picked up the burner and hit REDIAL.

"Who's this?" a small voice said.

Stay calm, Erin thought. "Hi, Hannah, it's Erin McCabe, one of your lawyers. Where are you?"

"It doesn't matter," Hannah replied.

"Of course, it matters, Hannah. We're all worried you may want to hurt yourself, and we don't want to see that happen."

"No one cares. No one understands how they're torturing me."

"Hannah, people care very much. Think how devastated your mom would be if she lost you."

"She's already lost me. Some judge says I have to be with my dad, and he thinks I'm a freak."

"Being with your dad is only temporary. There's a hearing coming up in which a different court could fix things. And I know it seems like your dad doesn't care, but I really think he does. He's just confused," Erin said, her own dad's struggles circling in the back of her head.

"Everyone's confused, but no one knows what it's like to be me."

"I know what it's like, Hannah."

"How would you know? You may mean well, but you don't know what it's like for me."

"Actually, I do, Hannah. I'm transgender too. I was assigned male at birth, just like you. And I struggled with who I was and how people felt about me for a long time."

"You're just saying that to try and stop me."

"No, Hannah. I'm telling you the truth. I know all about transitioning. I went through it. You and I have a lot in common. I'd really love to talk to you about it. Sometimes it helps to know someone else who has gone through the same things and is doing okay."

"Yeah, well, I bet your dad didn't try to change you and tell you that you were nuts," Hannah said.

"Actually, he did all those things," Erin said. "But like you, I was very lucky because I have a mom who loves me very much and just wants me to be myself and be happy, just like your mom wants for you. As hard as it was for me at times, knowing my mom loved me kept me going." Erin swallowed, trying not to get emotional. "Hannah, where are you? Let's you and I sit and talk."

As Erin waited for a reply, she listened to the background noises, hoping for a clue as to where Hannah was. She could hear the sound of cars, so at least Hannah was still near a road.

"Hannah, are you there? Don't leave me, Hannah. I need to talk to you. I think I can help you, and I think you can help me."

"How can I help you?" Hannah replied after a long silence.

"Because I'm hurting too."

"Why are you hurting?"

"Because my dad just died. And it's really hard to lose someone you love."

"I thought you said your dad tried to stop you."

"He did. But that doesn't mean I didn't love him. He was wrong, and sometimes what he said really hurt me, but in his own way, he acted the way he did because he thought he was protecting me from a world that wouldn't understand me. He thought he was helping, even though he wasn't. But even though my dad made mistakes, it doesn't mean he didn't love me. People sometimes make mistakes." Erin took a deep breath. "Let's talk, Hannah."

"I don't want to go back to the doctor who tries to change me or go to some summer camp to make me a boy."

"You won't, Hannah."

"How can you be sure? No one can be sure."

"You're right. No one can be sure. But I'm really confident that it'll be okay. Your dad was the one who called your mom, terrified you were going to hurt yourself. Your dad just wants you safe. And Logan and I will be there for you."

As she was talking, Erin was flying down the Parkway and now was only about five minutes from South Amboy. She took the exit for Route 9. She knew about a mile down the road there was an exit for Smith Street that would take her to Route 35 and the Victory Bridge.

"Why do these adults talk about me like I'm some kind of freak? I don't know why on the inside I'm a girl, but on the outside I'm not. Why don't people believe me?"

"Because people are always scared of people who aren't like themselves. But you're not a freak, Hannah, any more than I am. And I'm a lawyer, with a boyfriend. I have a business partner who's a great guy, and family and friends who love me. It will get better, Hannah. Trust me, it will."

"I . . . I don't know if I can do it."

"Do what, Hannah?"

"Survive."

"You can, Hannah. There'll be a lot of people who will be there to help you. You're going to grow up to be an amazing woman. And maybe, someday, you'll be there to help someone else. We all have to help each other."

Erin made a right-hand turn onto Route 35. The Victory Bridge loomed a block away. The sun had just set, and dusk was settling in. She had to find her before it got dark.

"Talk to me, Hannah. Let me help. Please tell me where you are."

As Erin made her way up the bridge, she stayed in the right

lane of the two southbound lanes, watching for a solitary figure on the sidewalk. *Come on, Hannah. Where are you?*

"Hannah, honey, you still with me?"

"Yes."

Thank God. "Hannah, I'm on the bridge going from Perth Amboy to Sayreville. Am I close to where you are?"

Erin reached the apex of the bridge, her car halfway in the bike lane and the right-hand lane. Despite a fifty-mile-per-hour speed limit, she flipped on her emergency flasher and slowed to a crawl on the way down, hoping she had guessed right. If she didn't, with the twilight quickly fading, she might not get a second chance.

"Tell me how I can help make things better for you?" Erin said, anxious to get Hannah talking.

"Were you always sure you were a girl?" Hannah asked.

"Yes. I always knew," Erin said, surprised and elated she had asked. "And people didn't believe me at first when I told them, but this is who I've always been."

"Are you happy?" Hannah's voice was now thin.

"Yes, Hannah. I'm very happy, and you will be too."

Cars sped around Erin and horns blared behind her, but her focus was ahead of her. As Erin neared the end of the bridge, a sense of dread enveloped her. And then, there she was. Erin recognized her immediately from the photos they had used at Michelle's bail hearing. Hannah was trudging up the sidewalk, a cell phone in her hand, a backpack strapped to her back.

Erin pulled her car as far to the right as she could, but she was still partially blocking the right lane. She grabbed her BlackBerry, checked the side-view mirror to make sure she could open the car door, and jumped out. She ran up onto the sidewalk and stopped in front of Hannah.

"Hi, Hannah. I'm Erin."

Hannah looked up, her expression registering her fear, her pain, her weariness.

"It's going to be okay, Hannah. You look tired. Let me help you with some of your things," Erin said, offering her hands to Hannah, who slipped her backpack off her shoulders and handed it to Erin. She almost dropped it to the ground, it was so heavy. "What do you have in here, rocks?" Erin asked.

Even though Hannah's face was only illuminated by the streetlight overhead, she appeared to blush. "Um, some weights."

"Why are you carrying weights?" Erin asked.

Hannah stared down at the ground. "I read somewhere that they used to weigh people down when they threw them into the water. So, I thought . . . it would . . . you know."

Erin unzipped the backpack and peered inside. There were four sets of strap-on ankle weights, and a few metal bars that looked like the inserts into a weighted vest. Erin reached in, moved things around, and there was the pistol. She knew very little about guns, and what she did came from the cases she'd handled in which a handgun was involved. But she knew enough to wrap her hand around the handle, making sure her fingers weren't anywhere near the trigger.

To the touch, it wasn't what she expected. She expected something cold and metallic, but it was like holding a solid piece of plastic. It was warm, almost inviting. And as she gently lifted it out of the backpack, ensuring it wasn't pointed at Hannah or herself, she was surprised by how light it felt. She pulled up her top and gently tucked it into the waistband of her jeans.

"How about we give your mom a call, so she knows you're safe?"

Erin hit REDIAL. Michelle picked up on the first ring.

"Hi, Michelle. I have Hannah with me, and I think she'd like to say hello," Erin said, just as a voice boomed behind her.

"Put the phone down."

Erin turned, confused. As she turned, she handed the phone to Hannah.

"I said put the phone down, now!"

Standing about ten feet away was a bald man with a faint goatee who looked vaguely familiar. He was holding a gun pointed directly at Erin.

"Now!" he commanded again.

Erin looked over her shoulder at Hannah, whose eyes were wide with fear.

"Put the phone down, Hannah. He has a gun," Erin said, hopefully loud enough for Michelle to hear her and call nine-one-one.

Hannah crouched down and put the phone on the ground.

When Erin turned back to the mysterious man, it came to her—Michael Gardner, Townsend's personal lawyer. She had seen him in court several times during Sharise Barnes's case.

"Good. Now, McCabe, I don't know who your little friend is, but he doesn't have to see what's going to happen. Just send him on his way, and he'll be fine."

"It's she!" Hannah screamed. "I'm a girl."

Gardner snorted. "What, are you out recruiting new members, McCabe?"

Erin turned to fully face Hannah. "Go ahead. Just start walking away, and when you get up the sidewalk a little bit, start running. I don't want you to get hurt. Please, Hannah. Just go."

As Erin spoke, she reached into her waistband and removed the gun, hoping it was covert enough that the man behind her couldn't tell.

"Go ahead," Erin said, her eyes pleading with Hannah to leave.

Hannah took a few tentative steps backward.

"Go," Erin said more forcefully, causing Hannah to turn and start walking away at a quicker pace.

"Turn around, McCabe. I want to see your fucking face when I put a bullet between your eyes.

Erin had seen enough police shows to know to grip the gun with both hands. She could only hope Costello was right and that, when she pulled the trigger, the gun would actually fire. She figured she'd get off one shot, two if she was lucky. She wasn't sure why, but in that split second before she turned around, she thought of her dad. *See you soon.*

Erin spun around, raising the gun chest-high, and pulled the trigger. The sound was louder and the recoil stronger than she expected. Before she could even bring the gun back down into a firing position, she heard three bangs, and a clang on the railing behind her.

Everything seemed to slow down. Somewhere behind her, Hannah was screaming. Erin wasn't sure whether she hadn't been hit or if she just hadn't felt it yet, but as she brought the gun back to a firing position, she saw Gardner sway and then drop to his knees. As she watched in disbelief, he fell face-first into the pavement. The momentary thought that she had just killed someone was shattered by Hannah's wails.

Oh my God, has she been hit? Erin spun around and ran to Hannah, who was crouched on the sidewalk up ahead.

"Hannah, are you okay?" Erin said, dropping to her knees next to Hannah. Realizing that she still had the gun in her hand, she placed it on the sidewalk. "Hannah, talk to me. Are you okay?"

Hannah looked up at Erin. "You're alive? I thought he killed you." She buried her head in Erin's chest and sobbed. "I thought you were dead."

Me too, Erin thought. "It's okay. I'm okay."

The squeal of the police sirens echoed in all directions, and then a cacophony of voices grew louder. *The cavalry has arrived,* Erin thought, folding her arms around Hannah and holding her tight. Somehow, she and Hannah had survived.

"You," a man's voice bellowed. "Hands up where I can see them."

"It's okay, officer. There's two of us here."

As Erin began to raise her arms, a second voice hollered, "There's a gun!"

Oh shit, she thought.

CHAPTER 39

Wednesday, July 15, 2009, 9:30 p.m.

MARK AND SWISH BURST THROUGH THE DOORS TO THE WAITING area of the emergency room at Raritan Bay Medical Center, frantically scanning the room, looking for someone they knew. Swish suddenly grabbed Mark by the arm.

"Logan," Swish called out, hustling over to where Logan was pacing the waiting area. "What's going on?"

"Damn if I know. No one will tell me a fucking thing," they said. "I told you everything I knew when I called you. Erin had just called Michelle to let her know that Hannah was safe, but then Michelle heard gunshots and screaming, and frantically called nine-one-one. That's what I know. When I got here, there was a small army of law-enforcement types going in and out of the emergency room, and I have no fucking clue as to what's going on. The only thing the triage people will tell me is that Michelle and Paul Costello are here. So, I assume I'm in the right fucking place."

"Does anyone know if Erin is here?" Mark asked, his heart pounding.

Logan gave Mark a "who the fuck are you?" look.

"Logan, this is Mark, Erin's boyfriend," Swish said, after seeing Logan's look.

Logan seemed to relax. "Sorry. Not a clue. They won't tell me a thing."

"I'm going to find out," Mark responded, heading over to the counter.

"Hi. My name is Mark Simpson. I'm trying to find out if my wife is here," he said, knowing if he said girlfriend, he'd get nothing.

The clerk looked up at him. "What's her name?"

"Erin McCabe."

"I thought you said it was your wife."

"She is. What century are you living in? She kept her maiden name."

"Date of birth?"

"August 4th, 1971."

She typed the information into the computer. "Yeah, she's here."

"Is she all right? Can I see her?"

"I have no information on her condition, and no, you can't see her."

"Why not? I'm her husband. I demand to see someone immediately who can tell me how my wife is."

Swish and Logan had made their way over to the counter.

"Mark," Swish said, "call Sean back. Hopefully, he'll know something."

Mark took out his phone.

"I'm sorry, sir. You can't use your cell phone in the hospital," the clerk said.

Mark looked around the waiting area and counted five people on their phones. He closed his eyes and exhaled. "I'll be right outside the door."

Two minutes later, he walked back in. "Anything?" Swish asked.

"He's on his way. They won't tell him anything either." Mark didn't know what it meant that even Sean couldn't get information on Erin, but it left him feeling sick to his stomach. "I'd better go call Peg."

Ed Champion knew that for Abhay Patel to be calling him at nine thirty p.m., something had to be breaking.

"What's going on?" he answered.

"I got a call a few minutes ago from the team that monitors situational awareness alerts put out by local law enforcement. There was a shooting in Sayreville around eight thirty tonight—multiple rounds fired, one person known dead. Tentative ID on the known deceased is Michael Gardner."

"What? Are you fucking kidding me? Gardner?"

"Wish I was," Patel replied. "Apparently, the deceased had documents showing multiple IDs, so we're not certain yet. But a motor vehicle check comes back to Gardner, and the victim fits Gardner's physical description. I sent a team down there to gather info."

"Shit. They know who shot him?" Champion asked.

"You sitting down?"

"Yeah," Champion replied, resignation creeping into his voice.

"Erin McCabe," Patel answered.

"Sweet Jesus. You can't make this shit up," Champion responded. "Did you let Pitts know?"

"He's on his way to the hospital now. From what I'm told, McCabe and another person at the scene were taken to Raritan Bay Medical Center. And assuming your next question is why—the answer is, I don't know."

"I know you've already thought about this, but without Gardner the already slim odds of us getting to Townsend just went to zero," Champion said.

"Yeah, there's a lot more to this that I haven't put together yet," Patel replied. "You want me to call you after I hear from Pitts?"

"Yeah, sounds good. I won't be able to sleep anyway," he added with a small laugh.

Thirty minutes later, Pitts walked up to the counter of the emergency room and flashed his credentials.

"FBI Special Agent Gerard Pitts—I'm here to see Detective Kavanaugh," he said.

"Gerry," a voice called from across the room. Pitts turned to see his former colleague, Duane Swisher, walking toward him. "Hey, Swish," he said warmly, extending his hand. "Nice to see you."

"Likewise," Swish replied. "Any chance you're here because of a shooting tonight on the Victory Bridge?"

"I am, but if you're going to ask me for info, I don't have any. That's why I'm here, to find out what the hell is going on."

"I believe my partner is somehow involved, but the hospital won't tell us anything. I don't know if she's hurt or what her status is. Her name is Erin McCabe. Anything you can tell me?"

Gerry gave him a sympathetic look. "Honest, Swish. I really don't know anything. Once I get back there and speak with the detectives, if there's any information I can get to you, I will. Promise."

"Special Agent Pitts?" a voice called from the door leading to the medical section of the ER.

Pitts looked over his shoulder. "Yeah," he replied. He turned back to Swish. "Let me see what I can find out," he offered before turning and heading back into the ER.

The nurse led Pitts to a door and knocked. "Yeah," a voice called out. She cracked open the door. "Special Agent Pitts," she said. "Yeah," the voice called out again.

The nurse pushed open the door, and Pitts walked into a conference room where, by his quick count, ten people were either seated at a conference table or standing in various locations around the room. He vaguely recognized a couple of people as being with the Middlesex County Prosecutor's Office; he had no clue who the others were. A guy at the door asked to see his credentials, which Pitts showed him.

"I'm Assistant Prosecutor Phil Marsh, director of Homicide," a guy at the table said. "To what do we owe the honor of the FBI showing up at our little party?"

His tone was less than welcoming.

"I understand there's been a shooting and one of the victims may be an individual by the name of Michael Gardner. Is that accurate?" Pitts asked.

"It is," Marsh replied.

"What can you tell me about the shooting?" Pitts asked.

"What can you tell me about why you're here?" Marsh responded.

"Let's just say Mr. Gardner is a person the FBI has an interest in," Pitts said.

"Well, that tells me absolutely nothing," Marsh shot back.

"Good," Pitts replied with a wry smile. "Now, please tell me about Mr. Gardner."

Marsh's eyes narrowed. "He was shot. He's dead. We're still investigating the circumstances. Anything else you want to know?"

"Do you know who shot him?"

"We're working on it.

A woman suddenly walked in, causing those seated around the table to stand. She looked to be in her mid-forties, medium height, slim build, long blond hair, dressed in jeans and a prosecutor's office windbreaker.

"Tell me what's going on," she ordered, taking a seat at the table.

"Um," Marsh stumbled, "we have an FBI special agent here," he said, nodding his head in Pitts's direction.

The woman turned around and extended her hand. "Vanessa Talon, Middlesex County prosecutor. Nice to meet you."

"Thank you, Madam Prosecutor. Special Agent Gerard Pitts. Nice to meet you as well."

"Call me Vanessa. All these guys call me much worse behind my back." She turned back so she was looking at Marsh. "Jesus, Phil. Don't get your shorts in a knot because the FBI showed up at your party. You guys and your turf wars. Remember, I was with the U.S. Attorney's Office before I became the prosecutor." She let out a small snort and looked back at Pitts. "Bugs the shit out of them that I was a fed and not part of one of the local old boys' clubs." She returned her gaze to Marsh. "Talk to me, Phil," she commanded.

"There was a shooting tonight on the Victory Bridge, one person deceased. The deceased person is Michael Gardner. Age sixty-three."

"Wait," Talon interrupted. "Is this the Michael Gardner who's counsel to Senator Townsend?"

"Yeah," Marsh replied.

"Has anyone reached out to the senator? Is he in any danger?"

"We did connect with the senator's chief of staff and made him aware. As to whether the senator is in any danger, we're not sure at this point, but we alerted the state police to add to his security detail."

"Okay," Talon said, motioning for him to continue.

"There were two other people at the scene of the shooting. An attorney by the name of Erin McCabe and an eleven-year-old child by the name of Nicholas Costello."

"Okay, why are those names familiar?"

After Marsh explained why Talon knew of them, he continued. "We originally believed McCabe shot Gardner, but we no longer believe that to be the case."

"Why?" Talon asked.

"McCabe said she had taken one shot at Gardner with a Glock 9mm, which was recovered at the scene, and her statement of firing one shot is consistent with the clip in the weapon. However, a physical examination of Gardner's body indicates he was shot three times in the back."

"Sounds pretty convincing to me that McCabe didn't shoot him," Talon said. "Do we know who the second shooter is?"

"Not at this time," Marsh replied.

"And why was McCabe taking a shot at Gardner?" she asked.

Marsh scratched the back of his head. "At least according to the kid and McCabe, because Gardner was going to shoot McCabe."

"That's a pretty damn good reason, in my book," Talon said, her mouth curled into a frown. "Where are McCabe and the child now?"

"McCabe's in the room next door, and the child is with his parents in a room farther down the hallway."

"Why is McCabe in the room next to us?" Talon said, her face scrunched in confusion.

"She's under arrest."

"For what?" Talon said, her voice rising.

"Well . . . well, originally, for murder, but when we learned that she hadn't shot him, we decided to hold her for illegal possession of a firearm," Marsh said.

Talon shook her head. "This just keeps getting better and better. So where'd she get the gun?"

"The kid," Marsh replied.

Talon drew in a deep breath. "And, Philip, where did the child get the gun, pray tell?"

"From his father."

"Let me back up," Talon said, her frustration evident. "This is the transgender kid where McCabe is representing the mother that we've charged with interfering with custody, right?"

Marsh nodded.

"Okay. Why were McCabe and the child together on the bridge?" she asked, throwing her hands up as if pleading for an answer.

"The child had indicated that he was going to kill himself. McCabe was able to call the child and stop him."

Talon placed her arms on the table and folded her hands together. "Let me see if I've got this straight. McCabe saves a kid from killing him . . . themselves; someone tries to kill McCabe; someone else kills the person who is trying to kill McCabe; and we arrest McCabe, originally on murder but now on weapons charges. Do I have this right?" her tone expressing her incredulity.

"Um, yeah. Basically," Marsh replied.

"Who the hell is the genius that thought this was a good idea? We should be pinning a medal on McCabe, but instead we arrest her. I realize you all no doubt have qualified immunity to protect yourselves from your own stupidity, so she'll probably never be able to successfully sue your sorry asses for false arrest, but I can't believe this."

"Ahh, there's probably one other thing you should know about McCabe's arrest," Marsh said, a hesitation in his voice.

"Oh, do pray tell," Talon replied sarcastically.

"A couple of cops from Perth Amboy PD roughed her up a bit when they pulled her and the kid apart because they saw the gun lying next to her."

"Wonderful. Is she badly hurt?"

"No. Just some bruises."

Talon brushed her blonde hair back from her face. "And why are Mom, Dad, and the child in a room down the hall?"

"The hospital wants to do a psych eval on the child because he was admittedly suicidal. Neither Mom nor Dad wants the eval; they just want to leave with their child."

"And what's our dog in that fight?" Talon asked.

"Dad has sole custody, and the child refuses to leave with Dad," Marsh responded.

"I don't believe this," she said, standing. "Is McCabe cuffed? Of course, she is, because we have her under arrest." Talon raised her eyes to the ceiling. "Who has the keys to her cuffs?"

"The officer outside her door," Marsh replied.

"Local?" she asked.

"Arresting municipality," Marsh replied. "Sayreville PD."

"Anyone here with Sayreville?" she said to the folks in the room.

"I am," said a detective in the far corner.

"Good. Come with me,"

"Agent, you want to come with me too?" she said to Pitts.

"I'd love to," he replied with a grin.

"Oh," she said, spinning around to face Marsh, "we are dropping all charges against McCabe, and tell Beasley I want to talk to him. What happened tonight proves exactly what the child's mother feared was going to happen—they were going to drive the child to harm . . . themselves." She craned her head and looked around the room. "By the looks of all the testosterone in here, I'll presume I'm the only mother in the room. So, I understand exactly what the child's mom did and why. Maybe we're right on the law, but we're a hundred percent wrong on making sure we're doing what we need to do to protect this child." She scowled. "And if I hear that any one of you made a crack about me saying I was the only *mother* in the room," she said with air quotes, "I'll have your badge!" She turned, caught Pitts's eye, and winked. "Let's go see Ms. McCabe."

When Talon and Pitts were in the hallway, she asked, "You here because of McCabe or Gardner?"

"Gardner," he replied.

"Got it," she said.

The three of them walked down the hallway to where an officer was standing guard.

"I need you to uncuff the prisoner," the Sayreville detective said.

"Sure," the officer responded, turning and opening the door.

Erin was seated in a chair with her hands cuffed behind her back, riding an emotional rollercoaster—thrilled to be alive, upset that she had shot someone, and livid that, once again, no one would listen to her when she explained that she had acted in self-defense.

She was startled when the door suddenly opened and an officer walked in. Not knowing why he was there, she flinched as he walked next to her. He then went behind her and unlocked the cuffs, put them back on his utility belt, and walked away. Erin began rotating her arms and rubbing her wrists, trying to work out the stiffness that had resulted from sitting there with her hands cuffed behind her. *This is getting old*, she thought. As she was doing that, a woman and a man walked into the room, and a second man stood in the doorway.

"Ms. McCabe, I'm Middlesex County Prosecutor Vanessa Talon," she said.

Erin looked up. *What the hell is the prosecutor doing here?* "Nice to meet you," Erin said, trying to hide her confusion.

"This is Special Agent . . . sorry, I forgot your name."

"Gerard Pitts," he said.

"Look, Ms. . . . can I call you Erin?" Talon asked.

Erin, still baffled as to what was going on, decided to go with the flow.

"Sure," Erin responded.

"Good. Erin, I understand you were told you were arrested for murder and unlawful possession of a weapon. I'm here to tell you there will be no formal charges filed against you of any kind. I also want to personally apologize for what you've been through, and I will confess that I'm still trying to understand what happened tonight. That said, would you mind coming with me to talk to the child you saved and their parents?"

"Not at all."

"Vanessa," Pitts interrupted, "could I ask the detective to do me a favor? Out in the waiting room are some people waiting to get information on Ms. McCabe, which, of course, the hospital couldn't give because she was in custody. Is it all right if he goes out and tells them Ms. McCabe is safe and well and will be out in a little bit?"

"Of course. Is there anyone in particular the detective should ask for?"

"Yeah, Duane Swisher."

When the door opened and Hannah saw Erin, she jumped up and ran and threw her arms around her waist and buried her head in her chest.

"I saw them hit you and put handcuffs on you. I tried to tell them you saved me, but they wouldn't listen. I was so afraid I'd never see you again."

"I'm okay," Erin said, returning the hug and wincing at the jolt of pain in her rib cage.

Hannah broke off her hug and grabbed Erin by the hand, leading her over to where her parents were standing. "She saved my life," Hannah said. "She's just like me, and she's a lawyer."

Michelle threw her arms around Erin's neck. "Thank you," she whispered. "Thank you, thank you, thank you."

"You're welcome," Erin replied.

"I need to thank you too," Paul said, reaching out and shaking Erin's hand. "Hannah told us what you did tonight. I don't know how to thank you."

"Did you hear that, Erin?" Hannah said, beaming. "My dad called me Hannah."

"I noticed," Erin replied with a wide smile.

Prosecutor Talon stepped forward and introduced herself to everyone. "Listen, folks, I know everyone has been through a lot tonight, and I'd like to get you all on your way, but I understand we have a little issue. Mr. and Mrs. Costello, let me get a doc in here to talk to the two of you and Hannah. Hannah, I'm hoping you don't want to kill yourself anymore. Do I have that right?"

"Yes, ma'am," Hannah replied.

"Good. Assuming the doc clears Hannah to go home, I understand there's still a custody issue to deal with."

"Miss Prosecutor," Paul said, "we've had some time to talk. Or maybe I should say that I've had some time to listen. I know I've never been the dad Hannah deserved, but over the last two months, I have really managed to mess up her and her mother's lives. I've also stood by silent when things were said about them that just weren't true. I guess I was confused when I learned Hannah was transgender and changing her name, and I let a 'friend' at work introduce me to the folks at the ALDA. Honestly, I bought what they told me because I was embarrassed. But I realized tonight that I was wrong. There's nothing embarrassing about"— he paused—"my daughter. And if Hannah will let me, I'd like to be part of her life. And I can start by recognizing she belongs with her mother. We'll work it out."

Hannah looked up at Erin, who had tears rolling down her cheeks. "I remember what you told me tonight about your dad," Hannah said. "Is that why you're crying?"

"You are a very perceptive young lady," Erin said, a catch in her voice.

As they talked through things, it was agreed that because of the court orders and criminal charges against Michelle, until they could get the court to change custody, Paul would stay in Michelle's basement and, in that way, continue to technically have custody of Hannah. He had also asked to meet with the prosecutor to discuss having the charges against Michelle dropped.

It was almost midnight when Erin and Mark arrived home.

"You want a glass of wine?" Mark asked, as Erin collapsed onto the couch.

"Sounds good. We have anything open?" she asked.

"There's still some Grgich Hills Chardonnay."

"That sounds wonderful," she said.

He walked back into the room carrying two glasses of wine, sat down next to her, and handed her one. "Cheers," he said, tapping his glass against hers.

"Cheers," she responded. "And thanks," she added.

"For what?" he asked.

She leaned up against him and took a sip. "For putting up with all the stuff going on in my life. It's been a crazy month and a half."

"Don't worry about me. I'm fine. But you're right. You haven't even had time to grieve your dad. So, yeah, I'm worried about you." He hesitated. "Perhaps I'm being too optimistic, but with this guy Gardner dead, do you think all the efforts to ruin your life or, worse, kill you are finally over?"

She looked up at him with her bloodshot eyes. "No," she said without hesitation. "I suspect that Gardner didn't decide who lived or died, as evidenced by what happened to him tonight. He just followed orders. My guess is the plan was for him to take me out, and then he was going to be taken out. I just kind of screwed up the timing by taking a shot at him. According to what the prosecutor told me, my shot didn't even hit him, but whoever was waiting to kill him probably thought I was firing at them and went ahead. I have a feeling that someone will be very unhappy tomorrow morning when they find out I'm still alive."

"Who?" he asked.

"Townsend," she said. "Soon to be Governor William E. Townsend," she said with an air of resignation.

They both grew quiet, letting the implications of that settle in.

"Shit, that's not good," Mark finally said. "Do you think Townsend has you under surveillance? I mean, how did Gardner even know where you were tonight?"

"They found a GPS tracking device in his car. Which means somewhere on my car there's a transponder hidden."

She suddenly sat up, placed her wineglass on the coffee table, and scurried to grab her cell phone.

"What are you doing?" he asked.

His question went unanswered as she hit the preset for Swish's phone.

"Swish. Sorry to bother you so late, but the FBI agent that was there tonight . . ."

"Pitts," he said.

"Yeah, I saw him give you his business card."

"Yeah. Why?"

"You need to reach him now."

"Now? It's midnight. Why now?"

"Because we have to get the FBI to take possession of Gardner's car. I'm sure there's a transponder on my car, and that's how Gardner was able to follow me. I'm also betting that there's a transponder on Gardner's car, and that's how whoever killed him was able to follow him."

"Meaning," Swish said, his voice growing excited as he jumped in to finish her thought, "that the transponder would be traceable back to whoever was receiving the data."

"Bingo!" she said. "And given all of Townsend's connections, if the locals keep Gardner's car, any transponder that's there just might disappear."

"I'm on it," Swish said.

CHAPTER 40

Tuesday, July 21, 2009, 9:30 a.m.

"SENATOR, THANK YOU FOR AGREEING TO MEET WITH US ON such short notice," Ed Champion said.

"Listen, when the U.S. Attorney calls and says he wants to discuss the murder of my dear friend and personal attorney Michael Gardner, that's good enough reason for me to clear my schedule and make the time," Townsend said with a gracious smile. "I will confess, I didn't expect the entire entourage."

Townsend's calm exterior betrayed a sense of foreboding that was building like thunderclouds before the arrival of the storm. With his fake smile still pasted on his lips, Townsend's eyes swept across the folks from the FBI and U.S. Attorney's Office assembled in his conference room. But as his gaze settled on Gordon Paterson, he realized it was his presence that unnerved him the most. *What the hell is he doing here—especially with all the feds?* And as disconcerting as his presence was, the fact that Paterson's demeanor seemed different was particularly unsettling. No longer the sycophant trying to garner favor, he now appeared confident and at ease.

"Because of Michael's awful murder, I hope you don't mind, but I asked Frank McDonald, who I assume most of you know, to be here," he continued. "Frank has helped my family out in the past, and without Michael, I felt I should have someone here."

"I think we all know Mr. McDonald, and not only is he welcome, I'm glad he's here," Champion replied.

Townsend's unease grew. *Why is he glad McDonald is here?*

"If you don't mind," Champion continued, "I'm going to let Gordon, who I understand you are acquainted with, give you some information."

"Will," Gordon began, "when we've met in the past, I've assured you that we would uncover who murdered Bradford Montgomery. I'm here to tell you that my office, with the help of the U.S. Attorney's Office and the FBI, now have the answer to that question." Gordon paused, his expression hardening. "Mr. Montgomery was murdered by Michael Gardner."

"What! Are you out of your mind?" Townsend erupted. "How dare you come in here and malign Michael like that. The man isn't even dead a week, and you're trying to pin a murder on him. This is outrageous."

"That's a very serious allegation, Mr. Paterson," McDonald interjected calmly. Do you have anything to back that up?"

"We do. With the help of the FBI, we were able to discover that Arnold Welch's campaign server was hacked. The hacker has been arrested and has provided a statement implicating Mr. Gardner in hiring him. The FBI can also place Mr. Gardner in Avalon, New Jersey, on Memorial Day, the day Mr. Montgomery was murdered. In addition, a Travis Moss is now cooperating and has implicated Mr. Gardner in the arson at the home of a Rachel Stern, a close personal friend of Mr. Montgomery. Ms. Stern was targeted because her cell-phone records confirm that Mr. Gardner contacted Mr. Montgomery minutes before his death on a cell phone Montgomery had on Ms. Stern's plan. According to Mr. Moss, Mr. Gardner also ordered the murders of the individuals who actually started the fire at Stern's residence."

Townsend couldn't believe what he was hearing—they had put it all together. *Fuck!*

"Mr. Gardner," Paterson continued, "also had a tracking transponder placed on a vehicle owned by Erin McCabe, the original suspect in Mr. Montgomery's murder, which allowed for the tracking of Ms. McCabe's vehicle in real time. The monitoring device was discovered in Mr. Gardner's vehicle. We believe he followed Ms. McCabe with the intention of murdering her—a fact confirmed by statements from both Ms. McCabe and a child who was also at the scene. Finally, and most important, the Union County Prosecutor's Office has recovered the knife used to murder Mr. Montgomery. According to the statement of Walter Johnson, the knife was given to him by Mr. Gardner for the purpose of planting it in an apartment rented by Erin McCabe, who, as I noted, was the initial target of our investigation, and who is an attorney well known to the senator and Mr. Gardner."

"I've had enough of this," Townsend said, rising out of his chair. "I won't stand by and watch as you attempt to blame a man who honorably served his country and isn't here to defend his reputation. You think it's a coincidence that all these people are trying to pin the blame on Michael right after he was murdered? I suggest you all leave."

"Senator, I'm afraid we're not leaving just yet," Champion said, his tone commanding the attention of everyone in the room. "I'm going to provide you with your Miranda rights, so that's why it's good that Mr. McDonald is here to advise you concerning those rights."

"Miranda? Ed, are you suggesting that Senator Townsend is a target of your investigation?"

"Correct, Frank. My only correction would be that he's not *a* target of our investigation, he's *the* target of our investigation," Champion replied.

Townsend slowly sank back into his chair, trying to process what was happening. *Who can I get to stop this?*

Champion then proceeded to read Townsend his rights, and when he was finished, he handed the acknowledgment form to McDonald.

Townsend signed the form and glared first at Paterson and then at Champion.

"This is a setup, and I am not waiving my rights. Are we finished now?"

"No," Champion responded. "As a courtesy, and given that what I am about to tell you may impact your campaign, I want you to know that my office has convened a grand jury, and we are presenting evidence seeking to indict you on a RICO conspiracy. We are currently executing search warrants at your homes to seize your home surveillance system and computers. I have with me a warrant to seize your cell phone. You should also know that the FBI discovered a GPS transponder on Mr. Gardner's vehicle. Through that transponder we were able to locate the monitoring device. We have arrested two individuals, one of whom has admitted to being the driver of the vehicle that followed Mr. Gardner to the location where he was shot. That individual also implicated the second person we arrested as the shooter. Based on the serial number of the devices, we were able to confirm who purchased the device. A member of your staff provided a statement that it was done at your request, and he provided a copy of an expense voucher he supplied to your campaign to be reimbursed. The driver of the vehicle also implicated Victor Marion as the person who had hired him and provided them with the tracking monitor. Mr. Marion was also arrested over the weekend and has agreed to cooperate with the investigation and testify before the grand jury concerning conversations he had with you—in particular, a conversation at the White House Diner, which, unbeknownst to you, he recorded. Based on you invoking your Fifth Amendment right to remain silent, we will not ask you any questions, and unless you or Mr. McDonald have any questions of us, we will collect your phone and leave."

Townsend placed his hands on the table and leaned forward. "You are nothing but a Democratic hack trying to destroy me and my run for governor. I won't stand for this. I know some very powerful people, and I am not going to take this lying down. Frank will fight you at every turn, and when this is over, all of you," he said with a sweep of his hand, "especially you," he said, pointing at Paterson, "will rue the day you came after me. Now get out."

After a brief discussion with McDonald over searching Townsend's cell phone, the five of them rose.

"Call me if you wish to discuss anything," Champion said to McDonald, before they filed out of the office.

"Will, do you mind telling me what the hell is going on? When you called me, you told me you were concerned about Michael, but if they can back up half of what they just laid on the table, you have a serious problem," Frank said after they were gone.

"This is all bullshit," Townsend screamed. "They don't have anything on me. I told you I thought Michael might be up to some crazy shit."

"Will, I hear you. But we'll have our work cut out for us to prove that's all bullshit. Did you meet with this guy Marion, who they say taped you in the diner?"

Townsend put his hands on his head and began rocking back and forth. "We had breakfast. I have breakfast with a lot of people. He's . . . lying. He hated Michael, and this must be his attempt to get even."

"Will, let me meet with Champion next week and see if he's bluffing. We need to start working on this immediately, especially given the impact this will have on your campaign."

"You're right, but I need some time to collect my thoughts. They're just trying to destroy my campaign. It's nothing but a smear job, and I need to figure out how I'm going to deal with the fallout. I'm a survivor, Frank, and I'm not going to sit here and feel sorry for myself. I just need some time to figure out how I fight back, because I will destroy them."

"That's fine. But they already have a grand jury impaneled, so we need to get on this. Let me know when you want to get together. I'll also get a retainer letter out to you. Don't want to run afoul of the ethics rules."

"Of course. Do what you need to do," Townsend said.

Townsend walked McDonald out to the front office. "I'll give you a call later," he said, shaking McDonald's hand. "I'm glad I have you on my side."

After McDonald left, Townsend asked his receptionist if there were any calls.

"Yes, Senator. The phone hasn't stopped ringing. Mr. Corliss has called several times," she said. "He asked that you call him as soon as you finish your meeting so he can readjust your schedule for the rest of the day."

"Thank you, Judy. I'll get right back to him. Um, could you do me a favor? Could you walk down to the Dunkin' Donuts and pick me up a couple of jelly donuts? I didn't get any breakfast this morning." He pulled a money clip out of his pants pocket and peeled off a twenty-dollar bill. "And get yourself whatever you'd like."

"Of course, Senator," she said, grabbing her purse.

He walked into his office and closed the door.

Fuck. How did things get fucked up so badly? He momentarily wondered how his wife, Sheila, would react; she'd been a basket case since Bill had been killed. Either way, it wouldn't be good.

He walked over to his desk and unlocked the top drawer. He stared at the gun for several seconds before he took it out and laid it on the desk. He remembered his last conversation with Michael—the next time they'd see each other would be in hell. His hand shook a little as he took the Glock by the handle and raised it to his temple.

I wonder what it's like? Am I going to see Michael in hell, or maybe it's like Tony Soprano, fade to black—it's just nothing. Nothing sounds pretty damn good. Here's hoping for nothing.

CHAPTER 41

ERIN LET HERSELF IN AND MADE HER WAY TO THE KITCHEN, WHERE her mother was taking bacon out of a cast-iron skillet.

"Hi, Mom," she said, as she gave her mother a peck on the cheek.

"I hope you don't mind eating in as opposed to the diner. We just have so much to catch up on . . ." She stopped. "They're not saying much on the news about how Senator Townsend died. I was just wondering if you have any gossip on what happened."

"He killed himself," Erin replied without emotion.

Her mother moved the skillet off the burner, put down the spatula, wiped her hands on her apron, and led Erin by the arm over to the kitchen table. "How do you know that?"

"Swish and I spoke with an FBI agent who's part of an investigation," Erin replied.

"Why? Was he in trouble?" Peg asked.

"Yeah, from what they were able to tell us, it sounds like everything had finally caught up with him."

"Good," her mom said. "I know I shouldn't speak ill of the dead, but he was not a good man."

"No, he wasn't. I suspect a lot of people lost their lives because of him and his henchman."

As her mother sat in rapt attention, Erin proceeded to tell her everything that she could about what had happened since Memorial Day weekend.

"Oh, sweet mother of God," Peg said thirty minutes later when Erin was finished. "I'm sorry, dear. You came for breakfast, and here I am making you tell me about all these sordid things. How would you like your eggs?"

"Mom, before we eat, can we talk?"

"Of course, honey. What's on your mind?"

"Well, let's start with, how are you doing? I feel so guilty that I haven't been here for you. I mean, it's been two weeks since Dad died, and I've been mostly MIA."

Peg reached across the kitchen table and patted Erin's hand. "I appreciate your concern, dear. But there certainly have been a few things going on in your life. Please don't feel guilty. I'm okay. Honestly, it's not too hard during the day. I have plenty of things to do. It's from dinnertime on when things get hard. Your dad and I always enjoyed having dinner together. I'd tell him about my day, he'd tell me about his—we enjoyed each other's company. I miss that a lot. He was more of a television watcher than I was; I still prefer to read a book. But when we went to bed, it was nice to lie next to him . . ." Peg shot her an apologetic look. "I'm sure you don't want to hear this, no child can ever imagine their parents having sex, but we still had a good sex life. I know it's probably hard for you to imagine your father as a good lover, but he was. And I'm really going to miss that."

Peg wiped away a tear from the corner of her eye, then drew in a breath and exhaled.

"I can't tell you how many times I've played back his last night in my mind," Peg continued. "Wondering whether if I had been with him, I could have saved him."

"You know from what Sean told you that you couldn't have done anything," Erin interjected.

"Yes, dear. I know what Sean's told me. But Sean is also my child and, I suspect, willing to color the truth to make things easier on me."

"Mom, I looked it up. I really think Sean leveled with you."

Her mother frowned. "Well, my dear, as you well know, some of us feel guilty even when we're not responsible for what happened. Kind of like you feeling guilty over what happened the last time you were here with your father. How many times have you played that back in your mind?"

"Don't know," Erin said with a shake of her head. "Lost count."

"Exactly my point," Peg replied. "I've told you, and I know Sean and Liz have told you that your father felt awful about what happened and was looking forward to making things right with you."

Erin smiled. "I hate to throw your words back at you, but you're my mom, Sean's my brother, and Liz is my sister-in-law. It wouldn't shock me if you all agreed to color the truth to make things easier on me."

"There are times when you are frighteningly like me," Peg said with a sad smile. "Erin, your father loved you with his whole being. He didn't understand you at all, but if it's any consolation, I don't think he understood me either. It didn't stop him from loving me. But just because he struggled to understand you doesn't mean he didn't love you."

"Mom, I embarrassed him. Do you know how that makes me feel—to know that when people brought me up, he'd cringe?"

"Erin McCabe, you should not feel bad about that. How many times did Mark stop dating you before he finally came around to loving you? And why was it so hard for him? Because he was worried about what other people might think. He saw you as a reflection on him. Men are like that. Why do you think so many men dump the women they've been married to for years—often the mothers of their children—to marry a trophy wife half their age? It all has to do with the fragile male ego. Stop beating yourself up over that. Just like Mark, your dad would've gotten there."

Peg reached into her apron pocket. "Here, this is for you," she said, handing Erin an envelope.

Erin looked at the envelope and then at her mom. "Why are you giving this to me? This is the letter I wrote to Dad from jail."

"Look at the envelope," Peg replied.

Erin turned the envelope sideways so she could see a word

scrawled on the envelope. "'Save,'" she read. "I recognize Dad's handwriting. Why did he want to save it?"

"All he told me was he wanted to talk to you about it."

Erin slid the letter out of the envelope. She immediately noticed two phrases she had written that were underlined, *I love you*, and *I'm happy with who I am.*

Erin fought to hold back her tears. "Thanks," she whispered.

They sat in silence, both of them lost in their own thoughts.

"How do you want your eggs?" Peg finally asked as she got up from the table.

After they finished breakfast, they sat around chatting about Peg's health, Erin's relationship with Mark, Sean and Liz, and, of course, Patrick and Brennan.

"Speaking of the boys," Peg said, in her usual way of saying something totally unrelated, "I was reading an article about a lawsuit in New Jersey over surrogacy, and it made me think about you."

"Why? I'm not exactly in the position to be a surrogate mom."

"Well, you told me once that before you transitioned you had banked your sperm in the hope that it might help save your marriage."

"That's true. I did."

"Is it still banked?"

Erin gave her mother a quizzical look. "Yeah."

"Think about it. You could have a woman act as a surrogate and carry your baby and have a child of your own."

"I guess," Erin said.

"Have you ever thought about being a mom?"

"Yeah, I have," Erin replied somewhat wistfully.

"So."

"So, what?" Erin replied.

"Think about it." Peg stood up and came over to where Erin was sitting, leaned over, and hugged her. "You'd be a wonderful mom." And then, almost as an afterthought, added, "And we already know I'm a wonderful grandmother."

CHAPTER 42

Tuesday, August 4, 2009

IN THE DAYS AFTER TOWNSEND'S DEATH, WORD HAD GOTTEN OUT that he had committed suicide, but despite rumors, no one seemed to know why. Then, as a series of guilty pleas occurred in state and federal courts in which the plea allocutions referenced Gardner and sometimes Townsend, several newspapers had run articles trying to connect the dots and explain how all the pleas were related. Finally, Nancy David, the New Jersey reporter for WNYC, broke the story that put all the pieces together.

Logan was finally able to get custody of Hannah returned to Michelle. Of course, it was made easier by Paul's consent and, despite the objections of the ALDA, his agreement to dismiss his lawsuit seeking custody. As part of the agreement, Paul was given liberal visitation rights.

Erin and Duane had met with Middlesex County Prosecutor Vanessa Talon, and she agreed to dismiss the charges against Michelle now that the custody issues were settled.

With both Gardner and Townsend gone, Rachel finally came out of hiding. And although neither said anything, Erin suspected that despite the differences in their ages, Rachel and Logan's relationship had developed into something more than a platonic friendship while they were living together.

* * *

"Happy birthday," Swish said from the doorway to Erin's office. "What are you doing here? I thought you were finally taking some time off. It's your birthday, for crying out loud."

Erin beckoned Swish in with a wave of her hand. "Thank you," she said with a wide grin. "I'm leaving soon—honest. I just have a few things to take care of before I take off. Plus, I promised Hannah I'd try and get to the courthouse later. Her name-change hearing is today."

"Good for her," he said. "Also, just so you know, I did receive the order dismissing the criminal complaint against you in Cape May. I'll prepare the paperwork to get the record of the criminal complaint and your arrest record expunged so you can honestly say you've never been arrested."

"Thanks," Erin replied. "It kind of stinks that you have to affirmatively move to have your records and arrest expunged, even when you're completely exonerated. I'm sure there's lots of people who don't know that or can't afford to do it."

"Unfortunately, that's very true."

"And I know that I have to make a decision as to whether I'm going to sue the Cape May Correctional Center. But right now, I prefer not to think of any of that stuff. Although I did get an interesting voice-mail message from Sylvia Walker's attorney."

"Who's Sylvia Walker?" Swish asked.

"The woman in my cell who I thought was going to testify that I confessed to her."

"Oh yeah. What happened with her?"

"Her attorney struck a plea deal, based on a motion to suppress I told her to have him file and her willingness to testify against the officer who had approached her to set me up. Not sure what she pled to, but he said she was being sentenced to time served, and both of them wanted to thank me for my help."

"Sounds like you did pretty good as a jailhouse lawyer," Swish said with a laugh.

"Thanks," Erin replied, giving him a dirty look. "Listen, Mark and I are going to be in Bradley Beach until at least August 16th. I really hope you, Cori, and the kids come to visit."

"Let's play it by ear. You really need to get some R and R—something I can guarantee you won't get if the four of us are there."

"You know how much I love your family. It's never a problem."

"We'll see. You go and have a good time, and enjoy your birthday."

She got up from behind her desk, went over to where he was standing, and wrapped her arms around him. "Thank you, Swish. I don't know that I could have survived this mess if it weren't for you being with me every step along the way. I owe you."

"All you owe me is to come back rested and healthy."

"Thanks, big guy. You got it."

Gordon Paterson stood next to his mother, staring down at the headstone that bore his father's name.

"Why did you want to come here, Gordie?" his mother asked.

He put his arm around her shoulders and gave her a gentle hug. "I know how Dad dreamed that one day I'd be the Cape May County Prosecutor. But a couple of months ago, I decided that I wouldn't sell my soul to get the job. I decided it was more important to do what was right, even if it ruined my chances of being prosecutor."

His mother stared up at him. "You did the right thing, Gordie. I know how much your dad regretted helping Townsend. I know he'd be proud of the choices you made."

Gordon leaned over and kissed his mother on the top of her head. "I hope so. I always wanted to make Dad proud of me," he said, choking on his emotions.

She squeezed him a little tighter. "He always was, and I'm sure he still is."

Hannah stood between her parents, trying not to fidget.

"Can I have appearances, please?"

"Good afternoon, Your Honor. Logan Stevens on behalf of Michelle Costello, the mother of the minor child, seeking to allow her to formally assume the name Hannah Costello."

"Paul Costello, pro se, Judge. And I'm Hannah's father."

"Thank you. The record should reflect that counsel alerted me prior to this afternoon's hearing of the confidential nature of this afternoon's proceeding and the desire of Michelle and Paul Costello to avoid any unnecessary publicity concerning these proceedings. Accordingly, I have held this matter until the end of the day, and other than the parties and my staff, no one else is present. I will enter an order at the conclusion of today's proceedings that, except for the formal judgment that the parties will need to effectuate the formal name change for their child, all other matters in connection with this case will be sealed."

"Thank you, Judge," Logan said.

"Counsel, I have read all the papers submitted in connection with this matter, including the certification of your client. I note for the record that the minor child is present in the courtroom with her parents. I just have a few questions. Ms. Costello, is everything contained in the complaint true and accurate?"

"It is, Your Honor."

"I understand that Hannah has been going by that name for approximately six months now, which under New Jersey law is permissible because we are a common-law name-change state, and so, Ms. Costello, this is your application to allow your child to formally assume the name Hannah Costello. Is that correct?"

"It is, Judge."

"Mr. Costello, I understand you had initially opposed this application, but that you have changed your position. Is that correct?"

"Yes, Your Honor. It is."

"And so that the record is clear, you are now in agreement that your child should be allowed to formally assume the name of Hannah Costello. Is that correct?"

"It is, Your Honor."

"Thank you both. All of the paperwork being in order, and both parents having consented, I will enter an order allowing the minor child to assume the name Hannah Costello. Under the court rules, my order will not be effective for thirty days, but let me be the first to say congratulations, Hannah."

"Thank you, Judge," Hannah said, barely able to contain her emotions.

"I hope your parents will take you out to celebrate, because this is a very special day in your life. I wish you all the best. Court is adjourned."

Paul and Michelle circled around Hannah.

"Thank you, Mom," Hannah said, giving her mom a hug. Then she turned and looked at her father, and the tears began to stream down her cheeks. "Oh, Dad, thank you so much."

"You're welcome, Hannah. Hopefully, I'll be a better dad from now on. You deserve that."

When they walked out of the courtroom, Erin and Mark were waiting in the hallway. "Hi, Hannah," Erin said.

Hannah ran over to her and hugged Erin.

"What's that for?" Erin asked, sporting a wide smile.

"For saving my life," Hannah responded.

"Well, then," Erin said, wrapping her arms back around Hannah.

"What was that for?" Hannah asked.

"For saving my life," Erin said, putting her arm around Hannah and walking her over to where Mark was standing. "Remember I told you I had a boyfriend? Well, this is Mark. And, Mark, this is Hannah."

"Hi, Hannah," Mark said. "A pleasure to meet you."

"Nice meeting you too," Hannah said, her cheeks turning red.

The three of them walked over to where Logan, Michelle, and Paul were standing, and Erin introduced Mark to everyone.

"I really haven't had a chance to talk to you since what happened a couple of weeks ago," Erin said, turning to Michelle and Paul, "but I wanted to congratulate you on working things out. And I know both of you already know this," Erin continued, her gaze settling on Hannah, "but you have an amazing daughter."

"Yes, we do," Paul said.

CHAPTER 43

THEY SAT OUT ON HER DECK, HAVING A GLASS OF WINE, TAKING IN the light from the almost full moon dancing on the ocean.

"Dinner was delicious," she said. "Thank you for a wonderful birthday."

"You're welcome. But it's not over yet."

She turned her head coyly and smiled. "Anything in particular you have in mind?"

"Perhaps," he replied, with the goofy grin of his that she loved so much.

"You ever think about being a mom?" he asked, seemingly out of left field.

"What makes you ask that question?"

"Well, I watched you with Hannah, and the other day at your mom's when Cori asked you to give Alysha a bottle. You just seem to light up around kids."

Erin sheepishly looked down at the deck. "Well, I know you're aware that there is a little physical impediment to me being a mother."

"There's a lot of women who for one reason or another can't become pregnant who nonetheless become mothers—adoption, for example."

"There is also the fact that I'm not married and have no desire to be a single mom."

"There's a way to fix that too," he said. He got up out of his chair and stood in front of her. Slowly, he knelt on one knee. "Erin McCabe, you are the most amazing woman I've ever known." He reached into his pocket, took out a small jeweler's box, and opened it to reveal a diamond ring. "Would you do me the honor of marrying me?"

Erin couldn't believe what was happening. Her heart was racing with joy, her hand started shaking, and tears formed in the corners of her eyes. "Yes. Oh my God, yes!"

He took the ring out the box and gently guided it onto her finger. When he was done, she held her hand out in front of her. "Oh, Mark, I can't believe this. It's beautiful," she offered.

He slowly stood and, taking her hand, helped her out of her chair. When she was standing, she threw her arms around him and gave him a passionate kiss. After they finally broke their embrace, she stared into his green eyes. "Thank you for the best birthday ever," she said.

"It's still not over," he replied with a smile, taking her by the hand and leading her inside.

ACKNOWLEDGMENTS

To my readers, thank you for investing your precious time in reading (or listening to) this story I created. I hope you've enjoyed reading it as much as I enjoyed creating it.

I owe so much to my agent, Carrie Pestrito, at Laura Dail Literary Agency, who, over the last five years, has helped guide me through three novels. Thank you, Carrie. Similarly, to my amazing editor at Kensington Books, John Scognamiglio, thank you for all your help and sage advice. John, you are the best.

I also want to thank all the people at Kensington Books who have worked so hard to make this novel the best book it could be. And to all the folks at Kensington who work behind the scenes to help promote my books. I am so grateful to have such a great team working with me.

As I was with my first two novels, I am indebted to Andrea Robinson, an independent editor, who was faced with the horror of my original draft. As she was in the past, she was incredibly helpful with her thoughts, suggestions, and edits. Andrea's input has made this a much better book—trust me on that.

To the people who have read various drafts of this along the way—Gerry Carbine, Lori Becker, Janet Bayer, and Jan Gigl— thank you for your help. Special thanks to Lisa Spiegel and Brian Neary for their support and encouragement and to Celeste Fiore, for reading and commenting on the draft and for providing the inspiration for me to include a nonbinary character. I have learned and continue to learn so much from Celeste.

To Jan, my best friend and the mother of our children, thank you for sharing my journey. To our sons, Tim and Colin, our daughter, Kate, granddaughters, Madison, Gwen, Alice, Caroline, and Abigail, and daughters-in-law, Stephine and Carly, you get thanks for just being you. I love all of you more than you'll ever know. To my sister Virginia, niece Casey, and cousin Lynn, who have shown up at so many of my events they know my story better than I do—thank you for your support. And to my mom, who passed away in December 2020. It is no secret that Peg McCabe is an homage to my mom. As long as Peg lives on in my books, I feel like a part of my mom is still with me.

These are especially difficult times for the trans and nonbinary communities. We are under attack by people who deny our very existence and seek to take away our basic human rights. So, to everyone in the LGBTQ+ community and especially those in the trans and nonbinary communities, thank you for your strength and inspiration.

Finally, one of the things that I have discovered about being a published author is that occasionally a reader will reach out and email me concerning one of my books. Sometimes those emails can be very impactful. Right after *Survivor's Guilt* was published, I received an email from a wonderful woman, who thanked me for my book but went on to tell me that not all transgender people were as lucky as my characters. That led to a series of emails in which she told me about her daughter, who, after being outed and bullied for being transgender, had taken her own life. I was heartbroken for her, and for her daughter. Unfortunately, theirs is not an isolated story. Every year, we lose hundreds of trans and nonbinary people to violence, and although I cannot acknowledge everyone by name, I do want to acknowledge all the trans and nonbinary individuals who have lost their lives because of hatred. And to all the people who have lost a loved one, I hope you find peace in the memories they gave you while they were here.